THE TALE OF
THE DRAKANOX

by Deby Fredericks

A character index can be found in the back of the book.

Indicia

Minstrels of Skaythe

Where dark sorcery rules, they seek to restore a
forbidden power — hope!

More by Deby Fredericks

E-books
The Weight of Their Souls
The Gellboar
*Wyrmflight, a Hoard of Dragon Lore**

Wolfsinger Publishing
*The Seven Exalted Orders**
*Trials of the Eighth Order (forthcoming)**

Dragon Moon Press
The Magister's Mask
The Necromancer's Bones
Too Many Princes

More by Lucy D. Ford

E-books
*Aunt Ursula's Atlas**
*Masters of Air & Fire**

*Also available in paperback

The Tale of the Drakanox

Dedication

If you question the world,
If you believe violence is not the answer,
If you want a better way than
racism and rivalries...

This book is for you.

Chapters

BEFORE

I t was time. Past time. But Ar-Thea didn't want to say goodbye.

Dark eyes lingered on her six magelings as they crowded into the main room of the ramshackle farmhouse. She couldn't really call them magelings any more, for a mageling was a child. The skinny boys she remembered had become young men who all but burst the room with their wide shoulders. Shy slips of girls were filling out into curvy fullness. Like all the people of Skaythe, they had a sturdy built, handsome brown faces, wavy black hair done in ponytails or topknots or braids. Her adoptive brood were all but grown.

Ar-Thea loved them so much. She had tried to teach them with patience and care. It had worked, hadn't it? Here they were at the supper table, with barely enough room for everyone. Most young mages would be squabbling viciously, carving out space for themselves. Even murdering each other for a better score on some wretched exam.

In Ar-Thea's house, white teeth flashed in laughter. Black eyes were bright and trusting. Meven, the first of her magelings, clung to the dignity of an older sibling. She pushed her chair back, annoyed by the antics beside her. The brothers, Berisan and Alemin were always tossing oranges or sweet potatoes back and forth. Lorrah, the youngest at just 14, did her best to get into their game. Tisha danced a bit as she carried empty dishes back to the kitchen. Keilos tapped an array of cups with his spoon, trying to bring forth a melody.

How she was going to miss them!

But Ar-Thea had been delaying what must be. Foolishly, selfishly. The layered sight of foretelling flickered before her. Most of the time she saw scattered images, possibilities to choose from. Lately they had collapsed into one. She knew what she must do, yet she hesitated. It would be cruel, a sort of curse.

Perhaps Keilos sensed something. He had been darting glances at her during the meal. Now he asked, "Ar-Thea, what's wrong?"

She blinked, drawn back from her distraction. Her first impulse was to lie and reassure them, as any mother would. She wanted to say everything would be fine, when it wouldn't. But there was no more time. The blow had to fall. Tonight, before it was too late.

If it wasn't already.

"Is it a foretelling?" Hesitantly, Keilos questioned her.

The younger teens kept up their noisy game until Meven reached over to grip the back of Alemin's neck with ice cold fingers.

"Ow, Meven!" He jumped, protesting.

Berisan fumbled the orange they were juggling between them. Lorrah grabbed it with a triumphant yip. They all turned to yell at Meven, who silenced them with her imperious stare.

"Pay attention," she scolded.

Keilos repeated, "It is a foretelling." It was no longer a question, but his puzzled frown showed that he still trusted her.

Ar-Thea nodded, suddenly feeling the weight of sixty

years. She hadn't noticed the time passing so much, as her magelings enlivened her life and there was always the need to keep them moving in search of herbs or anonymity. Recently her joints were stiffer. Her belly got rounder. Silvery curls were streaked with raven black, where formerly it had been reversed.

The magelings were all watching her. Ar-Thea said, "My children, it is time to travel." They nodded, accepting her words. Ar-Thea's family traveled most of the year. They harvested herbs and minerals to make into medicines, which they sold in villages along the way. Yet a moment of confusion crossed Keilos' face. Something was different, but he didn't know what.

"This year, I cannot go with you," Ar-Thea said.

"What?" Tisha hovered in the kitchen door, wash rag dripping in her hand.

"Why not?" Berisan echoed the alarm she saw around the table.

"Don't look like that," Ar-Thea chuckled. "You know our routes. You've gone with me, some for as long as ten years."

"Twelve years," Meven corrected, unblinking.

Lorrah pushed her shoulder. "You don't always have to be right, Meven." Meven brushed her hand aside.

"I'm getting older, maybe you didn't notice," Ar-Thea said mildly.

"You aren't old," Alemin tried to soothe her.

Anxiously, Keilos stuck to the main question. "What is your premonition?"

Ar-Thea's heart broke for them. She couldn't say the words, but she had to say something. "There will be trouble," she answered gently. "I will be hurt."

"I can heal you," Tisha immediately offered.

Slowly Ar-Thea shook her head. "Not from this."

"So you need to stay here, where you're safe." Alemin's expression cleared. The boy was ever an optimist.

"Yes." Ar-Thea avoided Keilos' eye. "I need to stay here."

Berisan was a little more savvy. He unconsciously leaned forward as if to protect his brother. "What kind of trouble? Raiders?"

"Tigers?" Lorrah set the orange down, embarrassed now to be holding it.

"Neither of those," Ar-Thea answered, "and you let me worry about it."

Keilos pushed back the long curls from around his face. His expression was doubtful. He also had premonitions, and they must have been showing him something. Luckily for Ar-Thea, most foretelling was personal, regarding only oneself. There were still some secrets she needed to keep.

"She's right," Keilos spoke softly, hardly believing. "We will leave without her. Within three days?"

"But —" Tisha's eyes were wide with panic.

"I wish I could go with you, my children," Ar-Thea murmured. "I have only ever wanted to keep you safe. If I go this year, it... will not be helpful."

Meven and Berisan both frowned, picking up on something they couldn't quite name. How could the magelings be safer without their mentor? To keep them from dwelling too much on that, Ar-Thea clapped her hands as she did to call them for lessons.

"Now then, magelings. I have taught you many things in the time you've been with me. Before you begin your journey, there is one more lesson I have to share."

Tisha tossed the washrag back into the kitchen and returned to the table. With restless, worried expressions, the students settled in to listen.

"We are renegades. You know this. My methods are radical. I have taught you to use *vitalis* instead of *lethentros*. Not to take things just because you can. To offer compassion no matter who needs it. Now, I will tell you why."

Lorrah leaned back a little, a crimp in her brow. This wasn't like one of their ordinary lessons.

"When I was young," Ar-Thea began, "hunter-guards took me to the temple school in Nimthar. I barely made it through and wasn't given a chance at the three rituals that could have helped me establish a career." Meven shuddered and nodded. She knew the ordeal of a temple school. Ar-Thea had rescued her from one.

"Nobody wanted a failure like me in their household," Ar-Thea continued. "For years, I scraped by as a wandering herbalist. I thought my life was meaningless."

More nods rippled through the watching students. Herbalism was the same familiar profession she was teaching them.

"Along the way I became friends with an older mage, Ar-Cerroth. People said he was in his dotage, his mind wandering. We all know *lethentros* drives mages mad." It was a peril she had warned them of many times. "Still, Ar-Cerroth seemed less dangerous than most other mages I knew, and he liked my salves. There was another man, Ar-Lannon, who joined us at times. He never would say how he got by in the world. But, after we had known each other for some time, Ar-Cerroth offered to tell us a story. I thought nothing of it. Mind wandering and all."

"Now be careful." Ar-Thea lowered her voice, betting that the lure of secrecy would weave a stronger spell than any of her own. "This is a story that is dangerous to know. That is because it is true, and it tells a history the regime does not want you to know."

She paused, hanging on a knife's edge. There would

be no turning back from this moment.

"In ancient times, it is said, all people were magical. There was no division of mages and commoners, of rich and poor, or even of men and women. We call those people the Shining Ones. Knowing that all were equally blessed, they shared a mutual purpose to bring happiness and welfare to every person.

"The Shining Ones raised up a great civilization. It boasted every marvel that magic could provide. No one wanted for food or companionship, for all things were held in common. Nor were the people judged for any failings. Human frailty was met with compassion rather than anger. Error aroused not disgust but forgiveness."

Alemin and Berisan shared a bewildered glance, but no one interrupted.

"The cities of the Shining Ones prospered and grew to cover all of Skaythe. Even now, some of their works endure. Their ancient roads stitch our world together long after their time.

"But we know that for every light there is a shadow. After the summer, winter must come. The Shining Ones, too, had their opposite. These were the sadistic Devourers.

"The Devourers came from everywhere, and from nowhere. They fed upon magic, and all the things of magic. The Shining Ones could not fight them, for their spells were consumed. They could not hide, for their very essence was magical and the Devourers were drawn to slaughter them.

"Soon the Shining Ones were gone forever. Their great cities crumbled, and everything they had made was swept away."

A breath of shock passed among the magelings. This wasn't how they thought the story would end!

"There had been those few who were born without magic, or whose magic was malformed in some way. These broken ones were regarded with pity and maintained with all kindness. After the Devourers, they were all that was left.

"Alas, these were no Shining Ones. Some did not wish to share in common. They seized what they wanted to keep it for themselves. So were the rich divided from the poor. Some desired to hold and control the ones they loved. So were the men divided from the women. And some, who yet held a feeble ember of magic, set themselves up as rulers over those who had none. So were the mages divided from the commons.

"This is the end of the story. For the Shining Ones are lost, and now we must struggle in the dregs of our world that the Devourers left behind."

Silence reigned. Ar-Thea sensed their emotions, the struggle between sensible disbelief and the longing to trust her. They listened to her story much as her younger self had to Ar-Cerroth, thinking only to indulge a feeble old man. Ar-Lannon had scoffed at it all, and left soon after. But the story had taken root in Ar-Thea's heart. The lore of the Shining Ones had turned a forty-year-old woman, jaded and childless, into a quiet crusader who collected runaway magelings. She kept them out of the temple schools and taught them to follow a different path. Now, the knowledge passed to her students. Their lives, too, would be remade.

"That doesn't..." Tisha began, but faltered.

"It can't be real," Meven accused.

"It was real," Ar-Thea corrected softly. "When a flower drops its seeds onto the earth, we often cannot see them. Who is to say where those seeds may sprout in the future?"

The students stirred, eyes wide and lips opening for questions to burst out. Ar-Thea clapped to signal the end of the lesson.

"No more for tonight. You must think on this story, my children. We have the meal to put away, and packing begins tomorrow."

"But... Where will we go?" Lorrah blurted.

"Where and how are for you to decide," she told them. Ar-Thea rose and went to her tiny bedchamber, where stars shone through a gap in the thatching. Through the thin walls, she heard Meven asking Keilos what else he foresaw.

She took a deep breath and blotted her eyes. That story had such power. It had changed her life. Now it would change theirs. They hadn't asked for this, and no one could predict how much they might suffer because of it. That was why it was a curse.

Yet, her children must go forward without her. They thought they needed her, but Ar-Thea knew better. She had built this group carefully. Six was enough to watch out for each other, but not so many as to draw attention. They would have to keep moving, as she had until now.

Herbalism probably wasn't the solution for them. Berisan was the only one who had any aptitude. Besides, it was too clear a link to her own subversion. Whatever they chose must help them avoid detection as they worked, in their own way, to defy the cruel regime.

No matter, now, if her direst foretelling came true. Her children would keep the lore of the Shining Ones alive until the day when Skaythe was freed from the torment of Dar-Gothull's evil reign.

I — RENEGADES

H ere we go," Sergeant Piyaro murmured to himself. The village of Opshar was just coming into sight, and it was important to make the right impression.

He raised a bone whistle to his lips and blew a shrill signal. Hawk Squad was spread out a little on the trail, but now they hurried into ranks of four, with Piyaro at the head. His second, Cothyr, fell in behind to make sure none of them ran off.

Opshar was an ordinary village in the County of Pulgoll. Stone huts with thatched roofs huddled in a bend of the river that looped across the valley floor. Each hut had a wall around it to protect their vegetable gardens from pilfering, and for defense. On the river, fishermen cast their nets from flat boats. Ahead of the hunter guards, the dirt track widened out into a market plaza. A stone tavern with a shadowy porch rose among rows of wooden stalls displaying common wares. Faint notes from a pipe lilted through the murmuring of peasant farmers beneath the hot tropical sun. It was just the sort of place for a renegade to blend in. Though not well enough, apparently.

By itself, this was a nothing village. Yet it was everything for Hawk Squad. What they did today would make or break his squad.

A rising murmur followed the hunter-guards. Villagers stopped what they were doing and jumped to alertness. If the people were nervous about a squad of guards appearing, that was as it should be. Piyaro kept a stolid face, while his dark eyes took in important details like side paths and gaps between walled huts. Something was off here. The folk were concerned, but not truly afraid. He missed the days when fear made the peasants cooperative.

As they reached the plaza, Ragis muttered behind him, "On the right."

"I see it."

Someone dashed ahead, trying to stay behind the line of market stalls. Could that be the renegade? He wasn't wearing mage robes. That might not mean anything. A renegade would be trying to disguise himself.

Piyaro tried to keep the runner in sight. His view was broken when a well-dressed young man strutted out to meet them.

"Finally, the count sent someone!" The fellow spoke eagerly, yet with a hint of indignant whine. Piyaro made note of his fine trousers and tunic, both edged with embroidery. A gleaming satin ribbon tied his black topknot. He seemed over-dressed for a village like this, but it gave Piyaro hope that the bounty might be better than expected.

However, the interruption had also made him lose track of the runner. Piyaro glanced back, catching two of his men with a glance. "Circle around, try to figure out where he went."

"Yes Sergeant." The guardsmen broke from the file and moved into the crowd, Ragis going left and Rowlan going right.

Piyaro nodded to the man who had come to meet them. "You're Aulgrip, the Headman?"

"I'm his nephew, Kinson." An avid expression fired his sleek brown face. "The renegade is right over here. You can get him before he runs. Come on!"

The babble of voices had quieted, but now it rose again. Piyaro, watchful, scanned the brown faces with wide noses, dark eyes, wavy black hair held back in topknots or ponytails. They wore rough tunics and trousers or dresses with white blouses. Typical peasants, except that instead of scattering, they gathered closer. All of them were scowling.

A man yelled at Kinson, "What are you up to, boy? You ain't the headman." Someone else went bolting off toward the tavern.

Sergeant Piyaro noted these reactions even as Kinson brushed them aside and strutted further into the plaza. The guardsmen followed. The cheerful piping got a little louder. The area was a rough oval edged with stalls displaying hand crafts and foodstuffs. The small stone tavern was the most prominent building. Piyaro glimpsed activity under the shaded porch, but it didn't seem to signify anything.

A closer flicker of movement caught his eye. He turned quickly, looking for that runner, but only saw a group of boys chasing each other. Across the square, he spotted the piper crouched beside a vegetable cart. His face was shadowed by a round hat of woven reeds. Nearby, a pretty woman bartered with a customer.

The man who had been running appeared out of the crowd. He rushed up to the piper and babbled urgently. Words faintly reached Piyaro.

"Sand, Sand, come quick! Ressa's cut herself with the skinning knife. It's bad. You have to come."

In reaction, the piper and his woman both looked around sharply. The piper started to get up, while the woman dropped what she was selling and pushed her customer out of the way. Before she could get around the cart, Kinson pointed dramatically across the square.

"That's him! He's a renegade. Quick, before he gets away!"

Something made Piyaro think he and his squad were

being used for petty reasons. Not that it mattered. He needed this bounty. "Which one?" he asked. It could have been the woman or the piper, or even the runner who seemed to be warning them.

"The worthless vagabond," sneered Kinson.

That still didn't answer Piyaro's question. He wasn't from Opshar and didn't know the vagabonds from the villagers.

A startled silence rippled across the plaza. Again, Piyaro noted that the locals appeared upset but not shocked by the accusation. The piper got up, though the runner tugged his arm with increased urgency. He faced Hawk Squad without surprise.

Here was the renegade. Piyaro would have known it just from the grace of his movements and his resolute expression.

"Shit." Piyaro's feet seemed welded to the earth, unable to rise for that next step. "He's one of *them?*"

Behind him, the guardsmen murmured warily. They recognized it, too. This wasn't just any runaway mage. It was one of the golden renegades.

A terrible and brilliant memory seared Piyaro's mind. The renegade witch danced inside a circle of pale golden light. Ar-Dayne poured a fountain of fire on her, but she did not burn. Instead, she breathed it in. Flames transformed into a shimmering wave of impossible serenity. Even on the edge of battle, it had been hard to resist the warmth and softness flowing over them. Count Ar-Dayne threw everything he had at her until he fell, spasming, while she stole his power and perverted it into that seductive feeling.

All the certainty in Piyaro's world went down with Ar-Dayne, and they didn't even know the witch's name.

The renegade, "Sand," wore the same expression of gentle inquiry that the golden witch had. He held the pipes loosely in his hand. As he turned to calm his friend, the woman came out from behind her cart. She had some kind of heavy bag on her back, but defiance lit her face. As she placed herself between Hawk Squad and the renegade, Piyaro noted two blades sheathed at her side. Bright black eyes roved along their line, assessing each one of them. This was no mere peasant woman. She was a fighter, calculating the numbers as surely as Piyaro himself did.

All right, this might not be easy, but she was one and he had many. The renegade wasn't even likely to fight, if he was like the other one.

"Ready," Piyaro barked. Metal clinked lightly as he readied his shield and loosened his sword. The guardsmen prepared as well, pushing back onlookers and spreading out their line.

The woman smiled a little, with murder in her eyes. One foot slid back. Her shoulders settled as she relaxed into an easy combat stance. Hesitating, the renegade reached toward her.

"Yamaya," he began.

"You slime." Yamaya's voice lashed across the plaza. She wasn't talking to Piyaro or Sand, though.

"Keep your place, woman," Kinson taunted. "It's too late for you to save your precious renegade."

More of the villagers came out of their booths in ones and twos. Some hurried to the renegade's side. Others yelled at the soldiers, despite having no arms to back it up.

"Let him alone," they called. And another, "He hasn't done anything."

Piyaro had never seen the like. Everyone knew mages were dangerous, fit only for hatred and fear. They hurt people without thinking about it, burned houses and fields in their warring against each other. Nobody would ever run to defend one.

The guardsmen glanced at Piyaro, seeking guidance. In turn, he looked to Kinson, whose handsome face twisted with scorn.

"Get out of the way," he sneered to those closest. "I'm trying to protect the village."

"Bullshit." Somehow the woman, Yamaya, made her voice known through the crowd's growing roar. "Get it through your head, Kinson. I'm never marrying you."

"Who wants an uppity bitch like you?" Kinson retorted. "You had your chance."

Thin wails pierced the noise, a baby crying. The renegade turned, concerned, but then another girl, younger than Yamaya, darted up to them. Yamaya shrugged her burden loose, and the girl rushed it away. With a slight shock, Piyaro realized the burden was a padded sling holding a tiny infant. That changed things again. If this was the renegade's baby, he would have something precious to fight for. The babe's mother didn't take her eyes off Piyaro and the Hawks for a moment.

The villagers' increasing fury was focused on Kinson rather than the Hawks. "This ain't your job," yelled a man wearing the tall leather boots of a fisherman. Someone else cried, "Kinson, what are you doing? We need him."

Piyaro seriously considered leaving Kinson to deal with his own mess, but the grim truth was that Hawk Squad still needed the bounty for arresting the renegade.

"What's going on?" a new voice called out. The villagers quieted as an older gentleman strode down the tavern steps and pushed his way through. Recognizing Piyaro as the sergeant, he said, "I'm Headman Aulgrip. What brings the fine hunter-guards to Opshar?"

Piyaro concealed a grimace at his oily tone. "We have a writ," he started, but the fierce woman cut in with a menacing glare for Aulgrip.

"Did you send for them?"

"I assure you, Farmer..." Aungrip answered with feigned sympathy. Something in his emphasis on 'farmer' held unmistakable spite.

"So you did this on your own?" Yamaya stared at Kinson.

"Someone has to think of the village," the younger man retorted.

His uncle looked none too pleased by the admission. To make things worse, two more well-dressed men were hurrying up, ready to join the argument.

"Brother! I thought we talked about this," the first one said.

"You need to consult us before you make these decisions," said the other.

Aulgrip puffed up his chest, but he was clearly conflicted about whether to take credit for his nephew's initiative. "As a matter of fact..."

He didn't get to finish. The crowd was getting uglier, shouts and jeers overriding the village leaders. This had gone on long enough. Piyaro's men were hungry, and this whole situation was getting off track.

"Shut up, all of you!" he bellowed in a voice that would silence any number of unruly guardsmen. It worked here, too. "We are here by the count's order."

"The count. Which one?" Yamaya set her hands on her hips and tossed her chin.

"Your count, Ar-Azlor. Here is the writ." He drew a folded parchment from his belt and passed it to Aulgrip.

Piyaro couldn't read the message himself. His best scribe was one of the men he'd lost to that golden witch. Aulgrip's dark eyes roved the page, while his two brothers crowded close to read over his shoulder. A silent conference passed among them. Then Aulgrip gave a little shrug and passed the writ back.

He didn't appear completely sorry to say, "There's nothing to be done."

"Turn over the renegade, and everything will be fine." Piyaro's tone held a warning of what would happen if they didn't cooperate.

"That's not happening," Yamaya bit out.

Voices started to rise again. "This isn't right," called a woman from one side. "Who said any of you get to decide?" another man challenged.

"Aulgrip!" A burly fellow stepped up near Yamaya, hefting a sledge hammer. "I've lived here for fifty years, and this is the first time we've had something good in Opshar. One good thing!" He shook a single finger toward Aulgrip and his kin. "You'd let them take it away from us?"

All this time, the mage stood listening as they argued over his fate. Calmly, he asked, "What if I bought everyone a mug of Aulgrip's finest, and we talk about it?"

The headman appeared tempted, but Kinson spat with fury. "You're just trying to delay!" To Piyaro, he complained, "Look at all the trouble he's caused. Get him out of here."

That was the most sense Piyaro had heard since they arrived in Opshar, but the crowd erupted. "No!" "You can't take him!" "The only one who caused trouble is you," they raged at Kinson.

"Get away from me," whined the young dandy.

"It's the count's order," Aulgrip raised his hands in feigned helplessness.

The market plaza churned with confusion. A few people — the smart ones — were running off, but a lot of them grabbed up melons, metal pans and other solid objects. An older woman in a potter's stall was passing out heavy-looking stoneware pitchers and bowls. In half a minute, the renegade and his bitch wouldn't be the ones who were outnumbered.

Piyaro gritted his teeth. Hawk Squad had come to take down a renegade, not put a village to the sword.

"Ready," he ordered, and started forward. The guardsmen advanced at a steady pace, not rushing. "In the name of Count Ar-Azlor!"

The men fanned out, preparing to surround the mage. The shouting increased. Objects began to fly. Yamaya stepped forward, drawing her blades, but the renegade, Sand, hastily touched her arm.

Resigned, he said, "No, farmer. I'll do it."

"You?" she mocked.

"There's somebody depending on you," Sand told her. Yamaya glanced over, where her friend crouched behind a fish stall, cradling the infant protectively. As she hesitated, the renegade faced Piyaro with open hands.

Softly, he asked, "What have I done to offend the count?"

He sounded so reasonable, and so fake. Piyaro swallowed around a knot in his throat. Just like that witch in Seofan, innocently playing the victim. She'd taunted Ar-Dayne into attacking her, then drained him of all power. This man was a menace, and his supposed humility wouldn't work on Piyaro.

"You're a renagade," he snarled, and charged.

~ ~ ~

"Duessa." Bettain leaned over, the rumble of cart wheels concealing her ungrateful words. "Are we really sure about this?"

Duessa and Elldri looked up from the grass cord they were weaving in their laps. The lowlands of Yergha were thick with tough stems, which could be woven into many useful items. At the moment, Duessa needed a new pair of sandals to replace her tattered prison wear. Also, it gave them something to do while the cart jolted along the rough dirt track.

"Sure about what?" Duessa asked back.

"This." Bettain made a vague circular gesture, taking in their surroundings. Beside her, Elldri jumped a little. The youngest of them, Elldri usually didn't say much. She listened now in somber silence, while chapped brown fingers twisted and twined the grass.

Duessa grumbled to herself. Bettain had been looking at her sidelong all day, with unspoken questions hanging between them. The scars on her face and neck felt tight and itchy. She kept her hands busy so she wouldn't rub them. Why should Duessa have to coax the words? Bettain wasn't a child. In fact, she was probably a decade older than Duessa.

Irritated, Duessa asked, "What part are you not sure about?"

There were a lot of variables, after all. The three women rode in a prison wagon, its bed mostly filled by a large iron cage. Dust from the earthen track rose to screen the sight of several guardswomen riding alongside. Until this morning, Duessa, Bettain and Elldri had been riding in that cage. They were not prisoners, however. Quite the opposite.

Three days ago, they had been freed from the Larder, a notorious prison for the most vicious and insane mages of Skaythe. A new prisoner, the juggler Alemin, had been flung into the Larder about a month before that. He'd said all along that he had friends on the outside. It had still come as a shock when the friends actually showed up and sparked a mass escape. Now, every prisoner of the Larder was free. Most of them had scattered immediately. But not all.

"Did you not like that they gave us food and better clothes?" Duessa gestured to take in their peasant dresses, which were well used but sturdy.

"No," Bettain retorted.

When the three women escaped, their garments had been coarse gray robes and crude sandals. Those, along with their shaved heads, marked them as prisoners. It was why they'd had to stay in the cage, pretending to be captives of the hunter-guards. After a bit of careful bargaining in one of the towns, they had been given their current skirts and blouses, with tight bodices over them. To protect against Skaythe's burning sun, they had cut one of their prison robes into lengths that could be wrapped around their shaved heads in elegant sweeps. That made it easier to pass among the populace. Being able to sleep without nightmares was also a big relief. They could almost forget where they were running from.

Almost. After enduring the Larder's relentless grind of short meals and long hours of work, they all had been wizened and gaunt. Elldri and Duessa were starting to recover. Bettain must have been quite heavy at one time, for the ordeal had left her with sagging folds of flesh, like a half-filled waterskin.

"Then did you not like the part where they broke us out of there?" Duessa pressed. Despite herself, she rubbed the rough skin below her left eye. A phantom of old pain stirred at her touch.

"No," Bettain groused. "I'm not that ungrateful."

"Oh?" Duessa retorted. Bettain folded her arms and looked away. Duessa didn't like to draw attention to the puckered silvery net of burn scars that ruined her good looks. The scars made people uncomfortable. That could be useful at times, but it wasn't a weapon she wanted to use against her few real friends.

Inside the Larder, the three women had been a team.

They guarded each other from the ruthless prison guards, and from the other prisoners, who had been even more dangerous. Since their escape from the Larder, they'd had many chances to split up, but they hadn't done it. Maybe that was loyalty, or maybe it was fear of being on their own in Skaythe.

Now, it sounded like Bettain was thinking of going it alone after all. Duessa's stomach felt tight at the thought of losing a trusted ally. When Bettain had been quiet too long, she prodded, "Then what?"

"It's just..." Bettain gave an irritated gust of sigh. "I'd been in there for years. Every day just like every other. Screaming in the morning, screaming at night, and drudging in between." Bettain glanced at Duessa, then away. Her hands knotted in her lap. "I hated it, but I knew where I was. Now?"

She threw up her hands in a frustrated gesture. Alemin, their fellow escapee, turned around to look. He'd been riding on the wagon's front bench, beside the driver, Sethamis. His girlfriend, Lorrah, rode along close to that side. They both wore understanding expressions, but to Duessa's relief, they didn't say anything. This was something her team needed to settle for themselves.

"I get it," Duessa told Bettain. "We could count on each other, and nothing else." Elldri nodded, too. She came off a bit simple-minded at times. Duessa was never sure if she didn't understand things, or if she was too smart to open her mouth.

"I don't know where we are," Bettain admitted. "I barely know these people. I have no idea where we're going!"

Alemin chuckled to himself, and Duessa frowned. The juggler was a strange one, no doubt. Calm when everyone else was raging, laughing through the starvation and abuse in the Larder. It wasn't normal. Yet there was something about him that eased everyone's tension. He reminded Duessa of someone she hadn't thought about in years. Maybe that was why she trusted him, when trust was the stupidest thing to do.

"Okay, what's funny?" Duessa demanded.

"It's just, we're not as organized as you might think." Alemin spoke with the shamefaced air of someone who had farted loudly.

"We're figuring it out," Lorrah put in. The girl stuck to Alemin like a burr on his sleeve. It was cute, and also irritating.

The swish and thud of hooves over Ebruc's grassy plains made Duessa look around. Some of the guardswomen had heard their conversation and gathered closer. The sight of so many guards made Duessa nervous, even if they weren't from the Larder. The two groups hadn't been mingling much. They were too busy foraging and making camps and caring for their livestock. That needed to change.

"You have to admit, it's suspicious," Duessa said.

And Bettain snapped. "Nobody just gives people things."

It was true, they didn't know much about the hunter-guards, except that they had come to rescue Alemin, probably because of his girlfriend. Duessa had decided to go with them because they were all women. It considerably reduced the possibility of being raped.

Alemin shrugged, a sly smile on his lips. "Just call me nobody."

Elldri made a wheeze that might have been laughter, and Duessa growled, "Funny."

"But we don't know where we're going," Bettain repeated in a frustrated tone. Alemin started to answer, but Elldri spoke up first.

"We don't know the price," she lisped.

The space where Elldri's front teeth should have been told the story of how many times she'd been hit in the face. Duessa had no idea who had done that. You didn't talk about private things in the Larder. The knowledge could too easily be turned into a weapon. Still, when Elldri did speak up, Duessa was pretty sure she wasn't half-witted at all.

"Oh, I think we know the price," Duessa predicted with grim certainty.

"Do tell," came a cool voice from just beside the wagon.

Sergeant Zathi, who commanded Badger Squad, reined her sorrel in beside Lorrah's chestnut. Duessa's neck tightened with nerves, but this was no time to back down.

"You're hunter-guards, and you've left your post," she started.

Zathi parried the accusation. "Hunter-guards don't have permanent posts. We rove. That's come in handy recently."

Duessa kept on, "You're still warriors who serve Dar-Gothull. You must have something planned. It's a trap, or..." Zathi's expression said that was wrong. She pushed on. "Then we're all headed to meet up with your army. You brought us along to fight on your side."

"Because we'd be grateful, or something," Bettain added bitterly.

Duessa felt as irritated as Bettain when they all chuckled. "If only," one of the women said. It might be Keerin.

Another one smiled. "That would be nice." Was her name Giniver?

Zathi hesitated, then admitted, "Alemin is correct. We're not as organized as it may seem."

The three former prisoners exchanged glances of

anger and dismay. "You broke us out, but you don't have a plan?" Duessa rubbed her knuckles against the tight scars below her chin.

"We knew we needed to get Alemin out. We couldn't leave him there," Lorrah hastily explained. "But then —"

"When I was meditating, I learned that Dar-Gothull uses the Larder to feed off the mages inside," Alemin carried on. "If he's ever going to be overthrown, we had to take his food away."

"To weaken him, we had to let all of you out," Zathi said.

"Starving him would be fair, right?" the driver quipped.

"Wait. Weaken him?" Duessa pressed her hands to her temples. Her dark eyes darted from brown face to brown face, and rested on Alemin's patient expression. "This is one of your jokes."

"No," he answered. "I know it's a lot..."

"You want to overthrow Dar-Gothull?" Bettain was aghast, yet impressed. Elldri listened, round-eyed. "What, with the six of you?"

"Seven," Lorrah corrected.

"Eight," Alemin said.

"That's... not better," Duessa choked. However strange she had ever thought Alemin was, this was far beyond it. "You're insane! He's Dar-Gothull. He has the whole regime and all the counts, the temple priests, the hunter-guards, the..." She trailed off, finding herself momentarily unable to breathe.

"There are more of us," Alemin went on, soothingly. "We had to split up when one of our friends had a foretelling that he would be captured..."

"A foretelling?" she shrieked. That was worse than nothing.

"Hey, quiet down," scolded Jaxynne, the second in command. "People are working in the fields around here. Someone might hear you."

Mages and guardswomen then compounded the blunder by looking around, guilty as crows in a corn field. An orchard of spice wood stretched along one side the road, shadowed between the rows of trees. On the other side, a vegetable patch drowsed beneath the afternoon sun. A shallow river sparkled on just beyond it. On the bank, a pair of farmers worked a bucket and lever to irrigate the field. Neither of them seemed to care about the passing wagon.

"We were supposed to meet up again after six months," Alemin continued. "Right now, that's what we're doing. I have a sense of another one of our friends. We're trying to find her."

"While avoiding my sister," Lorrah added grimly.

"And we're getting the hell away from the Larder," one of the others added, cheeky.

"No. No," Duessa insisted. "You just want us for canon fodder."

"We need allies," Zathi corrected.

"Yeah, no kidding," Bettain laughed rudely.

"We don't have a plan because it's impossible to make a plan before we know who supports us," Zathi went on.

"Really, you're going to try this?"

Duessa's eyes pleaded with Alemin to say no, it was just tavern talk. The guardswomen were silent for a moment, and then they nodded among themselves. "Yes." "Yeah, sure." "What, you want to live like this forever?"

"It's time," Zathi said firmly. "Dar-Gothull's reign has distorted everything. It has to end."

She made a circular gesture, as Bettain had done. It encompassed all of Skaythe, where mages preyed on everyone else without consequence. Even lesser mages could be thrown into the Larder for defending themselves, and drained of their power by a nightmarish revenant.

Duessa and Bettain traded a stunned look. "You just decided that?" Duessa asked.

"Not only her," Lorrah answered. "We talked about it. We all decided."

"We made a choice," Zathi said.

Horrified, Duessa stared at Alemin. "Juggler, I don't know about this. We've already been through the Larder, that was bad enough, but it's Dar-Gothull. He's immortal. You know he can do worse if he wants, and you plan to take on the whole regime?"

Again, Alemin tried to soothe them. "Right now, we're just finding our friends."

"And getting away from the Larder," Lorrah added.

Duessa drew a deep breath, trying to settle herself, because they were scaring the spit out of her with this talk of rebellion. After all her scolding to Bettain for not being sure, now Duessa was the one who didn't know.

Bettain patted Duessa's knee and said, "Okay, that's something we can agree on."

~ ~ ~

The battle didn't last long. No matter how hard they charged, they ran into some sort of barrier. That faint golden glow scooped them up and flung them backward. Ragis and Cothyr, hidden in the crowd, had charged from the sides, but the renegade hoisted them off their feet and sent them tumbling several feet behind the Hawks' line. Jeering villagers and showers of crockery pursued them.

Headman Aulgrip and his brothers were nowhere to be seen. Only the renegade and his crowd of peasants advanced steadily, pressing the hunter-guards back before them. Except for the woman, Yamaya, the farmers and fishermen weren't trained to fight. They were smart enough to shelter behind Sand's barrier, emerging only long enough to throw whatever came to hand. Any time it looked like one of the soldiers might land a blow, that damned barrier appeared.

Despite everything they did, Piyaro found himself and Hawk Squad back at the edge of the village. Maddeningly, no one was even hurt. The guardsmen had a few bruises from thrown objects, but none were serious.

Finally, he faced the renegade and his bandit woman with only that sheer, invulnerable screen between them. Sand breathed lightly, a sheen of sweat across his face, but maintained his poise. Yamaya was ready with her knives.

"Friends!" Sand called. "Please, I need to talk to him." It took several tries before the taunts of the villagers died away.

Piyaro cursed at him in the gathering quiet. "This isn't the end of it."

"I understand," Sand replied with patience and regret. "But if you would, please tell Count Ar-Azlor that I won't be leaving. This is my home."

"That's right," muttered the villagers. Some looking nervous now that the adrenaline was fading, but most were defiant and resolute.

"The count says different," Piyaro snapped.

"I have no intention toward the count's seat," Sand said. "However, if he wants to come here, I would be glad to discuss it."

Piyaro gritted his teeth at the man's nerve. It would be suicide to relay such a message. Yet, obviously, there was no way to go any farther with the writ.

Grimly, he told his men, "Stand down."

The men stared at him, most of them disgusted that he gave up. Their possible rebellion would have to be dealt with, and soon. To his disgust, Kinson emerged from behind a wall. He said what the guardsmen wouldn't.

"What? You can't!" It was practically a child's squalling.

"That's right, Kinson," Yamaya bit out. "They can't." Dark eyes blazed as her weight shifted again, blades rising as if she was prepared to stab the man. "If you think you're going to take my hired man away, maybe you should go with them."

"Yeah, get out of here!" hooted the villagers, still on fire with enthusiasm."Go with them, if you think you're so tough."

"You're a traitor, Yamaya. You knew all along what he is, and you didn't turn him in. You... you're all traitors!" Kinson clenched his fists, and stormed off.

Piyaro watched it all, horrified and fascinated. No mage he had ever encountered inspired this kind of popular loyalty. *"Who are you?"* That was what he wanted to ask, but he couldn't let himself show it. Too many of his men had already deserted.

"Turn about," he grated. A few blasts from his whistle brought them back into ranks. Piyaro might keep a straight back, but loathing and disgust weighed on his shoulders. How had it come to this?

It used to be, when Hawk Squad marched into a village, the people would scatter in panic. Not from them, of course. It was Count Ar-Dayne the people feared. The mad lord, with his flaring crimson robe and fists full of lightning, had ruled the County of Sloram through a decade of blood and the dread of his furious temper. Anyone with sense ran away from that.

Maybe the count hadn't treated his guardsman much better than the commoners, but it had felt good to be part of something so grand and terrifying. People showed them respect, lest the count's awful shadow fall upon them.

No longer. Ar-Dayne was dead, and so was Piyaro's career.

The moment they brought Ar-Dayne back to Sloram, barely conscious after the battle with that golden witch, the keep's other mages had exploded into combat. They all wanted the count's seat. Ar-Dayne had died quickly, but the others had fought for hours. Their running battle had wrecked a third of the keep.

Afterward, the allegiance Piyaro had built with Ar-Dayne had become a liability. The new countess, Ar-Jeziak, wanted none of the old count's people around her. Hawk Squad had been dismissed, forced to seek other employment. No longer did they enjoy sturdy barracks and access to smiths who cared for their weapons and harness. Nor steady meals, either. Hawk Squad was at the mercy of wind and weather, scratching for jobs along with all the other hunter-guard squads in Skaythe.

Everything Piyaro had built was falling apart. From a strength of twenty-six, he was reduced to fourteen. Two of his men were dead, casualties of their ill-fated charge against a rogue mage and his bunch of marauders. Another two had been lost to the golden witch. His second-in-command, Hyurey, had lured four of the others away to start his own squad. The last pair had deserted on the way to this wretched village.

As Hawk Squad trudged away, Piyaro reflected on the grim reality. It might be just as well so many men had deserted. In their reduced circumstances, he had a hard time feeding those who stayed. Hawk Squad spent more time foraging than they did training.

Count Ar-Oshten of Prizom had no more trust for Ar-Dayne's former soldiers than Ar-Jeziak. He'd quickly moved them on from his county. Dunsaph wouldn't even let them pass the border. The only light in this bleak tunnel was that they had arrived in Pulgoll at a moment of opportunity. Count Ar-Azlor was getting reports of a renegade mage stirring up trouble in the village of Opshar. He wanted it handled without arousing the suspicions of his neighbors. If Piyaro could make it work, maybe this new count would take them on. All would be well again.

With that purpose, Piyaro led his squad into Opshar. But they had failed.

He could see the glint of frustration in the Hawks' eyes, the slump of their shoulders, but none of them argued. They'd all tried it, and fought as well as they could. They'd seen what happened. As Piyaro led them back the way they came, he swore to himself that this was not over. These renegades would be brought to heel. It just might take more than his few of Hawk Squad to do it.

~ ~ ~

Flames roared and leaped, as if they would join with the lowering sun. It was a farmer's hut that burned, the thatched roofing a ready food for the blaze. Just short of the fire's reach, Ar-Lizelle glared down at the corpse that lay at her feet. Her former prisoner was still shaved bald, scorch marks crossing the clothing he'd stolen to hide himself among the commoners. A perpetual grin of madness split the stubbled face.

Ar-Lizelle's pulse pounded in her ears, and familiar scouring ache surged through her veins with every beat. *Lethentros* was the fuel for her destructive magic. Effective as it was, it came at a price. She breathed steadily and waited for the pain to ease.

This hadn't been an easy fight. The fugitive's

madness gave him wild power. However, Ar-Lizelle had been warden of the Larder, Dar-Gothull's prison for insane mages. She knew how to deal with the likes of him. Haafeth had died choking, her fire whip snaked about his throat. Not once did he stop laughing.

That was no surprise. Haafeth had been closer to madness than the rest of the prisoners. Ar-Lizelle had no remorse for his death. The list of his crimes was long even before the peasant farmer he murdered, and the widow he had been terrorizing when Ar-Lizelle caught up with him. It was Haafeth who set their roof on fire, a futile attempt at distraction.

No, her only regret was that she had learned nothing about the whereabouts of the other fugitives who broke loose on that horrible day.

Ar-Lizelle clenched her fists, controlling her fury. After years of patient work, monitoring reports and questioning new prisoners, she'd finally had the chance to capture her worthless younger sister. Lorrah had left their father to die, and Ar-Lizelle to prison. Worse, she had become a subversive, working against the mages who rightfully ruled over Skaythe. But the hunt's promised ending was merely a ruse. Lorrah had lured Ar-Lizelle out of the Larder, and while she was gone, a bunch of fake hunter-guards had broken all the prisoners out.

Disgraced by the failure of security, Ar-Lizelle lived on borrowed time. Countess Ar-Khoreen of Yergha, where the Larder was located, had made it clear that she must bring those fugitives back, or otherwise deal with them. If she failed, she would be stripped of her rank and cast back into the Larder as a prisoner.

Ar-Lizelle stood rigid, gazing at the flames without seeing them. She had sworn she would never suffer that way again. A ghastly creature haunted the Larder, a revenant with slashing octopus arms paired to a human face. That creature called itself a Devourer. And what did it devour? Mages.

No. No, that fate must not be hers.

"Well, that's one down," a man joked behind her.

"Only nine to go," his fellow agreed.

"Are you keeping score?" Ar-Lizelle whirled to screech in her high voice. "Do you think this is some sort of game?"

"No, Warden," Endole hastily replied. He and Groff saluted.

By Ar-Khoreen's order, only two of the prison guards had come with her on this hunt. The others remained with Captain Morthem, who held the Larder for her return. If she survived to return.

"Let's go," she snarled, and turned away.

As they strode away from the battle site, other sounds penetrated the fire's greedy crackling. Several voices whimpered and sobbed. Ar-Lizelle glanced over, annoyed. On the other side of the farm yard, the widowed peasant woman huddled with her three children. The family wept as they watched flames dance over their home.

That wasn't Ar-Lizelle's problem. She hadn't told them to build their hut with cheap, flimsy wood and flammable thatch.

Still, those children were pretty young.

Ar-Lizelle released an irritable sigh. Turning back, she raised her hands and commanded the fire to come to her. Bright orange flames flowed in a sheet, like a banner blown by a fierce gale. Hot prickles of renewed pain surged through her veins. She cursed under her breath. Startled, the two guards jumped back as it wrapped around her.

The flames shrank as Ar-Lizelle blew out a breath, releasing excess heat. It was a simple exercise, drilled into every young mage who sought to control their power. Two breaths more, and with each one the flames died farther down. She flicked the last wisp of fire from her fingertips after the fourth exhale.

The peasant woman gaped at her in awe. The children's faces glittered with tear tracks and snot. Disgusting.

Yet her irritation was not only for them. Coddling a bunch of peasants was just the sort of stupid thing Alemin or Lorrah might have done. Ar-Lizelle refused to even think that she might be like them.

"There," she snapped at the woman. "You can get your neighbors to help fix it, I suppose."

"Y-yes," stammered the widow. "Th-thank you, my lady..."

"Shhh!" Ar-Lizelle hissed, even more annoyed with herself for giving in to this weakness. She stormed toward the horses, and her guards quickly followed.

The last village, pathetic as it was, had held something resembling an inn. If they hurried, they could get back to it before darkness fell. After that, she must study her charts. The fugitives had been clever enough to split up, forcing Ar-Lizelle to track them individually. Before she could even do that, she would have to call on each count as they passed, assuring them of her good intentions and begging permission to do her duty.

Her team still had a lot of ground to cover, and much hunting to do.

II — SCARS

D usk settled over Fang Marsh. Shonn watched from the roof of the houseboat Otter as the setting sun cast muted pink and gold rays across the placid waters around the landing. He was tired at the end of a long working day. Poling his small raft through the shallows, pulling up crab pots, foraging in the dense mangroves. *Otter* sheltered his extended family, and Shonn had to do his part.

He leaned forward to rest his elbows on the rail. Time with kinfolk was good, the evening meal of river grain and fish satisfying, yet he was restless. It wasn't only boredom that made him fidgety. Everyone here was kin. He knew them all too well. Even now, he heard muffled voices rising in a pointless bicker over the same game they played every evening. Shonn had an itch to travel, to meet new people — especially young women who were not part of his own clan.

A fish jumped, raising rings of brighter water. As the air became cooler than the water, mist began to creep over the lotus pools and among the mangroves. Frogs and crickets and other night creatures raised their shimmering chorus. Inevitably, Shonn's eyes strayed south and west, where a low hump rose above the vegetation.

The mage's tower was deceptively quiet, showing no lights. You could think no one was there. That was the way they wanted it. He shrugged a little, irritated, and jerked around to watch the sun's last rays creep up the brown rocks that crowned the hills beyond the Fang Marsh.

That tower had been empty for a long time, decades at least, but it was Addith's domain now. Shonn remembered how he had worked to help her settle in. Her and the boy she'd said was a foundling. Ozlin was a surly brat. He'd never had taken to Shonn. Despite the kid's interference, Shonn had almost gotten to her. He grinned a little, remembering the hunger of Addith's kiss. It wouldn't have been much longer before he laid her down in the sand...

But the truth came out. Addith was never who she said she was. The water clan she claimed probably didn't even exist. Her real name was Meven, and she was a runaway mage. He'd seen her throwing ice chunks around, when that mudmaw took a strike at the boy. The kid lit himself on fire, too. Ozlin was a mageling she tried to train, while they both hid from Dar-Gothull's regime in the depths of the swamp.

Shonn had tried to hide his reaction, but Meven had turned cold and he'd known it was over between them. There was never really a choice, anyway. He'd had to report to the Eshur city guards. If Countess Ar-Torix thought the water-folk were in league with a rogue mage, she could destroy *Otter* and everyone aboard her.

That's what Shonn had told his parents, and the others who protested that he'd turned against one of the water-folk. To himself, he could admit the truth. He'd suspected about Meven, and he'd been toying with her, part of the same boredom that still scratched between his shoulder blades. If he won her trust, he could gather more information, something to trade with the guards. He could even have blackmailed her, forced her to lie with him, or used her in some other way. Shonn still wasn't sure how. It had only seemed like a good thing to have a mage at his command.

He would have done it, if not for Ozlin wandering carelessly on the bank. But the mudmaw's attack had made it clear the boy would always come first. It grated on Shonn's ego to be second best.

Meven's parting words were clear: "I don't want to see you again." Unfortunately for Meven, she didn't get to decide. Countess Ar-Torix had made it clear that she still wanted Shonn to be an informant. He had to be sneaky, knowing his parents wouldn't approve, but maybe he'd have another chance at the ice witch after all.

With a scowl, Shonn turned away from his thwarted vision. A flickering light caught his eye. He glanced over, expecting to see fireflies or the sun's final reflection. Instead, a glow appeared among the distant rocks. It swelled brighter, flashed briefly. Yellow light streaked down the slope. Sparks trailed behind it, like embers falling from a brazier. Shonn blinked. It moved so fast – and it was coming closer!

There was no sound of hooves or wheels. No flames rose from that spot. The golden streak, soft and vaguely shaped, curved to follow the old silvery scar that crossed the plain beyond the marsh. The silence was eerie. After a moment's staring, Shonn stamped his sandaled foot vigorously on the roof of the main cabin. "Oberim, Kannat!" he called to his father and uncle.

The bickering quieted. Muffled steps came from below, and the houseboat shifted slightly as the two men emerged from the main cabin. Shonn pointed at the mysterious object gliding ever closer.

"Do you see that?"

"Huh," said Oberim.

The three of them watched in silence. Whatever it was moved swiftly and steadily, stretched out to twice the length of Otter. In a way, it resembled a cloud of mist lit by morning sun. Yet there was no sun to light it.

Uncle Kannat murmured, "What moves it? There is no wind."

"Moves it," Shonn retorted. "What *is* it?"

The angle changed as the creature got closer. There were hints of solid form within the cloudy mass. Two branching antlers, a wolf's head with tousled mane, followed by a long body like an eel's. Yet any shape dissolved almost before he could identify it.

Then it was past them, following the ancient track that went straight across the marsh. By now, other family streamed out of the cabin and crowded up to the rail. The youngest boys, Nog and Ravi, went pelting around to the other side of the houseboat. Their shrill cries joined the adult murmurs of confusion and dismay drifting up to the cabin roof.

"Have you ever seen something like that?" Oberim asked his brothers.

"We know where it's going," Shonn replied, hiding his glee with grim certainty. "That path leads to the mage tower."

The adults gazed up at him with warning in their eyes. "She said not to go back," Oberim cautioned.

"The Countess wants us to keep an eye on her," Uncle Delveer answered.

"It's not really a choice, is it?" Shonn said. Rather than join this old argument, he kept his eyes on that misty glow until its last glint flared between the mangroves.

"Meven keeps to herself," argued his mother, Daranna. "We need to leave her alone."

"If the guards from Eshur find out, there's going to be trouble." That was Shonn's older brother, Bonton.

"Who's going to tell them?" Daranna said. Everyone pretended that they weren't looking at Shonn.

"Anyone could have seen it," he answered, annoyed. "It was glowing in the dark!"

"Maybe he's right," Oberim said slowly.

"We should keep on Ar-Torix's good side," Kannat said.

"We should stay out of her business," warned old Criya, who was just about everyone's grandmother.

"Do you want me to follow it?" Shonn tried not to sound too eager. There were risks to traveling in the marsh at night. Mudmaws were more active, for one thing.

"No," Oberim decided. "We'll just report this and let the Countess figure out what it means."

"Yes, Father."

The family started to filter back indoors, but Shonn stayed on the cabin roof a little longer. Maybe this time Meven wouldn't get away from him.

~ ~ ~

The next morning, Shonn poled away from *Otter* in the gray light of dawn. A few crab pots were stacked on his long, narrow raft as a sort of camouflage, but he didn't plan to go crabbing. Nor was he bound for the Eshur docks, on the northern edge of the salt marsh, though that was what his family elders expected. Shonn pushed his raft along with swift purpose. The sighting was intriguing, but he meant to bring the countess more than that.

Already, he could see a change at the mage tower since last evening. Clouds of ghostly mist wreathed the structure, concealing it from view. Shonn had a suspicion about what it meant.

He approached cautiously, taking an indirect route through the braided channels of the mangrove swamp. In some places, he turned aside to avoid mudmaw pools. In others, he crouched to pass beneath low-hanging branches. If he was lucky, Meven wouldn't know these hidden routes yet. She had only lived in Fang Marsh for a few months. That wasn't nearly enough time to learn all its secrets.

Still, Shonn took his time. There were many ways to give himself away. Water was noisy, easy to splash. Wild monkeys might start screeching, or chattering birds might suddenly fall silent. Either one could give a warning of his presence. He would need all his swampcraft to spy on the ice witch.

Before long, pale blotches began to show between layers of leafy cover. Shonn frowned as a chilly draft flowed around him in defiance of the morning's rising heat. He should be getting close, yet there was an alternation in the sound of the water. Wavelets slapped against some obstruction rather than just swishing between the mangrove roots. Whatever this obstacle was, it hadn't been here before. He shifted the angle of his pole to turn the raft and skirt around what he suspected.

The cold intensified, so it was no surprise that the nose of his raft thumped against something hard and shining. Even with fog muffling the sunlight, the ice was stark white. It shouldn't have been possible in the heat of the marsh, but there it was. The damp chill clung to his skin, and his lungs ached a bit with each breath. Aside from the mist coiling off the ice, there was no sign of melting.

Not possible, Shonn repeated to himself. Well, what did that mean? With an ice witch around, the definition of what was possible obviously stretched a bit.

He turned his raft, seeking a way past the ice wall. There didn't seem to be an end to it. After a couple of fruitless efforts, he tied his raft to the mangrove roots. Grabbing a strong branch, he monkey-climbed to the top of the thicket. Like water, the leaves were hard to pass through without making noise, but he went slowly and soon raised a cautious head just above the level of the highest branches.

As he had suspected, Meven's tower was completely covered with ice. Glistening spires surrounded the structure, covering even the archway leading in. Around it, an impressive wall circled the landing area. This was what blocked the channels. The road was cut off, as well. Sheets of fog circulated in layers all around the old tower, chilling the air even beyond the immediate space.

Shonn had seen this before, when he followed Ar-Torix to confront Meven those months before. As unnatural and intimidating as it had been at that time, this tableau made even more of a statement.

The ice witch was expecting to be attacked.

He watched for a while, shivering as the cold of her vigilance penetrated to his bones. Nothing moved in the area around the landing, or on the rooftop with its fringe of fruiting vines. That was too bad. If Shonn had a chance, he might be able to talk her around. He could find out what that creature was, and what it had to do with her. Or, maybe, he just wanted to see her again.

Well, the tower was shut up tight, ready for danger. They must have a store of food inside. After a time, Shonn slid back down between the branches. The raft sloshed and swayed as he dropped lightly onto it.

Oberim might not have told him to come here, but Shonn was glad that he had. Even if he didn't know what that creature was, he did have other information to share. Solid, icy white information. Countess Ar-Torix would definitely want to know about this.

~ ~ ~

Duessa woke in the chill of dawn. Unlike the guardswomen, the Larder's fugitives had neither tents nor bedrolls. They slept crammed into the back of the Badgers' wagon. It was Duessa's turn to use the narrow bench. She caught herself just short of falling off and sat up, shivering.

A bubble of lantern light revealed the guardswomen's camp and its short row of blood-red tents. Horses and oxen were only vague dark shapes where they had been picketed the night before. Outside that limited area, it was barely light enough to see.

Rustling fabric alerted her when Alemin came out of the tent he shared with Lorrah. He wasn't heading for the cess pit, as Duessa was half tempted to do. Slow, stiff steps brought him around to face southward. A single hand rose to scratch through the stubble on his shaved head. Though the fields and groves around them were quiet, Alemin winced, as if a loud noise troubled him.

Duessa folded her arms against the cold. She couldn't figure out why they were awake. Below her feet, Bettain stirred and mumbled something. Elldri was open-eyed, too. When she saw Duessa's gaze on her, she rolled over.

A memory surfaced reluctantly. It was sunrise. That was when the wailing would always start in the Larder. Duessa shivered, and not just with pre-dawn chill. They were free of that place now. She hadn't had a nightmare since they left. Yet the fugitives still woke up to its call.

Images flashed through her. Fighting against the hard grip of guards. Screams ahead of them. They propelled her into the torture chamber with the Larder's warden, Ar-Wharon, gone mad and attacking the prisoners. Scattered corpses, blackened and stinking of scorched flash.

Duessa jerked upright and shook her head. She ran a shaking hand over her face. The scars were like that memory. Not always hurting, but they never went away. Wharon was dead and she was out of the Larder. Why did she think she would never truly be free?

"We need allies," Sergeant Zathi had said, while Alemin consoled her, "We're only going to find our friend." Both statements appeared to be true, yet they felt like bold-faced lies.

She should have expected this, Duessa scolded herself as she joined in the routines of breaking camp. Back in the wagon for another day's travel, she tried to settle her emotions. On the day of the escape, Alemin and Lorrah had been very interested in her training. They seemed to imagine some connection between their teacher, Ar-Thea, and her former mentor, Ar-Lannon. Which was hardly the recommendation they believed.

They assumed, mages and guardswomen alike, that the Larder's surviving mages would be excited to join in their insane mission of destroying Dar-Gothull's regime. Arrogant, that's what it was. Duessa frowned at the wooded hills rising along the border between Yergha and Kamuril.

Was she ready for a rebellion? Nobody could be ready for that. The idea was tempting, of course. Skaythe was a wreck of a nation, divided into counties that squabbled among themselves while Dar-Gothull fed off them all. Death and grief were constant companions.

And yet, the idea of doing anything about it was terrifying.

The Larder mages rode silently, carrying on their task of knotting grass into sandal cord. Occasionally one of them yawned. But they hadn't lost their sense of self-preservation. When Keerin, riding as forward scout, trotted back to Zathi, they all looked up sharply.

"Road's washed out up there," she called.

"Show me." The sergeant prodded her sorrel, Ember, and the two rode ahead. Jaxynne reined Cinder around to take the position Zathi had been riding.

"What do you think," called Alemin from his seat beside the driver. "Marauders?"

"Maybe it's a tax collector," Razeet said. Duessa nodded. Traders often used these back roads to avoid border posts. It was a scheme she, herself, was very familiar with.

"They'd just set up a roadblock, though," Giniver said from the other side.

"We'll know soon enough," Jaxynne replied.

Zathi and Keerin quickly trotted back. "Yep, it's washed out."

Before long, Sethamis hauled on the reins and called out, "Ho boys, ho now!"

Once the wagon had jolted into stillness, they all stood to see what was in front of the oxen. A small gully had eroded across the track at a long angle. Horses and people on foot would be able to get across with a little effort, but the wagon wheels were another matter.

"No tax collectors," Lorrah cheerfully reported. "Just another count who's too lazy to take care of his people."

Zathi, Jaxynne, Lorrah and Alemin joined in an intense discussion of how to get their wagon across the damaged area, or whether there was another road that didn't take them back toward Yergha and the Larder.

Duessa, having nothing to contribute, sat back down to brood some more. Allies, not fighters, that was what Sergeant Zathi claimed. Not likely. All her life, people wanted Duessa to fight. In the temple school, they said it was the only way. To survive in this world, you had to be vicious. You couldn't give in to the pain of *lethentros*.

That had never felt right to her. Even in the extremes of the combat training, when practice bouts could turn deadly, Duessa had known there must be a better way. She didn't want to be estranged from her family by the magic she was born with. She wanted to have better choices about her life.

Later, when she found out her mother was so ill, it had been no choice at all to steal the medicine that might save her. Mother had died anyway, but at least Duessa had been able to see her before it was too late. Then she was on the run, trying to find a way out of Busaren ahead of the hunter-guards. There was a water-folk landing near the fishing village of Liatho. That was where she met Ar-Lannon.

As a moon-runner, smuggling people and goods where they might not be welcome, he had presented an alternative. Escape from the hunter-guards, yes, but Ar-Lannon was a rogue mage, too. He offered training, companionship, and a rough sort of employment. So what if she had to become a moon-runner? Rogue mages didn't have many options. It had been a tough life, but she did gain another sort of family, with Ar-Lannon and his two other magelings, Gauer and Doromy.

Ar-Lannon was the one who told them the impossible story of the Shining Ones. In that long-ago utopia, Skaythe was a land of wonders where magic was shared freely. With a crooked smile, Ar-Lannon mocked the tale even as he hungered to believe in it. Duessa had been younger then, eager to take up anything besides Dar-Gothull's terrible laws. Only later, she had learned the limits of Ar-Lannon's loyalty.

"Duessa, Bettain?" It was almost a relief when Lorrah's high voice interrupted her thoughts. The younger mage gestured to the gully blocking their way. "Do you have any ideas?"

"Couldn't we just fill it in?" Alemin gestured to the washed-out road.

"With what?" Zathi asked. "I don't see a pile of loose gravel around here."

Duessa and Bettain stood up to look again. Sethamis was unyoking the oxen and leading them aside, while the wagon itself rumbled and bumped as Jaxynne directed Razeet and Keerin to unload the cargo bay underneath. The gully wasn't very wide. If they stretched out, the women could pass things to each other. It was just that the edges were crumbling and the wagon wheels obviously wouldn't make it across.

Alemin gave a wry chuckle. "All our great plans, thwarted by a washed-out road."

Lorrah pouted, but Duessa and Bettain laughed along with him. Strangely enough, Duessa was reminded of how the moon-runners sometimes moved their boats as they skirted the coast between Busaren and Prowth.

"We could pick it up," she said. It had been a while, but Duessa still remembered how to move things without crushing them.

"What do you mean?" Jaxynne straightened.

"Magic." Duessa thought that was obvious. "Some friends of mine, we had to get our boat over some rapids in a flood." No need to explain that they were moving stolen goods, trying to hide their traces from the count's guards. "It took four of us, though."

"Yeah, that's easy," Lorrah quickly inserted, and preened a little. "You know I can throw rocks with my magic, right? It's just a matter of lifting instead of throwing."

She looked to Alemin for approval, and he quickly squeezed her hand. "That's three of us. Who's our fourth mage?"

"Don't look at me," Bettain waved in denial. "Fire is my specialty. Let me know when you want to set it on fire."

"No thanks," Zathi answered drily.

Everyone looked at Elldri, who ducked her chin, eyes wide with concern. Then she lisped, "I can try."

"Great!" Razeet enthusiastically started shoving things back into the cargo bay.

"Hold on," Zathi said. "If it takes four of them, let's make it as light as we can."

Badger Squad moved quickly then, some of the guardswomen leading the animals around while others passed the luggage across and sorted it on the far side. Bettain and Razeet kept watch for any unexpected onlookers. Lorrah coached Elldri on the way to focus her power and lift a stone from the roadside.

After many fumbles, Duessa patted her friend's

shoulder. "Let us do the moving. You just help steady it."

They balanced their skills by having Alemin and Duessa switch places. He would help Elldri push from one side, while Lorrah and Duessa pulled it to them. Duessa summoned her power, gritting her teeth against the acrid sensation. Fortunately, the work went smoothly. Despite her youth, Lorrah was strong. Duessa was only sorry she hadn't stayed with Elldri, because the girl trembled and sweated with some emotion Duessa couldn't identify.

They soon had the wagon over the gap. While the guardswomen got on with the process of re-packing cargo and hitching the oxen back up, Duessa rested beside Elldri and Bettain. The younger woman stared into the distance without speaking. Bettain obviously wondered why Elldri was so upset, but neither of them asked. If Elldri wanted them to know, she would say it herself.

The wagon had been heavy, even when empty, but it roused more memories. Duessa and Ar-Lannon's other crew used to operate like this, crossing borders and generally getting into places where they weren't supposed to be. Working together had been easy, even fun. Until that last night.

Duessa had been the lookout. Hidden in the rocks, she had heard the tramp of booted feet and saw the hunter-guards coming. She'd sent up a small spark, the signal of warning. Duessa didn't know if her friends had seen it, but the hunter-guards definitely did. She fought as best she could, hoping someone would come to help her, but it never happened. Duessa had been taken prisoner. She didn't know whether Ar-Lannon and the others had fought and been killed, or left her there to save themselves.

The hunter-guards had asked a lot of questions about who hired Ar-Lannon and where they were going with their illicit cargo, but they hadn't talked about fighting with anyone else. There was only one conclusion Duessa could make.

Eventually she had been sentenced to the Larder for her thievery. So much for the Shining Ones, sharing one and all. Or so she had thought all these years. Until Alemin's friends turned up and broke everyone out of the Larder.

Yes, it was great to get away from the nightmares. To have full meals and learn to know the women of Badger Squad. For the first time in years, Duessa was free to make choices for herself, about her life.

It was nice, but she couldn't forget how Ar-Lannon, Gauer and Doromy had disappeared without a word. How did she know these people wouldn't abandon her, too?

~ ~ ~

By noon, Shonn was sweating in the muggy heat. He adjusted the waist of his short sarong and pulled a loose shirt of pale green swamp linen over his brown shoulders. A reed hat kept the worst of the sun off. Eshur's harbor was noisome compared to salt marsh and mangroves. The odor of rotten fish rose from the stagnant water. Larger ships rowed to the higher wharves, while a floating dock hosted an assortment of skiffs and rowboats. As Shonn poled his raft in, it was the only water-folk craft among them.

Maybe that was why the guard at the top of the stairs frowned and stalked down to confront him. A sharp gaze took in the empty crab pots on his raft.

"You're not selling anything, so what's your business here?"

"I have a report from Fang Marsh." Shonn stowed his pole and jumped over to the dock. He knelt to tie off his raft.

"And who are you?" The fellow folded his arms, blocking Shonn from coming any farther up the dock.

"Shonn, from the *Otter*." The questions were irritating, but Shonn knew better than to make trouble among the land-folk. "Countess Ar-Torix wants this information. Is Sergeant Hurth around? He'll vouch for it."

The guardsman shrugged, refusing to believe what Shonn said. "Wait here."

He ambled back down the dock and up the steps, in no particular hurry to cooperate with the water-folk from Fang Marsh. Shonn supposed he felt powerful now. What a jerk. Holding back curses, Shonn stepped over into a narrow patch of shade. This was why he hated coming to Eshur. No amount of trade goods made up for the attitude of the land-folk.

Time passed. Shonn stood sweating while the shade's edge crept farther along the dock. Maybe he should have offered a bribe. He did have another option, if the guard took too long. A lot of guards passed time at Fang Reef Tavern. One of them might know where Hurth was, or the barkeep might pay for the information.

Shonn didn't object to the notion of extra coin in his belt. If this was a random tip-off, like smugglers hiding out in the marsh, that would be one thing. But it wasn't. The countess was already directly involved in Meven's business. Going around her would not be a good idea.

He was just about to head for the Fang Reef Tavern when the dock shuddered underfoot. Looking up, he saw his original guard approaching, followed by a larger guard with more stripes on the shoulder of his vambrace. Hurth was a sergeant in the Countess' personal guard. He was armed with sword, club and whip. His face was broad and softly fleshed, but the bright black eyes sheltered beneath his heavy brow held a glint sharper than mere greed.

"You have something?"

"Yes," Shonn answered. He let his gaze stray past Hurth to that other guard, who loitered suspiciously near. Hurth turned to follow his gaze, and the eavesdropper edged back a little.

"That will do." Hurth's tone allowed no argument. When the fellow had moved off, he grated out, "Well?"

"Something came into Fang Marsh yesterday, at dusk. It was like a ball of yellow light, drifting without the wind's help," Shonn explained.

"Yellow light," Hurth repeated skeptically. "There's a lot of mist over the marsh at dusk."

"It wasn't a mirage," Shonn said. "The sun had already gone down, but it was still glowing. You could almost see shapes in it, but they didn't come clear. It followed the old road, where we went to the mage tower last time. Father thought Lady Ar-Torix would want to know."

Shonn made sure to mention that. It would make a lot of things easier if *Otter* kept a good reputation with the land-folk. Hurth nodded. He had been part of Ar-Torix's escort to confront Meven, those months ago. Dark eyes gleamed as he considered what Shonn was saying.

"Anything else?"

"I thought it was connected, so I went by this morning at dawn," Shonn went on. "The mage tower is covered with ice again, and there's another wall of ice around it, blocking the road. The ice witch is getting ready for trouble."

"There's fog there. We can see it from the keep." Hurth considered for a moment longer, then said, "It's good that you came. Follow me."

Spongy wood sagged beneath their feet as they moved along the floating dock. A couple of traders came down the stone steps from the town, but quickly got out of Hurth's way. As soon as they reached the top, the street and wharves were packed with people. Shonn took advantage of his companion's imposing presence to keep a steady pace. Also, it was easier than trying to find his own way through.

Eshur Holl was a warren of badly patched cobblestone streets, where moss coated both wooden shacks and stone warehouses. The air was unnaturally still, penned by too many walls. The noise and stench were tremendously magnified after the open landscape of marsh and mangroves. Shonn did his best to mark the turnings, all the same.

Soon enough, they crossed into the main plaza, where Dar-Gothull's temple stood tall and square. Four watch towers rose above the passing throng. The cast iron statue was huge, with a severe frown and black metal robes flowing as if in a strong breeze. Its left hand was raised, and an eternal flame burned in the palm. Shonn was glad that Hurth didn't stop to pay homage, since he hadn't brought anything to give in offering. He still felt as if the row of gargoyles along the roof's edge were glaring at him suspiciously.

He was a little surprised that Hurth didn't lead him past that, to the north gate. A fortified causeway led up to the countess' keep, on the bluff above the town. That was where they had taken him, the first time he met with the countess and revealed Meven's intrusion into Fang Marsh. But instead, Hurth went past Dar-Gothull's temple to another grim stone structure.

The temple school was just beyond the temple itself. It wasn't as tall, but still windowless and forbidding. More gargoyles lined the roof. Here was where young mages took their training, kept imprisoned by sternly vigilant hunter-guards. A pair of these guards flanked the cavernous entrance. Hurth saluted and gruffly asked if the countess was still there. After being told yes, he waved for Shonn to follow.

It was a little cooler once they got out of the sun, but no breeze made it past those walls. The atmosphere inside was stifling. Shonn couldn't see any smoke, though there a strange odor and something in the air made his eyes sting. Blinking, he followed Hurth through a reception area and straight back to an interior courtyard.

There were windows here, a few large ones on the ground floor and many smaller ones above. A low wall divided the courtyard into two squares, where layers of stony benches sank down to a pair of arenas. In one of them, students in plain brown robes watched their fellows spar. A red-robed instructor was scolding one of them.

"You're holding back," he snapped. "Do you want to die?"

Above that arena was a larger seat, elegantly carved and cushioned. There lounged the woman Shonn had come to see.

He would have known she was here, even if she hadn't been facing him. Objectively, Countess Ar-Torix was no more beautiful than any other woman her age, yet Shonn found it impossible to be objective. There was something about her that drew every eye. Perhaps that her crimson robe was cut enticingly low, while her midnight braids were done up high. Pearls gleamed in those coils, and at her ears, neck and wrists.

You couldn't trust a mage, especially not the nobility. Shonn knew that as well as anyone, but when he was in her presence, all caution faded. He wanted nothing more than to kneel at her feet. Hurth led him toward the throne. With what remained of his senses, Shonn wondered how Hurth and the others of her household stood it. He would be going crazy, constantly feeling the lure of someone who might kill him at a whim, and unable to reach for her.

Sizzles and pops echoed from the walls as the two students fought. The one who was being yelled at summoned a hail of sparks that sent some of the onlookers scrambling, but his opponent, a young woman, merely side-stepped. She swept a hand downward and shards of glittering ice formed under his feet. Trying to dodge, he fell and curled onto one side, clasping his elbow with a snarl of pain.

"Match!" cried their instructor, wholly disgusted. "Point to Nyette."

Polite applause echoed across the courtyard. Countess Ar-Torix joined in, but when she saw Hurth and Shonn approaching, her eyes narrowed. The instructor, noting her gaze, asked, "Countess, should we delay the next fight?"

"No, continue," Ar-Torix replied. Her cheerful smoothness was at odds with her wary gaze.

The previous two competitors returned to the stone benches. They glared at each other briefly, the loser still rubbing his elbow. The mage in charge called on two new competitors. Hurth stopped before the countess and saluted, fist to his chest.

"My lady. A report from Fang Marsh."

"I thought I recognized our friend from the water-folk," Ar-Torix smirked. As she shifted in her seat, a slit in her robe showed Shonn the shape of her legs. He tore his eyes away. "How is dear old Meven? I hope she isn't getting up to something."

From the gleam in her eyes, Ar-Torix actually hoped for a reason to go after Meven. Shonn wasn't sure if his news would satisfy that desire.

"I don't know, my lady," he began, and quickly outlined what he had already said to Hurth. Ar-Torix listened intently.

"How mysterious," she murmured when he described the cloud-creature. "Pale gold light, you say?"

"Yes, countess." Shonn went on with his tale. As he described the icy spires, Shonn could still feel a lingering ache in his lungs.

Even though the students were blasting fire at each other, the instructor made no secret that he was also listening. Hurth frowned at that, but since the instructor was a mage, he couldn't make an issue of it.

At the end, Hurth did put in, "This would explain the light our sentries saw last night."

"An explanation that explains nothing," Ar-Torix

mused. "Now why would Meven feel the need to defend herself, if she has done no wrong? This requires further exploration."

"Shall I send for your horse, Countess?" Hurth asked.

Pearls gleamed in the countess' hair as she considered. "Not yet. If this is some sort of trick, I'll not rush into it. Ar-Selviss."

The instructor quickly stopped the match and bowed. "My lady?"

Ar-Torix went on, "I believe it was Nyette who won the bout just now. In your opinion, is she ready for a different sort of challenge?"

"An excellent suggestion, my lady." Ar-Selviss smiled obsequiously. "The arena does not always prepare our students for conditions in the field."

The student in question was already on her feet. She was tall for a girl, and Shonn had the impression of an athletic build beneath her stiff brown robe. Black, curly hair fell to her shoulders, where it was cut off in a sharp, straight line. Two dainty hairpins, shaped as butterflies, held it away from her face.

"Command me, Countess," she cried.

"No need to get so excited." Ar-Torix laughed, a silvery sound that drew every man's eye to her. "I merely need you to venture into Fang Marsh along with my friend from the water-folk. Examine the ice wall with a mage's eye, and report back to me. Simplicity."

"I will make it so." Nyette's gaze was intense, in contrast to the childish note of the butterfly pins.

"Yes, yes." Ar-Torix looked past her and signaled Ar-Selviss to begin the next match. It may have been Shonn's imagination, but he thought Ar-Torix didn't want a younger woman getting too much attention. Not that she needed to worry, as alluring as she was.

Hurth tapped Shonn's shoulder, breaking Ar-Torix's spell. "Come on."

Reluctantly, he tore his eyes away from the temptation of the countess and followed Hurth back into the stuffy building. Shonn's eyes began to sting again. Nyette stopped in the reception area, where a narrow staircase led upward.

"I'm going to gather a few things," she announced in a brittle imitation of Ar-Torix's confident tone. Hunter-guards at the counter looked around at those words. To Shonn, she said, "I assume you don't want a troop of them escorting me."

"No," he immediately agreed. One passenger might fit on his raft, but not a bunch of them. "We'll want to move quietly through the swamp."

Wryly, Hurth asked, "Shall I explain that to them?"

"I'd appreciate it." Nyette hurried up the steps.

"This is more than I had planned on," Shonn complained, but Hurth was already walking away.

~ ~ ~

Ar-Lizelle sat near the hearth in that miserable excuse for an inn, running an impatient finger up and down a cut mark in the wooden table. Groff sat across from her, drinking what passed for their ale. A circle of nervous silence ringed the two of them. Locals edged by, afraid to disturb her in case she lashed out in anger. Which, to be fair, she might do if this waiting went on much longer.

Earlier, she had sent Endole out to circulate in the small marketplace. With any luck, he would track down a helpful rumor. People wouldn't speak freely to a mage, but they might open up for a somewhat friendly guardsman. Unfortunately, it meant wasting time that Ar-Lizelle might not have.

At last, she heard booted strides. Endole returned, and from his bright expression, he had good news.

"Well?" Ar-Lizelle snapped.

"One of the traders said their caravan passed a guard wagon a couple of days ago. Hunter-guards, all females." Endole paused significantly. Ar-Lizelle nodded, terse. The hunter-guards who deceived her crew had been all women. "They had a bunch of mages in a cage, but they weren't heading for the Larder."

She resisted the urge to jump to her feet. "Where was this?"

"The old highway," he said. "It runs east to west, then turns north. They could be bound for either Kamuril or Unthur."

"Wasn't the juggler arrested in Unthur?" Groff asked. "He wouldn't go back there."

"But he does have family in Kamuril." Ar-Lizelle had studied Alemin's origins thoroughly.

"Maybe he thinks they'll help him," Endole said.

"Perhaps." Ar-Lizelle pushed back from the table with a nod to Endole. "Good work."

Groff tossed back the last of his ale. "I'll get the horses."

III — EXPEDITION

L eading an expedition was not what Shonn had planned. He slouched down the steps to the floating dock, unwanted passenger following closely. Maybe he shouldn't have been surprised. The last time, Ar-Torix had insisted he come with her and her guards. If it got him any more information on Meven, maybe it would be worth it.

The student mage, Nyette, had obviously never been in a boat before. She wobbled and waved her arms for balance when the raft shifted under her feet. Land-folk were always funny to watch, as long as they didn't capsize your boat. Shonn bent forward to untie his line, and hid his mocking smile.

At least the young mage had sense enough to crouch near the center of the raft and steady herself on the stack of crab pots. She wasn't allowed to change her brown robe, but she'd swapped out her heavy boots and gauntlets from the arena. Leather sandals and a patterned scarf over her hair were better choices for the steamy marsh. She still looked like a lump of mud huddled nervously on the deck.

As Shonn poled away from the dock, Nyette spoke in a clipped tone. "What do I need to know about this ice witch?"

It wasn't quite an order, which was good since she wasn't quite a mage. She was also several years younger than

Shonn. It was annoying to answer to her, but this was what the countess wanted so he had to put up with it.

"She's older than you, not as tall," he began grudgingly. "She was dressed like a peasant at first. Wore her hair in a single braid, and she had a hat like this one." He tapped the brim of his reed hat. "Later on, she changed into our kind of clothes and pretended that she was one of us."

"What do you mean," Nyette interrupted. "Our kind of clothes?"

"A sarong, like this." Shonn swept a hand, showing her his short sarong and loose shirt of uniform, pale green. "Though the women wear it from their chest to their knees."

The raft rocked as Nyette peered over her shoulder. Black eyes studied him with the same intensity she had shown in the arena. He posed a little with the pole, rather than let her see how uneasy that made him.

"What is that fabric?" she asked with genuine curiosity.

"Swamp linen. Our women make it." Shonn couldn't think why she cared about this. Making swamp linen was a long process, which he had seen but fortunately never been part of. A man's work was fishing and hunting. "Swamp linen cuts the sun, but it dries quickly, so it won't rot in the damp air."

Carefully, Nyette turned back around. Shonn continued guiding the raft out of Eshur's crowded and stinking harbor. He expected more questions as they glided into the salt marsh, but she only looked around suspiciously. After a few minutes, she leaned over to trail a hand in the water. Then she gazed upward, studying the white puffs of cloud. Her shoulders rose and fell with several deep breaths.

The silence made Shonn edgy, so he decided to bring the subject back to Meven.

"Anyway, she called herself Addith, but her real

name is Meven. She tried to act like water-folk, gave my father some story about coming from a houseboat on Lake Bilseng. I could tell something was off."

"How?" Nyette interrupted.

"She didn't keep our customs." Shonn left it at that. There was a lot about water-folk life that land-folk didn't need to know. "She wouldn't come aboard our houseboat, hardly wanted to talk." Shonn remembered trying to strike up a conversation, thinking to woo an attractive stranger. The memory of her rejection scraped at his pride. "She lied to us about everything."

"Of course a rogue would do that." Nyette dismissed his complaint. "I've heard she had a mageling boy with her."

"That kid wasn't hers, and she told a fine story about him, too." Shonn poled harder as anger gave strength to his arms. "His name is Oz, or that's what she told me. I guess she was trying to teach him."

"Magelings belong in the temple school," Nyette said primly. Again she leaned over, reaching for the soft curl of the raft's wake. A rough stroke of Shonn's pole splashed her. She hastily sat back up, complaining, "Slow down."

"We have a job to do," he dared to retort.

"There's no rush." Nyette frowned at him, but then her fierce gaze veered away. Her tone was softer, almost longing. "I haven't been outside the Temple School in nine years. Except for festivals, but that doesn't count. We have to work."

Shonn raised his pole and let the raft glide, simply out of shock. He had little sympathy for mages, but she hadn't been outside that stuffy temple school in how long? It sounded unbearable.

He looked around, trying to see the salt marsh as Nyette must. A gentle wind brushed his legs and whispered among the reeds and grasses. It was hot and humid, yes, with nothing to shelter them from the sun. Yet wavelets shimmered on all sides. Instead of the harbor's stench, the air was ripe with scents of greenery and life. The deep breaths she took might not be a sign of panic, but savoring the fresh air beyond Eshur's reek of sewage and rot.

Ahead of them, the ice-covered tower stuck up above the mangroves. Layers of mist still drifted there, even in the heat of day. Shonn kept quiet until they reached the mangroves. In those shaded channels, the bright waters turned glossy and dark. Low-hanging branches threatened them, and he cautioned, "Watch your head."

Nyette gave a kind of sigh, then once again turned to their task. "I suppose you should tell me about her magic."

"I'm not a mage," he began, but Nyette cut him off.

"I know that," she scowled. "Just say what you observed. After what happened last time, Lady Ar-Torix was obsessed with ice magic. She wanted all the older students to try it. Everyone knows fire and lightning, she said, but ice would bring versatility to Eshur's forces."

The student mage raised both her hands, and Shonn felt the cold draft even before he saw the glitter of frost on her brown skin. When she folded her fingers into fists, mist feathered around them.

"I don't like this," Nyette said, "but if it gets me out of that place faster, I'll do it."

Her voice turned flat in a way that instantly made him think of Meven. It was an unwelcome reminder of all his frustrations. From what he had seen earlier, Shonn couldn't go directly to the mage tower's landing. The ice walls and spires were still there. He'd have to use a side path. One with bittersweet memories.

"All right." Shonn turned the raft down another channel. "What I mostly saw was when a mudmaw tried to eat the kid. It dragged him into the water." Nyette frowned, concerned. He supposed, being shut up in a school, she had never seen a mudmaw, either. "Meven covered them in a block of ice and yanked the whole thing onto the shore. Then she carved the ice with her hands, and let Oz out."

"She pulled the ice block." Nyette seemed to study her own fingers. "And the mudmaw, did it get away?"

"No, it was still stuck in the ice. She killed it by hitting its head and some ice spikes went in." The smoked meat was still feeding his family, but that was little compensation for Meven's deception.

"She had to touch it first? Interesting."

The young mage asked no more questions, and Shonn was glad enough to just steer his raft through a series of narrower channels. Soon enough, they emerged into open water that had been a mudmaw's pool. Lotus pads were already poking up along the edges. As they nosed up to the bank, Shonn saw that little was left of the beast but a few bones, well gnawed and scattered about the sand. The skull was mostly intact, with two round holes from Meven's fatal attack.

Nyette stepped off the raft with grateful speed, then spent a moment settling the thick folds of her brown robe. She went to examine the skull, while Shonn pulled the raft farther up the sand. The ice-clad tower loomed above the dark mangroves, reflecting the sunlight with painful brilliance. All around it, stark white patches showed through the trees.

"There's a trail over here." Shonn led Nyette past the clump of grass trees, where he had kissed Meven for the first and only time. Bitterness clawed at him, and he quickly moved past.

The path was blocked just beyond that point by a smooth and glistening sheet of ice. Even if Shonn climbed the nearest tree and jumped, he wouldn't be able to cross it. It felt like a personal comment. Meven knew he would remember the trail they had used so many times, and made sure to close it off.

"I do not wish to see you," she'd said. Apparently she meant it.

Knowing none of this history, Nyette bent low to study the base of the ice wall. She then straightened and glared at it, as if it was her enemy in the temple school's arena. "You say she carved the ice with her hands?"

"That's what it looked like."

Nyette raised both arms above her head, holding the fingers flat, as if her hands were blades. A downward slash, a slithering sound, and shards of ice peeled off the wall. After several passes, a pile of ice accumulated up to her ankles. Shonn stepped back to let the mage work. He could feel the cold in his lungs again, and he was amazed Nyette could stand the ice piling up around her sandals. Soon he saw greenery on the other side of the wall. A few more swift strokes widened the gap.

"It wasn't very thick." Shonn felt foolish for not even trying to cut his way through with his hunting knife. Nyette shrugged.

"It doesn't have to be. There's magic in it still. Look, it's trying to freeze itself over again."

Shonn leaned closer. The chunks on the ground were already melting, but the jagged edges gave light crackles as they began to fill in. Nyette flicked a few ice chips off her robe before she stepped through.

"Come along," she said, still wrapped in icy calm. "Even if the gap closes completely, I can get us back out."

The ground felt slick as Shonn followed Nyette along the trail. Clusters of leaves glistened with a sheer layer of ice. Some of them were darkened and limp, damaged by temperatures they weren't bred for. Thick fog clung to his skin as if it would freeze him, too. The cold made him cough. Aside from that, a few slow drips of water were the only sounds.

The walk was short, but memories stuck to him like the mist. Here was a cut branch where he gathered wood to make Meven's bench. There, he'd cleaned a catfish he caught for her. And now came the flattened paving in front of the entrance, where they had sat in the shade for hours, while Meven twisted sections of reed into cord for making a carry-bag.

What a waste of time. Yet, to Shonn's surprise, some of his anger fell away as they rounded the tower. Meven hadn't been the only one lying, he could admit. His flirtations had never been honest.

Nyette stopped, facing the structure. Black eyes roved the frozen facade with her usual keen focus. Thinking that she wanted a way in, Shonn stepped over to where clusters of vines were still cloudily visible through the whiteness.

"There's an archway past here," he said.

She didn't answer right away, but in a short while announced, "That doesn't matter. We can go back."

Shonn followed uncertainly as she turned decisively toward the trail they had come in on. He felt like a fool and didn't appreciate it.

"You don't need to talk to her?" he asked. "I thought the countess said..."

"I can't talk to her," Nyette cut him off. "No one is here."

"Not here?" Shonn felt even more like a fool, repeating her words. Why did the knowledge hurt him?

"They've gone," Nyette affirmed calmly. "There's *isalonis* and nothing else."

She must have seen that Shonn didn't understand what that meant, because she continued patiently. "This whole thing is a trick. Lady Ar-Torix was right about that, but not the way she thought. Your Meven must have feared someone would see her leave, so she gave us something else to look at."

"She's not my..." Shonn trailed off. Searching for a different explanation, he asked, "If she's gone, then why doesn't the ice melt?"

"I don't know how she did it," Nyette answered, "but it feels like a self-enforcing bond. The *isalonis* seems endless. The more ice it creates, the colder it gets, and the colder it gets, the more ice will form. She might have kept everyone watching this spot for quite a while."

Shonn stopped listening for a moment, trying to breathe around the ache in his chest. Just this morning, he had been thinking he would speak to Meven. Talk her around. Even put up with her surly brat, if it meant he got back into her life.

But her lies were better.

He followed the student mage back the way they had come. The fog was thicker, as if it would hide the trail, but soon enough they stepped back through the gap Nyette had made. The icy walls were definitely closing in. Broken edges caught at his shoulders like icy claws. Mist billowed from Shonn's mouth as he coughed, brushing frost off his shirt.

"What are we going to do?" he asked when he could get a breath without coughing.

"*You*," she stressed it, "will take me back to Eshur and be on your way. *I* will inform Countess Ar-Torix of what I learned, and *she* will decide what to do next."

That hurt, how she cut Shonn out of the matter. He didn't even know if that was what he wanted. Nyette stepped back onto the raft, gathered her robe, and settled down beside the empty crab pots. Shonn pushed off, chewing on his thoughts.

"We still don't know what everyone saw," he said, "or if it has to do with Meven and Oz being gone."

"You're right." Nyette's voice began to sound more normal and arrogant. "However, that may not matter. The ice witch has fled. If she's not in Eshur, there may be nothing Lady Ar-Torix needs to do. Aside from warning her neighbors that a powerful rogue mage is on the move, that is."

Shonn winced. Yes, rogue mages were dangerous. They had to be hunted down. But he couldn't help wondering what had made Meven leave so suddenly. Her deal with the countess seemed to protect her. Something had changed. It must have to do with that unknown, glowing creature.

As Shonn poled into the mangroves, Nyette reached up to brush the leaves with her fingers. Softly, almost to herself, she murmured, "She's clever. I hope I get to meet her."

Shonn had no answer to that. He'd always thought of himself as the clever one. Manipulating Meven's feelings to control her, and then sacrificing her to win the countess' favor. Yes, he'd thought he was smart. Look what it had cost him.

~ ~ ~

"I see you have no prisoner," Captain Jorus all but sneered in Piyaro's face. The accusation stung because it was true. Piyaro didn't try to deny it.

He said, "The peasants in Opshar revolted when I tried."

"Revolt — What did you do?" Jorus' already dark face flushed angrily.

"I served the writ," Piyaro answered plainly. "The rest, I will explain to the count."

At least, he dared to hope for the chance to explain

further. Either Jorus had left a few details out of his briefing, or there had been things he hadn't known. It did no good to use that for an excuse, or worse, accuse the man of lying about the situation in Opshar.

The captain of the count's personal guard stared him down, no doubt calculating the worth of his information against the risk of having a stranger, armed, so near the count. That's what Piyaro would have been thinking, if he still held Ar-Dayne's oath. Jorus gave a little irritable shrug, and nodded to one of the other guards nearby. The guard strode off with a nasty backward glance.

Jorus paced a little, looking Piyaro's squad over. The men mostly didn't flinch at his hard appraisal. Hawk Squad had tried to clean up before they reported back in, but lining up crisply couldn't disguise their bruises and lagging morale.

Piyaro waited, sweating along with his men in the sun-scalded bailey. Their heavy armor couldn't protect them from Skaythe's burning heat. A few of Jorus' men loitered nearby, obviously ready if he needed them. It irked Piyaro, the way these comfortable men-at-arms seemed to regard the Hawks as fledglings beneath their notice. Piyaro wouldn't let them make his squad slink away from this. For the sake of his men, he had to try.

After several long minutes, the guard opened the door for a mage in crimson robes. He could have been anyone, just a member of the count's staff, but the guardsmen straightened to attention. Piyaro saluted, and the rest of Hawk Squad did the same. This had to be Pulgoll's Count, Ar-Azlor.

Compared to Piyaro's old master, Ar-Azlor was the soul of dignity. His robe hung in folds, just so, and his short beard and topknot were neatly trimmed. The dark eyes were veiled and considering. He, too, looked over Hawk Squad with a condescending air. That was much preferable to him being on the verge of blasting anyone.

The count turned to the man who had led him in.

"Give them water and something to eat, let them sit down. Sergeant Piyaro, join us in Captain Jorus' office."

There was a moment's hesitation all around. Jorus clearly didn't want to share his facilities with these low-lives, and Piyaro didn't want his men sitting down, in a position of disadvantage. What could he say? They were in enough trouble without stirring up more.

"At ease," he told his squad, just before Jorus said, "Do it," to one of his men. Without being asked, Piyaro belted off his sword and passed it to over Cothyr. Captain Jorus seemed to appreciate the concession.

Piyaro followed the count, catching a faint whiff of floral oil, while Jorus came in behind him. They didn't go into the keep itself, but into a small office enclosed within the gatehouse. Jorus made a few unconscious strides toward the desk, but stopped himself. It was Ar-Azlor who seated himself there.

"I'm told there's trouble in Opshar?" The count spoke kindly, as if to a stubborn child.

"Something's going on there. Factions." Piyaro tried to hide his anger at their disdain. "Captain Jorus briefed me that Headman Aulgrip reported the rogue mage and wanted him out of there, but when we got to Opshar it turned out be his nephew Kinson who sent word."

Ar-Azlor considered that, stroking his beard. Piyaro continued.

"The rogue is called Sand. He was with a woman named Yamaya, and they had a little baby. Kinson said he wanted to protect the village from Sand, but he seemed like he was getting back at the woman. She yelled out that she was never going to marry him."

"So, this Kinson would use me for his petty revenge?" The count laughed without much humor. Meanwhile, Jorus opened a cabinet on the wall and drew out a folded chart.

"You said her name is Yamaya?" Jorus asked, while opening the chart over the desk.

"I think so." Piyaro agreed.

To Ar-Azlor, Jorus said, "That's one of Huld's. A daughter, I expect. She was paired with that mage Gabrith for a while, but they both haven't been mentioned in my reports for over a year."

"Do you think it's the same one? Maybe that's where they went." The count placed a careful finger on the map, and drew it over toward where Piyaro thought Opshar might be. With a hint of threat, he murmured, "I'm disappointed that the headman didn't report it sooner."

Piyaro didn't know what they were talking about. "Who's Huld?"

"A bandit chief," Jorus answered scornfully. He jabbed a finger at the first place Ar-Azlor had touched. "His base is at Cutrock Canyon, right on the border with Deeve. The bandits and their women always disappear over the border before we get close. Ar-Gevant won't do anything about it on his side of the mountains."

"Ar-Gevant wants to start something with me," Ar-Azlor said acidly. Piyaro was impressed by his restraint. Ar-Dayne would have been riding for the border with an army if he thought his neighbors were trying to start something.

That answered some of Piyaro's questions. The woman, Yamaya, definitely could have been a bandit. Still, he shook his head. "It's not the same mage."

Jorus bristled, but Ar-Azlor fixed his attention on Piyaro. "Do go on."

"Being a bandit doesn't match," Piyaro explained. "When Augrip read the writ, the locals were really angry. They started throwing everything they could, behind a barrier Sand made. They wouldn't let us take him."

"How hard did you try?" Jorus challenged.

"We fought," Piyaro wasn't so submissive that he'd let the insult pass. "We couldn't get past the barrier. He picked us up and threw us back." He shook his head with remembered frustration. "We could have lit up some torches and set a few fires, but that seemed to go beyond my authority."

He glanced at the count, and was relieved to see the man nod. "I appreciate it when hirelings don't raze my villages."

"Thank you, my lord." The slighting reference to hirelings chafed, but Piyaro would take what approval he could get. "What's important is, if this Sand was a bandit, nobody would flock to him like that. They would have let us take him."

Jorus listened with plain disbelief, but Ar-Azlor just kept stroking his beard. "In your view, Sergeant, did they act to defy my authority or to protect this rogue mage?"

"Protect," Piyaro replied without hesitation. "Nobody said anything against you, my lord. They were only mad that Aulgrip would let Sand be arrested. They said —" Piyaro searched for the words. "He was the first good thing that ever happened in Opshar."

"For that they would start a rebellion?" The count's poise slipped a little. After a moment, he seemed to realize he was repeating the gesture with his beard, and clasped his hands on top of the map.

"He must be compelling them to obey," Jorus suggested.

Some mages could do that, Piyaro knew. He felt a little ill, but he shook his head. "No. Sand is one of *them*. A golden mage."

"What in Dar-Gothull's name are you talking about?" Jorus mocked.

"Gold," Ar-Azlor repeated softly. The guard captain did a double take and shifted his bearing.

"This isn't the first time I've had dealings with their kind." Piyaro cleared his throat uncomfortably. "They're incredibly dangerous. Four months ago, maybe five, Count Ar-Dayne detected an intrusion in Sloram. We went after it, through the Hornwood and all the way into Seofan."

No need to get into how Ar-Dayne had killed two of Piyaro's guardsmen and maimed the third, Cylass, so he had to be left for dead. Somehow that golden witch had healed Cylass, stolen him more effectively than any charm.

"Seofan Valley is cursed," Jorus said. "Everyone knows that."

"I've heard rumors that the curse was lifted." Ar-Azlor waved for Piyaro to continue.

"The mage he pursued was a woman, very beautiful." Piyaro said. "She was inside one of those barriers, along with a guard of her own. There was a golden light around her. Count Ar-Dayne accused her of trespassing, but she said we weren't in Sloram any more, and he should let her alone. The way she talked..." He shook his head a little. How could he describe it? "It was perfectly polite, but also... disrespectful. Taunting. My lord didn't let things like that go."

"Yes, I remember his charming personality," Ar-Azlor said drily.

"Count Ar-Dayne attacked her, but whatever he cast had no effect. Fire, lightning, the witch never fought back. She just smiled and sort of danced." Piyaro shook his head again. He had been there, but he still couldn't belive it. "My lord poured fire on her, but she wasn't burned. It just disappeared. Then there was a wave of light. It felt to us like... an embrace? All the trees in the valley were dead, but they started sprouting leaves again."

Both men listened, Jorus frankly incredulous, but Ar-Azlor paying close attention.

"My squad are swordsmen," Piyaro went on. "This fight was beyond us. The witch, we never even heard her name, but she said to Lord Ar-Dayne that he was sick and she offered to heal him. My lord kept attacking her until he exhausted himself and fell unconscious."

"When you got him home, he was still weak? The household turned on him," Ar-Azlor finished.

Piyaro nodded. "Countess Ar-Jeziak had her own people in mind. That's how Hawk Squad came to be roving hunter-guards."

"A sad story, if true," said Jorus, still skeptical but not without sympathy.

"I tell that story because the barrier Sand used is the same. Transparent, a golden light," Piyaro said shortly. "He speaks in the same way, very reasonable and insulting. We should assume that he's just as dangerous as the witch."

"Anything else?" the count asked.

Piyaro hesitated. He had been dreading this question. When Ar-Azlor raised a brow, he forced the words out.

"Sand did ask me to tell you something. He claims that he has no intention to take anything from you, but he means to stay in Opshar. If you want to come see him, he'll be glad to talk to you about it."

"Talk about it?" Predictably Jorus was furious. "We don't talk to rebels, and we're not going to him. We'll send someone competent to drag him back here!"

Maybe he expected his count to agree, but Ar-Azlor leaned back, stroking his beard again, eyes narrowed in thought. "Ar-Dayne was a maniac, but the man was strong. It would be no small thing to take him down."

"Well, she did it," Piyaro said, "and you may risk the same if you go to Opshar. Not that I think you would pour fire on anyone," he hastily added. "Without a good reason."

Jorus glowered at that, but a small, grim smile lurked behind the count's beard.

"I'll need to consult with some of the mages in Prowth and Busaren. They were closer to Seofan Holl during the event," he said. "My lord Dar-Gothull has taken an interest in the matter, as well. He'll want to know that another of these renegades has surfaced. Once he gives me direction, then perhaps I will pay a visit to Opshar."

"With archers?" Captain Jorus asked hopefully.

"For now, we'll let the peasants revel a bit and see if they come to their senses," Ar-Azlor concluded. "Maybe Aulgrip will do his job as headman, and sort it out by himself."

As Piyaro watched the count and his captain discuss it, the deepest, most bitter jealousy he had ever felt stabbed its way into his heart. How much of his life would be different if his count had not been a maniac? If Jorus hadn't been ten years younger, Piyaro would have been tempted to challenge for his command. Now, the best he could hope for was that Hawk Squad had served well enough to be paid for their trouble.

Striving to keep an even tone, he cut in, "Then, my lord, shall my squad be paid and be on our way?"

Immediately Jorus straightened, folding his arms with a smug expression. "Paid for doing what?"

Jorus might have been willing to use Hawk Squad and cast them aside, but his count chuckled again, softly. The way he did it was not exactly reassuring.

"No, Jorus. These men won't be leaving my service." His captain didn't like that at all, but Ar-Azlor turned to Piyaro. "You and your squad are witnesses to something extraordinary, Sergeant. There may be more questions yet."

"Then I suppose I can find a use for them," Jorus grumbled.

For a moment, Piyaro couldn't seem to draw a breath. Answering to a grudging commander might be almost as bad as serving a mad count. Yet Ar-Azlor's leniency, ominous as it was, provided exactly the security and opportunities he wanted for his guardsmen. How could he complain?

"My lord." Chest still tight, Piyaro bowed to his new employer. "We will serve as best we can."

~ ~ ~

Ar-Lizelle led her two guards at a fast pace, hoping to make up the time lost while she danced attendance on Countess Ar-Khoreen in Yergha. They had not yet found the ancient highway the trader had described, and they had to be careful where the horses galloped because of pits and runnels in the road. Grudgingly she allowed for stops to rest the horses at streams and in shady groves. Every moment was a frustrating waste of time.

She couldn't even ride her own horse, the chestnut Roxalen. That bitch, Lorrah, had stolen him along with the prisoners. Ar-Lizelle fumed about the loss, how her stupid sister had tricked her into leaving the Larder, then hit her with that cheap mind trick. The replacement gelding wasn't nearly as well trained. It wasn't red, either. Red horses were a mark of pride for any mage of Skaythe. Unfortunately, she had no time to acquire a better mount.

That theft was only the most recent of Lorrah's offenses. One more thing to get revenge for. After she let their father die, no penalty was too harsh. Ar-Lizelle scanned the road ahead, as if she could summon her treacherous sister and blast her on the spot.

At least she didn't have to worry about finding lodging. The lowlands had lots of little villages scattered among the vegetable fields and orchards of citrus or spice wood. There were also lots of carts, traffic that slowed the Larder's crew. Not as much as the hunter-guards with their wagon pulled by oxen, though. That was Ar-Lizelle's best hope. If anyone looked unusually nervous about spotting a mage, she could stop and question them.

The need for vengeance pulled her on, an urging she didn't try to deny. They alternated galloping with trotting, riding hard to catch up to with the fugitives. But as noon approached, a feeling gradually grew within Ar-Lizelle. Somehow, she felt, she had gone too far. She had passed it.

That was absurd, when she clearly hadn't passed Lorrah and those traitors on the road. What else could "it" be? Yet the feeling persisted. It niggled enough that she called an early halt for noon. There were no inns here, just a crude bench beside an orange grove. Groff watered the horses, and Endole gave her first share of their provisions. Ar-Lizelle chewed on the smoked fish roll while she pondered what she could possibly be sensing.

Their best lead was in Kamuril, to the east. That was on her right hand as they faced the road. Whatever nagged at her was to her left. Ar-Lizelle glared west, as if she could accuse her own instincts of falsehood.

Yet she was certain someone was there. Her mage's senses gave her a whiff of sun-baked stone and fearful sweat. She drew a deeper breath, filling her lungs with scents of damp earth and greenery. This was an orchard. How could she be smelling the Larder?

Maybe it didn't matter. Much as she wanted to find that fake guard wagon, there were ten fugitives, and only one of them had been dealt with. If another prisoner was nearby, she might as well deal with it. That, or she would have to come back later.

As soon as they had eaten, and she was back on her horse, she grudgingly turned its head to the west. The two guards exchanged puzzled glances, but didn't dare to question. Over the next few hours, Ar-Lizelle let intuition guide her down this lane and across that field. She didn't like it. A mage should be in control of her power, not the other way around. It was scant reassurance when her sense of "it" became more vivid.

At long last, they emerged from the farm lands and saw the ancient highway scrolling before them. High, rugged hills lumped up on the far side of it, with a well built road winding toward what clearly was a pass into Unthur. Yet another village had been planted on both sides of the roadway. On the near side, the banner of Yergha floated on the breeze above a large stone building. Across the narrow strip of silver, a similar sized building displayed the banner of Unthur.

"Shall we check in at the border post?" Endole suggested. "Maybe they've heard something about the fugitives."

It wasn't a bad idea, yet Ar-Lizelle hesitated. The trace she had been following had nothing to do with this. Nor was she obligated to explain herself to menials.

"When I'm ready," she snapped.

Ar-Lizelle remained in the saddle, scanning the landscape for some indication. Her eyes narrowed in on a rocky clutter off to the right. Wisps of smoke rose from the chimney hole of a square stone kiln with a stub of chimney. Rubble walls surrounded it and a substantial pit filled one corner. There were also several irregular heaps of objects she couldn't identify over the distance.

"What do you think," she asked. "The village midden?"

"Most likely," Endole agreed.

"Not a bad place to hide," Groff added. "Lots of cover, and junk that could be useful if you're desperate. Good thing we're upwind of it, though."

Indeed, Ar-Lizelle blessed her scant good fortune that they weren't breathing in the midden's stench. If it worked like the one in Hagazes, just outside the Larder, they would shovel their refuse into the kiln on a regular schedule. Whatever couldn't be burned, they would heave into the pit and fling a bit of dirt over it.

Just now, as she watched, a lone figure emerged from behind the kiln. It moved from heap to heap, occasionally pausing to extract something from the leavings. The man stayed low, head rising furtively. Whoever it was hurried back behind the kiln. It could just be a beggar. There was no sign of the ragged gray robe her prisoners had been forced to wear. Yet something in the movements was familiar.

"There you are," she hissed to herself.

"My lady?" Groff asked.

"That's one of them down there," she informed him. "Remember, I want to talk to him."

Ar-Lizelle snapped the reins and her horse trotted swiftly toward the midden. As they approached, she tried to figure out who that was. Definitely a man, so that ruled out Duessa, Bettain or Elldri. Maybe this was Ferrant or Noluss. If she was lucky, it might even be Illen. He and the juggler had been relatively close, in the Larder. If anyone had an idea of Alemin's plans, it would be Illen. Turning him against Alemin would sweeten her revenge.

The two guards spread out behind her, just as they had when they cornered Haafeth. If the fugitive ran, one of them would be in position to cut off his escape. As she approached the fence line, Ar-Lizelle's voice rose in a shrill command.

"Come on out. We know you're there!"

The wind gusted, feathering smoke away but unfortunately not clearing much of the rank odor from the midden. She waited a moment, studying the broken pottery, torn clothing, smashed furniture, and other objects waiting for the kiln. The two guardsmen walked their horses aside, approaching more stealthily.

"You aren't fooling anyone," Ar-Lizelle shouted. After a moment, she caught a flare of reflected light on a bit of formerly-polished metal. Whoever it was had summoned fire.

A moment later, he rose and strode out from behind the kiln. Ar-Lizelle had guessed wrong. It wasn't Illen, Noluss or Ferrant. Kyanon had acquired peasant clothes, rough trousers and a sack-like shirt, but he looked as hungry and tired as ever. His shaved hair had grown out a bit, so that it stuck out in tufts. Still, he squared his shoulders and stood to face her.

Maybe it wasn't Illen, but her idea still could work. Kyanon wasn't a weakling, like Ferrant, nor a madman like Haafeth. He had a practical nature, as she recalled, and it seemed he still had some gumption.

"Don't come any closer, Lizard!" That was the inmates' insulting nickname for her. As he raised his fist to cast the first bolt, Ar-Lizelle waved her hand to dismiss the threat.

"Are you in a hurry to die? I'd rather talk to you."

"What's there to talk about?" he yelled, a little hysterical. "I'm not going back there!"

'Oh, you are going back," Ar-Lizelle vowed sweetly. "No one escapes the Larder, Kyanon. Not really. That doesn't mean it has to be painful." She paused a moment, letting him think. "Ar-Chindu died in the breakout, did you know?"

"It wasn't me," he grunted, "so what about it?"

"I happen to need a new second, that's what."

Kyanon straightened a bit, wary of the suddenly changed subject. "Is this a trick?"

"I don't have time for tricks."

"Good luck with it," Kyanon said, but Ar-Lizelle noted a moment's hesitation. In fact, he was curious. She could use that.

"It is lucky," she said. "You don't even have to fight for the position. Normally, if the warden's second is killed or promoted away from the Larder, the count of Yergha will send a replacement. How do you think I got stuck with an incompetent like Ar-Chindu? Ar-Khoreen dumped him where he couldn't do much harm, so she thought." Ar-Lizelle rolled her eyes. "However, the dear countess isn't offering me much in the way of resources at the moment. That being the case, I have to find a replacement on my own."

Kyanon's gaze darted left and right, realizing that the Larder's warden had only the two guards as an escort. He relaxed a bit, and the flames puffed away from his fist.

"Is that how you became Ar-Wharon's second?" he asked.

"The situation was different, but yes." Ar-Lizelle felt no need to get into the details of how her father's fatal plot had left her a condemned traitor, until she fought her way to becoming Ar-Wharon's second. "You'd still be a convict, just serving your sentence in a different capacity. Why not enjoy a few perks? Or," she let her tone darken, "you can die here, in a midden."

The man's mouth tightened, acknowledging the indignity. Ar-Lizelle remembered a little of his record. Once a proud mage in Nimthar, now he was just a beggar, scrounging through trash heaps for the scraps he needed to stay alive.

Maybe Kyanon was that desperate, but he was smart enough to keep asking questions. "There has to be something else."

"Yes, of course there is. We're hunting for the rest of the prisoners who escaped. Will that be a problem?" Ar-Lizelle watched carefully for his reaction. "I know you must be anxious to see your good friend the juggler again."

Kyanon's lip curled. "We're not friends. He was a convenience."

Ar-Lizelle allowed herself a moment's smugness. With this, she doubled her striking power — by recruiting one of Alemin's former allies, at that. Kyanon didn't seem to have any hesitation about following orders when it came to his fellow prisoners, either.

"Then I invite you to join me, Ar-Kyanon," she said. "We'll get you cleaned up, and while we eat, you can tell me everything you remember about those idiots who dared defy the Wizard King Dar-Gothull."

Kyanon eyed her, then glanced again at the approaching guards. Just as she thought he might refuse, he sketched a bow. "I don't mind if I do, Warden Ar-Lizelle."

IV — HUNTED

H ey, Duessa." Alemin called cheerfully.

"What?" She turned quickly, aware that Elldri and Bettain's heads snapped up, too. Living in the Larder left one with certain reflexes.

A gusting wind carried the fragrance of citrus leaves across the roadside pullout, where Badger Squad had set up their camp. The three of them were preparing the wagon for sleeping. They were close now to the high hills between Yergha and Unthur, and the wind was cold. Clouds ran before it. Duessa hoped they wouldn't be rained on during the night.

Alemin strolled over, hand in hand with Lorrah. "Do you want to meditate with us?"

Lorrah didn't look quite certain of this offer. Not that Duessa blamed her for being protective, since Alemin was the only man surrounded by other women who were all variously athletic and attractive. With her scars, Duessa didn't consider herself in contention.

"More meditation?" Bettain groaned. "We did that in the Larder."

"I did that," Duessa corrected her. Meditation had been Alemin's idea to communicate without the guards knowing. Duessa didn't think Bettain had tried very hard.

Alemin smiled. "I know you had some success, but

there's more we can do. After today, it's obvious we should learn to cast together."

Naturally, Lorrah agreed with him. "Working as a team would be really helpful. Let's not waste the chance."

Duessa and Bettain both eyed them. Lorrah and Alemin didn't seem to understand the risks. In the temple school, everyone fought alone. You might give away your best strategy to someone who turned into a rival. Even when Ar-Lannon trained his magelings, they could only work in pairs. The others had to be lookouts.

"So you want to train us like an army?" she asked suspiciously.

"What's wrong with an army?" Razeet called over from the stove, where some of the squad had gathered to clean their equipment. The others had gone to groom their horses.

"Not just that." Alemin tried to reassure Duessa. "We can do a lot of things, not only in emergencies when the road is gone. If we start to work together, we can discover what they are."

"Like what?" Bettain pursued. Elldri watched anxiously.

"You remember that we were trying to communicate through the tower, right?" he said. "If we get to know each other well enough, we can hear each other over longer distances."

Lorrah nodded. "That's how I knew where Alemin was, and it's how we're trying to find Tisha." When they all didn't jump at the chance to meditate, she got irritated. "Well, if they don't want to," she complained to Alemin.

"Don't get mad. Things were rough in the Larder." He laid a calming hand on Lorrah's shoulder. To Duessa, he said, "It's all right if you need more time. We have to build trust. What if you just watch, for now?"

"That sounds pointless," Bettain said.

After a moment, Duessa said, "Maybe I'd try it. The Badgers have sentries, so we wouldn't need to worry about watching our backs."

"Good point," Alemin said.

Bettain groaned again, but Elldri was scooting away on the bench. When she saw Duessa looking at her, she shook her head vigorously.

Bettain was immediately concerned. "What's wrong?"

"No, I can't," Elldri whispered between the fingers that covered her mouth.

"Casting? Sure you can," Bettain scolded fondly. "I know we weren't supposed to, back in that shithouse, but everybody did. Sneaking it in was part of the fun."

Elldri shook her head again, her gaze focused inward. What she saw there must have been terrifying.

"Let her alone," Duessa said. "When we tried before, I reached out to both of you, not the other way."

"I never saw Elldri work a spell," Alemin said. The girl refused to make eye contact..

"Just go slowly and build your strength," Bettain advised.

"Sure." Lorrah jerked a thumb over at the guardswomen. "They'll tell you how many times I tried to summon fire and only made this vile fume appear."

Giniver looked up from oiling her armor. "It was pretty bad," she laughed.

From inside her tent, Zathi called, "I don't want her casting wild spells around here, if she's out of practice."

"We'll only be meditating," Lorrah called back.

Elldri's arms were trembling. "I don't want to."

"Well, then how do you plan to defend yourself?" Bettain's worry made her voice harsher even than usual.

Duessa watched them for a moment. Except for that worst day in the Larder, when the former warden tried to slaughter them all, Elldri hadn't been this closed in. Duessa didn't understand it, but she wouldn't let her friend be bullied.

"She said no, Bettain," Duessa spoke firmly.

Alemin said gently, "It's all right. You don't have to."

"I'll give it a try, though." Duessa rose from the wagon's bench. "You should, too, Bettain."

"Why me?" Bettain clearly wanted to stay and keep pestering Elldri.

"It's been four years since I got to practice anything," Duessa said. "How about you?"

Grudgingly, Bettain answered. "Seven years. Maybe more."

The mages all looked at Elldri, who twitched in a way that might have been meant as a head shake, no.

"Well, I won't pass up training where my partners aren't trying to kill me. You're not too old to learn new things, are you?" Duessa teased.

"I'm not old at all!" Bettain jumped up and struck a pose, lifting her skirt to show off her thick ankles. "I'm experienced." Lorrah and Alemin both broke into laughter.

"Is that what you call it?" Smirking, Duessa turned back to the others. "Where do you want to do this?"

~ ~ ~

"Tell me about these so-called hunter-guards," Ar-Lizelle said.

The Yergha border post had a guest room for visiting mages. It was small and would be crowded, but after watching her personal coin dwindle, Ar-Lizelle took it. Her new second had bathed and shaved, his hair oiled to tame the spikes. His crimson robe was not in perfect condition, being a second-hand from the post's stores. Still, Ar-Kyanon smoothed the folds with visible satisfaction.

Groff had fetched lamb skewers from a nearby tavern, and Ar-Kyanon had made his disappear with almost magical speed. Ar-Lizelle ate more gracefully, but if he was done, there was no reason he couldn't start talking.

"There were seven of them. Three warriors, three archers, and the ox driver. All women, like you heard." Ar-Kyanon glanced at Endole, who nodded respectfully.

The two guards ate their meal separately, in a corner. There had been a bit of awkwardness as the guards adjusted to the notion that their former prisoner, who they hounded at will, was now second in command.

"Their sergeant said we couldn't all come." Ar-Kyanon sneered a little at some memory. "They dumped us off right away, at a waterfall. Gave us different clothes and some food, I guess so we'd leave faster."

"Yes, we found that." Ar-Lizelle remembered the spot, especially with the hoof prints of her stolen horses in the mud on the bank. Unfortunately, the fugitives hadn't lingered there long enough for her to pick up any traces of their magic. "Did you get any of their names?"

"No, they were careful. That girl Lorrah was the only name they mentioned." He shook his head, cutting off Ar-Lizelle's next question. "Wouldn't say where they were going, either. "

"They were prepared, came in with a plan," Endole said. "It wasn't a spur of the moment decision."

"Obviously," Ar-Lizelle snapped. The guard flinched from her irritation. "The false writ, the count's stamp, the ink, it all took time to make." Lorrah had done a good job, but Ar-Lizelle wouldn't give her obnoxious sister the credit. Ar-Chindu still should have been able to see that it was fake.

"Ar-Kyanon," Groff spoke tentatively.

"Yes, Groff?" The man clearly enjoyed his newfound superiority.

"Did everyone else leave when you did?" Groff asked.

"Mostly. Duessa and Bettain were still talking to the sergeant when I left. Elldri was with them, too."

"Oh?" Ar-Lizelle asked. Then she shrugged. "That's no surprise. Those three always did stick together."

"It could be a problem when we catch up with them," Ar-Kyanon said. "Two of us, with two guards, against their three."

Ar-Lizelle was already frowning to herself. On second thought, this might be important.

"Alemin was one of the minstrels Lorrah travels with," she said. "They won't divide forces. Those renegades are always trying to recruit more mages, too. Theoretically, if they all did travel on, it wouldn't be three mages against us, it would be five."

The guardsmen exchanged glances of dismay.

"Five is a lot. They'd start fighting among themselves pretty quickly,"was Ar-Kyanon's cynical prediction.

"Our three were a team already," Endole dared to correct him.

"No, I've studied these renegades." Ar-Lizelle gritted her teeth, remembering all the reports she had gathered over the past few years. "Individually, they're weak, but they don't fight each other. They'll try to bring our three into their group."

"Join some renegades?" Ar-Kyanon scoffed. "Duessa's a lot smarter than that. Bettain, too."

"Not everyone has your sense of self-preservation," Ar-Lizelle said. "The minstrels had six already. Adding our three would make nine in all."

"Theoretically," Ar-Kyanon said.

Quietly, Endole said, "Nine mages is an army."

"With their squad of guards," Groff added. "It was the archers that took Ar-Chindu out."

Ar-Lizelle released a small, bitter sigh. This was forcing her toward a decision she didn't want to make. "As if that's not enough, we're going to have to call on Count Ar-Gammord."

"In Unthur? I thought they were seen heading toward Kamuril," Ar-Kyanon objected.

"They were, but we had to ride west to collect you." Ar-Lizelle cocked an eyebrow. He shrugged, unrepentant. "We'll lose too much time if we try to chase them east, even though our horses are faster than their wagon. It's better to go north, through the hills, cross Unthur, and try to get into Kamuril ahead of them."

After days spent studying the charts with Endole and Groff, she was quite sure of their route. The rest of it, though, was not so certain.

"Unfortunately, Ar-Gammord is a paranoid ass," she said. Older mages often lost touch with reality. From her one brief meeting, as Ar-Wharon's assistant, he was well on his way to that. "We don't want him riding up on our tails with his household guard. We'll have to visit, even if it does waste time."

Ar-Kyanon nodded. "Point taken." Then he glanced down at Ar-Lizelle's plate, where one of her meat skewers was untouched. "Are you going to eat that?"

"Yes." She smirked at his disappointment.

~ ~ ~

Two more days bumped by as the Badgers' wagon followed its winding dirt track through the rugged hills between Yergha and Unthur. Somewhere in the middle of the hills, they intersected the Shining Ones' highway. The smooth road shot straight north, as if it had been laid down by a bird in flight. It helped the Badgers picke up speed.

As they reached the rolling plains between Kamuril and Unthur, the imperative to *get away from the Larder* faded. The band still moved with purpose, though the Duessa and her friends hadn't been told their destination. At a noon rest, while Elldri helped Sethamis water the livestock, Duessa and Bettain pulled Alemin aside.

"You have a purpose for this, right? We're going somewhere?" Duessa demanded.

"Sort of." Alemin ran a hand over the bristles where his shaved hair was growing out. "We're trying to find our friend, Tisha. Berisan and Meven are too far away, but Tisha is closer."

"Who's Tisha, exactly?" Bettain asked.

"She's a born healer. We need her," Alemin vowed. "When we meditate, we can get a sense of her direction."

"Your girlfriend says she talked to you across the distance," Bettain said. "But not with this Tisha?"

"With me, she did." Alemin glanced over, where Lorrah was going over the charts with Zathi and Jaxynne. He smiled fondly, as if he couldn't quite believe his luck. "I was in the Larder then. It seemed built to channel magic. Besides, nobody suspected we could do it, so they weren't watchful. But now..."

"Now the Lizard will be alert," Bettain finished.

Duessa frowned. As much of a bitch as the Larder's

warden was, she had stopped Ar-Wharon's rampage. They shouldn't call her names.

"Fine," Duessa said, "but that doesn't answer our question. Where do you think we'll finally end up?"

"According to Zathi, there's a tower in the middle of the Hornwood," he said. "That's where Keilos found the reservoir of *vitalis*. Eventually, we'll want to gather there to draw on the stored power."

"In the Hornwood?" Duessa and Bettain exchanged glances. There were a lot of stories about that place. None of them good.

Bettain gave a shrug. "Maybe nobody will want to chase us in there?"

The three of them who had escaped the Larder were already shaking their heads. Alemin spoke for all of them.

"That won't stop Ar-Lizelle. Which is why we have to find our other friends on the quiet, and get to the Hornwood before Ar-Lizelle finds us."

Duessa was at the point of giving in to his vague logic, when she caught what he had said. The certainty of it.

"Wait. You think she's coming after us herself, instead of putting out a bounty with the hunter-guards?"

Now it was Alemin who looked puzzled. "Can't you feel it?"

"Feel what?" Bettain demanded.

"Ar-Lizelle. She's following us." Alemin's dark eyes flicked between them, taking in their skeptical reactions. "After everything we went through in the Larder, it feels like we're still connected. Maybe we always will be."

Bettain's shoulders shifted uneasily. "That sounds more like a parasite than a connection."

Alemin grinned a little as he strolled off toward

Lorrah. "You both need to work on your meditation."

"Easy for you to say," Duessa retorted.

Meditation was harder than she remembered. Alemin and Lorrah went into the trance as naturally as breathing, but Duessa found success frustratingly elusive. The ground where they sat was too hard, or there were twigs that stabbed at her knees. Bettain was even more restless, constantly shifting around or just breathing too loudly.

When Duessa first learned meditation from Ar-Lannon, it had been no more than a calming exercise. She'd been terrified, running from the hunter-guards. According to Ar-Lannon, her wildly flaring *lethentros* was a beacon to draw all sorts of attention. If Duessa wanted to travel with his crew of moon-runners, she couldn't be a liability.

After they left her for the hunter-guards, she hadn't done it much. What was the point, when she was already captured? But she hadn't totally given it up, either. With the terrors of the mage's prison, she had needed to calm herself more than ever. Duessa only meditated during rest times, when she was locked in her cell. No one could come at her then.

She had never been as stupid as Alemin and meditated in front of the other prisoners. Nor had she really considered that the Larder itself could affect a mage's craft. When Alemin had claimed he could communicate through the tower, Duessa had tried it for herself, but only succeeded in a vague way. The best she had done was exchange brief impressions with Elldri and Bettain, like birds flitting through the branches, half-seen. It was embarrassing that a simple working should be so difficult.

"Meditation," Bettain grumbled, perhaps attempting to conceal her own failures. "I'm saving my energy for the real casting."

"Maybe so," Duessa said, while in her memory throbbed that need to not be a liability. "If Ar-Lizelle is chasing us, don't you want all the warning you can get?"

~ ~ ~

A lot went on in the first few days of Hawk Squad's engagement in Pulgoll. There was new livery, and their gear was inspected. Piyaro was proud that, despite the squad's adverse circumstances, most of it was battle worthy.

Hawk Squad was assigned to quarters, packed in with another squad in a way that reminded them they were latecomers, not planned upon. Piyaro gave his men strict orders to cooperate, and then had to fend off the other squad trying to dump all the cleaning on them.

The following morning held an early meeting where Captain Jorus introduced him to the other sergeants. Each of them greeted him with professional courtesy but no warmth. With a patronizing air, Jorus had Piyaro split his men up and pair them with others to walk the walls and corridors. It was a good enough way for them to learn the keep's layout. It also kept the Hawks under Jorus' eye. Piyaro couldn't fault his caution. In fact, Piyaro would probably have done the same if Ar-Dayne had dropped a dozen new men into his ranks without warning.

Only later did he learn that the Hawks had been pulled out separately and questioned by one of Ar-Azlor's junior mages about the events in Seofan Valley. Piyaro should have expected that, but still, it rankled. If his men were being questioned, he should have been there.

Now, on this third day, the squad was starting to get comfortable in Ar-Azlor's service. Piyaro had found an afternoon time when he could work with his men in a training ring out in the bailey. The familiar drills and sparring were a relief after weeks of uncertainty. Piyaro was well aware of other sergeants casually wandering through to observe. It spoke well of Jorus' command that his officers took an appropriate interest.

Eventually one of them, whose name Piyaro couldn't

remember, stopped to talk. "What is that?"

The Hawks were running a drill where they sprinted a few steps and dropped into a crouch when Piyaro blew his whistle.

"Dash and duck," he said.

"What's it for, when a mage is aiming at them?" the other man guessed.

Dourly, Piyaro said, "It's for when your count is a lunatic who doesn't care if he blasts through the forward line."

"Great." The other sergeant drawled sarcastically.

Piyaro blew his whistle, watched his men leap back up, and then winced as Ragis stumbled. The fool was left a pace behind and scurried to catch up. That was the third time this session.

Ragis had been off since Seofan, and Piyaro knew why. The man was a skinny suck-up who had attached himself to a brute called Ennow. Ennow was a reliable fighter, until he got the nasty idea to advance himself by shoving other guys in front of Count Ar-Dayne. That trick had cost Piyaro three good men, but one of them finally stabbed Ennow back. He hadn't lasted for the trip back to Sloram.

Hawk Squad all knew what Ennow had done, and that Ragis hadn't tried to stop it. Now nobody wanted to stand near him. A lone fighter was vulnerable. He kept falling over his own feet, and it was his own doing.

Piyaro blew a halt. "Ragis!"

Reluctantly, the man trotted toward him, while the rest of the squad relaxed between relays. The other sergeant huffed a laugh. "Have fun with it," he said. "And when you get done, Captain wants a word."

"Thanks." Now Piyaro had that to worry him while

he barked at Ragis to brace up. They'd only had this post for two days. Surely he hadn't screwed up badly enough for the captain to want a word already.

He sent his men to clean up, and hurried to the guard captain's office. Jorus wasted no time. "My lord has a mission for you. Come look at this."

Piyaro approached the desk, where Jorus had spread his chart out again. A packet, wrapped in thin leather and bound with red cord, lay over to the side. Jorus pressed his finger to the small square marking Pulgoll's position, then moved it across the parchment.

"This is Eshur, to the south of us. Countess Ar-Torix is our ally." Jorus lifted the packet. "You are taking this letter to her. My lord wants you to tell her everything you told him about these golden mages in Opshar and Seofan Holl."

Piyaro accepted the packet. The captain's contempt wasn't quite so pronounced, he noted. This was real work, not some excuse to get Hawk Squad out of Pulgoll.

"Do we wait for her reply, or come back after delivering it?"

"Wait for directions," Jorus said.

Piyaro nodded. However, he hadn't forgotten their last briefing, and the important facts he hadn't been told about the situation in Opshar.

"Anything else you can tell me?" he asked.

"Don't get smart. I didn't know any of that crap." Jorus scowled, correctly understanding the reference. "But since you mention it, don't go through Deeve." He poked at another small square, on a river mouth between Pulgoll and Eshur.

"The count who's trying to start something," Piyaro remembered. Jorus grunted. Piyaro studied the coastline, where narrow inlets outlined what looked like swollen fingers of land. "How do we get by? Deeve is right on the sea."

"There's a landing down in the mangroves, Oyster Rocks." Jorus tapped the chart. "The water-folk go up and down the coast. If you pay them well, they'll skim you right across the strait. Report to the bursar. She'll issue the funds and provisions."

"Understood. Thank you, Captain." Piyaro didn't want to say it, when the man was such an ass, but it meant a lot to be trusted with a mission after the way the last one turned out.

Jorus straightened, arms folded across his chest, and seemed to study Piyaro with a different eye. "There's another squad heading out to Prizom, as well. I'll need one of your men to go with them."

"My number is already down," Piyaro protested.

"We need an eye witness to talk to Count Ar-Oshtur. Don't worry, we'll take care of him," Jorus taunted a little.

Just for that, Piyaro decided to send Ragis. The man needed a break anyway. Maybe he could get in with a squad who didn't despise him. "All right, I have someone in mind."

Jorus nodded curtly, and said, "This thing in Opshar isn't just a peasant revolt, Sergeant. We're into something big."

"If all the counts are comparing notes, I'd say you're right." Piyaro wasn't some greenhorn, who needed this warning. He hadn't forgotten about those golden mages, either.

"Get back as fast as you can."

~ ~ ~

The Badgers made good progress on the ancient highway. Rainy lowlands gave way to dryer grassland, where mixed herds of horses and cattle grazed. Teams of herders with long-legged dogs watched over them. The Badgers' wagon passed a few villages, but chose not to stop. Ground fowl took wing as they passed, often enough that Jaxynne rode with her crossbow ready, so that some of them went into the Badgers' cook pot. Thus there was no reason to stop, and many good reasons not to.

The squad fell into a routine. In the mornings, the guardswomen trained on horseback while the mages watched over the camp. Bettain often joined them, generating flames or loud bangs to condition the horses against panicking. In the evenings, it was reversed. The guardswomen tended their gear and kept watch while the mages practiced their meditation.

Only Elldri refused to even talk about trying it. She preferred to help Sethamis look after the oxen. That was becoming a real puzzle.

"Are we really sure she's a mage?" Lorrah asked quietly, when Elldri was out of earshot.

"She has to be," Bettain insisted. "The Larder is a prison for mages."

"Yes, but she didn't brag about what she did to be sent there," Duessa said. "Not like the guys did."

Alemin put in, "I never heard her talk about casting." Then he shrugged, smiling impishly. "Actually, I never heard her talk much at all."

"No, you're right. She doesn't," Duessa agreed.

"Do you think she came from a temple school?" Bettain asked doubtfully.

"I doubt it," Duessa said. Nobody that timid would have survived the combat training, at least not in Busaren.

Duessa tried not to let that concern her, because the

meditation was working for her at last. Five or six days after she began to focus her mind on it, she started to sense the flow of energy among them. Bettain's power was a tight ball of thorns, angrily coiled upon itself. She and Duessa both blazed with *lethentros*, the energy of pain and death. It was the same with almost everyone. *Lethentros* was the dominant power all over Skaythe.

Alemin and Lorrah were different, though. Their power felt soft and warm, like the glow of firelight they sang about sometimes.

"It's *vitalis*," Lorrah assured them breezily, "the power that comes from all living things. It feels a lot better than *lethentros*."

"As long as there's sunlight, we can draw power," Alemin echoed.

Bettain was very skeptical. Duessa would have been, too, except that she had heard about *vitalis* before. In the moon-runners' camp, Ar-Lannon had taught them about sources of power besides *lethentros*. Sources that didn't make you irritable and unstable. *Isalonis* was rare, a power of ice that could only be drawn from the highest peaks of the Gavalar Mountains, near Dakadoz. And there was *vitalis*, which he knew almost nothing about.

Looking back, Duessa could recognize her teacher's yearning for a better way. He'd been half ashamed, self-mocking, when he told them about the search for something so impossible.

Duessa hadn't seen much point in it. She was comfortable with *lethentros*. The burning in her veins, and the way it scorched her mind as she released it. Those things made her strong. She hadn't seen the need for another source, and she had never found one.

Except now, finally, it was there before her. Alemin and Lorrah sat still and calm, just a few feet away. They faced each other with knees nearly touching and seemed almost to breathe as one being. Duessa watched the energy flow between them, such an intimacy that it was embarrassing to witness.

Yet, to her surprise, she now saw what she couldn't have seen before. Alemin's *vitalis* was not pure and golden. There were dark stains at his core, something like bruises. You wouldn't see it on his skin. He and Lorrah were circulating their energy to try and clear it away.

Tendrils of their healing energy brushed past her, as lightly as walking through cobwebs. Duessa was shocked at how much she wanted that. *Vitalis*, a power that made her feel good. It could soothe her fears instead of leaving her cut up inside. And she wanted what came with it — this minstrel band she had barely heard about. Friends who would come when she needed them, instead of running to save themselves. Someone who would try to heal the bruises at her core.

But such a gift wasn't meant for Duessa, a bloody-handed bitch of the Larder. She was too scorched inside. She pulled away, trying to regain her focus.

It was obvious Alemin was willing to teach her and Bettain their ways by showing off the *vitalis*. All this meditation was probably nothing but a strategy to get them interested. If Duessa wanted that power, she would have to learn everything over again. Not wanting to be a liability was all well and good, but to completely re-make herself might be going a bit too far.

~ ~ ~

"Is that... Ferrant?"

Ar-Kyanon stared upward as they rode toward the Unthur city gate. Following his sight line, Ar-Lizelle noted the gibbets and crow-cages hanging along the city's wall. A gusting wind rocked them slowly. Swirls of rotten stench carried to the traffic on the road below, provoking many disgusted grumbles from the travelers.

The occupant of the nearest cage had a shaved head, clear sign of a condemned prisoner. He or she slumped motionless, but didn't appear so gone in decay as the others. It was even possible that prisoner still lived. Reluctantly, she extend her mage's senses, probing for any remaining intelligence.

"Whoever that was, they're dead." Ar-Lizelle teetered between disgust at the odor and satisfaction that another of the fugitives may have been accounted for. "I suppose we should ask, at some point."

"Well." Ar-Kyanon murmured with grim sarcasm.

Behind them, Groff shook his head. "The fool must have tried to sneak through."

"I told you Ar-Gammord's paranoid," Ar-Lizelle said.

Unlike the ill-fated prisoner, she had travel documents signed by Count Ar-Khoreen of Yergha. She also had the dogged patience to sit through the interview at the border post and do check-ins along the way. It all took too long, but this tasteful display of Count Ar-Gammord's justice demonstrated perfectly why it was necessary.

The city's walls were of brown stone, drab and unlovely under mid-morning's harsh sun. They were surrounded by a dry moat lined with more jagged rocks. A broad stone bridge crossed the moat toward a sturdy but equally ugly gatehouse. The route was lined by people and carts waiting to pass the guards. Ar-Lizelle had no intention of wasting yet more time. She and Ar-Kyanon were mages, and rank had privileges. Straightening her back, she trotted her horse forward. Some of the queue burst out with protests when she rode past them, but quickly fell silent when they saw the crimson robes.

Ahead of them, the guards who were searching the carts turned at the clatter of hooves on stone. One of them shouted into the gatehouse. A higher-ranked guardsman came out and bowed, but glanced between them, uncertain who was in charge.

"My lord, my lady, have you any documents?"

"I am Warden Ar-Lizelle, of the Larder Prison. My assistant, Ar-Kyanon." So named, he dismounted and presented the letter. The guardsman read it, and passed it back.

"Welcome, Warden Ar-Lizelle," he saluted. "What is your business in Unthur?"

It was an ordinary question, but she was annoyed that he had doubted she was in command. Nor did she have any intention of feeding rumors to Unthur's spy network.

"I will discuss my business with Count Ar-Gammord," Ar-Lizelle told him. "Who should my assistant see about arranging a courtesy call?"

He gave her the name of the aide who kept the count's schedule, and also suggested an inn which, he said, was not too far from the keep. As they passed beneath the echoing vault of the gatehouse, Ar-Kyanon sniped, "Oh, your assistant will take care of it?"

Ar-Lizelle waited for the city's buzz of carts and voices to conceal her reply. "Are you complaining? I can have you put up in the cage with Ferrant, if you prefer." When he shook his head, she went on, "Our appearances are important. We can't do anything to provoke the count's anxiety. Although, as long as you're there, maybe you can find out if that really was Ferrant."

"As you say," he muttered, disgruntled.

Behind them, Endole cleared his throat. "Warden. Should we assume they'll spy on us?"

"Yes, so stay alert."

"Maybe one of the guards should stay with the horses, to be certain they aren't tampered with," Ar-Kyanon suggested.

"Unless that would make them even more suspicious," Groff put in. "Begging your pardon."

"Keep your eyes open for another inn, as well," Ar-Lizelle said. "There might be a reason the count's guards want us to stay at that one."

~ ~ ~

Between two folds of land, the Badgers found a small lake fringed all around with reeds. Zathi immediately called a halt. They camped beside it for a day, washed themselves, rested the animals, and caught up on the minor mending that had built up as they went. Somewhat to her surprise, Duessa felt the first cramps and spotting of her monthly courses. During the stress and starvation in the Larder, she hadn't bled consistently for a couple of years.

Fortunately, when traveling with a group of women warriors, there were rags enough to share. Lorrah helpfully showed Duessa how to circulate *vitalis* through her abdomen in a way that relieved the worst cramps. Now that was a practical reason to learn their ways.

After that all-too-brief pause, they kept on across the rolling plains. The silvery highway made several sharp diagonals, for no apparent reason, but mostly it led north. In the far distance, the mountains of Prowth were faintly visible. It would still take many days to reach them.

At the lakeside, Alemin had collected a few stones that had a bit of sparkle to them. In the evenings, he would goof around with his juggling tricks. Lorrah played her violin and Razeet spun amusing tales. They all took turns entertaining the group. But with Alemin's art, there was more. Duessa saw now that he was also generating *vitalis* by juggling. She felt it often, that he was reaching with his mind — no doubt seeking this friend of his.

When he came out of his trance, he would tell Zathi,"Still more north. She's making her way from somewhere northeast."

"We were supposed to meet in Nibbok," Lorrah would chime in. "Maybe she's trying to get there."

Or Alemin would ask, "Can we find a way more east? Unthur isn't a good idea."

"Oh yeah," Bettain cackled. "You said that you laughed at the count there?"

He grinned a bit, and repeated the tale of how he'd intervened to protect an innocent man, but Count Ar-Gammord had accidentally intercepted a rotten egg. Alemin had been arrested for the insult.

"And that's why I can't go back there," he said when everyone had stopped laughing.

"He's a mad one, by what I hear," Zathi said. "I'd steer clear anyhow."

"No kidding, if he condemned someone to the larder just for that," Lorrah exclaimed indignantly.

After a few more days, they came to a branch in the road. One branch curved gently east, almost as if by Alemin's request. Duessa was glad to see rugged hills on the near horizon. If they needed to hide out, she'd have a chance of finding a good place.

Her thoughts weren't completely easy, though. If the Badgers kept on, they'd go through Prowth, bypass the cursed Seofan Valley, and wind up in Busaren. Duessa was surprised by a twinge of anxiety.

Once, Busaren had been her home. She hadn't thought about the knife-edge ridges and shadowed valleys in years. What was the point of going back? Her mother was dead, and the rest of the family had probably forgotten all about her. She was a mage, after all. Born of their blood, but then become a monster.

So they must think. Her family — what was left of it — knew she had run from the temple school, but they might not welcome her bringing a pack of fugitives to their doorstep. In fact, they might assume she was already dead.

The other question was, what about Ar-Lannan or her fellow magelings, Doromy and Gauer? She could try to find them, the way Alemin was searching for his old friend Tisha. Yet they'd left Duessa to the hunter-guards. Why would she even want to see them?

Duessa got a headache thinking about it. Best to deal with that if it happened. Besides, she had other things to focus on. She was finding the meditation easier and easier all the time. Like Alemin with his juggling, she had little else to do as they rode along in the Badgers' wagon.

She began to see it more easily, the difference between *vitalis* and *lethentros*. She could close her eyes and know who was around her. Oddly enough, drawing in *vitalis* made her scarred face tingle and itch. The power seemed to linger in that area, like the fabric of her dress getting caught on a splinter. It was annoying, that even *vitalis* didn't like her scars.

Duessa sensed something else, too. Elldri did no casting herself, but she seemed keenly aware of all they were doing. Perhaps painfully so. She flinched sometimes, for no visible reason. It was strange that Elldri had no aura. Even the women warriors, who had no magic, still radiated of life.

Except for Elldri. It was hard to tell, but Duessa thought there was something after all. Perhaps it was *lethentros,* so concentrated and dark that it felt wrong, alien. What she sensed was thick, slick and oily, a blackness which oozed out the scent of char. Duessa couldn't put a name on it, but she understood why Alemin was worried.

Elldri seemed to sense her interest. She pulled in on herself and quickly scooted off whenever the wagon pulled over for a rest. Bettain would have gone after her, but Duessa stopped her.

"What's gotten into her?" Bettain grumbled.

"She's... sick, I guess. You still can't sense the energies at all?" Duessa tried to keep the question neutral, but of course Bettain was annoyed.

"What I *sense* is that meditation is boring, and I want to fall asleep!"

"Well, don't," Duessa snapped back at her. Turning to Alemin and Lorrah, she said, "You can feel it, right? Like black sludge, and it stinks of burning. What's wrong with her?"

"I don't know if she's sick, exactly," Lorrah answered, "but I've never felt anything like it."

"I have. In the Larder." Alemin's dark tone made all of them double-take. Duessa frowned, but quickly realized that he wasn't suspicious of Elldri, so much as worried.

"Do I want to know?" Duessa asked.

Quietly he said, "It's the same as the revenant."

"What?" Bettain exclaimed angrily. "Nobody but you even saw that."

"Trust me, you don't want to see it." Alemin looked away, swallowing against the memory of horror.

Duessa shuddered, too. An evil revenant haunted the Larder, preying on the prisoners. Her cell had been close to the stairs. She had heard the echoes of Wharon's dying shrieks. An agony no doubt reinforced by the Larder's resonating structure.

"No," she choked. "It can't get us here. We left it!"

"I don't know about any revenant, but your friend needs help." Lorrah leaned in urgently. "Tisha is the only one who might be able to heal her."

V — PURSUIT

T he count's keep was surrounded by a second moat with even more jagged rocks lining it. Ar-Lizelle and Ar-Kyanon crossed a drawbridge of sturdy timbers and entered another ugly gatehouse. Only Endole came to guard them. Groff had taken Ar-Kyanon's suggestion and remained at the inn to safeguard their belongings. Inside the gatehouse, they were searched and their weapons secured. Endole didn't like it, but Ar-Lizelle had warned him not to complain.

"We just have to get this over with," she snapped.

Upon entering the actual keep, they were met by Ar-Gammord's assistant, a very tired young mage who introduced himself as Ar-Vennic. In an urgent yet apologetic tone, he said, "I must ask you to take off your boots. The count does not like people making too much noise."

"Whatever will help my lord feel most comfortable," Ar-Lizelle kept a steady tone and followed her own advice to not argue with the strange demand. Ar-Gammord must have declined quite a bit if he couldn't tolerate the simple sound of people walking around.

A cringing servant helped the Larder team take off their travel-worthy boots and put on soft leather slippers embroidered with Unthur's crest. Even Endole received the same deference, much to his bemusement. Ar-Kyanon, on the other hand, gave every evidence of enjoying the attention.

"May we now proceed?" Ar-Lizelle tried not to let her impatience show.

"Thank you for your understanding." Ar-Vennic appeared slightly shamed but grateful that they didn't make a scene.

The slippers were too thin for comfort on the hard stone floor, but they did quiet the footsteps. In fact, the entire household lay under an unnatural hush. Servants scurried, visibly timid, speaking in anxious whispers. Like any wealthy household, the keep was decorated with rich wall hangings and finely carved furnishings. Everything was the same color, a muted green. It seemed Ar-Gammord couldn't handle bright colors, either.

Hanging lamps sent angled rays to light every corner. Yet, the order of the house was so perfect and absolute, one might think that no one really lived here.

Ar-Vennic guided them through a small courtyard before the keep's residence. A narrow slot of sky shone down on a painfully groomed formal garden. Balconies in all sides were ideal for archer posts, and there were doors behind the shrubbery that could easily admit soldiers. Before them, a wide stair led up to a small terrace where an armored door was flanked by soldiers they could actually see.

It reminded Ar-Lizelle of the entrance to the Larder. That was unnerving. A prickle of heat ran through her veins, but she breathed steadily, calming herself. Ar-Gammord's security was ridiculous, when all they needed was permission to travel through.

Beyond that door was an antechamber, two stories high and again featuring the balconies. Ar-Vennic paused outside a smaller doorway. A loose curl dangled by his face and he frantically brushed it flat before pressing his hand to a crest on the door. Ar-Lizelle felt a brief pulse of magic before a bolt clicked and the door swung inward.

Just within, a new set of guards searched them again.

Ar-Lizelle scanned the chamber. It was a formal reception room with a modest conference table and chairs. The textiles were all of that same dull green. On a side table, trays of refreshments and a silver carafe had been laid out. Two servants stood nearby with downcast eyes and their hands folded meekly in front of them.

Beyond the table, a small fireplace glowed. Near it, a red-robed figure watched intently as they were searched. Count Ar-Gammord had a wide, hooked nose and heavy jaw. Silver streaked his thinning black hair and topknot. The count's face was markedly thinner than she recalled, grooved as if sculpted by an unkind hand. However, the deep-set eyes glared at them with vivid attention.

Again, Ar-Lizelle's power roused against the possible threat. Beside her, Ar-Kyanon's breath halted momentarily, so she knew he also sensed the danger. It was a normal reflex when meeting any unknown mage. She met the count's gaze without flinching.

Ar-Vennic approached the count slowly, bowing. He murmured, "My lord count, Warden Ar-Lizelle is here from the Larder. You recall that you approved her visit?"

"Come on, then." Ar-Gammord stalked to the conference table. His posture was tense, too straight in the back. Ar-Vennic ushered the Larder team to join the count.

"Thank you, my lord," Ar-Lizelle said pointedly as the assistant held her chair. Her voice was naturally high and sharp, and everything about this made her want to pitch it even higher, just to annoy him. As it was, Ar-Vennic winced a little as he slid into a seat at Ar-Gammord's left hand. A thin leather case, papers, pen and ink were already set out there.

As they settled themselves, the servants glided over to offer wine and small plates of sliced fruit. Ar-Gammord watched intently until after Ar-Lizelle had taken her first sip. She wondered if he expected her to fall over, poisoned, before he would taste his own. *Paranoid*, she reminded herself.

"Thank you for seeing us, Count Ar-Gammord," she said. "I am Ar-Lizelle, Warden of the Larder Prison. We've met in the past, you may recall. This is my assistant, Ar-Kyanon. Our guardsman, Endole."

Endole gave a quick bow, and stepped back to stand with the servants at the side of the hall.

"Just what is this business that requires my attention?" Suspicion gave an edge to his voice. "Something you can tell no one else."

Was that a jab at her for refusing to answer the gate guard?

"I appreciate your time, and I assure you, I will not waste it." Ar-Lizelle sipped her wine again, finding it just pleasantly bitter. With that to smooth her throat, she repeated the bare facts of the Larder prison break, avoiding any hint of self-pity.

As he listened, Ar-Gammord held his predatory stiffness, except that his hands were always moving. Long fingers straightened an imaginary wrinkle in his sleeve, or picked at his collar. For a moment he frowned at a button on his sleeve, as if it had offended him.

Concluding, Ar-Lizelle said, "We are committed to recapturing every one of these fugitives. To do so, I ask your leave to cross the County of Unthur and pass into Kamuril, where we hope to intercept them."

"The Larder." Ar-Gammord sat back a little, hostility in his gaze. "That's where I sent that vagabond. The one who dared laugh at me."

"Just so, my lord," murmured Ar-Vennic.

"Yes, Alemin was there," Ar-Lizelle confirmed through gritted teeth.

"Are you saying he's on the loose again?" Ar-

Gammord sat even straighter. His black eyes bored into hers like a pair of awls.

"Not for long," she answered, "if you have the wisdom to allow us passage."

"You let him escape?" As Ar-Lizelle had feared, Unthur's count was fixated on the wrong part of her story.

"My previous assistant was deceived," she repeated, but he didn't allow her to go on.

"And he's roaming around here in Unthur?" Ar-Gammord's voice was rising.

"As I said, we hope to intercept him or the others in Kamuril." Beside her, Ar-Lizelle felt Ar-Kyanon's rigid tension. Her energy was rising again, and this time she didn't completely resist gathering it.

Ignoring them, Ar-Gammord turned to Ar-Vennic with a sort of petulant triumph. "I suppose this explains why so many strange mages were showing up all of a sudden. Who was it again?"

The flustered assistant consulted his documents. "There was a Ferrant, and a Doromy."

Ar-Kyanon, who had been keeping prudently silent, murmured, "That's one more accounted for."

"What was that?" Ar-Gammord demanded.

"Ferrant was one of our escapees," Ar-Lizelle answered, "but I don't know this Doromy person. Where are they now?"

"Up in crow's cages, of course," Ar-Gammord snapped. "As I should have done with that juggler, it seems. Unthur has no room for these vagrants. They are too unpredictable."

"We didn't realize anyone might come looking for Ferrant." Ar-Vennic appeared slightly desperate as Ar-

Gammord's temper flared.

"My lord, you are most wise, and that is merely one less for us to worry about," Ar-Lizelle said. It was no surprise that Ferrant was dead, and she hoped a bit of flattery would appease the count long enough for them to do what they needed. "With your gracious permission, we would like to pass through and continue tracking the rest of them."

His withered brows twitched inward, suspicious of the flattery. "Yes, yes. I don't want you here, a bunch of incompetents who can't even keep your prisoners in their cells. Get out of Unthur!"

Dark eyes glittering, Ar-Gammord pushed his chair back with a jerk. The startled servants jumped aside as he stormed from the hall.

Ar-Kyanon gave a slight huff at his retreating back. "Reminds me of Wharon, right before he lost his mind."

"Quiet," Ar-Lizelle hissed. If Ar-Gammord heard them whispering behind his back, it would set him off again.

Ar-Vennic seemed to share her concern. He was already bringing out parchment from his leather folder. "It will be just a few moments as I prepare the documents."

"Thank you for your assistance." Ar-Lizelle cautiously relaxed. The scratching of *lethentros* in her veins faded slowly. She sipped her wine and enjoyed the sliced melon the servants offered. Catching Ar-Kyanon's eye, she subtly urged him to do the same. Abrasive as Ar-Gammord was, this could have been a lot worse.

~ ~ ~

Sergeant Piyaro had never spent any time on the water, so it hadn't occurred to him that he or the Hawks might get seasick. The half-day's ride across the strait on a bobbing water-folk raft had left him dizzy in a way that still hadn't cleared up. Some of the others had it worse, though. The water-folk made no secret of their amusement at the guardsmen leaning over the rail, cursing and heaving their guts up.

On the far side of the strait, they had come to a landing deep in the mangrove swamp. Luckily, there was only one path out, so they didn't have to do much more than walk straight until the reaction faded.

The Hawks now approached Eshur Holl from the north. They could see the city's sturdy walls in the distance. The countess' keep stood above the town on a high, rocky knoll. Walls, knoll and keep were all of the same brown stone.

A line of people had backed up at the city gate. With many sullen glances, they shuffled aside for the Hawks to march through. A city guardsman was assigned to guide them through the harbor town. Unlike the walls, the buildings here were worn down and rickety. The air was heavy with a stink of sea water and sewage.

At the base of the knoll, they were passed over to one of the keep's guardsmen. Piyaro's heart pounded with exertion as he followed their guide up the narrow, steep switchbacks. Beyond the cluttered fringe of the town, the glittering gray sea stretched out toward the vague shadow of Pulgoll's peninsula. Afternoon was fading, and they could see the sails of many small boats skimming back toward the harbor.

Once at the keep, the Hawks were escorted to a side courtyard where the countess' guards eyed them but left them alone. They rested in the shade of a colonnade. Piyaro even closed his eyes for a moment, though his head still spun a little. Soon a low-level mage came to fetch him.

"Remember," Piyaro warned, "you serve Count Ar-Azlor. Don't embarrass him. And don't answer any questions unless I'm with you."

"Yes Sergeant," they rumbled.

Piyaro followed his latest guide back through the

keep, to a large audience chamber. As he went, he compared this court to the other counts' courts he had known. Ar-Dayne of Sloram had whipped his staff to the point almost of panic. Whatever he wanted, he wanted it instantly, and they scurried frantically, trying to anticipate his whims. In Prizom, people wouldn't even look at the Hawks. Clearly, their former count's reputation tainted them.

In Pulgoll, by contrast, the courtiers and guards went about with purpose. They might patronize, but they were relaxed and secure. Piyaro hadn't been there long, but it was obvious no one was in fear of Count Ar-Azlor.

Here in Eshur, the atmosphere was different again. People moved with a kind of strut, shoulders back and heads high. The mage who led him, Ar-Engil, had his hair done flamboyantly, in a row of small topknots that left the rest of his black hair to curl free. His robe was of fine fabric, its silky sheen further ornamented with subtle embroidery. The impression of pride was better than desperation, but it made Piyaro wonder what this latest countess would mean for him and his squad. He didn't think they could get so lucky again as they had with Ar-Azlor.

Ar-Engil led him to a large audience chamber, where the high ceiling was screened by gracefully draped banners stitched with white dolphins, Eshur's emblem. Strands of fine chain hung among the banners, glittering in the bright lamplight. A number of richly dressed onlookers circulated around the main floor. At the far end of the chamber, more banners and sparkling chains drew the eye to a dais where the countess sat on an elaborate chair.

She was stunning, in a gorgeous red robe of silky fabric. It was cut low in the front, allowing her to make a fabulous display of jeweled and pearl chains. Even more pearls gleamed against her raven-wing hair that was coiled up high. There was something incredibly enticing about her. He couldn't take his eyes off her sleek figure and soft, full lips.

At that, Piyaro caught himself back. He wasn't a young fool to lust after forbidden fruit. Besides, after he got past that first impression, he could remind himself that Ar-Torix was not, in fact, the most beautiful woman he had ever seen. The golden witch from Seofan outdid her, though maybe not by much.

Piyaro had been so struck by the countess' glamor that he barely noticed the line of people waiting to have their petitions heard. His guide led him to the head of the line, much to the annoyance of the man who was supposed to be next.

Countess Ar-Torix relaxed in her chair, listening to the latest presentation while clearly enjoying the attention of her court. The nobles near her remained quiet, as Piyaro had first noted, allowing everyone to hear the man go on about repairs to the city docks. When the countess' dark eyes touched him and Ar-Engil, her gaze sharpened into true alertness.

In a purring voice, she cut into the presentation. "That will do, my good man. What exactly do you propose?"

"If we want trade to increase, there must be an investment in the port facilities," the fellow recited, though without much hope. "I propose a schedule of replacement for the three main piers. My associates are experts in these repairs."

Ar-Torix raised a jeweled hand. "I will need to see a detailed proposal. How much time do you need?"

"Thank you, countess! A week will be adequate."

"Then I will look forward to seeing you in a week."

The carpenter backed out, bowing and beaming. Ar-Engil urged Piyaro forward. They both bowed at the base of the dais. Piyaro was close enough to see that a number of courtiers and guards were partly concealed behind all the draperies around the dais. The countess directed one of her staff to send their own team of inspectors to make sure this work was truly necessary. Then her black eyes rested on him.

"Ah, a friend from Pulgoll. Welcome to my city." Her throaty voice rang in the hall.

"Thank you, my lady." Piyaro matched her volume with his firm tone. "I bear a letter from Count Ar-Azlor."

One of her guards stepped down to fetch it. Ar-Torix's dark eyes roved over the page, then rested on Piyaro again with cool intelligence. She refolded the letter and passed it to her guard, who brought it back down.

"Do you wish to send a reply, my lady?" he asked. Captain Jorus had spoken of answering her questions, but that might not be what the countess had in mind.

"This will require more discussion," she answered. "You are Sergeant Piyaro?"

"Yes, my lady."

"You came with your squad, I assume. We'll see them quartered for the night." She glanced at one of her guards among the drapes, who touched his chest and hurried off. Looking to Ar-Engil, she said, "Wait in the back conference room. Send for refreshments. Nyette will be joining us from the Temple School."

"Yes, my lady." Ar-Engil bowed, but with a trace of indignation, added, "Surely one of us can serve better than a student."

"Do you presume to know my mind?" The countess' welcoming aura turned cold and sharp as steel.

"Not at all, my lady." The mage bowed again, a bit sulky, though in Piyaro's mind the rebuke was well deserved.

Ar-Engil led him to a side door, half hidden by among the drapery. Behind them, Ar-Torix announced, "I shall hear three more. The others must return another day."

Beyond that side door, a corridor ran parallel to the audience chamber. On the opposite side of it a servant in livery was just opening a door into a smaller room. The elegant table and chairs were of carved spicewood, its fragrance softening the air. Mercifully, there were no more drapes here.

Piyaro sat quietly while the servant poured something for him and Ar-Engil, then set the carafe on the table and left the room. The mage studied Piyaro, while Piyaro savored the faintly sweet liquid and decided it was some sort of wine.

After a moment, Ar-Engil leaned forward with a sly air. "Is it true there's a rebellion up in Pulgoll?"

A bold question, even rude. Piyaro kept his face blank and voice neutral. "I don't think my lord wants me talking about things like that." After a moment, he asked his own question. "Who said so?"

Ar-Engil smirked into his cup. "I don't exactly remember."

This mage reminded Piyaro a little of Ar-Jeziak. Ar-Dayne had taken her on as a junior mage, but right from the start she had been poking into things, looking for any hint of weakness or influence. From Ar-Jeziak's perspective, Piyaro supposed it had paid benefits. Himself, he had no intention of getting tangled up in Eshur's court affairs. He sat stolidly and tried to enjoy his wine.

After a moment, Ar-Engil spoke again. "So you're saying there *is* a rebellion?"

Piyaro's jaw clenched. Every instinct warned that lying or refusing to answer a mage was dangerous. Yet, as he had only just reminded his men, he was in Eshur to represent Ar-Azlor. Even if the count's protection was all too distant at the moment.

"Don't put words in my mouth," he answered.

"I won't, if you just answer the question." The mage's

mouth quirked in a coaxing smile. "Really, you can tell me."

"Really, I can't." Piyaro sat stiff. This wasn't a matter for compromise. He'd just have to be ready to duck the mage's blast. "Your prying into my lord's affairs is unbecoming. I would hate to have to mention this to Countess Ar-Torix."

The mage gave a little snort and looked away, as if Piyaro was suddenly beneath his concern. "Have it your way."

Time dragged as Piyaro waited, all too aware of his companion's frustration. He sipped his wine, enough to keep himself busy but not enough to muddle his senses. Eshur might be Pulgoll's ally, but he couldn't forget what was at stake.

Both he and Ar-Engil straightened as the door opened quietly. A tall young woman in a brown robe entered. This must be Nyette, the student mage Ar-Torix had sent for over Ar-Engil's protest. A pair of pretty hair pins held waves of dark hair away from her face. They made her look very young. Dark eyes touched Piyaro with curiosity, then flicked away.

The girl took a seat on the opposite side of the table and composed her hands in front of her. Ar-Engil stared at her, as a fox would toward a hare. Piyaro's breath tightened in his throat. If Ar-Engil went after Nyette, what was he supposed to do? Help the student, or help the mage, or just get under the table?

Luckily, he didn't have to make that decision. The door opened again, and the countess herself strutted in, followed by a guard who closed the door softly and took up a position beside it. Ar-Torix settled gracefully at the head of the table.

"Well?" Her eyes were on Ar-Engil. Piyaro assumed she could sense his intentions toward Nyette, but that turned out not to be the case.

"He's not supposed to talk about it," Ar-Engil intoned in a mocking imitation of Piyaro's words, and he irritably brushed his loose hair behind his shoulder.

"Good." Ar-Torix gave a sharp little nod. "That will be all."

Ar-Engil slunk from the room, visibly discontent. Piyaro tried to suppress his offense that, apparently, the intrusive questions had been a test of his loyalty to Ar-Azlor. The aggression toward Nyette had seemed real enough.

The countess, meanwhile, gave an extended sigh. Piyaro stared as her intense glamor suddenly faded away. The countess was a normal, attractive woman with lines just beginning to appear at the corners of her eyes. A different indignation surged through him. That attraction was just an illusion, designed to trap men's emotions. It was humbling to realize how effective her strategy had been.

Now, the lines around her eyes made her look weary. The constant effort of holding that aura of attraction seemed to drain her energy. She was still decked in pearls, so at least that much was real.

Ar-Torix poured wine for herself and Nyette. The student sipped cautiously. Piyar shook his head when she extended the carafe toward him. More than ever, he needed all his wits.

"Well, Sergeant," Ar-Torix said, "I understand that you and your squad witnessed something unusual?"

"Yes, my lady." Piyaro was heartily glad to get to business. "By my lord Ar-Azlor's command, I am to answer any questions you may have."

"Let's begin with what you saw." Ar-Torix leaned back, rubbing her hands over the carved arms of her chair. A faint fragrance of spicewood rose in the air.

Piyaro set his cup aside and went into the familiar story. Ar-Dayne had gone in pursuit of one more mage, and followed her all the way through the Hornwood to Seofan Valley.

"Seofan," Ar-Torix cut in. "Six months ago?"

"Yes, my lady." Piyaro wondered what she had heard about it. "We finally caught up with the rogue mage, and we found a soldier I had to leave for dead. All of his injuries were healed. He only carried the scars on his arm."

"She healed him?" Ar-Torix repeated. Nyette glanced at the countess curiously.

"It seemed so. I've never heard of such magic, but I couldn't think of any other explanation," Piyaro said.

"Healing." Ar-Torix shook her head slightly, and raised her glass. Piyaro couldn't guess why she seemed so dissatisfied.

"Count Ar-Dayne fought the mage who was with him," he continued. "She's the one my lord Ar-Azlor may have mentioned."

"The mysterious golden witch," Ar-Torix spoke softly over the rim of her glass.

Piyaro went on with the telling, how the beautiful young woman had drawn Ar-Dayne's wrath and eventually destroyed him, all without leaving the safety of her barrier. Both mages listened carefully. Ar-Torix's dark eyes gleamed as her own thoughts ran behind them.

It was Nyette who asked, "She never retaliated?"

"Unless you count taunting him into violence." Perversely, Piyaro felt the need to defend his former count.

"No, it wouldn't be that," Ar-Torix murmured.

"Countess, you know of these renegades?" Nyette asked cautiously. Piyaro was beginning to wonder about that, too.

"I've heard of them, yes." Ar-Torix seemed to blink

back to alertness. "Would it surprise you to hear that this golden witch actually broke the curse over Seofan? After a century or more, reports are that moss and rascalweed are spreading from the edges in, and a number of the oleya trees have come back into bloom."

"No," Piyaro answered slowly, "it doesn't surprise me. I won't claim to understand your arts, countess, but what we experienced..." He trailed off. The rush of power in Seofan had been terrifying in its intensity, yet soft as a mother's embrace. Even for a man of forty, hardened by many battles, it had called up something deep within him, a child's longing to be loved and protected. Awkwardly he finished, "The trees leafed out before our eyes. If you say the curse has been lifted, I believe it."

"Let's get to more recent events, then," the countess said. "According to Ar-Azlor's letter, there's been an uprising and you saw another of these golden mages there?"

"Yes. A man this time, but we all recognized it." Piyaro shoved aside that guilty longing and related the events in Opshar. "He calls himself Sand. The peasants attacked us when we tried to arrest him."

"Sand. That's probably Berisan. Did he call on them to defend him?" Ar-Torix asked.

Piyaro shook his head. "It was pretty chaotic, with everyone yelling and throwing things, but the mage never asked for that. Like the witch in Seofan, he only defended them. The mob pushed us back out of the village, with just bruises to show." Shame prickled beneath his skin, for how useless his squad had been.

"Did they mention if he healed them?" The countess asked. Both Piyaro and Nyette regarded her with surprise.

"Possibly," Piyaro said. "The clearest thing I remember was them saying Sand was the best thing that had happened to their village. They were mad that the headman would let him be taken." A new thought came to him. "Is the healing a way to control them?" That could explain Cylass' defection.

Ar-Torix thought about it. "Not intentionally, so they claim." Then she snorted to herself. "There have been a number of unusual reports over the past several months. Your incident in Seofan, and something deep in the Hornwood that nobody seems to know much about. Now in Opshar. There always seems to be one of these renegades nearby. But I knew of them, a long time ago."

Nyette spoke up. "Does this have to do with Meven?"

"My dear old friend, who ran away from the temple school in Nibbok. She took up with some sort of wandering herbalist." Ar-Torix rolled her eyes at the memory. "Eventually she showed up here, and I dealt with her in my own way."

Piyaro didn't understand who the student mage meant, but it seemed like something Ar-Azlor might want to hear about. He listened carefully.

"I have a theory," the countess said. "Warden Ar-Lizelle, at the Larder, was collecting details on the renegades. As I understand it, she had another one of them captured there."

"They got one?" That was good news. Piyaro assumed he had been tortured for information, but Ar-Torix gave an irritable wave.

"Not for long. The Larder's been broken, all the prisoners set loose. Ar-Lizelle has gone quiet these past few weeks." She snorted again. "If I lost track of a dozen criminal mages, I'd be hiding, too. Dar-Gothull will take her soul for this."

"Attacked by the golden mages?" Piyaro tried to conceal his shock at the loss of Skaythe's most deadly prison.

"By a squad of fake hunter-guards, apparently." Ar-Torix refilled her own glass. "Details are scant there, too."

That would have to be quite a squad, in Piyaro's opinion. He'd seen the Larder once. Even partly ruined, it was formidable.

"Now Meven has also vanished," Nyette said softly.

"I thought I knew what she wanted. That I could use it to keep her close." Ar-Torix's eyes narrowed at some other thought she did not voice. Piyaro wondered if she, too, was at risk of losing her soul for failing to keep this Meven contained. He was glad to let that be Eshur's problem, and not his own.

"Something is moving beneath the waters," the countess brooded. "If, as I suspect, Meven has gone to join her friend in Pulgoll, then we may all be served by finding out what it is. So, you say this renegade in Opshar wants to negotiate?" Her dark eyes touched Piyaro's again.

"Yes, Countess."

"Then I agree with Ar-Azlor. If he wants to talk, we should talk."

"Are you really going to negotiate?" Piyaro could hardly believe it. The highest mages in the land wouldn't stoop to diplomacy with a bunch of peasants and rebels.

"I'm only making a suggestion. It's Ar-Azlor's decision, not mine," she answered smoothly. "However, if it gets us any useful information, I'd at least let them think we're negotiating, for a while." Looking to Nyette, Ar-Torix instructed, "You'll be returning along with Sergeant Piyaro and his squad. Get close to this renegade, if you can. Observe for me. And of course, assist Count Ar-Azlor in any way he asks."

That took Piyaro by surprise. He'd imagined Ar-Torix would send him back with a letter, not someone from her household. Nyette also appeared confused.

"Countess..." She hesitated, then gathered her nerve. "Why would you send me? Surely a fully trained mage would serve you better."

Piyaro's reply would have been that obviously a student was expendable. However, Ar-Torix gave a different explanation.

"Several months ago, I laid down a challenge for all my upper students," she said. "Only one of you rose to meet it. Only one of you has been out to Fang Marsh and has a sense for Meven's power. I think you're ready, Nyette. I certainly hope you aren't going to prove me wrong."

"No, Countess." Nyette's eyes flashed, maybe with fear but more likely youthful indignation.

Nyette was a smart one, Piyaro could tell. She knew the other mages would resent being passed over in favor of a mere student. Maybe that snake, Ar-Engil, had already been stepping on her tail about it. Piyaro was reminded of Hawk Squad, before everything went bad. Cylass had been a promising soldier, and even more valuable because he could read and write. But Ennow had served there longer, and Piyaro's favor had provoked his jealousy.

Not that it mattered now. Ennow was dead and Cylass was beyond reach. Piyaro was where he was, and he had the pieces of a squad to hold together. That was yet another reason to stay out of Eshur's affairs and get back to Pulgoll as soon as possible.

"When do you want us to leave?" he asked.

~ ~ ~

Shonn's father and uncles talked about leaving Fang Marsh as soon as Shonn told them how Countess Ar-Torix made him take Nyette over to Meven's tower, but it didn't happen. *Otter* stayed anchored at the landing. Days passed in the same way they had for every year of Shonn's life. There was still plenty to do, fishing, gathering fruit, helping his brother and father replace a loose rail where they stood to put their poles in the water. He slunk through it all, more restless than ever.

"What are you moping for?" Shonn's brother Bonton asked as they rubbed protective oil onto the new rail.

Shonn just shrugged. The pungent odor of ship's oil burned in his nostrils. "This stuff stinks," he said, not really answering the question.

Yes, these jobs were important. *Otter* was home to a family of fifteen, and she had to be kept in fit shape. But Shonn had done it all a hundred times before. Now that Meven was gone, it all seemed pointless.

"You're still thinking about that girl, aren't you?" Bonton chuckled when Shonn glared at him.

"Easy for you to laugh. You've been married to Miniber for four years." While Shonn's best prospect had lied about everything and then vanished.

Bonton wetted his rag with more oil before setting to work on another section of rail. After a moment, he said, "You did the right thing, you know."

Shonn's jaw tightened. "I thought so."

As consequences unreeled, it was harder to believe that. Even as strange and aloof as Meven was, it had been a thrill to pole his raft over and see her every day. Shonn rubbed sullenly at the rail's supporting post.

"We all depend on the countess' favor. She can drive us out of Fang Marsh any time," Bonton continued.

Shonn rubbed harder and harder with his oily rag. "So instead I drove Meven out." He stopped with a hiss as a shard of dried reed jabbed his thumb.

"She was never going to join our family." Bonton spoke with the smug assurance of an annoying older brother. "Miniber told me that Mother about begged her to stay, the first day, but she headed off. You knew where she was, but the rest of us never saw her again."

"Because she was in hiding." Shonn mumbled as he

sucked on his injured finger.

"Don't defend her," Bonton said. "Water-folk have to take care of ourselves first."

Mutinously, Shonn polished the rail. Bonton wasn't saying anything he hadn't told himself, until he realized what a mistake he'd made. Every day since, his eyes turned to the rocky hilltop where he had first seen that mysterious glow. He couldn't stop wondering where Meven had gone. Why did that creature take her?

The silence stretched, until Bonton suddenly nudged his arm. "You see that?"

His low, cautious tone made Shonn freeze. Bonton's oily rag released a single slow drop as he pressed it against the rail. He was facing toward the hills.

Shonn's heart leaped. He whipped around and spotted movement on the pale road that wound its way into Fang Marsh. That was the way Meven and Oz had come. Was it possible that the creature had returned? Was Meven back?

The sun had been up for hours, but patches of mist still drifted over the salt marsh. A small file of people came steadily in and out of sight. Shonn could immediately tell Meven wasn't one of them.

"Soldiers, you think?" Bonton asked.

"Looks like it." Shonn counted twelve men, heavily armored, with one more leading them. A slight figure in a brown mage robe moved among them, in a protected position. "I think that's Nyette."

"The student Countess Ar-Torix had you ferry around?" Bonton asked. "Did she say she'd be coming back?"

"Not to me." Without shifting his gaze, Shonn called out, "Oberim, on the road!"

The deck rolled slightly beneath their feet as Oberim

and the other men came over to the rail. Their father took a long look and said, "I guess we'd better get ready for company."

The strangers were still a good way off, but water-folk didn't take chances. The women and children who were on shore, gathering fruit, were quickly called back aboard the houseboat. Uncle Delveer scooped up the fishing gear he had laid out for repair. Working together, the men of the clan poled the *Otter* a good distance out into the lagoon. All the time, Shonn's head drummed with worry and excitement.

Meven might not be with them, but this probably had something to do with her. What could he do about it, that was the question. String them along, ask for news? That wouldn't work. Oberim was going to do the talking.

Maybe it was none of his business. Meven didn't want to see him. He should leave her alone. Shonn prowled along the rail, watching the landing.

"Would you sit down?" Uncle Kannat asked irritably. "You're making me seasick."

"But there's a girl," teased Bonton. Everyone laughed. Shonn's fists tightened around the jug of polishing oil, but he didn't dare throw it. Aunt Avera was helping Grandmother Criya sit down right behind Bonton. Instead he stalked off to put the oil away. Wringing out the polishing cloths, he imagined it was his brother's neck, instead.

After what seemed like days, the soldiers arrived at the landing. Their leader came forward to the end of the dock and called, "In the name of Countess Ar-Torix."

"He's not wearing Eshur's symbol," Uncle Delveer muttered.

"No, it's a heron. That's Pulgoll," said Miniber, who came from there.

"I can see it," Oberim answered evenly, before calling to the shore, "What does the countess want from us?"

"We need to cross over to Pulgoll," the sergeant called back.

Uncle Kannat leaned in to urge, "Ask them how much they'll pay."

Oberim gave Kannat a look before replying, "Our family is using this houseboat."

"The countess only requires your assistance for one trip. It should take less than a day," the sergeant called.

Shonn listened with increasing interest. They were headed for Pulgoll? And that was definitely Nyette standing among the soldiers. From the angle of her face, he was sure she had seen him. They had worked together before, on Countess Ar-Torix's behalf. Maybe she had even come here because of him.

"We have to stay on the countess' good side." Shonn parroted Bonton's words. Oberim quirked a sardonic brow, and Shonn knew he wasn't fooling anyone about why he was interested. Still, he was ready to try anything if there was a chance he could see Meven again.

"It's a fair point," Aunt Keesa said.

"Wait, though." Uncle Delveer burst out. "There's some kind of patrol boat the past few days. Could it be looking for them?"

"Not from Eshur?" Oberim asked.

Delveer shook his head. "No, from Deeve."

Everyone turned to gaze at the party gathered on the shore. What was the greater risk? Water-folk had to travel everywhere, and it was no good winning Ar-Torix's favor at the expense of Ar-Gevant's.

"Can it be done?" The sergeant sounded impatient with their muffled debates.

Resigned, Oberim shouted back. "I'll come over on a

raft. We can talk about it."

VI — THE CROSSING

I t took a bit of prodding to secure the water-folk's cooperation. The clan in Pulgoll hadn't been nearly as skittish. Piyaro understood when they told him unknown ships were moving about. Piyaro had left Cothyr in charge while he and Nyette went with the water-folk to see for themselves.

Now, they crouched on a sand bar, peering through a screen of mangrove branches. Pestering gnats hovered about Piyaro's face, and he could fairly taste the cloying odors of mud and salt water.

Far across the strait, Pulgoll's coast was a distant shadow. Closer at hand, small fishing boats with lateen sails bobbed on the swell. Nets briefly winked and flared as the crews flung them out. Unfortunately, a sleek, dangerous predator glided among them: a warship, long and low, propelled by banks of swift oars.

"Not a regular patrol?" Piyaro glanced over at the two water-folk kneeling nearby. Oberim's lips thinned as they surveyed the scene. The younger one, Shonn, fidgeted with a leaf on the bank.

"They definitely aren't from Eshur," Nyette said from slightly behind them.

"We know Eshur's patrols," Shonn said indignantly.

Oberim cut him off. "It doesn't matter. Deeve doesn't

belong here. These are Eshur's waters."

As they watched, the warship glided up beside one of the fishing boats. Several armed men stood up while they talked to the crew.

"Unless they're looking for someone." Piyaro considered the implications. Oberim slanted him a look, but nodded, neutral.

When Captain Jorus sent the Hawks from Pulgoll, he had specifically said to avoid the coast of Deeve. Piyaro had taken steps to avoid trouble, even following Nyette's advice to head south of Eshur and cross aboard the *Otter*, a different water-folk houseboat.

It was Nyette who asked the obvious question. "Do they know you're here?"

"Hard to say," Piyaro replied. Someone from Ar-Torix's court could have tipped Deeve's people. And for any reason, from petty revenge to a pocket full of coin. "I assume they won't try to land in Eshur, so the real question is, do we risk crossing?"

"*Otter* can't out-run them," Oberim said flatly, "and we don't want a fight."

"Can you hold them off?" blurted Shonn. Piyaro sympathized with the young man's energy, but he shook his head.

"We don't want a fight, either." The shifting footing on the deck would be a challenge for his men, not to mention their upset stomachs.

Nyette squinted across the water. "I don't think they have a mage."

"Then you could bluff them?" Shonn asked eagerly.

"Not as a student," she answered. "Perhaps I could fend them off, but we don't want a lot of ice to weigh down one side of your ship."

"Put it on their ship," Shonn suggested.

"Won't Eshur send out their own boats? Chase these fellows off?" Piyaro asked. They weren't much of a county if they wouldn't defend their border.

"Maybe," Oberim said, "but that doesn't stop another boat from patrolling on the northern shore. A lot of the land-folk places aren't friendly to us water-folk. Even with Eshur, it's chancy."

"Then we'll have to wait. See if they give up." Piyaro was reluctant, but he didn't see an alternative.

"For how long?" Shonn ground his heel into the bank.

"Don't be in such a hurry," Oberim frowned. "I've said you can go with them, if it pleases the countess. Just don't let your wanderlust get you killed."

"I won't," Shonn growled. Keeping low, he moved back from the edge of the branches.

Piyaro thought about that as they followed the water-folk. Shonn's restlessness seemed like more than mere wanderlust. As they moved back to their hidden rafts, he murmured a question to Nyette.

"Why are we taking him along, again?"

"Shonn is already part of this," the mage girl said. "He's loyal to Ar-Torix, and he knows Meven."

The last thing Piyaro wanted was to shepherd a swamp dweller into potential danger. Yes, Shonn looked strong and lithe, and he was armed with a bush knife. His sarong and thin shirt hardly protected against blades or arrows, however. Piyaro wasn't sure what the young man had to offer besides Ar-Torix's approval.

~ ~ ~

Little changed in the scenery of Kamuril as another

few days passed on the ageless highway. The hills rolled like a static sea, if the water was tall grass and sea foam was replaced by scrubby bushes. Each day showed the same birds, horses and cattle, the occasional village to be avoided. Distant mountains rose on the horizon, until Duessa could begin to pick out their individual features.

"Looking for something?" teased the archer, Razeet.

Duessa shook her head. "Not yet. We're too far south." It was a disappointment that she didn't recognize any of the peaks. There was regret, too, that she couldn't be fully joyful, so near to home.

A certain tension was building, all the same. Even if Alemin or Lorrah didn't cry out every morning, "We're getting closer," their excitement was evident. Even Duessa began to feel the tug of something approaching. The guardswomen seemed to sense it, too, in their way. They kept a sharper watch over the camp. Their lives had already been turned around, from pursuing rogue mages to working alongside them. Whoever they were about to meet, it would change things around again.

Change could be for the better, Duessa reminded herself. Alemin's anticipation was genuine, and she should be able to trust him. He'd said his friends were coming to get him out of the Larder, and no one had believed it. Not until they actually saw the wagon waiting to get them out of that nightmare. Why would he lie, after that?

Uncertain as Duessa might be, she also understood that these days on the road were her best chance to build her skills, and that time was coming to a close. She didn't waste it. As she learned more, she could almost begin to draw the warmth of *vitalis* into herself. The ragged channels *lethentros* had carved into her soul were smoothing out. She just couldn't quite bring herself to embrace *vitalis* completely. Many times, *lethentros* had been the difference between life and death. She didn't know what would happen if she gave it up.

Bettain had her own strategy for facing the future. One morning, while the Badgers were sparring, she hauled out the grimy, threadbare robes the former prisoners had worn in the Larder.

"Elldri," she called out. "Come help me with this. You can sew, right?"

Silently, the youngest prisoner studied their old clothes. Prison robes were too recognizable. Jaxynne hadn't thought it safe to trade them, so they had been stuffed into a box under the bench.

"Ugh," Duessa gagged a bit. The body odor wafting up from the box was all too familiar. It encapsulated endless days of hard labor, and afternoons in the stifling courtyard that passed as their rest period, with just a tinge of the Larder's sun-baked stone mingled in.

"I can do something with these," Bettain said tartly. "If we're going to be a group, we should have a uniform, too."

"Really?" Alemin looked over his shoulder, mildly disgusted.

"They reek," Lorrah added helpfully.

"What's your idea?" Duessa didn't know how to sew, but she didn't like her friend being mocked.

"They're all the same size, right?" Bettain held one up. "But they're thin. If we turn one inside the other, we can make them more sturdy. They're still mage robes, just not red."

Elldri lisped, "They go with the gray of the road."

"A fitting match," Alemin admitted.

"That's what I thought, too." Bettain nodded, obviously pleased to engage Elldri in something besides livestock care. "We came out of there with ten, but we've already torn one of them up for our head wraps. We can unravel the rest of that one for thread to sew the others, and there will be an extra if we need to make patches."

"Can you put in sleeve pockets?" As a moon-runner, Duessa knew the value of hidden spaces in clothing.

"I like it," Bettain grinned. "Hey, Jaxynne, do you have a needle and some pins?"

"She's off scouting," someone else called back.

"I have a needle for repairing tack, but it might be too big," Sethamis added. Then she wrinkled her nose. "Whew! They do need to be washed."

"Too bad you didn't think of it while we were at that lake," Lorrah said.

"Well, I didn't." Bettain shrugged that aside. "We'll have to work carefully. If there's enough thread, we can do a bit of quilting to hold the layers together and make them look more fancy."

Duessa wasn't sure they wanted to look like any sort of group. That would only make it easier to identify them. Reluctantly, she said, "I guess it'll give us something to do while we're in the cart."

The ancient highway made a grand sweep toward the east, roughly following the hills along the coast. Duessa couldn't tell whether they were still in Kamuril, or had crossed into Ebruc. She was glad enough to help with unraveling the torn robe. It was a slight revenge, to destroy something from the Larder without actually doing any harm.

As they rode along, the guardswomen debated whether to stop and trade horses with some of the local herders. One of the ones Lorrah had taken from the Larder had a distinctive spray of white on its neck that might make it easier to track them. The discussion halted when the group paused on the crest of a steeper hill to rest their oxen.

Their vantage overlooked one of those strange

intersections, where the Shining Ones' highways came together. A perfectly round pond was at the center, sparkling blue under the sun. Around it, the roads divided into sweeping curls, almost like tendrils of a vine. Common roads spread out to the east and west, while a silvery glimmer suggested that the ancient highway angled more to the northwest. A cluster of buildings had grown up around the pond.

"What is that, a guard station?" Duessa asked the obvious question.

"Can't be," Keerin answered. "They'd have a stockade at least. This looks more like a trading post. There could be some guards passing through, I suppose."

"From Prowth?" Lorrah asked. As if to reassure herself, she murmured, "I wasn't the one arrested, though."

So Alemin's sweet little girlfriend had a criminal past? Duessa stored that information for later teasing.

"We should be near Prowth by now," Jaxynne confirmed.

Everyone looked to Sergeant Zathi, who shrugged. "They'll notice if we don't stop to trade for supplies. Let's take down our pennant and cover anything else that might make us stand out."

The wagon kept a steady pace. Zathi and the others tied scraps of cloth over their pauldrons, where the squad's emblem was painted on. The actual pennant was on a short pole that went through a hole in the bench, behind where Sethamis sat to drive the wagon. Elldri and Bettain moved their sewing over so that Duessa could take out a couple of pegs and get the pole down. It fitted neatly under their bench. The pennant she folded and tucked out of sight until Jaxynne could store it somewhere better.

By the time that was done, the settlement was coming into focus. It had three main buildings of large timbers with mud stuffed between them. Smoke rose from one that might be a smithy, a convenience for travelers who needed to repair their wagons. Another had a striped awning that marked it as a trader. No doubt the last one was a tavern. Informal camps were spread around that main hub, using the curved bits of road to separate them from each other.

"Look, Alemin!" Lorrah stood in the stirrups, shading her eyes against the afternoon light. "Do you see it?"

"Finally!" The two shared a look of excitement and relief.

"Your friends?" Zathi asked.

"Yes, Tisha's there." Alemin eased back down, but Duessa could feel him stretching out with his senses.

"It's about time," Bettain groused. "I was starting to think this was one of your jokes."

"Nope." Alemin didn't even sound annoyed.

"What are we looking for?" Duessa demanded.

"That tent with the bold stripes, see it?" Lorrah pointed. "On the western side, diagonal from the tavern. It's what we used to attract people, when we were doing the minstrel shows."

Once she said it, the tent was impossible to miss. It was tall and conical, striped with orange, purple and green. Like the trader's striped awning, its vivid coloration would be helpful to draw attention.

"I guess you weren't trying to be discreet," Duessa said. Alemin just kept grinning, radiating relief and joy.

They encountered more traffic as they approached the trading post. People and carts moved around, especially near the pond. Someone was taking coin to water livestock or buy large urns of water. Dust rose around a makeshift corral, where some of the local herders appeared to be selling their animals.

"There's your horse trader," Keerin called to Jaxynne.

Sethamis guided the oxen around the outside, following one of the spiral paths. The guardswomen were watchful, and a few residents seemed to eye them in return, but Duessa didn't note anything they had to be worried about. The odd road formation seemed to mark this place as special, neutral ground. Nobody wanted to spoil that.

Even so, Elldri hunched low in the bed of the wagon. Bettain looked around boldly and muttered to her, "Don't worry so much. Nobody cares about us."

Duessa stayed focused on that gaudy tent. It was set on the very edge of the encampment, with a visible space between it and the road. Duessa wondered about the gap, but most of her senses were drawn to the energy around the place. *Vitalis,* matching Alemin's and Lorrah's. As their branch of road curved closer, she spotted a donkey grazing behind the tent, and a small hand cart near the entrance. A lone man stacked wood to make a bonfire in the center of the gap. He looked up warily as the Badgers' wagon drew near.

"Do you know who that is?" Alemin asked Lorrah. Before she could answer, someone else threw back the tent flap and hurried out.

Lorrah gave a happy cry. "Tisha!"

The woman who waved back seemed unremarkable, clad in a coarse peasant dress and hood. The figure beneath it was shapely, and she moved forward with unusual grace. The man with her set his last log down and aggressively moved between them.

Lorrah trotted toward them and impatiently swung down from her horse. Not to be left out, Alemin jumped from his seat, too, but he had the presence of mind to run behind the wagon instead of dashing in front of the oxen. Tisha appeared to be reassuring her protector when the two of them got there. They all collided in a group embrace.

"Ho boys, ho," Sethamis called as she hauled on the

reins. The wagon jolted slower, and came to a halt. There was a moment of general confusion as the mounted guardswomen gathered around, but respected the reunion before them. When she could, Duessa also jumped down from the back of the wagon.

The three mages laughed and cried, talking over each other. "I missed you so much!" Tisha said.

"I was afraid I'd never see you again!" That was Lorrah.

"Have you heard from anyone else?" Alemin asked.

"No, not since Sloram," Tisha replied.

All the time, their energies mingled and flowed, sharing power that went deeper than words. Duessa tried to ignore her stinging jealousy. Even on their best days, her crew of moon-runners had never shared such a bond.

Like Duessa, Tisha's companion stood a little apart. He was armed, she saw, though not as heavily as the guardswomen. Duessa wondered if he was Tisha's boyfriend. When he could get a word in, the man cocked an eyebrow toward the gathering of strangers.

"Lady, were you expecting so many?" Lady, he named her. A bodyguard, then.

They were a pretty big group, but it wasn't the quantity he referred to. The Badgers might have covered their colors, but they were clearly soldiers. The Larder crew, meanwhile, looked thoroughly shabby.

Zathi also dismounted, and nodded to the fellow with understanding. "Relax, we're friendly."

Tisha did take notice, then. Her eyes, an unusual light brown, moved between the Badgers and the women of the Larder, lingering for just a bit longer on the place where Elldri was trying to sit small in the wagon. Lorrah wiped her eyes as she stepped away from Tisha's embrace.

"These are our friends," she began.

Tisha laughed teasingly. "When you said people, I didn't think you meant an army."

"It's my charisma. I just can't help it." Alemin grinned, and shrugged with feigned helplessness. More somberly, he said, "We have a lot to tell you."

"I see that." Tisha's sly gaze noted the fact that Alemin and Lorrah were still arm in arm.

Duessa shook her head a little. If she'd thought Alemin was ridiculously easy-going, Tisha's presence was even more soothing. Being near her felt like standing in a softly falling rain, the kind that cooled you without drenching your clothes.

"We're not an army," Zathi put in. "Not any longer. We knew Keilos." Tisha's eyes brightened, and the sergeant filled in before she could ask. "He's not here. But then we met Lorrah, and Lorrah knew Alemin, and Alemin knew all of these." A little awkwardly, she finished, "It seems that our circles overlap."

Duessa stepped in quickly. "I'm Duessa. That's Bettain, and Elldri." She left off their origins until there weren't so many other people around.

Again, Tisha's searching gaze moved among them. Duessa couldn't believe she just accepted her camp being invaded. The woman was open and curious, without visible fear. Duessa felt a delicate brush of inquisitive power, lingering again on Elldri. Finally there was a hint of questioning concern.

"I welcome you all," Tisha said, "and I can see there's more than one story to tell. Let's try to get you all set up, and we can figure out who tells it first."

"Good idea," Jaxynne called from beside the wagon.

"Hey!" Someone called. Most of the group turned,

startled. A man in a nearby camp asked, "Are you still dancing tonight?"

"Of course I am," Tisha twinkled back at him. "Not 'til nightfall, though."

"Can't wait," the fellow leered.

Duessa wondered suspiciously what that was about, but Alemin was already hurrying off with Tisha and Lorrah. It was just one more question that would have to wait.

~ ~ ~

One of Oberim's people kept watch on Deeve's warship. As predicted, a pair of warships skimmed in from Eshur. The lone intruder made a hasty retreat. The *Otter* clan spent the morning unloading their essential supplies to a small hut on the shore, where the elders, women and children would wait for the larger houseboat to return. Piyaro allowed Hawk Squad to share a meal at noon, but as the afternoon lengthened, he cut them off from any more food.

"I want you ready for a fight," he said, "not emptying your guts into the sea."

Nyette spoke up. "Sergeant, I have an idea about the crossing."

Piyaro would be glad to hear something useful. "Go ahead."

"We have fog from the marsh most nights," she said, "even up in Eshur Holl. But at Meven's tower, the ice is causing fog all the time. I can do something like that for us."

Everyone looked south. Piyaro had heard rumors, but this was as close as he'd come to the ice-sheathed tower of rumors. It was a daunting and unnatural vision, indeed.

"That's a lot of ice, though," Oberim objected. "It could interfere with our steering."

"I don't plan to weigh the *Otter* down," Nyette said.

"If I freeze part of the lagoon, it will let me create a cloud of fog that will conceal the *Otter*. By the afternoon, when the mist naturally starts to build, we can move out with the cloud around us."

Piyaro had a moment's disorientation as he tried to picture the young mage freezing the lagoon. Still, who was he to say what a mage could do?

"Will we be able to see where we're going?" Oberim asked.

"I don't know," Nyette admitted. "If your mast is fully open, I might not be able to cover it all. But if we leave in the late afternoon, it will start getting dark. Once there's sea fog, I can let my cloud fade."

"What if it's dark when we get there?" Piyaro added to Oberim's question.

"We'll have to go fast," she said.

"We have torches fore and aft," Shonn supplied eagerly. "If your soldiers stay in the cabin, out of sight, anyone will think we're just water-folk coming for a visit. When our kin see us, they'll light their own torches."

Piyaro nodded respectfully to Nyette. "It's a better idea than I had."

"I'll get to work, then," she said.

Actually, it didn't seem like Nyette did anything. The Hawks went through last minute checks of their gear, while the young mage sat cross-legged on the smooth sand beside the shore. As time passed, though, he saw patches of white floating on the water near where she sat. They were small at first, and thin, likely to disappear as lapping waves washed over them.

The water-folk watched, murmuring interest, as the small ice plates joined into a wider sheet that thickened on the lagoon's surface. Just as Nyette had predicted, tendrils of mist began to hover over the water. The sun was beginning to lower as Nyette raised her hands, caressing the air. Thicker and higher billows of fog began to wreath the *Otter*.

"Let's get aboard," Piyaro called.

Hawk Squad got into line, the boarding plank flexing beneath their armored weight as they went aboard. Nyette came with them, guided by Cothyr. Her young face was set with concentration. The three water-folk men who would crew the *Otter* hugged their wives and children, while Shonn got even more hugs and kisses from the rest of the clan. Many warnings about being careful and not trusting land-folk followed him up the ramp.

At last, everyone was aboard. The slow tilt and bob of the houseboat settled after most of the men had gathered in the main cabin, surrounded by low cushions and bunks of the water-folk's daily lives. Fog swirled on every side, muffling the sounds of the crew scampering about, calling advice to each other. With a gentle lurch and glide, the water-folk started them off.

It was time to find out what gauntlet Deeve's count had throw down before them.

~ ~ ~

The crossing started like a dozen others before it. Shonn worked in tandem with Uncle Kannat, pushing his pole deep and helping *Otter* work its way through the maze of the mangrove swamp. Nyette's mist came with them in billows and drifts. It wasn't hard to find their way, since they knew the channels well, but still his shoulders tingled with the thrill of this secretive passage. That, or it was the effort of moving the large houseboat.

As they emerged from the mangroves, the rhythm of the water changed. No more did roots and branches soften the tide. The houseboat fell into the slower, deeper up-and-down of open water. Delveer and Bonton had the youngest families, so they had stayed behind to protect the rest of the clan. Only Shonn and Kannat were there to haul on the ropes and raise *Otter's* lateen sail. Nyette's sea fog did nothing to still the wind, and the houseboat surged into motion as the sail snapped out and went taut. Shonn could almost imagine the ship was as eager to move as he was.

On the cabin roof, Oberim watched the water for obstacles ahead of them, as much as he could. Nyette stood with him, and the sergeant, Piyaro was beside her, looking slightly bilious but determined. The rest of the soldiers were in the cabin, hunkered down. Shonn had never understood why land-folk would be afraid, but with the choppy sea spitting and spraying, he could almost see it.

According to Piyaro, the Hawks had crossed from Pulgoll on a houseboat called *Pelican*. Oberim knew where their landing was, and he called instructions to angle the sail in that direction. The work fell into a pattern as the afternoon light grew longer. Slowly they crept toward the lumpen gray land on the north side of the strait.

All the time, his heart beat a little harder. Shonn couldn't believe he was really doing this. He loved his family, but it annoyed him to take direction from his father, and his uncles, and his brother, and occasionally his mother and grandmother. Not to mention the months of boredom in Fang Marsh. He was a young man, not meant to stay among the mangroves forever. Soon he would leave the *Otter* behind.

After some time, Nyette gave in to Oberim's request and allowed her sea fog to dissipate. She came down the ladder and went to rest in the cabin. Oberim and Piyaro kept a wary watch, but Shonn already knew there were no other ships nearby. He watched the gray land grow higher and more distinct, folds of the land springing out as the sinking sun painted them with yellow light and deeper shadows.

Eager to see what lay ahead, Shonn scrambled up the narrow ladder to the roof. With a slight shock, he found himself face to face with Oberim.

They shared a glance, startled and ill-at-ease. Then Oberim looked away, pretending to scan the rolling water. Sergeant Piyaro glanced around, too. Dark eyes flicked between them. Then the ladder creaked beneath his armored weight as he descended.

Shonn's shoulders itched again. He wanted to slide back down, too. Oberim had already argued with him half the morning. Why shouldn't the rest of the words go unspoken? Shonn was a man, after all. He could make a decision without his father's approval. But, it was also true that he didn't know when he would be back to the *Otter*. A bit stiffly, he moved up beside Oberim.

"You really mean to do this?" Oberim's voice was low, private.

"If Meven's there, I have to."

"There's more than one woman in the marshes."

Shonn shifted restlessly. This was nothing they hadn't already said.

"Young men roam around," he answered defensively. And it was true. A man might wander for weeks and months, if the family had bitter arguments, not to be settled, or if there were no young women to keep them there. It wasn't something Shonn had planned. Like Bonton, he had expected to meet a fetching woman at the clan gathering and persuade her to come aboard the *Otter*.

That hadn't exactly happened.

"But with land-folk?" Oberim allowed his worry to show. "You don't know them. And a mage?"

"That's why," Shonn replied. "They haven't said so, but they're going after Meven."

"You don't know that."

"There's no other reason," Shonn said. "Nyette said it herself. They only want me along because I know Meven."

"And you want to get in the middle of it? That's mages, son. They have their wars and such. We humble folk of the marsh just keep out of it."

Shonn nodded. That was the wisdom he had grown up with. And if truth be told, he had little trust for the men of Hawk Squad, with their sharp edges and armor, and their closed-in faces. But that only made it more urgent he didn't let Meven stand alone against them.

"I know what she said," Shonn admitted, "but she still might need my help."

Oberim snorted. "She's a mage. She doesn't need help."

"That's not the point." Shonn scuffed his sandal over the bristling thatched roof. "I thought we had more time."

In those weeks with Meven, he had thought he had forever to win her over. She'd been very attached to her vine-covered tower, and to the scrawny boy she was caring for. He'd never thought she would leave it. Even now that she had, he expected that she would be back someday. But did he want to wait it out?

"There's never enough time," Oberim said quietly.

Shonn remembered it clearly, the last time he saw Meven. She had been so cool and controlled, the day she confronted Ar-Torix. Invulnerable, needing no one. But he also remembered kissing her, the heat awakening between them. Meven might conceal it, but there was a heart under all that ice.

"I made a mistake," Shonn said. "I shouldn't have sold her out to the countess' guards."

"You want to apologize?" Oberim had never said whether he approved of Shonn's decision to betray Meven's presence. But for the first time, it sounded like his father respected what he was doing.

"I don't know what I'll say to her," Shonn said. "Fix it, or something."

"Then that's a good enough reason to go."

Shonn grinned and dared to relax, having finally won his father's real approval.

Dusk was falling, but they were almost across. Sergeant Piyaro came back up to the roof, casting his gimlet eye over the sea. Impatiently, Shonn lit the lamps on *Otter's* fore, castle, and aft. He leaned on the rail, where fresh oil was beaded with spray, and stared eagerly toward the shore.

Almost at once, his prediction came true: lamps flickered to life at the edge of the mangroves. They bobbed a little, and Shonn picked out small shapes outlined by the glow. Water-folk on a raft, ready to guide them into the mangroves.

Now Shonn was running again, turning the sail to bring the *Otter* about, and then quickly lowering it. With the remaining momentum, they glided toward the welcoming lights.

It was strange to think that he wouldn't be coming back with his family. Instead, he would travel with these land-folk in all their armor and with the young mage Nyette, who thought he would be useful somehow in talking to Meven. Would he ever return to these too-familiar decks of home?

~ ~ ~

The bustle of arrival had been more complicated than usual. The Badgers set up their tents near the big one, and staked down their livestock with Tisha's donkey. The good news was that the Larder mages didn't have to sleep in the open wagon. Tisha's tent was so huge that there was room for her and Cylass, Alemin, Lorrah, and ample space still left. Better yet, Tisha explained that she and Cylass had been traveling as rag-pickers, so her saddlebags and hand cart were stuffed full of spare clothing and housewares. Alemin and Lorrah eagerly reclaimed some of their belongings, but Tisha remarked on how threadbare Elldri's skirt was. She offered for her, Bettain and Duessa a chance to look through the bags as well.

"This Tisha's too good to be true," Bettain muttered, even as she shook out a peasant blouse with a tear in the front. She was having trouble finding anything big enough for her.

"Why are you surprised? These are Alemin's people." Duessa shrugged. She wasn't finding anything she needed, but she didn't miss the haunted expression in Elldri's eyes as the girl held up a peasant dress. Gently, Duessa said, "That's too big for you. Try this one."

Wrapped in her own thoughts, Elldri nodded and made the switch. The tactile darkness of her aura coiled and knotted within her.

Softly, Duessa told her, "This is Alemin's friend. She would never hurt you. All right?"

With a guilty start, the younger woman flicked deer-dark eyes to her, and then away. She nodded spasmodically, but said nothing, as usual.

"And if she did, she'll have to deal with me," Bettain added stoutly.

That was absurd, in Duessa's opinion, considering how much they owed Alemin and his friends. She understood, though. Nobody was so generous without some motive. Duessa would always have assumed as much, except that she didn't feel anything suspect in the glow of the woman's energy. Unlike Elldri.

By the time they got their sleeping arrangements made, and thanked Tisha for her kindness, it was time to cook supper. The Badgers set up their portable stove, and Cylass insisted in sharing the work with Razeet. He was unmistakably protective of Tisha, and considered the chore his personal duty. Alemin sat and ate with Tisha and Lorrah, talking about some sort of performance, while Duessa and Bettain held their own protective vigil over Elldri. The younger woman had begun her courses earlier in the day but not told anyone. Bettain helped her with the rags and Duessa tried to teach her Lorrah's trick for soothing cramps, but the effort at healing seemed to vanish into the blackness of Elldri's aura.

"You'd rather be in pain?" Duessa asked irritably, convinced that Elldri was refusing to be helped. The younger woman wouldn't look at her.

By the time they cleaned everything up, dusk was falling. Cylass lit the bonfire outside Tisha's tent, and folk began filtering in from the surrounding caravans. Duessa was glad enough for the distraction. She had known Alemin was a juggler, and Lorrah practiced the violin, but she had assumed those were just a way to pass time during long hours of confinement in the Larder, or to relieve an evening's boredom. Or they were some kind of obsession.

It turned out, they really were performers in a minstrel show. That was what they had been planning during supper. Soon Duessa was seated in the Badgers' wagon, alongside Elldri and Bettain, with Sethamis on their other side. They had a good view of the area.

The bonfire crackled and blazed. Cylass collected coins, and the cleared space Duessa had noticed when they arrived was quickly filling. Zathi had the Badgers space themselves out, keeping an eye on the crowd, though from Duessa's vantage it didn't seem that anyone was looking to make trouble. She waited with some skepticism, wondering what this "minstrel show" was really about.

The noise died away as notes of Lorrah's violin penetrated the babble. The young girl strolled out from the tent, having given up her red robe in favor of a fancy dress glittering with beads. She played a series of folk songs. The locals seemed to know some of them, and they clapped in time to the music. Then Lorrah stepped back, and a slender young man bounded out of the tent.

"Is that Alemin?" Bettain choked. Elldri sat up with startled grin.

The man was barely recognizable in a flowing ruffled shirt and tight leather trousers. A broad hat with bobbing plumes disguised his shaved head. He bowed flamboyantly and set down a basket of assorted objects, just as Lorrah began to play again. Alemin started with five oranges, moving through a series of complicated patterns, even where the oranges appeared to be moving in opposite directions. Soon Tisha sauntered in. The audience gasped and yelled as she threw in different things from the basket. There were hoops woven from reeds, then small clay cups, and what looked like balls of scarves tied together. One at a time, he tossed back what Tisha gave him and juggled the new objects instead.

But Tisha kept throwing more and different things, until the juggler staggered dramatically. The audience roared with laughter when he finally missed his beat and a painted stick fell on his head. Duessa felt her scars pulling as she grinned. Alemin fell backward in defeat, only to leap up and wave to the cheers.

"He's pretty good," Bettain yelled over the sound of applause.

Duessa heard Keerin call to Zathi, "Hey! We should sell punch or something."

"The tavern might not like us taking their business," Jaxynne called back.

"We won't always be near a tavern, though," Giniver put in.

Looking down along the wagon, Duessa saw that even Elldri was smiling past her tucked-up knees. In fact, it was strange to see so many people sitting together without any tension. Most people in Skaythe were hard and suspicious. Here they laughed and relaxed together. Lorrah returned to the center and began another series of folk songs. One or two people sang along, somewhat rustily. Their anticipation was building, the energy sparkling higher, yet the crowd wasn't as agitated as they should be.

Belatedly, Duessa recognized what the minstrels were doing. Their performances had set up a flow of *vitalis* through the throng. She could practically see it in the reflected glow of the blazing bonfire. It was massive, because there were so many, yet it was hardly more than a gentle breeze blowing through the throng. Just as when Lorrah worked to heal Alemin's spirit, the enchantment lightened their hearts without them knowing.

Duessa leaned over a little to say, "Can you feel it?"

"What?" Bettain called, as if she couldn't hear over the nosie. Elldri tilted her head anxiously, and Duessa suspected she could feel the *vitalis* but didn't know what it was.

Alemin's slow drumbeat interrupted her thoughts, and the audience went quiet with rapt anticipation. Lorrah's violin drew out a sultry melody, and the tent flaps billowed. Cylass, the bodyguard, appeared in a leather jerkin, with a short sword at his side. He stopped at one side of the stage area, arms folded sternly. The audience leaned forward, ignoring him, as the music skipped faster.

Out came Tisha, her rough peasant dress exchanged for colorful layers of skirts and fluttering sleeves. Black curls were pulled up high above her pretty face, with something woven into them that twinkled like stars in the night. The dancer extended a hand, acknowledging the roar of approval, just before the music sped up. Bare feet hardly seemed to touch the dirt as she spun and danced, circling her hips with superhuman flexibility. No one appeared to notice that she radiated more light than the bonfire could explain.

It was an enchanting performance. Most of the men, and a few of the women, stared lustfully at the dancer. Even Duessa felt her pulse quicken, and she had never been attracted to other women. Even more than the *vitalis* conjuring, it made her want to dance, too. Some of the audience seemed to feel the same way. There were a couple of times when men jumped past the fire and Cylass strode forward menacingly. Mostly, the audience drank in the mood, whether Tisha danced a simple country dance or one of her acrobatic routines.

Duessa grabbed a moment to turn and see Elldri's reaction. The younger woman breathed heavily, eyes dark and wide. She was obviously trying to decide whether she should run.

"It's okay," Duessa whispered. "They won't hurt you." But a shout rose from the crowd, and she wasn't sure if Elldri heard her.

After several dances, Lorrah drew her violin down into another sultry trill. Tisha was breathing hard, her flesh gleaming with sweat in the flickering light of the bonfire. Cylass' dour stare kept back a number of lusty admirers. In the deepening pause, Alemin swaggered out to join her, beating his drum softly into a new rhythm. Lorrah followed, the violin under her chin, and flowed into a simple melody that brought them back to where they began. Alemin and Tisha began to sing.

The light of your fire draws me ever,

A tie that no distance or time can sever.

Sure as the sun rises at dawn,

The hope in our hearts will go on.

It wasn't perfect singing, especially since Tisha's breath was still choppy, but some in the crowd seemed to know the song. Scattered voices joined in, including a couple of the hunter-guards. When the tune finished, they bowed their way into the tent. The audience cheered and chanted, but they weren't stirred up by Tisha's erotic performance, so much as filled with contentment.

Duessa shook her head as she joined in the applause. It was hard to decide if these minstrels were genius or insane, casting a spell over so many people. Even if it didn't harm them, it was taking a risk. Despite that, Duessa couldn't resist breathing it all in, just like the rest of the audience did. How often did anyone get a chance to relax without fear?

Bettain turned to her with an astonished expression. "What the hell was that?"

"If you'd been doing your meditation, you would know," Duessa retorted.

"No, I mean, I was expecting a riot when she came out in that dress," Bettain persisted.

"You're complaining that there wasn't a riot?" Duessa teased. "It felt to me like..."

She trailed off. Duessa couldn't have said what it felt like. Only, she was certain that this was what she'd been working toward, even if she hadn't known. It was Ar-Lannon's broken promise, this sense of hope. That no matter how hard their lives were, there was still so much to live for.

In a quavering voice, Elldri whispered, "It feels like a gift."

"Yeah, you're right," Duessa exclaimed. "And it's for everyone. Even a couple of fugitives from the Larder."

"Or a bunch of broken-down guardswomen," Sethamis added from Elldri's other side.

"Whatever it is, they had me seeing it, too." Bettain rolled her eyes and groaned, "We're doomed."

VII — THE TELLING

The minstrel show was over, but the women of Badger Squad remained vigilant. The rapt audience dissolved into smaller groups and wandered off to their own camp sites. Some of them tried to sing the final song. Soon all that was left was a thin haze of dust rising in the bonfire's flickering light. Duessa moved past Cylass, who was now guarding the entrance to the striped tent. Elldri had stayed behind, joining Sethamis for a final check on the horses and oxen.

"I swear, that girl should have been a farmer," Bettain grumbled.

"Maybe she was." Duessa barely paid attention to her friend's familiar complaint. Several blankets had been hung inside the minstrels' tent, allowing for privacy. Behind them, Tisha, Lorrah and Alemin changed back into their ordinary clothes. Emerging, Alemin shook out his flashy shirt and inspected one of the cuffs.

"I think this tore when I caught that knife," he complained mildly. Spying Duessa, he grinned. "Like the show?"

"I don't know what you guys have planned," Duessa said, "but I want in."

Lorrah smirked as she laced up her boots. "Took you long enough to decide."

Tisha appeared next, still untangling the thread of glittering beads from her riot of curls. "And you?" She glanced at Bettain.

The older woman shifted irritably. "You'd better tell us where you're going with this."

"We did tell you," Alemin answered.

"That bunch of nonsense?" Bettain waved his protest away. "You aren't going to take down Dar-Gothull with song and dance, so be serious."

The minstrels deflated a little, disappointed that she wasn't wildly enthusiastic. Duessa was just relieved that Bettain had decided not to walk away. It would have been surprising after the time she spend sewing on the gray robes, but it was still good to know.

"Actually, I think they might," Duessa said. Bettain frowned at her, until she turned back to the minstrels. "But Bettain's right, too. We need concrete details."

"I agree." Zathi came in behind Duessa, forcing her to step out of the way. "We've been scattered too long. Each group has its own information and ideas. It's time we brought it all together."

Tisha nodded soberly. "There's a lot to tell."

"Yes, there is," Alemin said, with weight of his own.

"Hold onto that." Zathi strode back out of the tent. Through the thin walls, they heard her order Giniver to set watches around the camp. "We don't want anyone listening in."

"Yes Sergeant."

"Keep an eye on that bonfire," Jaxynne added. She brought in one of the Badgers' lanterns and turned the flame down slightly before hanging it from a support post.

The group settled in that circle of light. Duessa and

Bettain sat next to Lorrah and Alemin. Zathi and Jaxynne were across from them. Duessa was glad only the two officers had joined the discussion. The tent was big, but it would have been a tight fit for all fourteen of them. Tisha completed the circle with her bodyguard, Cylass, who was urging her to drink from a waterskin.

"Don't fuss," she murmured. "The show went well."

"You still need to rebuild your strength, Lady," he answered.

"Yeah, what was that show?" Bettain demanded.

"Hold on," Zathi cut in. "I know we all have stories to tell, but it's best to start with the hard news."

"Yes," Tisha said, suddenly grave. "Can you tell me what happened to Keilos?"

Jaxynne looked away, but Zathi remained unflinching as ever. "We arrested him in Prizom and were taking him south, to Dakadoz, but we had to go through the Hornwood. Things kept happening."

"What things?" Cylass asked, satisfied that Tisha was drinking from the skin he offered.

"There was a giant badger." Jaxynne paused a moment, as if expecting an argument, but Cylass's brows merely twitched in the briefest of frowns.

"We fought it off, with Keilos' help, but our horses and oxen got loose and ran away," Zathi went on. "While we were searching for them, we encountered a strange fog that burned when we touched it. Keilos told us it was a drakanox. Maybe *the* drakanox, the one that destroyed Seofan Holl."

"It's not destroyed." Tisha's brown eyes brightened. "I have to tell you about that."

"Wait, though." Lorrah raised a hand. "One story at a time."

"Keilos protected us from the drakanox, but we had to take shelter inside a strange tower. The creature trapped us there." Zathi's jaw tightened slightly.

Now Alemin perked up. "A tower?"

Duessa suspected he was thinking of the Larder's tower. Zathi seemed to have the same idea.

"Yes, though not exactly like the one in Dakadoz, or the Larder. This tower is much larger, with several buildings around it. They're overgrown by the Hornwood. We explored a few of them and couldn't make sense of the layout. As near as Jaxynne can tell from the charts, it's right at the center of the Hornwood."

"And the Hornwood is at the center of all Skaythe," Jaxynne said. "We also found a few of those roads connecting to it. My charts don't show the highways, just the different counties we've traveled through, but it seems like all the roads lead into the Hornwood."

"That makes sense," Alemin said thoughtfully.

"Keilos kept telling us about his minstrel knowledge, but he didn't know anything about the tower. He did say it was full of that energy you mages use. The golden kind, not the red," Zathi said.

"*Vitalis,*" Lorrah supplied.

"Like I said, the drakanox had us trapped inside. Keilos drew from the reservoir of *vitalis* and created a..." Zathi shook her head briefly. "A giant man made of light, and he was trying to calm the drakanox."

"A man made of light?" Tisha marveled.

"But, one of my guardswomen cut his throat," Zathi said heavily.

Lorrah gasped, tears coming to her eyes. Alemin silently put his arm around her shoulders, his own expression strained. Duessa felt Bettain shift a little, beside her.

"Thersa really hated mages. She kept telling us not to trust him," Jaxynne explained dully. "So as soon as everyone was busy..." She raised her hands and made a chopping motion above her lap.

"Why?" came Lorrah's strangled question.

"She thought Keilos was controlling us," Zathi said. "She was trying to stop him."

Tisha's eyes glittered with tears before she pressed her sleeve to her face. Cylass wrapped one arm around her waist.

"The giant man was still there," Zathi went on, her voice clipped. "It seemed that the drakanox was tearing it apart, but they merged somehow. It spoke to us with Keilos' voice and flew off. We aren't sure what that means."

"Then he is not truly dead," Tisha smiled despite her tears. Everyone regarded her doubtfully, but Tisha seemed certain. "Some part of him is still alive."

"I don't know whether to hope," Zathi answered.

Duessa and Bettain shared a glance. That chopping motion of Jaxynne's didn't leave a lot of room for interpretation.

"Wait." Alemin shook off his dismay. "When I first got to the Larder, Ar-Lizelle was questioning me. She said there was some kind of magical event in the Hornwood, and something in Seofan Holl, and something else in Eshur. Could Keilos... transforming, have been the Hornwood event?"

"Maybe," Jaxynne said. "Did the warden say when this was?"

He shook his head. "No, just that she was looking for a pattern."

"She was looking for me," Lorrah said bitterly.

"Regardless." Zathi was just as stern as ever, but somehow calm and assured. "The Badgers know where that tower is. However, none of us are mages. Our plan was to gather any of you minstrels that we could find, so you can decide what to do with the power there."

Duessa shook her head, disgusted. This was the kind of story she expected to hear in Skaythe. A mage could do something amazing, and have his throat cut for it. By all common sense, she should be running for her life. Why did she not feel afraid?

~ ~ ~

Piyaro had suspected that the torches came on too quickly after Shonn lit the houseboat's lamps. He was right. Soldiers from Pulgoll were waiting when they got to the water-folk's landing.

At first, he didn't see the soldiers. Not one but two of the big houseboats were already there. Great ripples of reflected torchlight streaked the dark water as one of them poled laterally across the lagoon, making room for *Otter* at the dock. Piyaro thought it was *Pelican*, the houseboat they had crossed on two days before. On the beach, fire pits glowed in the gathering darkness. Two water-clans had gathered to share warmth and food. Over to one side, a row of tents had been set up. A small cluster of guardsmen in Pulgoll's crimson kept an awkward space between themselves and the water-folk.

On the dock, a number of the water-men stood ready to catch the *Otter's* lines. When Piyaro and his men emerged from *Otter's* cabin, Oberim and Kannat were being swept into a round of greetings and embraces. Shonn hesitated, looking between the soldiers and his kin, before Kannat hooked an arm around his neck and dragged him into the group.

Most of the Hawks weren't as seasick as they had been after their first crossing. They hoisted their waypacks and followed Piyaro down the dock. No one offered to hug them, but one of the older women did ask, cautiously, if they were hungry.

"Thank you," Piyaro said. "They can eat, if they have the stomach for it."

The sergeant who led the Pulgoll guards was right behind her, so Piyaro sent Cothyr to figure out the meal arrangements while he stayed to talk. Somewhat to Piyaro's surprise, Nyette lingered beside him. Her dark eyes sparkled as she took in the scene with keen interest.

The other sergeant stepped forward. He looked familiar, perhaps from one of the meetings Piyaro had been to. They traded salutes, and Piyaro nodded toward a row of large tents that had been set up on the level sand.

"Is there room for more?"

"Yes, we planned for that." Amren, that was his name.

"I appreciate it."

"They're yours." Sergeant Amren spoke with a shade of the smugness Piyaro remembered so well. He offered a small parcel. "New orders."

Piyaro accepted it, mulling the implication that the Hawks would not be returning to Pulgoll with Amren and his squad. The sparse torchlight made it impossible to read anything, so he tucked the parcel under his arm. It was also a convenient way to avoid showing that he couldn't have read it, even with good light.

In return, Nyette offered her own small parcel to Sergeant Amren. "A letter for Count Ar-Azlor."

Amren eyed her a moment before taking it. Then he turned away, as if determined to ignore a girl mage. "The food's not bad. Come on up."

As they walked up the beach, Piyaro asked, "What news? Did the rebellion quiet down?"

"It's not spreading any more, that's all I know." Now that his delivery was complete, Amren seemed disinterested in conversation.

Piyaro hadn't realized the uprising was spreading. He considered the implications, keenly aware of paper crackling as he followed his counterpart toward the fire pits. He accepted a low, wide bowl mounded with river grain and some sort of roasted fish. As he carried it toward the tents, he couldn't help noticing that Oberim and the other water-folk men were sitting in a close discussion while they ate. That looked interesting. Piyaro wondered how much of their conversation Shonn might be persuaded to share with him.

He joined his own men, and found Nyette at his shoulder again. Softly, she suggested, "After we eat, I'll be happy to read that for you."

"Thank you, miss." Piyaro kept a stony face. He didn't know how she could tell, but at least she didn't shout it out. Lots of people couldn't read, but Piyaro was supposed to be a leader. He concentrated on eating. Later, he knew, he would have bed spins from the sea crossing. At the moment, his empty stomach was shouting at him.

By the time they were finished, it was fully dark. The water-folk cleaned up and gathered around one of the fire pits, sorting themselves by age and gender. Younger children ran around or tussled in the sand, paying no heed to such things as rank. The singing began, soft and pleasant, with a slow rhythm like the rise and fall of sea waves.

Piyaro might have enjoyed more of it, but Nyette caught Shonn's eye and beckoned him over. As the water-man came over, brushing sand from the back of his short sarong, Piyaro passed his letter to the young mage. She opened it carefully and angled it toward the nearest torch.

"What's going on over there?" Piyaro asked as Shonn joined them.

"*Pelican* stays around here most of the time, but *Seal*

is from the north coast, beyond the cape. They say there's fighting up there."

"Hmm," Piyaro murmured. That didn't match what Amren had told him.

"They've cleared the area and come down this way earlier than usual," Shonn finished.

Nyette also paused to listen. Then she glanced around, taking in the watchful eyes of Hawk Squad and the pretended disinterest of Sergeant Amren.

"I understand now," she murmured, and quietly folded the letter before passing it back to Piyaro.

"What does it say?" Piyaro didn't like having to ask, but what choice did he have?

Instead of answering, Nyette looked to Amren. "Are you aware of our destination?"

"No, miss. We're only delivering the orders and getting this letter." Amren put on a dutiful air, but that didn't mean he wasn't interested.

"Then this conversation is not for you," she told him. Amren' brows twitched, showing a flash of resentment at taking orders from a girl, even if she was a mage. Nyette turned to Piyaro and suggested, "Shall we walk aside?"

Her glance invited Shonn as well, and she led them down toward the dock, where no one was able to eavesdrop. With soft music flowing behind them, Piyaro asked, "You said you understand something?"

With a trace of irony, she answered, "I believe I know why we, particularly, were chosen for this task."

Her vague statement made Piyaro uneasy. The three of them eyed each other, perhaps trying to decide if the others could be trusted. This time it was Shonn who demanded, "What do you mean?"

"Hawk Squad is not returning to Pulgoll," Nyette began.

"I guessed that," Piyaro said. Remembering Amren' smugness, he wondered if the other sergeant really didn't know Hawk Squad's orders.

Shonn crossed his arms, frowning impatiently.

"Your job," Nyette told him, "is to guide us through the mangroves, around the cape, to the town of Opshar."

"Through the mangroves?" Shonn's frown turned to quick understanding.

"Opshar is where the revolt started," Piyaro mused.

"We're going toward the revolt?" Shonn asked sharply.

"Not so loud," Piyaro cautioned. After encountering the roots of that rebellion, he understood why the lad would be worried. "We couldn't totally avoid being seen while we crossed today, but it sounds like they want us to stay out of sight from here on."

Nyette quietly told Shonn, "Your people might want to spread out, in case one of those boats from Deeve risks coming into the mangroves."

Shonn nodded, accepting her concern. "I'll warn them."

"All right," Piyaro said. "Why are we going to Opshar, and what did you mean that you understand now?"

"The renegade, Berisan, offered to talk." Nyette looked to Piyaro for confirmation. He hesitated over the change of Sand's name, but nodded sourly. "I am going to talk to him."

"I remember that." Piyaro also recalled that Countess Ar-Torix had said they should at least pretend to talk. "As a delaying tactic?"

"I have instructions." Nyette evaded that part of the question. "As to the rest, I'm sure you are correct about concealing ourselves in the mangroves instead of going through the mountains. Shonn already said the water-folk don't meddle with land-folk, so no one should suspect his connection to Countess Ar-Torix. However, Berisan is apparently an old friend of Meven's, and she may be in Opshar. The countess isn't certain."

Shonn said nothing to that, but Piyaro didn't miss his eager gaze. Nyette continued, "Hawk Squad is only recently attached to Count Ar-Azlor. Again, your association isn't widely known."

Piyaro rubbed the back of his neck. These layers of secrecy were not surprising, considering how many counts were involved. It still wasn't reassuring.

What in Dar-Gothull's name was this all about?

"What about you?" Shonn asked.

"Why was I, a student, chosen over mages who are fully trained and more experienced?" Nyette smiled wryly. "It is *because* I am still a student. Before we can leave the temple school, we have to pass three rituals. It's how Dar-Gothull controls the counts and all the other mages."

"I stood guard for some of those," Piyaro said. There had been blood and shrieking, and he had been relieved when Count Ar-Dayne found an assistant to lead the rituals for him.

"Adult mages are bound to Dar-Gothull's will. Countess Ar-Torix is, and your Count Ar-Azlor." For all Nyette's youth, her expression was sly and cynical. "But I, as a student, am not yet bound. Thus, their discussion with the renegades can remain private."

Shonn stared at her, and finally asked, "What are we doing, that needs to be so secret?"

Nyette gave a little shrug and repeated, "I have my

instructions."

The water-folk's music drifted down from the campfire, a peaceful counterweight to the worries that dragged at Piyaro's mind. Everything Nyette said pointed back to his initial suspicion: that they were expendable. If events took a wrong turn, it would be easy to sacrifice them. Piyaro tried to shove those thoughts away.

"What we're doing," he said firmly, "is following orders. Count Ar-Azlor has done right by Hawk Squad. We'll see his work through."

That made it sound simple, but it wasn't. From Shonn's slight frown and Nyette's cool smile, they knew it, too. Piyaro had a suspicion about what Nyette was being sent to negotiate. After all, there was really only one thing a bunch of counts would want to keep secret from the Wizard-King who owned their souls.

～ ～ ～

Bettain burst out, "Why do you have to do anything with this power in the Hornwood? It's better to keep our heads down. They'll forget about us after a while."

"Not soon enough," Lorrah answered with grim certainty.

"Because of Keilos," Zathi said. "I know we arrested him, but by the time we went through all that, we were... friends, sort of. He told us the story of the Shining Ones and why the minstrels are working against the regime. We want to make it right, for him."

"The story of what?" Bettain looked around suspiciously, realizing that everyone else knew something she didn't. "What's this story about?"

"It's some mage lore passed down by our mentors," Duessa told her. "I'll tell you later." Bettain folded her arms irritably, but Duessa turned to Alemin. "You said the second big event was in Seofan Holl?"

"It's what Ar-Lizelle claimed," he agreed.

"Then it's my turn." Tisha sat up straighter, brushing the last moisture from her face. All eyes turned to her. "After the Minstrels split up, I was supposed to go to Ortach. We talked about hiding, but I've always remembered the story of how Seofan Holl was conquered and remained cursed even after a hundred years. I decided to go there and see if the curse could be broken."

Tisha sounded almost apologetic. Duessa was surprised that she had been so bold. Tisha seemed gentle and pretty, not the daring type.

"You rebel," Alemin teased.

Tisha twinkled a smile at him. "It had just been a few days, and I was passing through Sloram. There was a battle, the count's guards against some marauders. I could hear the cries of the wounded. Once it was safe, I went to see if I could help."

Lorrah played at shock. "*You* ran toward a battle?"

"No," Tisha confessed. "I hid while the guards went by. But Cylass was still crying out, so I followed his trail."

"Count Ar-Dayne was very territorial," Cylass said. "He wouldn't tolerate any other mages in Sloram. The marauders had a mage." He pulled back a shirt sleeve, revealing a maze of vivid red scars all along his left arm. "The count blasted through our line, and hit me along with the bandits' mage and two others of our guard. They were killed. My arm was ruined. My squad, the Hawks, left me for dead." He looked over at Tisha, reverence shining through his stolid exterior. "My lady saved me."

"Anyone would," Tisha murmured.

"Not just anyone has your skill," Alemin replied, and Lorrah nodded beside him.

"Keilos told us if he healed our wounds it might

change our thinking," Zathi said warily. "Was that the case for you?"

"Maybe," Cylass admitted. "After all the pain I'd been through, it wasn't easy to think about going back to Hawk Squad. They'd abandoned me, but technically I still served Count Ar-Dayne. If he knew I was alive, he would order me to tell what I knew about Lady Tisha. I swore my oath to her, so I could protect her secrets in return for my life."

Duessa understood why Cylass' devotion went beyond Tisha's beauty. With that kind of power, she could see why Alemin and Lorrah were so anxious to join forces with her.

"I didn't want a guardsman," Tisha went on, "but Cylass was right. It helped us both. We traveled the rest of the way to Seofan Valley, but Ar-Dayne was still chasing us. We didn't reach the Holl itself before he attacked." She wrinkled her pretty brown nose in distasteful memory. "I had to absorb everything he threw at me, and shunted it into the ground. That's when some of the trees burst into leaf."

"You didn't fight back?" Duessa frowned, skeptical.

"No, I only defended."

The words could have seemed self-righteous, but Duessa thought Tisha was sincere. Her claim about absorbing Ar-Dayne's power was even more interesting. That was something to follow up on, when she got the chance.

"And you really broke the curse?" Lorrah was impressed.

"I didn't know that would happen." Tisha rubbed behind her ear. "It was pretty exciting, though!"

Bettain leaned toward Duessa. "Making the trees burst into leaf, no big deal," she snorted under her breath. Duessa chuckled.

Jaxynne said, "While we were traveling, we heard that Count Ar-Dayne had died."

Tisha sighed and ducked her head pensively. "I'm not surprised. He drained himself, trying to kill me. There wouldn't have been much left if he had to fight again so soon."

"Don't blame yourself," Cylass interrupted. "He should have left you alone. We weren't even in Sloram by then."

"It depleted me, too," Tisha said. "I haven't done a strong casting since Seofan Holl."

"You've healed people along the way," Cylass said.

"Only simple wounds," she answered.

"If you can reach this big tower of theirs, that might not be a problem." Duessa muffled a yawn. After a full day's travel, she was feeling tired, but they hadn't even mentioned escaping from the Larder yet.

"That explains two of the incidents At-Lizelle mentioned," Zathi said.

"Then what happened in Eshur?" Lorrah asked. "Does anyone know?"

"She said there was a tower covered in ice. That has to be Meven," Alemin answered. "No one else uses *isalonis*."

"That you know of," Zathi said.

"That seems kind of flashy for her," Lorrah answered doubtfully. "She always wanted to hide in the back of the tent."

"She'd be really powerful in the right conditions," Tisha said. "Isn't Eshur on the sea coast? There'd be plenty of water for her to freeze."

"It sounds like that's what she did," Duessa said, though Ar-Lannon hadn't taught her much about *isalonis*.

"So your friend is probably in Eshur." Zathi glanced at Jaxynne for confirmation. "That's pretty far off."

"Not a short trip," Jaxynne agreed.

"What about my brother?" Alemin asked. "Has anyone had word from Berisan?"

The other two mages shook their heads, but before anyone else spoke, Cylass came to his feet in a smooth motion.

"My lady." He spoke a low warning. Hand on his sword hilt, he padded toward the tent flap.

In the startled silence, they all heard the sliding crunch of footsteps passing by. Duessa's stomach clenched. Was someone sneaking around outside, listening to them? Everything they had said tonight was treason!

~ ~ ~

Ar-Lizelle was in her office at the Larder, but the familiar location had changed. Papers were strewn about her desk, obscuring the daily agenda she consulted so often. She scowled at the mess. This sloppiness was unacceptable. She reached behind her, seeking to pull her chair in close so she could set things right. Her fingers closed on empty air.

"Ar-Chindu!" she barked, thinking this might be some trick of his. She had always suspected her assistant had schemes of his own.

When she turned to where his desk should be, it wasn't there. Behind her, there was no chair. Sudden dismay coiled in her gut. Something was amiss. This was her office, but it wasn't, either. At least the door was in the right place. She strode to it, yanked it open, and halted as a gust of rank, cold air blew into her face.

Startled, Ar-Lizelle teetered on the edge of a vast abyss. Outside her office, the Larder was in ruins. Collapsed walls and scattered stones blocked the corridor in both directions. A narrow strip of paving led to the ragged remains of a stairway. A ceaseless roar came from far below, as from a powerful wind or churning tide. Only her office remained well lit, poised above the gulf.

This couldn't be! Those prisoners might have escaped, but the Larder had been standing strong when she left.

Ar-Lizelle's heart pounded, but she forced in a hard breath of dank air. This wasn't real. She clung to that thought. Ar-Lizelle was a mage, highly trained in arts of the mind. She wouldn't fall to some mirage.

"Not real," she repeated defiantly. It had to be a dream, or some other vile casting. To understand this was no consolation, however. Ar-Lizelle never had such dreams. Never... Except when she was in the Larder.

She closed her mouth over a panicked moan, and her fingers tightened on the doorknob until they twinged with a cramp. She forced herself to shut it and let the knob go. No matter the appearance, Ar-Lizelle knew that she wasn't in the Larder. She couldn't be doing this mad thing.

"I must wake up!" That shrill tone of command was usually directed at Ar-Chindu or some other fool. Now she lashed herself with it.

"Very good, Ar-Lizelle," spoke a voice behind her, dry as the rattle of wind-blown sand.

A raw gasp escaped her control. She knew that voice. It was what she most dreaded, all the time she pursued the escaped prisoners. Rigid as the doorframe, she forced herself to turn.

It was there, at her desk. Ar-Lizelle saw the horribly familiar, skull-like grin matched with the shaved head and ragged gray robe of a prisoner. Panic squeezed her lungs, driving out breath. Behind her was only the long fall, but before her was worse. The revenant that haunted the Larder had come for her. Where could she go, how could she escape this death?

Ar-Lizelle stood straight. She would not be treated so, as if she was a wayward prisoner and this creature was the warden.

"You can't be here," she accused, but her harsh voice wobbled.

"Poor Ar-Lizelle," crooned the revenant. "Did you really think you could avoid me?"

"You belong in the Larder. I am not there. I'm —" Ar-Lizelle cut off. Did she want to tell it where she was?

Maybe she wasn't even sure herself. An awful thought pierced her mind, that all of it — her travel, allying with Ar-Kyanon, enduring Ar-Gammord's suspicion — was the dream, and this madness was reality.

"I'm not there!" she repeated.

The revenant laughed, baring a terrible grin layered with shark teeth. "Don't you know? Once you have been in the Larder, you can never escape. Warden or warded, guards and unwilling guests — we are bound to each other. I know that you've felt it."

She shook her head, denying any connection to this filthy wraith, even if his words were all too like what she'd said to Ar-Kyanon, not long ago. The revenant glided forward, bare feet seeming not to touch the stony floor. She was forced to retreat into the space where Ar-Chindu's desk ought to have been. Every moment, she dreaded its awful transformation into the monstrous, squid-armed beast that had devoured Wharon and so many others.

"The Larder is within you, Ar-Lizelle," it insisted. "It is rooted to the foundation of your soul. Thus, I am always within you. I know what has happened. The Larder has been broken. You permitted this."

Ar-Lizelle could not deny the chilling accusation. "I

wasn't there. If I had been —"

If she had been there — what? Could she, alone, have held off ten rioting mages and their half-dozen false hunter guards? Ar-Lizelle faltered, and the revenant thrust itself into the gap.

"No, you went off to chase your sister," it interrupted. "Your family grudge was more important than your duty to me. The only reason I haven't devoured you yet, is because you have been so devoted in seeking my prey."

"The prisoners?" Here was something Ar-Lizelle could understand, through her panic. She vowed, as she had to Countess Ar-Khoreen, "I will track them down. I will bring them back..." Then she stumbled over an unfortunate fact. "Such as live."

"I know. I have faith in you, Ar-Lizelle."

The abrupt change, from sinister accusation to paternal reassurance, was even more frightening than any threat had been. Somehow, she had to retaliate.

"What do you mean," she cried. "My duty to you? I'm the warden. I run the Larder. You are only a small part of it. A ghost from its past."

"A small part?" The revenant corrected her with deadly intensity. "I am all of it. All of *us*. The devourer of souls, the ruler of all Skaythe from the seas to the mountaintops. You who dwell in the Larder have been living within *me*!"

Knowledge struck Ar-Lizelle like a mage's bolt, as dreadful as it was impossible. Yet no one could look upon this creature, even in a dream, and not realize the truth. He was Dar-Gothull, the Wizard-King!

"My lord... Majesty! Forgive my rudeness," she stammered. Pain burst in her knees as she knelt abruptly. Had she thought this was merely a dream? If only she could still believe that!

"There, there," the revenant consoled her with oozing contempt. "There's nothing to worry about as long as you continue to hunt my scattered flock. Bring them together, like a good shepherdess."

"Any of the counts might deny me passage," Ar-Lizelle said. He waved her to silence.

"The counts will not defy me. You all know how I hunger for souls, and there is a great feast being laid for me." Dar-Gothull's eyes went past her for a moment, savoring some image that only he could see. "None of them will wish to be part of it."

Ar-Lizelle shuddered. She didn't want that, either. "As you say, Majesty."

～ ～ ～

Slow footsteps grated closer in the tense silence. Everyone in the tent got quiet as a shadow loomed against the striped canvas. After a moment, Duessa dared to breathe. By the angled lines around the shoulders, it was just one of the guardswomen on patrol. A slight squeaking joined with the movement.

"That sounds like Keerin." Zathi's voice was a thread. She and Jaxynne had gone to flank Cylass as he came to the tent flap. With a slow hand he pushed the flap open. Slivers of dancing yellow light penetrated the tent. Elldri shuffled past, wrapping her shoulders in one of the thin blankets from the back of the wagon. She crouched not far from the bonfire, which had burned down considerably since the height of the performance.

Moments later, more footsteps approached. Familiar voices accompanied them. "Do you think I should?" Razeet asked.

"Sure, you're a good storyteller," Keerin answered. "They could use another act. You should ask them."

"Maybe I will," Razeet said.

The two sisters picked up long branches and started cautiously pulling the bonfire apart. Elldri jumped back as sparks showered upward into the darkening sky. She blinked against the smoke, and rubbed her eyes.

"Sorry, we need to put this out," Keerin apologized.

"She needs to get that greave fixed," Jaxynne said. Cylass lowered the flap, and the three of them rejoined the circle.

"Sounds like she wants to get into your minstrel show," Bettain teased Alemin.

"She is pretty good," Alemin said to Tisha.

"Never mind that," Zathi firmly redirected. "What about your other friends?"

"It's not much, but I might have something," Alemin said. "One of the nightmares in the Larder showed me glimpses of *vitalis*. Just sparks in the darkness, really. I saw one in the north, that might have been Tisha near Seofan, and a closer one west of me that must have been Lorrah. A more white one, far to the west, would be Meven in Eshur. The only other one was even farther northwest, in Pulgoll or even Dunsaph."

"That has to be Berisan," Tisha suggested encouragingly.

"I hope so," Alemin said.

"At least we know he was alive then," Lorrah said.

"That's not a short trip, either," Jaxynne said.

"We can head to the Hornwood and be halfway there," Duessa countered.

"That's the obvious plan," Zathi said.

"Wait. Before we get excited, you still have to hear my part," Alemin said. "About the Larder and the Devourer."

"The Larder?" Tisha repeated, shocked.

"We were there, too," Duessa complained. Alemin grinned briefly, and settled himself facing Tisha.

"All right. So. I was arrested. It was in Unthur, and it's a long, stupid story. They sent me to the Larder. It was full of horrible lunatics and criminals." He smirked at Duessa and Bettain.

"What's horrible was having to put up with your juggling all the time!" Bettain scoffed. Lorrah and Duessa both laughed at that.

Zathi cut in, "Can we get on with this? I'd like to sleep sometime tonight."

"Right. So much happened..." Alemin hesitated, then sighed. "We had nightmares every night, and the tower itself seemed to scream with thousands of voices at dusk and at dawn. The warden, Ar-Lizelle, turned out to be Lorrah's sister, who had been doing research on us to try and find Lorrah." He rubbed the back of his neck awkwardly. "I guess we weren't as discreet as we thought we were."

"Based on how easily the Badgers tracked down Keilos, you weren't," Jaxynne answered drily.

"Well, the Larder is not an ordinary building," Alemin went on. "It's of ancient construction, like the highways. After a few days, I found out I could focus my thoughts into it. I worked at it during rest periods. I saw things that were happening around the building."

"I always felt that I could hear strangely around the highways," Tisha murmured.

Alemin nodded. "From that, there were two things I learned. First, the Larder has a revenant. I thought it was the ghost of a prisoner who had died, and I tried to avoid it, but it chased me. Ar-Lizelle and I confronted it, in spirit." His face twisted, recalling unpleasant memories. "It called itself the Devourer, and it threatened to kill Ar-Lizelle. Later, it did kill someone else by devouring their soul."

"A Devourer?" Tisha pursued. Alemin nodded grimly.

"I remember that day," Duessa added.

"We all felt it," Bettain said, "and most of us aren't sissies like Alemin."

"Thanks for your support," Alemin grumbled. "The second thing I learned was that the screaming comes from hundreds of ancient spirits that are trapped there, in the Larder. Near the end, I was able to understand some of it." He shook his head, amazed. "Those spirits were the Shining Ones. I saw them."

Tisha straightened, her eyes glowing with surprise. "They're real?"

"They *were* real," Alemin corrected. "There was a whole community who lived around the tower. They received *vitalis* through it, I think using the highways as conduits." The excitement faded with grim memory. "They showed me how the Devourers arrived and drained the life from them, but somehow they were bonded to the tower. Even being drained couldn't destroy their spirits. They're still trapped there."

"After all this time?" Tisha murmured.

Lorrah shook her head. "It's hard to imagine."

Jaxynne said, "At our big tower, Keilos wrote his name on the wall as a way of connecting to the *vitalis*. Maybe that's why he still exists, in some form, after his body had died."

"What does it mean, though?" Bettain interrupted. "Even if it's true, that's all ancient myth."

"Well," Alemin drew a deep breath, shaking the memories away. "Ar-Thea told us Dar-Gothull is probably a Devourer, feeding off of souls to sustain himself. It seems like she was right."

"Don't forget what Alemin told us, right after we escaped," Duessa said. "Dar-Gothull uses the Larder to feed on the mage prisoners. It's why they had to get us all out."

"I also think," Alemin went on, "that he's able to cast his mind through the highways. Physically, we know he lives in the capital, Dakadoz, yet he was able to speak to me in the Larder. So, even though they're handy, we might not want to always rely on the highways. We especially might not want to reach out for Meven or Berisan that way."

Around the circle, they nodded morbidly. No one wanted to give themselves away to the wizard-king's regime. After learning how close they had already been to the murderous tyrant, speed was more urgent than ever.

"Those back roads are pretty rough." Duessa spoke from experience. "They could slow us down, when we need to be moving faster."

"Not if we work together," Jaxynne said. "Look how easily we got across that washed-out road."

Duessa was willing to accept the compliment, but then she tensed, distracted. Something had moved past her, like the faintest touch of a breeze.

"What's that?" She looked around, and saw that the other mages in their circle were turning toward the same source.

Tisha had stopped talking a short time ago. She sat now, eyes closed and breathing slowly. Her open hands rested on her knees as if to meditate, but in the middle of a conversation? It was just like when Alemin did his trances in the Larder. The faint ripple brushed past Duessa again.

"What's going on?" Bettain asked warily. Alemin shook his head slightly, even as Lorrah leaned forward.

"Tisha," Lorrah said softly. "What do you see?"

The dancer's brows twitched, and after a moment she blinked her eyes into focus. "My foretelling isn't as strong as Keilos or Ar-Thea, but yes. We should go there."

"The Hornwood?" Alemin pressed. Tisha nodded.

However, Duessa noted, Tisha's gaze drifted past him, to the tent flap. Flaring sparks and charcoal thunks told that the two guardswomen were still working to tame the bonfire. That didn't seem to be what held Tisha's attention. Again, her smooth forehead tightened with concern.

"Then we'll leave in the morning." Zathi stood, slapping dust off the back of her trousers.

The others began to stir, realizing how long they had been sitting there, talking. They had all been carrying the burden of knowledge, and it was a relief to share the weight of it. However, the mages remained where they were until Tisha nodded somberly.

"Yes, we should move quickly."

As Zathi and Jaxynne headed out of the tent, Duessa glimpsed Elldri again. The youngest mage still crouched near the remains of the bonfire. The dull glow of the coals barely lit her face, and her eyes were heavily shadowed.

Duessa rose stiffly. "We're done, Elldri. Come on in."

With a startled blink, Elldri gathered her blanket. It was subtle, but Duessa thought she deliberately walked around the outside of the tent, avoiding Tisha.

"What did you decide?" Elldri lisped.

"Not so much decide." Bettain shuffled over to where their three mats were laid out. "We already knew what we need to do."

"We learned a lot more detail, though," Duessa said. "It's a lot to think about."

"You're not kidding," Bettain said.

Duessa tried to settle down with her mat and thin blanket. So many stories were blurring together in her mind, but at least they had a clear goal in that mysterious Hornwood tower. The pleasant glow of the minstrel show still lingered in her mind. The only thing to disturb it was the way Tisha's gaze had seemed to penetrate the tent. Duessa had a suspicion that she was looking right at Elldri.

Yes, Duessa was aware of Elldri's aura, black as tar and suffocating if she pressed too closely. Yet Tisha had spoken of a foretelling. Was there something else they should know?

VIII — THE SCATTERING

I n her dream, the vision of Ar-Lizelle's safe office dissolved abruptly. She dropped screaming into the void and fell out of the nightmare with a gasp. In the darkened room, someone loomed over her.

"Get away!" She shoved at whoever it was, rolling backward and coming to her feet even before she fully realized that she had touched an actual, solid person. Ar-Kyanon also leapt away. They glared at each other, flames roiling about their fists.

Ar-Lizelle panted, taking in a blurry view of the room. Everything was jumping in the firelight from their hands. There were rough mats on the plank floor, a night stand with an urn of water. An oil lamp was bolted to otherwise bare wooden walls. On the other side of a narrow bed, Ar-Kyanon was poised for combat. Three other beds were lined up along the wall, their blankets tossed by use. Her two guardsmen watched anxiously.

"Warden." Anger dug deep grooves around Ar-Kyanon's eyes. "You were yelling in your sleep."

The petulant words stung her to full wakefulness. This was the latest inn they stayed at, somewhere near the border of Unthur and Ebruc. Its tangible reality proved that the return to her office in the Larder was only a foul illusion.

"A nightmare," she snapped. Even now she sweated, her heart beating hard. Black waves of her hair, taken down for the night, clung to her damp face. Perhaps her throat was a bit sore, as if she had been yelling, but she had no intention of apologizing.

"Yeah, I said that." Ar-Kyanon straightened, and the flames flickered away from his fists. The two guards relaxed, and sheathed their swords.

"No," she croaked, rubbing her throat. "It was one of *those* nightmares."

The three of them regarded her anxiously. Endole licked his lips nervously. "Like from the Larder?"

Ar-Lizelle nodded grimly. "It was a visitation. The revenant."

"Really?" Ar-Kyanon sank slowly onto his own bed. Brown fingers dug furrows in the stubble growing thicker over his skull. "The juggler talked about it, but I never knew whether to believe anything that guy said."

"Alemin wasn't a liar. Isn't," Ar-Lizelle made a sour face. For a moment she studied her two guards. Normally, she wouldn't involve a couple of menials in mages' business, but they had been faithful to her for this long. She needed them ready to face what might be coming.

"The revenant is real enough," she said. "It's something the wardens pass on between us. Assuming we made it back to the Larder and received Countess Ar-Khoreen's approval, I would have told you the details then."

"With the tentacle arms?" Ar-Kyanon repeated warily.

"And the shark teeth." Ar-Lizelle didn't appreciate him fixing on minor details. "I said so after Wharon died, remember?"

"How can it find you, when we aren't in the Larder?" Groff wanted to know.

"That was my question, too." Ar-Lizelle straightened

on her bed, as if she sat behind a proper desk. "Every mage who takes the crimson robe must pass the rituals that bind us to Dar-Gothull's service. According to the revenant, those who serve in the Larder are chained even further, to it and to each other. It can find any of us, at any time."

Which made her wonder, had the revenant — she couldn't quite make herself call it by Dar-Gothull's name — been reaching out to the escaped prisoners, too? What might it have said to them? Perhaps it had offered someone the chance to clear her out of the way, and take her place as warden.

"I don't suppose you've had any nightmares," she half-accused Ar-Kyanon.

"Vaguely. Mostly at dusk, about the time..." He cleared his throat. "About when we would have heard the wailing, if we still were there."

Ar-Lizelle wasn't certain how much that reassured her. Behind Ar-Kyanon, the two guards exchanged anxious glances.

"Even if we aren't mages?" Endole burst out.

Ar-Lizelle felt a rush of angry heat at the interruption, but the thread of panic in his voice reminded her of her own recent terror. "I can't answer that," she admitted. "This information is new to me."

Ar-Kyanon's brows quirked with confusion, but he slowly nodded. "Back in Yergha, I think I felt you coming. At least, I knew something was coming, and it had to do with the Larder."

"If this is true," Ar-Lizelle said, "then I expect we can use it to find the rest of the prisoners. I had to be quite close before I could track you, but that should take care of itself."

Groff nodded. "We'll get closer, soon enough."

"Huh," Ar-Kyanon said thoughtfully. "You know, the

juggler mentioned something like that, right before we all broke out. He said that we're connected through the tower."

"Of course he did," Ar-Lizelle sighed irritably. "That man had an absolute gift for penetrating the Larder's defenses. It was maddening."

Her assistant gave what might have been a sympathetic smirk. "He talked in riddles, that's for sure."

"All right, so we have to keep looking," Endole said, as if reassuring himself.

"Look harder, you mean," Groff answered.

"You're not wrong," Ar-Lizelle said. "There's more, something even dear Alemin probably didn't know." They gazed at her, and she enjoyed a moment of bleak pleasure in their unhappiness. "That revenant claims to be Dar-Gothull himself."

All three of them stared, shocked. After a moment, Ar-Kyanon quipped, "I guess that's when you started screaming?"

"No." She cut that off, unwilling to let them consider any weakness on her part.

Ar-Kyanon had the nerve to look intrigued. "What it claims, is that possible?"

"That's all I know," she answered. "The revenant called itself 'devourer of souls' and it says that everything in the Larder, and all of Skaythe, is within its being." As she quoted from the fading scraps of her nightmare, she held herself rigid so she wouldn't tremble like a child in front of her underlings.

"Do you believe it?" Kyanon pressed.

"We know that Lord Dar-Gothull devours souls," Ar-Lizelle said. "So does the revenant. Can you think of any other soul-eaters in Skaythe?"

"That was just in a nightmare, though," Groff said. "I've heard some mages can send bad dreams. Maybe it's someone from Count Ar-Gammord's court, trying to break down your confidence."

Endole nodded with frantic agreement. They were scratching about for an answer, just as Ar-Lizelle had. She shook her head. This couldn't be so simple.

"In the nightmare, I completely believed it. Now that I'm awake..." She paused before admitting, "I wish I didn't believe it."

Ar-Kyanon had been watching her narrowly. "This could be something we can use, though. Dar-Gothull's favor is valuable. If we find all the prisoners, then we should benefit from it."

Ar-Lizelle didn't see much use for that favor, if they never escaped the Larder. Not that she would ever give voice to such a disloyal thought.

Groff said, "People can claim anything. Is there a way to prove it?"

That was sensible. It helped her shake her fears away.

"Lord Dar-Gothull said he would order the counts to help us collect the rest of the fugitives. If they all start cooperating, perhaps we'll have an answer." Turning to Ar-Kyanon, she said, "You're right. We should use this to as much advantage as we can."

~ ~ ~

After Nyette read Piyaro's letter, Shonn went back to the water-folk's fires. He sat up late with the men from *Pelican* and *Seal*, getting their opinions about the best route to the northern Pulgoll coast. Shonn listened carefully. Water-folk didn't write everything down, the way land-folk did, but the *Seal* clan recommended a trail from Oyster Rocks as their starting point. He would have to take into account how encumbered Piyaro's men were by their heavy gear when guiding them through the mangroves.

Early sun was just penetrating the mist over these mangroves. It wasn't his familiar Fang Marsh, but Oyster Marsh couldn't be that much different. *Pelican's* crabbers set off early to drop their pots in the water. Sergeant Amren roused his squad to march back to Pulgoll. Piyaro and the Hawks busied themselves packing up and figuring out how to carry the tents with their other gear. Shonn planned to forage as they went, so he took only a few provisions from *Seal's* stores.

After that, he shared one last, thumping embrace with his father before the *Otter* poled away from the dock. Oberim and Kannat wanted to get back to their families. Oyster Rocks was going to be crowded with both *Seal* and *Pelican* anchored there. It might strain their food supplies. A couple of men from *Pelican* had offered to go back and help out on *Otter* for a while. Shonn was glad to know they had enough hands for a safe crossing back to Fang Marsh. He watched for a moment as *Otter's* familiar lines faded into a bank of fog — normal morning fog, without Nyette's assistance.

"Hey." Piyaro's gruff voice drifted down the beach. "Let's get going."

Shonn cast a glance at the crew assembled on the sand. A dozen guardsmen, in their metal skins, and one young woman. Nyette had temporarily given up her brown mage robe in favor of anonymous peasant garb, and moved her two hair clips to hold back a short braid.

Were these land-folk truly to be his companions? Now that *Otter* had gone, Shonn felt its loss. For all his life, he had been among those he knew, even a bit too well. Now all these strangers would surround him. He had no idea if he could trust them. Still, they would be in the swamp. He would have the advantage, if an escape became necessary.

"Ready." Shonn hoisted his shoulder bag and settled his work knife on his hip. The foot path began at the northwest end of the beach, where lotus pads and reeds crowded up to the shore. He led the way toward it.

~ ~ ~

With the dawn, a plume of dust rose over the way station. Many of the travelers were striking camp and taking to the roads. Tisha's garish tent came down along with all the others. Sethamis hitched up the oxen and the Badgers stowed their gear. Duessa was glad that no one seemed to be paying attention to their preparations. It was better if nobody noticed which way they went.

As planned, the Badgers headed out to the west on a simple road of packed earth. It wasn't as bad as the washed out track they'd gone through Yergha on, but a main road into Ebruc. There was room enough for considerable traffic, and indeed, their group was hardly alone on the way. Duessa hoped that wouldn't become a problem.

The Badgers rode their horses, as usual, while most of the mages were in the wagon. Alemin had the front bench, with Lorrah nearby on her chestnut, Torch. Tisha and Cylass walked behind, Tisha leading her donkey and the bodyguard pushing their hand cart. From the way Cylass' dark eyes roved among their fellow travelers, Duessa suspected he preferred the rear guard.

For the first hour, Duessa, Elldri and Bettain sat in the back of the wagon, working on Bettain's sewing project. Duessa tried resolutely not to stab herself with the needle whenever the wagon wheels encountered a rut or stone. Eventually, Tisha passed Riprap's lead to her bodyguard and lithely jumped up. The dancer settled herself beside Duessa with a nod and a smile. Elldri kept her head down and edged away on the bench.

"What's going on?" Bettain immediately frowned, looking from Tisha to Alemin and Lorrah.

"Nothing bad," Lorrah quickly assured her.

"We should talk, as mages." Tisha smiled

encouragingly.

"What about?" Duessa asked. She wanted to trust them, but this sudden convergence wasn't reassuring. Elldri's hunched shoulders and downcast face were perfectly understandable.

"Elldri." Tisha gazed at her earnestly. "Don't be afraid."

"If she wants help, she'll say so," Bettain snapped.

At the raised voices, some of the riders glanced over, Duessa noted. Zathi, of course, was immediately aware of anything that had to do with her squad.

"Calm down," Alemin said to Bettain, and to Elldri, "We aren't going to hurt you."

"But someone did," Tisha went on softly, still focused on the youngest mage. "As a healer, I can sense your pain."

Duessa felt a twinge of resentment, that Tisha was stepping into the role of leader. In the Larder, it had been Duessa who rallied the surviving female mages and built their alliance against the hostile and dangerous men around them. Still, she had to admit, in terms of understanding *vitalis*, she was barely a novice. Tisha was modest, but she was clearly the most powerful of all the mages. Add to that Lorrah and Alemin's enduring trust. That was the measure of it, in Skaythe.

Elldri had no answer for Tisha. She sat perfectly still, dark eyes focused on nothing they could see. Only a slight tremor of her hands gave her emotions away.

Duessa tried to reassure her. "All that time, we stood together. I won't let anyone hurt you now." She glowered at Alemin and Lorrah. "But, even I can tell you're sick, Elldri."

For once, Bettain didn't argue about it. Elldri closed her eyes, keeping still as a rabbit under a bush when falcons were on the wing.

"You don't have to suffer," Alemin coaxed.

"Won't you let us try to heal you?" Tisha said.

"You can't." Elldri spoke in a strained whisper. "The Larder was bad, I know, but it was the right place for me."

Duessa choked a little. "That's not true!"

"That's impossible," Bettain cried. "Nobody deserves what we went through in the Larder. And you were there before me."

Elldri closed her eyes, and her face got thinner as she sucked in breath through the places where her teeth had been knocked out. Duessa did a quick calcluation. She'd been in the Larder four years, and Bettain said she'd been there seven. If Elldri had already been in the Larder then —

"How long were you in there?" Duessa asked, appalled. The other mages around them looked equally shocked. "You can't be more than fifteen. What were you, eight, when they condemned you to that?"

"I don't know how old," Elldri whispered.

The rhythm of hoofbeats on dirt changed subtly as the guardswomen reined closer to the wagon. They no longer pretended that they weren't listening. Only Cylass maintained his position, leading Tisha's donkey in the wake of the wagon.

"I know what I did to be in there," Bettain choked when Elldri didn't answer, "but you were a little kid. How could you have a death sentence?"

Elldri wrapped her arms around herself and trembled. When Duessa looked at her with her magical senses, the blackness of the girl's aura was so deep that her features were hard to distinguish.

"Let her breathe," Duessa said.

The others eased back, and Zathi wrily put in, "Once again, I'd prefer not to have wild spells going off around here."

"Once again, we can shield," Lorrah reminded her tartly.

Tisha spoke gently to Elldri. "Your wounds are deep. You must have carried them a long time." She leaned a little forward, never flinching from Elldri's living darkness. "But let's look at this a different way."

Elldri hunched around her silence.

"You can sense our power, right? The *vitalis,* what does it feel like to you?" Tisha asked.

After a strained silence, Elldri whispered at last, "It hurts, like boiling water."

"Really?" Lorrah exchanged a dismayed glance with Alemin. "It shouldn't hurt."

"Just leave her alone, then," Bettain cried.

"I can't." Tisha's cheerful demeanor slipped at little at that. The dancer was serious, almost angry. "Nobody should have to live like this. Always being afraid, always in pain, it isn't right."

Always being afraid was ordinary life in Skaythe. Keerin interrupted the tension with a joking retort. "Careful, someone might think you're a rebel."

Relieved laughter filled the wagon. Duessa noticed that Elldri even cringed from that. Tisha was right. There had to be a better way for Elldri. Even if she didn't see it.

"Quiet down." Zathi scowled around the area, making sure no other travelers were close enough to hear.

"Well, what about this," Duessa said. All eyes turned to her. "I didn't take to *vitalis* right away. I couldn't even see it at first." Bettain nodded. "And I don't even know the name for the energy that's inside Elldri, but we can't expect her to switch over in one day." To Tisha, she said, "Take slow steps. A few minutes at first, let her get used to it."

Tisha didn't look very happy, but she nodded. "Slow steps."

Elldri didn't answer that, but Alemin appealed to her. "Can you think about it?"

"Lady," Cylass suddenly called.

Everyone turned to see Tisha's donkey pulling at his lead. The wooly gray beast flopped his ears back and tried to reach some taller weeds at the roadside. When Cylass pulled him up short, he brayed a little in frustration. Tisha laughed, releasing her strong emotions.

"Riprap," she scolded, jumping lightly down. "You had all night to graze."

Alemin cast a final glance at Elldri before turning forward, while Bettain and Duessa went back to their sewing. Once everyone was distracted, Bettain said to Elldri, "Don't worry about them. I'll look out for you."

Based on the blackened turbulence of Elldri's aura, Duessa wasn't certain how much longer that would continue to be true.

～ ～ ～

Ar-Lizelle's group headed onward in the earliest dawn. She had been meaning to take on more supplies, but the memory of that dream visitation drove her like fire at her heels. Over the next several days, she led her team northward by every available road.

Always, the revenant's mocking voice pursued her: "I have faith in you, Ar-Lizelle."

The fugitives were somewhere ahead of them. Ar-Lizelle could sense it. She had flashes of intuition — a sense of movement that was not her own, unfamiliar voices, or the distant rumble of cart wheels. That must be the bond the revenant spoke of. Or possibly it was desperation.

"A bit more to the west, I think," she informed Ar-Kyanon.

"If you think so." His tone spoke of blaming her for whatever went wrong.

Ar-Lizelle scowled, but let it go. They had been pushing their horses as far and as fast as they could, until Endole appealed to let the beasts rest. Obviously, the horses weren't the only ones feeling the pace.

Ar-Lizelle begrudged every inn they stopped at, for another enemy pursued her as well. This one was less deadly, but still insidious. The store of coin she had brought with her was draining fast. As a mage, she could take what she wanted, of course, but her mother came from a merchant family. She taught that spreading a little coin around would often buy more cooperation than threats.

Unfortunately, they had been on the road for weeks now. At this rate, the promise of Dar-Gothull's favor would soon be the only coin in Ar-Lizelle's possession.

Concern about money dogged Ar-Lizelle as their latest road dipped between two hills and revealed a border town. Two diplomatic posts faced each other across the pale slash of the border road. Unthur's banner floated above the settlement on their side, while the far side — and the larger spread of buildings — displayed Ebruc's. They trotted their horses into town at a polite pace. Ar-Lizelle guided her horse toward Unthur's official buildings, where they could take lodging without payment.

In a low voice, Groff called to her. "Warden, doesn't it seem like there are an awful lot of guards around here?"

"What do you mean?" Ar-Lizelle argued, but now she saw what he meant.

The border road street was crowded with horses and

men at arms striding about in a businesslike manner. Most of them wore Ebruc's symbol, a vulture with wings outstretched. There were guardsmen in all the shops along the street, and the taverns sounded unusually busy. Unthur guardsmen were also visible, in a smaller number, watching cautiously across the avenue. Closer at hand, a pair of Ebruc guardsmen flanked the entrance to the Ebruc border post. They seemed to be watching Ar-Lizelle's party with particular interest. Just as she noted this, one of them turned to hurry inside.

"Those aren't a city watch," Ar-Kyanon observed. "It's someone's personal guard."

"Yes, I can see," Ar-Lizelle retorted, not bothering to lower her voice. A mage should be bold, and not whisper as if they'd done something wrong.

"I'd guess they're connected to Ebruc's count," Endole added. "Who is it again?"

"Ar-Kilohn," Ar-Kyanon said. "What do we know about him?"

"Ruthless and out for himself, same as all the counts," Ar-Lizelle said. "My father dealt with him, when he worked for the count of Prowth. Ar-Kilohn is more or less reliable. At least, he was a few years ago."

They reached the Unthur border post. Ar-Lizelle dismounted and swept inside. She was glad to see that a stout stone gateway framed the armored door, and it was in good repair. Ar-Kyanon followed, while the guardsmen remained outside. In the foyer, a large tapestry showed a map of Unthur and Ebruc. Ar-Lizelle went to study it, while Ar-Kyanon arranged for their lodgings.

Her attention was distracted, however, by a subtle feeling that she was being watched. Ar-Lizelle brushed it away, but the sensation persisted. What was it Groff had said, right after her nightmare? That some mages could try to cloud her senses. Considering that she was about to leave

Unthur, it wasn't likely to be someone from that side. That left Ebruc's forces as the main suspect. Frowning, she half-turned toward the north, where Ebruc's border post squatted across the way.

Illusions and other mind games were a weakling's trick, so her father had taught her. That didn't mean someone wasn't trying it. Ar-Lizelle fixed in her mind a bloody image of what she would do to anyone who toyed with her.

"Warden Ar-Lizelle," a humble voice interrupted her concentration. She turned to see a neatly dressed servant standing in Ar-Kyanon's shadow.

Her second preempted the servant. "We have rooms."

"It's about time." Once again Ar-Lizelle brushed away that intruding thought, and went to inspect the lodgings.

The suite was on an upper floor, three rooms with narrow windows overlooking the street. Two of the rooms were bedchambers, appropriately separating the mages and guards. Between was a common room with a table and chairs. Since Endole cared about the horses so much, Ar-Lizelle sent him off to secure fresh mounts. She also dispatched Ar-Kyanon to the Ebruc border post in search of letters of passage.

As soon as he returned, and she knew whether any diplomatic hurdles had appeared, she fully intended to enjoy a hot bath. In the meantime, Groff watched the door and Ar-Lizelle prowled around the windows, taking a better look outside. She quickly confirmed her impression that the outpost was more fortified than it first appeared. The square walls were of thick stone, enough to resist most magical blasts. An angled roof below the windows ran down to a sentry walk, which was partly concealed by the entry gate's high facade. Although the windows were narrow, a mage could open them and get down to the sentry walk.

Perhaps this was all common sense, although Ar-

Lizelle hadn't heard of any particular bad history between Unthur and Ebruc. It could just as well be evidence of Count Ar-Gammord's paranoia.

From her vantage, she watched Ar-Kyanon emerge from the opposite border post. He briefly turned back as he exited their own armored gate and appeared to be speaking with someone. Ar-Lizelle watched him cross back. Was that tension in his stride?

When he returned, her second announced, "Well, that was interesting."

Ar-Lizelle merely eyed him. She refused to beg for information.

"That place is full of mages," Ar-Kyanon went on as he settled into a chair across from her. "At least three, possibly more. They're circling like vultures over there."

Ar-Lizelle grimaced at the joking reference to Ebruc's symbol. "That answers some of our questions about Lord Dar-Gothull's influence."

"Not only are we granted passage into Ebruc, we are eagerly welcomed," Ar-Kyanon went on with mock sincerity. "In fact, we are cordially invited to join them for an early supper."

Ar-Lizelle frowned. These other mages seemed to have the same idea Ar-Kyanon did about winning the wizard-king's favor. She wasn't happy to have any more competitors under her feet.

"It sounds like they don't know what this is about, exactly, but they're eager to find out. Did you get any names?" Ar-Lizelle asked.

"Ar-Talvoy made the actual invitation, on behalf of Ar-Ishahl. There was another one, a fancy dresser. I didn't hear his name." Ar-Kyanon's shoulders twitched uneasily. "I didn't like the feeling he gave me."

Ar-Lizelle dredged up a memory from years ago. "If I recall, Ar-Ishahl is the son of Count Ar-Kilohn. The guards are probably there to protect him."

Groff cleared his throat, and when she looked at him, suggested, "That's a lot of guards for one man, even a count's son."

"Unless he's trying to make a statement," Ar-Kyanon answered thoughtfully. "How is Ar-Kilohn's health?"

"I haven't heard of any difficulties, but one's health is always at risk when ambitious mages are involved." Ar-Lizelle rose. "I'm going to get cleaned up, and then, I suppose we'll just have to ask them what they want."

Ar-Kyanon smiled mockingly. "Maybe they'll even tell us."

~ ~ ~

The mangrove swamp was not a comfortable place for Piyaro. It was humid, even when they passed along trails shaded by thick foliage. Sweat gathered beneath metal armor, soaking their gambesons and arming caps. Grit from the mud got into everything else. There also were families of shrieking monkeys, and flocks of birds that burst up into their faces. The tart smelling oil Shonn gave them did little to keep the mosquitos off.

In his light shirt and sarong, Shonn didn't seem to notice any of it. He constantly paused to grab some cluster of fruit from a vine or dig up a nest of turtle eggs that Piyaro would never have known was there.

"Fresh food is fine, but this can't delay us," Piyaro scolded.

"Hungry men won't fight well," Shonn pointed out, and he led them on.

Despite his complaint, Piyaro had to give the lad credit. Most of Skaythe was covered in fields or open, dry forest. To his eye, the mangrove swamp was dense and inscrutable. Thicket upon thicket wove together in a living maze. They could have slashed their way through with swords, but Shonn was quick to remind him that this would leave an obvious trail for any who followed. Not to mention dulling their blades.

Despite the challenges, Shonn would always find some path through. Sometimes it was on narrow tracks, little more than game trails. Other times, they stepped into the mangroves themselves, finding hidden tunnels there created from branches bent and lashed together by coarse rope. They had to walk bent over in places, and Piyaro's back felt it.

Cothyr complained, "I thought you water-folk went everywhere on rafts."

Shonn shrugged. "It's too tight through here. Besides, we don't have six spare rafts to lend out for a group this size. And I'm the only one who would know how to steer it right."

"It's fine," Piyaro cut on. "This keeps us out of sight, as Lord Ar-Azlor commanded."

"Yes Sergeant," Cothyr grumbled.

Their third day on, the Hawks confronted a narrow bridge where seawater gurgled and swirled just a foot below. The wood looked flimsy, and slippery with moss. Piyaro was immediately concerned about the weight of armored men on the unstable span. Most of Hawk Squad could not swim.

"We'd better cross one at a time," he said.

"Let me take a look," Shonn answered, and he skimmed across without a care.

Even Nyette, who seemed to be reveling in the adventure of travel, regarded the water warily. "How deep is this?" she asked.

"Good question," muttered Cothyr.

Shonn glanced over casually. "Not bad. You can

stand up." Then he teased, "Probably."

"Will we sink in the mire?" someone else wanted to know.

"I wouldn't let you drown," Shonn scowled indignantly. "If you're that worried, we can tie a rope across and you can hold onto it."

The guardsmen exchanged a lot of glances as everyone wondered who Piyaro would send across first.

"Wait." Nyette rolled her eyes. "I can do better than that."

The young mage stepped out on the span and stretched out her hands. The damp heat turned abruptly colder. With a series of pops, the thick frost built up on the bridge. She made a sweeping gesture and teetered a bit, but water followed her movement. Waves surged up and froze into a wider platform. She stepped out carefully, building the platform as she went. The stuff was strange, clear in some places and milky white in others. It shone where the sun struck it.

"What is that?" Cothyr asked suspiciously.

"Ice," Shonn called across.

"Looks slippery," another man frowned at wisps of fog that curled up from the frozen surface.

"Do you have a better idea?" Nyette called over her shoulder.

"Quit complaining," Piyaro snapped. They couldn't go back on their mission. Once it looked like Nyette was safely in reach of the far side, he jerked a thumb at the man who had been worried about slipping. "Rowlan. Get out there."

"Yes Sergeant." Rowlan shuffled all the way, cursing under his breath.

"Cothyr," Piyaro ordered. After that, the men didn't need to be told. They lined up and went across. Piyaro made sure they were safe before he crossed himself. It wasn't a comfortable experience, with muddy water gushing just under his feet, but he kept a steady pace and it was done soon enough. A few gestures from Nyette sent the ice bridge splashing into the channel, and they followed Shonn onward.

Not much farther on, they came to one of the water-folk's landings, nestled against a rocky knoll. Catfish Pool, as Shonn named it, wasn't as large as the last landing. Sheets of stone covered half the ground surface, so that the vegetation gave only sparse cover. Still, the hut would offer someplace identifiable as a camp.

"We'll stop to rest here," Piyaro ordered. "Everyone check your gear and make sure there's no mud in it."

"While you do that, I'll listen for a bit," Nyette said. "It doesn't seem like there would be any mages out here, but it never hurts to be careful."

"Then I'm going to collect some oysters," Shonn announced. Taking a small net from his shoulder bag, he loped off into the mangroves.

The men groaned gratefully as they stowed their gear in the water-folk's hut. Piyaro divided them into shifts, some to keep watch and some to clean their gear. The rest he sent to the lagoon to wash their gambesons and themselves, in roughly that order. Before long, water fountained high as the guardsmen fell to rough-housing. The men who were cleaning their gear out watched enviously. Piyaro kept an eye on the lot of them, making sure no one was actually trying to drown one of the others, while his hands were busy oiling his greaves, especially between the fine plates around the feet and ankles.

The sun glided overhead. Nyette informed him she sensed no mages or other peril nearby. Piyaro was starting to wonder if Shonn had decided to leave them here, in the middle of the swamp, when the young man returned with a net full of shellfish. Those would take time to cook, and it settled the question of whether they marched on that day. The men were enthusiastic, however, and quickly jumped up to help start a fire in the sand pit.

In some ways, Piyaro regretted taking the time. Their mission apparently was urgent, and it was even more important that Hawk Squad was successful. However, keeping their morale up could be part of that. Young and energetic as the guardsmen were, they had been pushing hard for weeks and needed to let off steam.

Shonn wrapped his catch in wide leaves and set them in the coals to cook. Then he jumped in, too, supposedly to give a basic swimming lesson. Before long, the whole squad was in the lagoon, shouting and laughing. Silty water and bits of vegetation scattered far up the beach.

Only Nyette and Piyaro stayed on shore to keep watch. Nyette declined several shouted invitations to join them, though she didn't seem to mind the flirtations.

"Is the water too warm?" Nyette called back with exaggerated sympathy. "I can cool that off for you."

Once they all settled down, Piyaro called them back up to pitch their tents and other chores. There were hooks on the side of the water-folk's hut, no doubt meant for storing rafts and oars. They worked just as well to hang the wet gambesons until they dried.

By the time the oysters were fit to eat, Piyaro had had a chance to look over his charts. They were nearly to the point of Cape Pulgoll, where they would turn northeast toward Opshar. However strange the paths, Shonn had them traveling faster than he'd thought.

As dusk fell, he returned his guardsmen to maintaining their gear and keeping watches. To Shonn, he nodded his approval of the food and shelter. "This will do well, lad."

~ ~ ~

The invitation from Ar-Ishahl was suspicious, but Ar-Lizelle was determined not to be spooked. She took her time washing, and combed fragrant oil into her hair before twisting it into a high coil. Ar-Kyanon's hair was still very short, though no longer obviously shaved. Instead of trying to hide it, he had the sides cropped even closer and left the top in spiky curls. Thus he turned a symbol of his imprisonment and shame into a fashionable choice.

Both wore fresh robes, claimed from the border post's stores, rather than their dusty ones from the road. Aside from a pair of black jade studs in Ar-Lizelle's ears, neither wore jewelry. She hadn't expected to need anything fancy on a mission to chase down escaped prisoners. Of course, as one of those prisoners, Ar-Kyanon had no jewels of his own. Ar-Lizelle hoped that wouldn't matter. This was a business discussion, after all. It wasn't as though she meant to woo any of them.

Before they crossed to Ebruc's post, they formed a basic strategy. "Let me do the talking," Ar-Lizelle instructed. "They'll focus on me anyway, I expect. That means you two can watch for anything odd."

"Sounds fun," Ar-Kyanon murmured.

"Yes, Warden," Endole said.

The two mages strode across the broad silvery stripe of roadway, with Endole following. The border post loomed ahead of them. It, too, had a fortified gate. The tips of a spiked portcullis were visible beneath the stony arch. They made Ar-Lizelle think of shark's teeth, but she reminded herself with grim purpose that every door on this journey had been some kind of new threat. Ebruc's outpost was no different. A guard stepped forward to meet them.

"Warden Ar-Lizelle," she announced, and was glad of her high, penetrating voice. "I am expected."

Not waiting for confirmation, she strode past the startled guard. Another pair of guards snapped to attention and hurried ahead as they passed beneath the portcullis. The secondary door was metal clad, and those two guards pushed it open for her. The other side was a shadowy foyer. Ar-Lizelle glimpsed flapping sleeves as someone hurried toward them. Whoever it was slowed abruptly and took the last few steps at a sedate pace.

A mage bowed, jeweled chains winking against his crimson robe. Before she bowed curtly in return Ar-Lizelle had the impression of a slightly older man with hints of silver at his temples.

"Welcome, Warden Ar-Lizelle. I am Ar-Talvoy, aide to Lord Ar-Ishahl. Thank you for coming so promptly."

His tone was almost accusing, his expression harried. Perhaps he hadn't expected her to come at all, but assumed she would slink away to avoid meeting Ar-Ishahl.

"I appreciate the invitation." She stressed the last word just a little, reminding him whose idea this was. "It will be good to have a civilized conversation. You've met my second in command, Ar-Kyanon?"

"A pleasure to see you again," Ar-Kyanon bowed, keeping his face smooth and neutral.

"Quite so, indeed. This way, please."

Ar-Talvoy hurried back the way he had come. Ar-Lizelle followed him deeper into the building, flanked by her companions. She barely heard Ar-Kyanon's comment, "At least we can keep our shoes on this time." She chuckled, and Ar-Talvoy glanced back at them warily.

The meeting chamber was small, its plain walls and furnishings hastily covered by richer hangings and fabrics. None of them quite matched the others, either in color or style. A table laid for five occupied the center of the room. As at Unthur, a handful of servants stood ready near tables of refreshments. There were also a handful of guards spaced out along the walls at attention, as if they were part of the decoration. Their weapons and armor appeared quite functional, however. She was briefly aware that Endole paused, measuring their number.

Ar-Talvoy hustled toward a stone hearth where ornate metalwork guarded a small blaze. Two other men in mage robes were seated in chairs draped with more swatches of fabric. They leaned in close conversation, but turned swiftly as Ar-Lizelle entered boldly, Ar-Kyanon following.

"My lord, this is Warden Ar-Lizelle." Ar-Talvoy announced it as if he had discovered her identity all on his own.

Both men rose with genial smiles, but the one who stepped forward wore a crimson robe decorated with rich yellow embroidery. Far more jewels circled his sleek topknot and decked the shoulders of his robe. In his ears were bits of shell carved to resemble animal claws. This had to be Ar-Ishahl.

"Welcome, Warden." Ar-Ishahl gave a quick but courteous bow, yet his eagerness had an undertone she couldn't place.

"It's an unexpected pleasure to encounter such hospitality," Ar-Lizelle lied, and she bowed just as quickly and faintly as he did. In truth, she was now regretting that she didn't have more jewels of her own. By birth they were nearly of equal rank, but his showy attire made her feel like a threadbare shadow. No doubt that was intended.

"You have met Ar-Talvoy," the count's son wore too wide a smile. "May I also introduce Ar-Javan."

The man in question was younger, not as ornately decked out, but notably handsome and with a winning smile. Instead of a topknot, he wore his hair shoulder-length, in loose waves.

"Delighted to meet you." He bowed low, but his brilliant dark eyes remained on Ar-Lizelle's for far too long. She deliberately broke the contact.

"My assistant, Ar-Kyanon," Ar-Lizelle began, but Ar-Ishahl was guiding her magnanimously to the table.

"Come, warden, join me."

IX — FRAUGHT ALLIANCE

T hey all settled, with a bit of jostling for place. Ar-Ishahl insisted on seating Ar-Lizelle beside him, while Ar-Talvoy and Ar-Javan both tried to get on his other side. Ar-Lizelle didn't want to be bracketed by strangers, and made sure Ar-Kyanon got the seat next to hers. Ar-Talvoy ended up sitting farthest from Ar-Ishahl, and he couldn't conceal his anxiety. Ar-Lizelle could almost have felt sorry for him. He was somewhat older, and clearly worried about being passed over. To compensate, Ar-Talvoy waved ostentatiously to the servants, who began to circulate with goblets of wine.

"I trust your journey has been successful, Warden Ar-Lizelle?" Ar-Ishahl sounded cheerful and relaxed. A bit too cheerful, actually.

"In part." Ar-Lizelle assumed he was fishing for information. She wanted to know a few things herself. "Ar-Kyanon tells me you are eager to be of assistance."

"Yes, of course." It was Ar-Javan who replied. He leaned in, trying to make eye contact. Beside her, Ar-Kyanon shifted restlessly.

Ar-Ishahl quickly spoke to reclaim the center of attention. "We all must do as our mighty king Dar-Gothull commands."

Ar-Lizelle nodded at his pompous declaration and

ignored the lackey, Ar-Javan. "In what way would you aid me?"

"My father has sent soldiers to augment your forces, which I'm told are few." Ar-Ishahl appeared kindly, yet made sure to point out the weakness of her position.

"We understand that you pursue a number of mages who escaped from the Larder," Ar-Talvoy cut in. Ar-Ishahl was not pleased by the interruption. It was useful to see where their rivalries were.

"What else to you know of my purpose?" Ar-Lizelle sipped her wine and found it unpleasantly sour. So much for the quality of their hospitality.

"There are rumors that these escaped prisoners may already be in Ebruc." Ar-Ishahl maintained his friendly manner, but now with a hint of warning. "My father will not tolerate this. However, we know you are doing your best with limited resources. Only tell us where they may be, and we will direct our forces immediately."

Limited resources, he said. Ar-Lizelle raised her goblet again, hiding her irritation at his patronizing tone. What he really wanted was to capture the fugitives before her, and take the credit for all she'd done.

The servants returned with steaming bowls half-full of stewed meat and vegetables. In the pause, she found her eyes straying back to Ar-Javan. He continued trying to capture her gaze, and smiled as if they were alone in the room. She deliberately looked away. What was he playing at?

While her thoughts pursued that question, Ar-Lizelle tasted the stew and murmured, "This is quite nice."

"My lady warden?" Ar-Ishahl pressed, still with that false joviality. "We stand ready to aid you."

"There are seven prisoners not accounted for," she told him. Beside her, Ar-Kyanon made a show of enjoying his food. She hoped he was as alert to the undercurrents as she was.

"That many?" Ar-Talvoy was immediately concerned.

"I don't believe all of them are in Ebruc," Ar-Lizelle refused to give way before veiled accusations. "They scattered, no doubt seeking their home ground. However, it's likely that a group of them are traveling together. These are who Lord Dar-Gothull most wishes to recapture."

"Recapture, not kill?" Ar-Javan asked with genuine curiosity.

"They will return to the Larder," Ar-Lizelle permitted no debate on that point. Then she shrugged. "If they live."

"Who are these valued prisoners?" Ar-Ishahl blustered. He drank from his own goblet to hide the cracks in his confidence. For a count's son, he was remarkably unnerved by the mention of Dar-Gothull's name.

"Duessa, Bettain and Elldri were the only surviving women in the Larder. They had an alliance of some years, and I believe they will have stayed together. As for the others..." Ar-Lizelle spooned up her stew, savoring the spices. "Alemin is part of a larger group, foolish subversives who roved around working to undermine his majesty Dar-Gothull's power. Another mage is with them, Lorrah." Ar-Lizelle spat her sister's hated name. "Somehow she hired half a dozen female mercenaries. They disguised themselves as hunter-guards and infiltrated the Larder while I was away."

Ar-Talvoy's alarm deepened. "Five mages, and as many mercenaries?" The soldiers along the wall listened intently.

"That's quite a number you let roam into my county." Ar-Ishahl maintained his genial tone, but no longer bothered to conceal the insult.

"I didn't let them. They fought their way free." Ar-

Lizelle held back her anger. No good would come of antagonizing these mages, even if they felt free to disparage her. Besides, Ebruc wasn't his county. It was his father's.

"It sounds as if they have some skill," Ar-Talvoy worried aloud.

"Not enough to stay out of prison," Ar-Ishahl answered scornfully.

"They do have some skill." Ar- Lizelle remembered all too well how she had assumed her little sister was helpless prey, and how painfully she had learned her error. "How many soldiers did you say the count sent along?"

"Wait, you say they're all women?" Ar-Javan directed a coy smile toward Ar-Ishahl. "That's something I can work with."

The two men exchange smirks. Ar-Lizelle, watching sharply, realized what she was sensing. Ar-Javan's handsomeness concealed something rotten. The way he kept trying to catch her eye seemed more like a covert attack than a charming mannerism.

"Explain what you mean." She tried to keep an even tone.

Ar-Javan smiled, and it made her skin crawl. "I'm a specialist in acquiring information."

"Very useful, I'm sure." That wasn't truly an answer, but Ar-Lizelle didn't need one. Something in this was familiar. She'd felt it earlier in the day, that someone was impinging on her thoughts. Here was the spy, then.

"It is," he murmured with false modesty, Then slanted a tempting glance under his brows.

Ar-Lizelle occupied herself by finishing her food. Since she arrived, she could see how Ar-Javan had been trying to insinuate himself. He must hope to engage her affection, but she had no intention of playing that game. For all their outward friendliness, these still might be her enemies.

"I don't advise trying it," she said. "That might work on commoners, but our former prisoners will not be deceived so easily."

Ar-Javan nodded smoothly, but from the momentary quirk of his eyebrows, he was taking that as a challenge rather than accepting her warning. Ar-Kyanon may have felt that, too. His shoulder went stiff beside hers. Turning from Ar-Javan, Ar-Lizelle focused on Ar-Talvoy and Ar-Ishahl, who seemed to have some sense of priorities.

"If you're interested in actually capturing the renegades," she said, "in the past they have disguised themselves as a traveling minstrel show. I suspect they're going to try that again. You'll want to have your men listen about for rumors of such a thing."

"Ebruc is large," Ar-Ishahl bragged. "Can you give us more of an idea where they'd be?"

"Initially I thought Kamuril, because Alemin had family there, but they've gone past it," she told him. "Now it seems they're moving west. They'll be crossing Ebruc over the next days or weeks."

"How can you be sure?" Ar-Ishahl pressed.

"It's none of your business how I know. Believe me or don't, as you wish." Ar-Lizelle reached for her limited store of patience against these repeated challenges. "What matters more is that they may also have a feel for where I am. They will retreat from me. But they will not be so familiar with the three of you." She paused to let them think about that.

Ar-Talvoy saw it at once. "My lord, if we divide our forces and move westward, while Warden Ar-Lizelle gets behind them, to the east, it's possible she can drive them into us. Then we'd be matched, five to five."

"That is one solution," Ar-Lizelle agreed. As another advantage: it would keep their troops out of her way until she needed them. "It depends how many guards you actually have."

"There are details to be arranged, of course." Ar-Ishahl resumed his helpful manner, still without answering her question. She wondered if he was trying to fool her, or himself.

"Then let's talk details," Ar-Lizelle said.

By reflex, she was suspicious of how easily Ar-Ishahl took to her plan. Or rather, how he thought he could take it over. That must be what this was all about, for him. Ar-Ishahl wanted to steal the credit, and enhance his own standing to succeed Count Ar-Kilohn one day. The other mages surely had their own aspirations.

Ar-Talvoy immediately urged, "Let me take ten guards and move toward the village of Lown."

"I won't need any," Ar-Javan said, and he leered a bit. "I prefer to work alone."

Ar-Lizelle listened as the three of them fell to debating and ignored her completely. With any luck, their rivalries would keep them busy.

Watching, she considered the Ebruc mages. At first, she had thought she and Ar-Kyanon were at a disadvantage. Their unadorned robes were too simple, almost severe. By comparison, their supposed allies were sleek and plump. Yet, how long had it been since these soft, house-bound mages fought their own battles?

Pretty as they were, Ar-Lizelle trusted herself and Ar-Kyanon's strength more.

~ ~ ~

In the days of travel after the minstrels performed, more changes took shape. Badger Squad hadn't exactly been moving at leisure, fleeing from danger as they did. Yet now there was a deeper urgency. Duessa felt it, and she was sure the others did, too. Their enemies were gathering. There would be no true safety until they reached the cover of the Hornwood. She hoped that whatever Zathi had uncovered there would be powerful enough to hold up against the looming menace.

With this pressure, they continued their training of body, mind and horses. Sethamis didn't want the animals to be injured in a panic, and Zathi didn't want any riders thrown at the wrong time. From the way she said it, this was something that had happened before. Even Tisha with her donkey joined in the controlled regimen of sudden bangs and flashes.

When the guardswomen trained, Cylass now joined them. Duessa wasn't much of a judge, but she thought he was skilled. The guardswomen seemed to enjoy having a new sparring partner. At the end of the second practice session, Sergeant Zathi called them all together.

"Listen up. Now that we have Tisha and Cylass, it's time we made some changes in our training."

"What are you thinking of?" Alemin asked.

"We've each been working with our own," Zathi said. "Mages with mages, archers with archers, warriors with warriors. But when we're under attack — which is not an if but a when — they won't come after just the mages or the warriors. It will be all of us, and we won't have time to sort out a strategy once we're in the middle of it."

"Yes, I agree," Jaxynne said. Others in the group murmured agreement.

"Makes sense," Duessa said.

"We've seen what Lorrah can do with her barriers, and we know Tisha and Alemin can cast that as well," Zathi went on. As usual, Lorrah preened a little. "My thought is to team up in pairs, a mage with a guardswoman. The mage protects her warrior from spells, and the warrior keeps other swords from getting too close."

"So I would team up with Cylass," Tisha said. That was obvious, and Cylass probably wouldn't tolerate anything else.

"Right," Zathi said.

"Or Sethamis with Elldri." Jaxynne aimed a teasing smirk at the driver. "Since we know they'll both run to help the animals anyway, they should just be assigned to protect the livestock."

Sethamis turned around and made a face at her, but Elldri's somber face did brighten a little.

"Having pairs would give us more flexibility," Giniver said.

"As long as we don't get too spread out," Duessa cautioned. "Fighting in a crowd might be a nuisance if we get in each other's way, but it's still better than trying to stand alone."

"It's good thinking, though," Alemin mused. "Everyone knows mages and warriors hate each other. No one will expect us to work together."

"That's all well and good," Bettain challenged, "except not all of us know the barrier spell."

"We'll teach you. It's easy," Lorrah brushed that aside.

"Do we have time for that?" Duessa asked.

"Well, wait," Keerin said from the other side. "You three already know it, right? Just make one big barrier to cover us all. Then Bettain and Duessa can cast through it."

The guardswomen liked that idea, but the minstrel mages were shaking their heads. Tisha said, "It's solid. They can't cast through it."

"We'd have to let it down for the archers to shoot or the guardswomen to fight," Lorrah said.

"So we could all be pinned down?" Razeet made a face.

"We have the day before us," Zathi said briskly. "Everyone do your thinking and talking. We'll decide on a strategy to try out."

"Sounds good, Sergeant." Tisha agreed.

And Duessa nodded, too. Zathi was a good leader. She set them a challenge, then gave them space to solve it.

"I'll tell Cylass." Giniver reined her roan, Cinder, around to the rear. With an inner sigh, Duessa noted how Elldri jumped away. She was starting to wonder if Elldri would do anything but cower when battle was upon them.

~ ~ ~

Even with all the negotiations and not-so-subtle posturing, Ar-Lizelle and Ar-Kyanon managed to enjoy the meal Ar-Ishal had provided. She even picked up a bit of palace gossip from Ar-Talvoy when Ar-Ishal was talking to his soldiers. Ar-Lizelle had finally got the count's son to admit he had 30 guards with him. From the way he slid around the number, she suspected he really had more.

Unfortunately, she could not avoid being assigned ten of them, from Ar-Ishal's own guard. It was a clear statement that, though Ar-Lizelle and her group were outwardly welcome in Ebruc, they did not have complete freedom. Ar-Ishal's men outnumbered her two, and that was going to be uncomfortable.

The party from the Larder were graciously invited to stay in Erbuc's border post, but she put that aside with the truthful statement that they already had lodgings for the night. The tag-along guards were bad enough. Ar-Lizelle had no intention of sleeping in a building with a group of mages she didn't know. Especially not Ar-Javan.

As they walked back, Ar-Kyanon murmured, "They're going to spy on us, you know."

"I'm sure," she said. "Unfortunately, I don't see how we can stop them."

"All kinds of things can happen on the road," Endole suggested, with obviously false concern. "There could be a tragic accident."

"Maybe it will come to that," Ar-Lizelle said, then shook her head. "Let's not start something too soon. We might actually need them."

They re-entered the Unthur waypost and trooped up the stairs. Groff met them anxiously at the door of their suite. Once in private, they briefed him on what had been decided.

"It could work," he said. "They know the land. They can help us get around more quickly than we would on our own."

"Ar-Ishal and Ar-Talvoy should know where the minstrels may try to run though," Ar-Lizelle acknowledged.

"The concept is good," Ar-Kyanon agreed. "It's the execution I'm concerned about. Those mages aren't fighters. Look at that Ar-Javan. He won't dirty himself. He wants to talk his way around people."

"Yes, and he isn't nearly as cute as he thinks he is," Ar-Lizelle snapped. For all that, the mage's image still lingered in her mind with unwelcome familiarity. She shot a glance to her second in command. "If you catch me acting like a fool around him, just kill me."

Ar-Kyanon flashed a sly grin. "I was thinking we could invite him to the Larder. You can play with him there."

There was half a question in his smirk. Did Ar-Lizelle ever take pleasure with the prisoners whose lives she controlled? She knew that Wharon, as warden, had sometimes summoned female prisoners to his quarters.

Palinna had almost been a regular. She was also the first to die when Wharon lost his grip.

Ar-Lizelle had never stooped to that. She would not risk a filthy prisoner having his hands on her. Some of the guards could possibly have been trusted, but then they would expect special treatment. There were male harlots in the taverns, as well, but none of them had struck her fancy.

Or perhaps, now that Ar-Kyanon himself was no longer a prisoner, he had some idea that she was open to flirtation. If so, he was even less trustworthy than one of the fugitives.

Coldly, she informed him, "I am far too busy for such games."

~ ~ ~

In the evening's camp, the warriors gathered close to the fire, debating ideas and formations for fighting alongside the mages. Those mages themselves formed their usual circle to meditate. Duessa was getting used to the flow of energy, though the sharing of emotions that came with it still made her uneasy. Such intimacy wasn't part of any other training she'd had. To show any weakness still seemed like an invitation to betrayal.

Their true goal, though unspoken, was to reach Elldri. The young mage would sit nearby, after some coaxing from Bettain, but she could only stay still so long. Any touch of *vitalis* for more than a few seconds made her jump up and dash off. The passing of several days hadn't made it any easier. Lorrah and Tisha traded worried glances with Alemin.

In their deep communion, Tisha's thought murmured, *"I've never seen one person with so many scars. It's not only her teeth. She's had so many broken bones. Both arms, her ribs, her skull."*

Lorrah winced. *"How is she even alive?"*

"They're old injuries, long healed, but the scars go deeper than just bone. No wonder she's so sensitive," Tisha said.

Duessa fumbled to add her thoughts. *"Done by magic?"*

"I can't tell," the healer replied.

"What could have happened?" Alemin projected horrified concern. Duessa sensed that he was ready to jump up and follow Elldri.

"No!"

The other mages jumped at her sudden cry. Embarrassed, Duessa spoke the words out loud. "Bettain is right. She'll tell us if she wants to. Just let us talk to her. You keep trying to reach your brother."

"All right." Alemin nodded appreciation.

Bettain had been sewing while the others were busy, but she was already striding after Elldri. Dusk was settling on the plains, and they could lose her in the night. Duessa hurried to catch up with Bettain.

"We should just let her alone." Bettain stopped to look around. "It's all right if she isn't like you guys. Why should she be? I'm not," she finished belligerently.

Patiently, Duessa replied, "Elldri's power could kill her. Is that what you want?"

"Mages die all the time. We flame out. You know that." For once, Bettain sounded less defiant and more defeated.

"This young?" Duessa asked.

A few weeks ago, the constant complaining would have set Duessa's own temper flaring. Now, she could recognize Bettain's gnawing worry. Elldri was a friend to Duessa, but Bettain was much more maternal and protective.

It burned like mage fire that she didn't know how to help.

Fortunately, Elldri hadn't gone far. Duessa spotted the blackness of her aura among some rocks, like an unhappy lump of charcoal in a dormant fire.

"Over there." Duessa moved slowly to reassure her friend. Tisha's list of old injuries revealed things Duessa had seen before, but not recognized. Yes, she knew Elldri's cheeks were sunken because of her missing teeth. Somehow she hadn't noticed that the girl's nose was flatter than it should have been. Her hair was still short, barely showing any curl, so it was easy to see the cris-crossed scars that would have been hidden by longer hair.

"Elldri?" Duessa crouched nearby, not approaching too closely. "I get it, you know."

Dark eyes flicked up to her, haunted.

"You're used to having one kind of power," Duessa went on. "It hurts, but it keeps you safe. That's hard to let go of, right?"

Elldri sat still as if she wanted to become one of the stones.

With a guilty glance toward Alemin, Duessa confessed, "I haven't totally stopped summoning *lethentros,* either. I'm trying with *vitalis,* but... I might still need it."

"We don't know what's coming at us," Bettain agreed.

"I guess I want the option, if the Badgers aren't enough to keep us safe." Duessa turned back to Elldri. "That day, in the Larder, you told Alemin that he needed to say what happened to him. And you were right, but you yourself won't tell us something important."

"Because I forgot," Elldri choked. "I forgot how bad it is. When I tried to help move the cart, it all came back again."

"Dangerous? It's just casting," Bettain scolded. "We

all do it. I don't get why this is so hard."

Elldri shook her head. "I can't use magic. It all comes back and it... I'm... not safe."

"I don't know what that blackness is," Duessa said, "but I understand if you don't want to let your power go. It's not good for you, though. You know that? You can hurt yourself if you hold onto it."

"I'm not holding it," Elldri answered, a mere thread of sound. "It's holding me. It won't let go."

"What do you mean?" Bettain frowned. "Anyone who's born with power can train it the way we want."

"Where did you learn this, anyway," Duessa asked. "At a temple school?"

"No, I never went." Elldri breathed deeply, as if fighting back sobs. "My parents kept me home."

It was brave of her to say so much, Duessa thought, but she couldn't help thinking how wonderful it sounded, to be saved from the temple school by a family who loved her. Even if her mother still got sick, so many things would have been easier.

"I wish my parents had let me stay," she sighed.

"Not like that." Elldri's voice was barely audible as she pulled in on herself again.

Duessa thought about that, studying all the scars Tisha had named off. She wondered about the ones that couldn't be seen. What kind of home life gave a young girl broken arms and ribs and ruined her teeth?

"It sounds like they were pretty rough on you," Duessa said. Once again, Elldri huddled against the rock.

Bettain frowned again, but in a thoughtful way. Slowly she said, "You know, I might have heard of this. It was at my temple school, a course for advanced students."

Duessa looked over, surprised. "I didn't know you went to a temple school. Which one?"

"It's in the past. I try not think about it." Bettain shrugged uncomfortably. *"Voromnil* is a power even worse than *lethentros*. It's capable of destroying all life. Things wither or rot." She eyed Elldri with concern. "It's pretty rare. Our tutor said the only people who can use it are already dead. I thought he was joking."

"That's..." Duessa fumbled for words. She studied the thick, tarry blackness that enveloped her friend. A power to destroy all life sounded too much like the drakanox that wiped out Seofan Holl at Dar-Gothull's command. Before she could stop herself, Duessa blurted, "Elldri, did you... die? Or almost die?"

Stricken, Elldri stared between them. Her breathing came in choked gasps. Even if she didn't speak, the answer was obvious.

"Who would do that?" Bettain clenched a fist and her voice rose. "I'll find them, Elldri. Just tell me where. I'll —"

"Hey, Elldri!" Sethamis' cheerful voice called from the camp. "Ready to check the horses?"

Elldri leapt up and darted off toward her favorite chore. Duessa and Bettain both cursed, yet it was also a relief to break the tension.

"That girl." Duessa gave a tired laugh.

"Aren't they supposed to take care of their own horses?" Bettain complained.

It was true that each guardswoman cared for her own horse, just as Tisha looked after Riprap. But it was also true that Sethamis's unnecessary tasks gave Elldri the comfort of working with animals who never asked questions she didn't want to answer.

Bettain shook her head. "This world isn't kind to

magelings."

"It isn't kind to anyone," Duessa replied grimly. One day, perhaps, she and the minstrels could change that. As it was, she needed to get back over and tell the rest of the mages what Bettain said about *voromnil*.

~ ~ ~

After their confrontation, Elldri distanced herself from the other Larder mages. Duessa kept hoping Elldri would get her bearings, but she didn't want to ride in the wagon. She walked behind instead. Sometimes she held the donkey's lead. Other times she plodded along with her head down. Duessa was certain Cylass slowed his handcart at times to avoid leaving her behind.

There was good reason to be watchful. Ebruc was more populous than Kamuril. The rolling hills had leveled out into fields of vegetables or grain, where small villages crowned the few low hills. Straggling lines of trees outlined the streams. The Badgers encountered more people than before, either on the road or near it. With the skills honed in her moon-running days, Duessa kept a sharp eye for anyone paying too much attention as they passed. Bettain sat next to her on the bench with her sewing. The gray robes had been doubled up as much as possible, and Bettain was now darning on patches of colorful fabric, taken from Tisha's remainders. The idea was that whoever wore them would appear as if they belonged in a minstrel show rather than a rebellion. The work kept her hands busy, but did not prevent her casting anxious glances behind the wagon.

Even in camp, Elldri hardly spoke. The only ones she seemed comfortable with were Sethamis and the oxen. It was painful to watch her drift away from them. Elldri was a friend, someone she depended on in the dangers of the Larder. Duessa asked herself, privately, how far they could trust this stranger Elldri had become.

At the end of a morning's practice, Duessa noticed Tisha having a long conversation with her boyfriend before they all headed out in the wagon. The rising dawn threw long shadows before them as the wagon rolled out of the copse of trees where they had been camping. Tisha sat straighter, leaning to peer ahead between Sethamis and Alemin.

"What's wrong?" Duessa asked. She didn't pitch her voice low enough. Zathi and Lorrah both took note.

Tisha seemed to make a decision. "A feeling. We shouldn't be going this way."

"We have to go this way to get to the Hornwood," Sethamis answered.

Again Tisha studied the horizon. "Something lies ahead of us. A danger."

"Is this a foretelling?" Zathi asked. "Like Keilos?"

The pretty mage shook her head. "Keilos saw distinct images. My gift is not so precise. I only sense that due west is a bad idea."

"That's not surprising, is it?" Zathi reasoned. "We've been slinking through, but we had to know the alarm would be raised sometime."

Frowning, Alemin said, "I feel something too, only mine is from behind us."

"Your brother?" Bettain asked hopefully.

"No, I'd have felt him much sooner than this," Alemin said. "Anyway, this isn't anything good I feel."

His words raised a specter that Duessa feared more than anything else. "Do you think it's her?"

All the Larder mages shared that flash of worry, that the hated Warden Ar-Lizelle was closing in on them. Lorrah had her own reasons to be worried.

"You think it's my sister?" she asked with disgust. "We need to move faster."

"I don't know Ar-Lizelle," Tisha said, but she urged, "Let's think about this more."

Any reminder about the Larder made Duessa glance behind them. Elldri walked along beside Cylass' cart, stroking the donkey's neck. She seemed to be buried in her own thoughts. Duessa shook her head slightly. Elldri said the Larder was the right place for her. Was she purposely slowing down, hoping to be caught?

Surely not! Elldri had been as eager to get out of the Larder as any of them. But if she did try to surrender, what then?

"My charts show a cutoff north, around Ebruc Holl," Jaxynne offered. "That will take us into the Hornwood, but far to the east of where we should be."

"It would still be cover," Razeet said.

"Travel will be slower if we have to go off the road," Sethamis immediately replied. "We've done that before, remember?"

"Lots of beasties in those woods," Giniver said. The other guardswomen groaned at some memory.

Tisha didn't argue with them, but her expression said she didn't think a cutoff to the north would be enough to ward off the danger. However, Lorrah was not so restrained.

"You shouldn't ignore our premonitions," she said a bit sharply. "The closer we get to Ebruc Holl, the more guards will be around. Is there any way to turn north sooner?"

Zathi appeared irritated, but she shook it off. "You're right. I shouldn't brush off any information. Next rest, we'll look at those charts again."

"I'll take a peek, too," Duessa offered. "There might be a back way that gets us through quietly."

~ ~ ~

It was exhilarating to thunder across the plains of Ebruc, with her crimson robes flaring and a squad of guardsmen following close behind. At last, there was nothing to stop her. Ar-Lizelle reveled in the fear on peasant faces when they saw her bearing down on them. Whatever concern she had about Ar-Ishahl's motives, it was useful to have all the perks of a count's support. Fresh horses were ready at every outpost, and no innkeeper dared to charge for their stay.

In each village of any size, she sent some of Ebruc's men to talk with the regular guards while Ar-Kyanon called on whatever passed for a local dignitary. Endole or Groff would mingle with the people in the markets. All of them brought along descriptions of Alemin and his misfit band.

On the fifth day, her diligence was rewarded. Both Groff and the Ebruc soldiers brought back excited rumors about a circus on the border with Kamuril. Many rumors fixated on a gorgeous dancing girl, but it was the mention of a very funny juggling act that caught Ar-Lizelle's attention.

"That's him! At last," she crowed. Alemin's juggling obsession would be his undoing.

Initially, she had rushed her force eastward, almost to the border with Kamuril. There they turned north. There was a trade road from Prowth to Ebruc, and Ar-Lizelle suspected the fugitives were trying to mingle with the flow of traffic. However, for the past half-day, she had been aware of an inner tug to the west. These rumors confirmed that the fugitives were acting exactly as she had predicted.

"Go get Ar-Kyanon," she snapped to Groff, and she ordered the soldiers, "Bring our horses around. It's barely mid-day. We have plenty of time to travel on."

This was perfect. Ar-Lizelle would drive the fugitives into Ar-Ishahl or Ar-Talvoy's force. They would be trapped. At least, that was the goal as they had spoken it at the border with Unthur. What Ar-Lizelle really wanted was to intercept the renegades first. She had a few words for the lot of them, those rebels who dared humiliate her before the wizard-king Dar-Gothull.

Soon they were galloping on, making peasants scatter before them. No matter what else happened, Ar-Lizelle would have her victory. Her faithless sister would die, and the rest of them would be in bonds, where they belonged. Ar-Lizelle's life would be secure.

It was only a matter of time.

~ ~ ~

In Shonn's opinion, the hardest crossing was at the very tip of the cape, where rocky cliffs fell almost vertically to the water. Only a thin shoulder of land allowed them to move between those cliffs and the surf. A constant screech and whine of sea birds came from up and down the massif. The mangroves, which he counted on for protection from the worst of the sun, and from prying eyes, became patchy with long stretches of reeds and marsh grass.

The men of Hawk Squad had become accustomed to travel in the mangroves, and no longer struggled to keep pace. However, there were several times when they had to stop and crouch in the reeds while small boats sailed by. These mostly appeared to be fishermen, but Piyaro didn't want to take the chance of being seen. Shonn watched the western horizon, where clouds were clotting together.

"If it storms, we'll be completely exposed," he warned Piyaro. "There's nothing to keep the waves from floating us right off this little patch."

"Understood," the sergeant said. The group moved off as soon as the small boat was past them.

Clouds continued thickening, until the cliff above was shadowed by them. Wind gusted, and the surf took on an angry growl. Shonn was relieved to round the cliffs and move back eastward, into the shelter of the mangroves. The thick vegetation blunted the worse of the wind and tide as they reached another landing, Sea Grazer Marsh.

If not for the storm, they would have had hours more to travel, but there was no avoiding this pause. Rain began to pelt down as they struggled to get their tents up. It was going to be a long, soggy afternoon.

X — REVENGE

I n the cold morning, the Badgers were already up and training. Duessa meditated as dawn painted the sky with fiery hues. Breathing deeply, she tried to follow the steps Lorrah had demonstrated.

Creating a barrier was similar to the casting she already knew so well, and yet it was exactly the opposite. When she prepared to strike a target, she pictured the full fury of what she wanted. But now, instead of the harsh burn of *lethentros*, it was soothing *vitalis* that answered her call. Rather than launching a burst of fire, Duessa's will raised a wall. Or, it was supposed to.

Bettain sat nearby, helpfully plinking her with pebbles. "Is it supposed to do something?" she teased as the first ones bounced off Duessa's knee.

"If you think it's so easy, you should try," Duessa's cheerful retort was a bit strained. Lorrah breezily assured her that the spell wasn't difficult. It would be embarrassing if she couldn't keep up with a teenager.

Drawing on her annoyance, she sharpened her will. "Try it now."

Bettain's next pebble slowed visibly. Duessa felt it strike her barrier, almost like the movement of her sleeves in the wind. The pebble didn't stop, however.

"Be certain." Alemin was juggling nearby, his eyes

half-closed in meditation. "Think of it like, 'nothing else gets through here.'"

"How about just no?" Rather than certain, Duessa felt irritated. Apparently that was enough. The image came clearly, a sheet of metal that nothing could penetrate. In her mind she barked, *"NO."*

A visible glow formed, irregularly shaped, but brightening and firming up as she went. Bettain's next pebble bounced away.

"That's more like it," her friend encouraged.

To Duessa's surprise, a larger rock flew in. She flinched at the unexpected movement, and the missile punched through to strike her chest. "Hey!" she rubbed at the burst of pain.

Zathi and the warriors had just come back from their morning run. "It's a good start, but you have a ways to go," Zathi informed her.

"Thanks?" Duessa grumbled.

~ ~ ~

"We have to be getting close," Ar-Lizelle said when Ar-Kyanon returned from his errand without news.

"I feel it, too," he agreed. The two guards nodded hopefully.

She didn't know why she was trying to convince them. They would follow whether they believed she was right or not. The men she had sent from Ebruc's guard were still out exchanging their mounts. Ar-Lizelle took the moment to rest in a tavern. After days of riding without pause, her hips and back no longer ached as they had a first. Still, it felt good to sit in a chair instead of on a horse.

The tavern maid bowed as she set goblets of wine in front of Ar-Lizelle and Ar-Kyanon. As she took the first welcome drink, the maid asked, "My lady, will you be staying to eat, or do you join the other mage who passed through?"

The question instantly spoiled Ar-Lizelle's mood. "What other mage?"

"Ar-Javan," said the maid, with a trace of a longing smile. "So charming."

"Ar-Javan?" Ar-Lizelle fumed. She had been right. That fool was trying to steal the credit for everything she had done!

"When did he leave?" Ar-Kyanon spoke smoothly, as if the matter was unimportant, but the waitress had already seen Ar-Lizelle's reaction.

"Not more than two hours, my lady," she replied in an appeasing tone. "Was he supposed to wait? I'm so sorry, I didn't get any message."

"None of your business." Weariness forgotten, Ar-Lizelle took a deep drink and directed an angry glance at one of Ar-Ishahl's men. "Go find the others, and get our horses ready."

"We can still catch up," Ar-Kyanon said. Then he teased, "Are we going after the prisoners, or Ar-Javan?"

It wasn't a bad question, and it cooled some of Ar-Lizelle's anger. They shouldn't rush into conflict with Ar-Ishahl's ally, now that they were so close to their goal.

"Ar-Javan was at dinner with us. He heard their numbers. If he decides to take foolish chances, it will be on his own head," she answered coolly.

Ar-Kyanon glanced around, making sure none of Ebruc's men were near enough to listen. "If he tangles with them first, it could be to our advantage. He'll draw them out, wear them down."

"That isn't the point." Ar-Lizelle drank a little more to quiet her temper. Still, she fretted as she watched the door for word that their horses were ready. "There's no way I'll let a late-comer get between me and my prisoners. Not in all Dar-Gothull's void."

Ar-Kyanon nodded slowly. "I couldn't follow you if you said anything else."

~ ~ ~

Duessa kept a nervous watch as their wagon bumped over the rugged farm track. Jaxynne had managed to find a northward branch from the main route, one that had long ago led to Seofan and Busaren, the counties on the northern coast of Skaythe. The farm houses were sparse here, which meant fewer people to note their passage.

That should have been reassuring, yet Duessa's neck twinged with tension. A group their size, heading into the middle of nowhere, was sure to stand out in a way they didn't want. On the driver's bench, Alemin turned around to share a worried glance.

"You feel it, too?"

"Yeah," she admitted.

"It's the Lizard," Bettain confirmed. "And someone else. I don't know who."

"Maybe Ar-Chindu?" Alemin said.

Duessa thought about it. "Didn't he get shot?"

With a grim smile, Bettain turned to the rear. Elldri trudged along, leading Riprap as usual. The younger girl was also looking around, alert to the danger they all sensed. Tisha was walking behind, with Cylass. She offered a faint hope. "We're closer to the Hornwood."

Since the day before, a fringe of trees had been darkening the horizon, and they had camped the night among a sparse grove of hornpines. The trees were tall and straight, sparsely leaved, with white bark grooved like deer horns. That distant shadow was the Hornwood, their hoped-for sanctuary. Duessa's hope of refuge there was dimming.

Lorrah, riding beside the wagon, reached to clasp Alemin's hand. "This is not good."

"You said it," Bettain grimly agreed.

Giniver rode up behind Lorrah. "If even Bettain feels it, maybe we should stop running. The fight is going to find us. It would be better to find a place where we can make a stand."

"It's still pretty open here," Jaxynne said. "Not much of a place to defend."

"No, I don't think we should stop," Tisha said. "That doesn't feel right."

"The wagon is slow, I know," Sethamis apologized. "Even if everyone got off and walked, the oxen can't go much faster before they wear themselves out."

"Maybe the mages should take the horses and ride ahead," Cylass offered. Duessa immediately wondered if he planned to go with Tisha and leave the rest of them.

Tisha turned to her boyfriend in shock. "Don't even think about that. We're training as teams for a reason."

"Lady. You mages are the ones who must get to the Hornwood," Cylass said.

"We still need you," Tisha insisted, and Duessa was sure she meant more than just for protection. The guardswomen didn't like his idea anyway.

"No thanks!" Jaxynne said. "We've been training the horses all this time. I count on my bond with Cinder to hold steady so I can shoot."

"Yeah," Keerin complained. "I just barely got Smoke."

"That's right." Razeet patted the neck of her bay, Tinder.

Zathi was also shaking her head. "Once we got separated, we'd never find each other."

"We found each other once," Lorrah said.

"The Badgers do have a good tracker, you know," Jaxynne added from the other side of the wagon.

"Not in the middle of the Hornwood," Alemin replied.

"You're assuming we even get there," Giniver said.

"Listen to me." Duessa tried to find words for what had been bothering her. "I know it looks quiet, but that's just because the locals are hiding. If they think we're running from the count's guards, they'll turn us in first thing."

"How do you know?" Lorrah asked.

"I was a moon-runner," Duessa reminded them without shame. "When farmers leave their fields in the prime of the workday, it's a sign that someone is lurking about. Maybe they think we're the someone, or maybe there are other troops nearby. Regular folks, they just want to stay out of the way."

That quieted everyone. Zathi spoke into the gap. "All right. We still need to get to the Hornwood. It has the best cover, even if it slows us down. Meanwhile, everyone stay alert. We aren't there yet."

Everyone was tense and quiet as the wagon rolled on. The guardswomen rode close, snapping to alert at every odd noise. Duessa still felt the creeping sense that Ar-Lizelle was nearby.

"What's that up ahead?" Keerin asked in a low, wary voice.

"Just a man," Lorrah answered, but in a puzzled tone.

She was right to be wary. A lone person was at the roadside ahead of them, fussing with his horse. Duessa eyed him as they drew closer. He was plainly dressed but notably handsome, with loose hair rippling down to his shoulders. As they got there, he stepped into the road without any fear.

"Ho, friends. Can you help me? My horse has come up lame." Indeed, the animal was in the tall grass, tossing its head and visibly limping.

Sethamis immediately called, "Ho boys," and pulled on the reins. "What happened?"

"Setha," Zathi rebuked. "I know you love animals, but this isn't the time."

"Sorry, sergeant," the driver mumbled, but she still was focused on the lame horse.

"You don't want to travel with us," Lorrah said to the stranger.

"But I do. I think we should all be good friends." He smiled with great sincerity, yet also, Duessa thought, surveying the hunter-guards as if they were a tree full of ripe oranges and he was about to take his pick. Her scars began to itch in warning. No ordinary person would be so poised in the presence of this many hunter-guards.

"He's a faker," Duessa murmured. "Alemin, tell them."

Sethamis still hesitated. "But the poor thing. Could we at least take a look?"

Zathi rode forward. "Move aside," she ordered, but the stranger's smile only widened.

"I'll be so much safer with you fine guards," he said.

Power came off him, a poisoned cloud enveloping their squad. Intruding thoughts assured Duessa that this was a good man, someone she could trust. He only needed help. And he was devastatingly handsome, besides.

"Hey!" she blurted. Elldri also jumped, pulling

Riprap's lead backward.

Bettain called, "What's wrong?"

A moment later, Alemin cried, "Don't do that," and Lorrah choked out, "Stop it!"

Duessa acted on instinct, rejecting the intrusion with an inner *"NO."* Some of the others may have struck back, because the man staggered momentarily.

On the opposite side of the wagon, Jaxynne stood in the stirrups. She scowled at the stranger. "Are you trying to dominate us?"

"Calm down," he coaxed, while Duessa felt the attempted seduction coil across her skin like an oily breeze. "There's no reason we shouldn't be friends."

On the driver's bench, Alemin glowered. "We are not going to be friends."

"That's enough!" Lorrah said. Duessa didn't know what she did, but the temptation faded as suddenly as it had come. Sethamis jumped and shook her head, rubbing her forehead.

"What am I doing?" she mumbled.

"Out of the way, mage." Zathi's steel was out, and Giniver reined around to bracket him.

Tisha's expression was uncharacteristically stern. "Warping people's minds is not acceptable. Please move aside."

"Please? This is no time for fancy manners." Bettain stood up in the back of the wagon, flames wrapping around her fist.

A sickening smirk replaced the enemy mage's winning smile. "You fools are welcome to try and make me move."

The whole wagon crackled with tension as the

guardswomen grabbed their weapons and the mages raised their fists in answer. In that moment of poised action, Razeet stood up in the stirrups, staring back the way they came.

"Sergeant, on the road!"

Duessa dared a backward glance. Dust rose along the track behind them. Horses and riders were coming up fast. The itch in Duessa's scars spread and sharpened into real pain.

"Alemin?" Zathi asked in a low, hard voice.

"It's her," he confirmed.

"Drive, Setha!" Zathi moved as if to kick that enemy mage, but he had jumped back out of reach and raised his hands to do some casting of his own.

Lorrah whirled her chestnut and called out, "Eyes!" A bright flash dazzled Duessa even though she was looking backward. The enemy mage yelled and stumbled back. Several horses jumped at the flash, but their training kept them under control.

"Get up, boys!" Sethamis snapped the reins and the wagon lurched into motion.

Behind them, Cylass was calling, "Get to the wagon." He pushed Tisha forward, then snatched the donkey's lead from Elldri's hand. "Let him go. He'll run faster on his own."

Both woman ran to the wagon, while Cylass grabbed the handles of his handcart and swung it around so that it partly blocked the road. Sword drawn, he sprinted to catch up with the others. Within moments he was boosting Tisha up. Elldri's face was drawn with fear as she jumped on next. Cylass came last, urging them both further into the wagon's bed so he could defend the rear.

Thundering hooves filled the air as riders closed the gap. Though the two oxen grunted with effort, the wagon moved only a little faster now than when they were trudging along normally. The donkey loped along easily beside it. The rattle of his saddlebags added to the general noise and fear.

The enemy mage had recovered from whatever Lorrah did. Bursts of flame arched after them. Lorrah turned her horse back and deflected the flames with her barrier. Duessa watched anxiously, trying to repeat in her mind how Lorrah acted with such precision.

"How are we supposed to do this?" Bettain called over the thudding of hooves. "We didn't practice being in the wagon and you guys riding."

"We work as a group," Tisha said. "I'll shield the left side of the wagon, while Lorrah defends the right."

"I'll watch forward to protect Sethamis and the animals," Alemin said, which made sense since he was still on the front bench.

"Good," Zathi called. "Guards, find your partners."

"Duessa, I'm here," called Keerin, bringing her dun up in Lorrah's usual spot.

"Hey," Bettain tapped Duessa's shoulder. "Can you push them off their horses with your barrier?"

"I'm not that good," Duessa answered. She liked the idea, though. "Lorrah, can you?"

Lorrah and Zathi had already dropped back. Thwarted, the enemy mage was running back to his horse, which she assumed was not actually lame. Riprap brayed a little with the distress of being separated from Tisha.

Every moment, the riders pursuing them drew closer. Duessa's heart pounded with helpless dread as details came into focus. Ar-Lizelle was in the lead, a savage grin on her face. Her exultation leaked through their strange bond of the Larder. Trying to shake that away, Duessa turned toward Elldri. The younger woman was cramming herself between the bench and the hunter-guards' metal cage. Duessa reached a hand back to squeeze her knee.

"It's okay," she said, although it wasn't. "We're all here."

"That's right," Bettain said, and then, "Tisha, trade me places."

Cylass was glad enough to let Tisha move to the middle of the wagon so that he and Bettain were shoulder to shoulder at the back. When she had settled in place, Tisha began swaying side to side, shoulders dipping and rising as her back curved and her hands caressed the air. Even seated, she was trying to dance.

Despite the circumstances, Duessa had to ask, "What are you doing?"

"Raising power." Tisha sounded a bit embarrassed. "It's hard for me to sit still."

Duessa was reminded of Alemin's constantly juggling when they were in the Larder. It had seemed like a weird compulsion, but he said it helped him to focus.

"It isn't the strangest thing happening right now," Razeet said from beside the wagon.

Cylass paid no attention to them. He watched the approaching force with a dourly calm, analytical eye. "Twelve guards, three mages," he reported to no one in particular.

"Five mages, six guards," Jaxynne shot back. The tallies weren't encouraging, but Zathi rallied them anyway.

"This is not beyond our strength," she called. "Take care of each other, and we can do it."

The guardswomen shouted together, "Aye Sergeant!"

The enemy galloped closer. Duessa couldn't stop thinking how scared she had been, the last time a bunch of guards charged toward her. The tearing pain as they grabbed her by her hair. Hard blows, and the vile taste of blood in her mouth. All that mixed with newer images. Flames in her eyes, her hair scorching, the agony of a fiery grip on her neck. A shaking hand rubbed the throbbing scars that she was forced to carry.

Duessa couldn't protect herself either time. Why did she think this situation would be any different?

Beside the wagon, Keerin matched paces with Razeet, who had her crossbow loaded and was fussing with the bolts in her quiver. The sisters reached out and clasped hands, no words spoken.

Duessa lowered her hand, drawing on *vitalis* to steady herself. This wasn't like last time. One important thing was different. Today, Duessa wasn't alone.

~ ~ ~

They were here! Ar-Lizelle scanned the familiar faces from the Larder. There was Duessa, with her disgusting burn scars, and fat Bettain, with Elldri hiding behind them. Alemin sat turned around on the driver's bench. A strange relief mixed with the rising heat of battle. Soon they would be reunited, those missing pieces of herself. They would toil under her command, as was right.

Then there was Lorrah, daring to prance around on Ar-Lizelle's stolen horse. Oh, how her cursed little sister was going to pay for that! Still, Ar-Lizelle couldn't focus only on Lorrah. That had been her weakness, and look what it cost her last time.

"Those bitches," Ar-Javan complained as he brought his blood bay up on her right. Loose hair blew into his face, and he jerked his chin to flip it away.

"We told you they wouldn't be fooled," Ar-Kyanon called from the other side.

"Fuck you," Ar-Javan snarled.

"No thanks," Ar-Kyanon retorted.

"Quiet! Save it for the enemy," Ar-Lizelle yelled at both of them. "Ar-Kyanon, stay at my left. Endole! You and Groff stay with us."

"Yes warden," they chorused.

"Thessal," she shouted to the Ebruc sergeant. "Your advice!"

"I thought you were in charge," Ar-Javan sneered, but Sergeant Thessal seemed to appreciate being consulted.

"Are we striking to capture or kill?" he asked.

"Capture if possible," Ar-Lizelle replied.

"Then we can fan out, come at them from both sides," the sergeant answered, "but we have to do it fast. Our horses can't keep this pace forever."

"Understood," Ar-Lizelle called back. They had been riding hard, and there was a chance their mounts could fail them.

Ar-Kyanon said, "Focus on one of them, try to get her out of the wagon."

The sergeant nodded. "Subdue one, then pick off the next."

"Only the mages," Ar-Javan interrupted. "Those guardswomen are traitors. If we take a few of them alive, I'll get them to talk."

"They were never my prisoners," Ar-Lizelle answered. "I don't care what you do to them."

Ar-Javan replied with a disgusting leer.

~ ~ ~

The pursuing guards caught up almost without trying. The oxen were that slow. Ar-Lizelle was grinning, confident of victory. Duessa felt a strange sensation in her chest. Even if they were enemies, somehow they still belonged together. She shook her arms and hands, loosening her shoulders and trying to shed the unwelcome connection. That was when she noticed another familiar face.

"Hey, is that Kyanon?" she burst out indignantly.

Alemin and Bettain both snapped around. Even Elldri took a scared look.

"Seems like it," Bettain gave grim confirmation.

Alemin stood on the bench, holding to the back for balance. "Kyanon, what are you doing?"

A sneer twisted his mouth. "What does it look like? You traitors are coming back to the Larder."

"You'd take sides with the Lizard?" Bettain yelled.

Ar-Lizelle scowled at the insulting nickname, but Kyanon shouted back.

"That's right, because she made me a decent offer. I'm her second, when we get back. What did all of you give me?"

"A way out," Lorrah called defiantly.

Kyanon retorted, "Here's some food, and off the wagon you go."

Duessa felt a momentary hesitation. Was this in some way their fault? But Bettain yelled back at him, "Oh no, you don't get to blame that on us."

"We had no reason to trust them," Zathi called to the mages. "This just shows we were right."

"All it shows," Ar-Lizelle taunted, "is that your fine words about kindness and acceptance are a lie."

"That's not true," Alemin answered, but Duessa shouted louder.

"We were in it together. Every day the screaming, the starvation —"

"Oh, woe is me!" Ar-Lizelle mocked

"Was that all a lie?" Duessa's scars puckered and stretched as she shrieked at Kyanon, the way she had wanted to shriek at Ar-Lannon, Doromy and Gauer for all these years.

"Together? Only if I was a girl," Kyanon shouted back. "I always knew you'd turn on me, Duessa. You and those two leeches."

"Give it up," Cylass interrupted. "How can we slow them down?"

"We talked about this," Jaxynne said from the left side. "We have to shoot their horses." Sethamis threw her a hurt look, but didn't argue.

"They're in range now," Razeet urged.

Duessa tried to control her temper. "Do you have to stop and aim? You'll be left behind!"

"In about the next minute, it's not going to matter," Razeet answered, grim but determined.

~ ~ ~

Keep the traitors distracted, Ar-Lizelle thought to herself. Don't let them find their balance. She called to Lorrah, "Give me back Roxalen, and I'll go easy on you."

Lorrah laughed mockingly. "I won her fair and square. She's mine now!"

"Not for much longer!" Ar-Lizelle stretched out her hand, slowly allowing her fire whip to coil out. Ar-Kyanon's horse snorted, but he managed to keep control of it. "Oh my mark," she called. The people on the cart raised their own hands in defiance.

She cracked her whip, aiming at the flank of the

sorrel their sergeant rode. Sparks burst and scattered, on Lorrah's barrier. Ar-Kyanon followed with a blast of fire, also deflected, but it kept their attention on him while the Ebruc guardsmen veered aside, getting into position. Ar-Lizelle lashed harder, testing the barrier's strength. After a moment, she realized that only two of them were attacking.

"Ar-Javan!" she yelled. "Do your part."

"Your whip keeps scaring my horse," he complained. It was true, the blood bay was tossing its head and whiffing anxiously. It tried to dart aside. Ar-Javan managed to curb the horse and conjured a halo of lightning around his fist.

"Strike together," Ar-Lizelle ordered. "No slacking off."

"Watch it," Groff called suddenly.

In the moments she had been distracted, the fleeing guardswomen had suddenly changed their tactics. Two of the warriors and the archers had turned about and were forming a wedge. Before she could react, they turned their horses and charged, coming straight for Ar-Lizelle!

"Revenge!" they all cried.

~ ~ ~

Duessa watched and waited for Tisha to lower her barrier so she and Bettain could launch their bolts. She closed her mouth on a gasp as *lethentros* surged to her calling. It passed through her body like a hive of stinging wasps.

"Did she say Ar-Javan?" Jaxynne demanded.

"You think that's him?" Keerin's face had been set, prepared for the fight, but now she turned murderous.

"We don't know it's the same one," Zathi corrected, with a steely gaze over her shoulder.

Jaxynne countered, "What if it is?"

After a moment, Zathi nodded curtly. "Giniver, you and Cylass stay here. Keerin with me. Lorrah, Jazynne and Razeet, follow."

"Yes sergeant," the chorus was a bit ragged as they urged their horses into place and then all wheeled together.

"Revenge!" Zathi exclaimed, and the others answered her, "Revenge!"

"What are they doing?" Bettain cried, waving a fist at the enemy guards who were swiftly moving the encircle the wagon. "We're being surrounded, and all the best fighters just leave?"

Tisha said, "This is personal for them, but I don't know why."

Duessa leaned around to ask, "Who's this Ar-Javan?"

Alemin shook his head, too, but Sethamis called back, "Thersa was one of us Badgers. She was abused by a mage and lost her previous position. Alemin, keep your eyes front. Don't let them hurt Star or Moon!"

"Can we worry about that later?" Cylass cut in, and Duessa turned with a start.

Five of the enemy guards were trying to come alongside the wagon. Dark grins split their faces, and their weapons gleamed with vicious promise.

Bettain cried, "Give us an opening!"

"Be ready." Tisha's pretty face was sad but resolute. "You'll have a count of five."

Too-bright steel flashed as the soldiers swung toward the wagon, but then yelled with frustration as their weapons deflected off the shield. In the moment of recoil, Tisha pushed. Her barrier slammed outward, and she murmured, "Now."

The barrier flickered away. Duessa and Bettain

released their bolts. The guardsmen raised their own shields, calling encouragement to their horses as flames roared around them. Bettain launched bolt after bolt, alternating between the two men in the front. Duessa's flame was different, more golden than yellow. She couldn't think about that now. The soldier nearest her was ready to swing again.

Instead of aiming at the guard, Duessa focused her power on his mount. There was a padded blanked under the leather and wooden saddle, cloth with a short red fringe. Nothing that would tangle in the rider's gear, but still a point of weakness. Duessa set it on fire. The horse began to twist and jump, squealing as it tried to get away from the flame.

"Good one!" Bettain clouted her shoulder as Tisha's barrier snapped back up. She'd forced one of her targets to back away, too.

Their moment of shared victory was shattered by Elldri's despairing shriek.

~ ~ ~

The two renegade guardswomen charged at Ar-Lizelle, brown faces ruthlessly intent. Lorrah was in the rear, with the archers, but the glimmer of her shield formed a wedge in the air.

"Out of the way!" Ar-Lizelle reined her horse left, avoiding the slicing edge. Ar-Kyanon cursed as her mount slammed into his. The bolt he was aiming at the archers went wild. Lorrah's hands swept wide. Ar-Lizelle felt the impact on her shoulder and knee as the barrier slammed open between her and Ar-Javan.

"Warden!" Endole was at her side, protecting her from the oncoming warriors. Groff likewise moved to protect Ar-Kyanon, crying, "Get behind me!"

Ar-Lizelle's inferior horse squealed and skittered wildly out of the way. By the time she controlled it, the two renegades were a little past her, shouting and crowding Ar-Javan away. She had a moment to realize the guardswomen were using the exact strategy that her soldiers proposed. What she didn't understand was why.

"You remember Thersa?" one of them yelled. "That was my partner, you bastard!"

"She died because of what you did!" The sergeant swung her shield and narrowly missed Ar-Javan's neck.

"If you... want to... tell me about it..." The mage still tried coaxing them, though his horse's jumping roughened his voice.

"Hit them," Ar-Lizelle commanded. Ar-Javan was obnoxious, but she still needed him. Ar-Kyanon blasted with fire, and she lashed with her flame whip, but Lorrah's damned barrier was still there. "Stop it, you little bitch. Your fight is with me."

Lorrah smirked a little, safely back with the archers and hiding behind her barrier. Roxalen was hardly sweating even now, which was all the more reason Ar-Lizelle wanted her horse back. Lorrah shoved harder with her barrier, forcing them away. Glancing over her shoulder, she said to the archers, "Do you have the shot?"

"Soon as they disengage," one of them answered. The other was focused down the length of her crossbow.

What Ar-Lizelle saw, but they didn't, was how the Ebruc soldiers on the right of the wagon were executing their own plan. Two of them engaged the lone guardswoman, keeping her from protecting the passengers. Another pair rode in close enough to grab someone. Alemin whirled, but before he could stop them, a shrieking and struggling figure went to the ground. The wagon kept moving, but the two soldiers jumped from the saddle to pile on it. A shrill voice rose in panic.

"Sounds like Elldri," Ar-Kyanon remarked with stony indifference. "Groff, come on!" He reined around to join that side of the fight.

The two guardswomen whirled their horses. "Shit!" the sergeant yelled, and they both spurred back toward the wagon. Lorrah also turned to look, but the archers never lost their focus. There were two loud snaps, and two nasty thuds. Ar-Javan's horse squealed and reared up. Ar-Javan made no effort to control it. As Ar-Lizelle watched, he toppled from the saddle with a pair of bolts embedded in his chest.

"Yeah!" cheered one of the archers, but Lorrah called out, "Hurry!" She and the two archers spun their horses, following their comrades to the wagon.

Ar-Lizelle spared a moment to be sure Ar-Javan wasn't moving before she spurred her own horse. "After them!"

There was no way she would let Lorrah get away again. Or that was what Ar-Lizelle intended, until another rising shriek pierced her mind like a fiery spear.

~ ~ ~

"Elldri!" Duessa cried.

She only had a moment to glimpse the struggling pile as the wagon rolled past. A guard straddled Elldri's back, twisting her arm up and back. A second one strode close enough to aim a kick at her head.

"I'm coming!" Bettain tried to crowd between Tisha and Cylass, but the guardsman pushed her back from Tisha, who continued her swaying dance.

"Don't get off the wagon," he warned.

The next moment Tisha called, "Shield your thoughts!"

Before Duessa could even decide what she meant, Elldri's shriek crashed into her mind. Her soul was splitting, torn apart from within. Something dark and horrible flooded through her. Alemin and Bettain were bent over, clutching their heads and wailing together as if they had all one voice.

It was like the Larder again. The anguished howl reverberated inside and outside her. In a dim way, she heard Cylass demanding what was wrong, and some vague reply from Tisha. Duessa could only rock and keen with terror.

Yards behind the wagon, a dark blur erupted where the soldiers had tackled Elldri. Duessa thought it was a fountain of blood, darker than mage robes, but then it fanned out into jagged tentacle arms. The pressure in her mind eased. She blinked and tried to understand.

The squid-like horror hovered, Elldri's face amid blackened scraps of fabric. Her toothless mouth stretched in a hideous O. There was more screaming, but it came from the men who had been beating her. Shark-toothed tentacles shoved them off, but also carved flesh and slithered through gaps in their armor. Blood spattered around her. Elldri's tentacles drove into their throats, silencing their cries, but then came worse — a sickening flood of desire to rend and kill and consume, not their flesh but their very souls.

There was so much of it. Too much. Duessa's mind went momentarily blank as the sensations overwhelmed her.

"No, no," Bettain was moaning. Alemin stared with dreadful recognition.

Duessa gagged and choked out, "Elldri's a devourer?"

XI — SOUL STORM

N o!" Ar-Lizelle screamed, not even knowing what it was she rejected.

Ar-Kyanon bent over his horse's neck, hands clasped to his head. "Stop, make it stop!"

All thoughts of battle or revenge were swallowed in that rush of alien desires. This had to be some new trick, or... It was too vivid, too real. She clung to the saddle and tried to make sense of it.

Both sides reined around in confusion. Horses whinnied and galloped past. Ar-Lizelle's mind didn't want to accept the reality, but it was there — the revenant from the Larder. No longer a mere nightmare, or a psychic presence. It was here, in open daylight, draining the life from those soldiers. Its hunger ignited like a furnace, and the fuel for it was their souls.

"Is that... Elldri?" Ar-Kyanon was wild-eyed and sweating.

"Yes." Ar-Lizelle heard her own voice high and shrill with fear. "It's the same link, how we felt we were getting close to them."

"I can't keep it out of my head!" Ar-Kyanon moaned.

In the wagon, Alemin, Bettain and Duessa were hunched over and yelling, just like Ar-Lizelle and Ar-Kyanon had. Their friends reached for them, offering reassurance. For some reason, that brought Ar-Lizelle a little back to herself. Yes, this was bad, but she would not cry. She was the warden of the Larder, a fully trained mage, and she was done with this weakness.

Somehow Groff and Endole kept their horses nearby, and they babbled questions. "What is that?" and, "Are you all right?" Ar-Lizelle assumed they had also felt something, though they were not mages. Endole rubbed his forehead under the rim of his helmet and Groff was a bit unsteady in the saddle.

"That," Ar-Lizelle declared, "is Elldri. It is also the revenant from the Larder. Before you ask, I don't know how."

"That is?" Endole grimaced.

Elldri dropped the husks of the two soldiers she had devoured. The Ebruc soldiers gathered some indignation on behalf of their fallen comrades. With wild cries, they galloped with swords bared, reaching low to slash at the revenant. Somehow, without legs, Elldri flung herself up at them. More screams echoed over the fields as she whirled like a blood-soaked dust devil, tentacles whipping around to seek new victims. Driven by animal instinct, their horses whinnied and bucked, trying to get away from the fiend.

"What are we supposed to do?" Groff muttered, stunned.

The Ebruc guards tried to slash through Elldri's corded arms, but it did no good. The tentacles whipped around them, and the revenant used that to launch herself. Elldri was an empty, maddened beast, ravenous for souls to fill the chasm within her. She swung between the men, leaving bloody gashes and vacant eyes. The air was full of dust and the bright stench of blood.

"I am the Warden of the Larder and this mad thing is my responsibility. Come on!" She spurred forward, ruthlessly curbing her horse when it tried to veer away. In a commanding tone she cried out, "Elldri, stop! Give up this instant."

Elldri did pause, and Ar-Lizelle sensed a faint recognition. Just as Elldri knew her friends on the wagon and avoided attacking them, she understood that Ar-Lizelle was part of the Larder. They were connected. And somehow Ar-Lizelle knew that the Larder had been Elldri's refuge from a world of unbearable torment.

Ar-Kyanon raged, "Get out of my head, Elldri! I'm not listening to this."

"Leave her alone!" Bettain roared back from the wagon.

"Shut up, you bitch!" Ar-Kyanon raged at Bettain. "Nobody cares about your feelings, Elldri. Get your damned crying out of my head!"

Ar-Lizelle, too, hated these raw emotions that didn't belong to her, but Elldri's answering wail told her the rejection was a fatal cut. Through the bond, Ar-Lizelle felt something slip, then shatter. Even later, she was never sure who it was that broke.

"Stop!" she cried, but it was too late.

Ar-Kyanon drove his barely controlled horse the last few feet to the wagon. He fired blast after blast to incinerate that monster and all the traitors who sheltered it. He never reached it. One of their mages still had a barrier up, and even if she hadn't, Elldri was a screaming black storm of torment. She never flinched from his fire bolts and engulfed him in a mass of tentacles.

"Stop," Ar-Lizelle demanded, retreating despite herself. So many pains, stabbing and slashing all over, compressed Ar-Kyanon into a howling package of agony. In seconds it turned to numbness, a cold too deep to bear. All his power and life drained into Elldri's voracious maw.

"Let him go!" Ar-Lizelle lashed with her whip, a

reflex of her anger and fear. This couldn't be her fate. She wouldn't accept it.

The creature who had been Elldri hurled itself off Ar-Kyanon, and his horse immediately bucked his limp body to the ground. Ar-Lizelle saw only darkness as the seething mass of tentacles enveloped her. There was so much pain that it didn't hurt at all. She was screeching and suffocating as spreading numbness dragged her down into nothingness.

~ ~ ~

The wagon shook wildly as the smell of blood drove the bawling oxen to reckless speed. Duessa and Bettain leaned on each other, while Alemin sagged in the front seat. Of all the mages, only Tisha and Lorrah were not affected by Elldri's hellish broadcast.

"Protect yourself, Alemin," Tisha called. Duessa realized Tisha was trying to shield them, but with a different barrier than she used against physical force.

"That won't work." Duessa croaked. Her scars throbbed with the tension.

"We're connected to her because of the Larder," Alemin said.

"Stop it, Elldri. Just stop," Bettain chanted, unheard.

Duessa tried to focus beyond Elldri's emotional storm. Ebruc's soldiers were dropping back in confusion. So many were dead, including the sergeant, who had been in the first group that grabbed Elldri. Duessa felt the burning hunger as the devourer engulfed Kyanon.

"What can we do?" Lorrah stood in the stirrups, her voice shrill with worry. "She's attacking them!"

Duessa tried to figure out why that mattered. Weren't they enemies? The rest of the Badgers were regrouping. Zathi rode up beside Giniver, finding out how bad her injury was, while Keerin met up with Jaxynne and Razeet.

"Good shooting," Keerin said.

"Thanks," Jaxynne answered absently. The compliment hardly seemed important compared to the horror on the road behind them.

"Now what?" Razeet asked.

"Stop the wagon!" Tisha tried to push between Bettain and Cylass. "Alemin, Lorrah, help me."

"What?" Clyass grabbed her arm just before she jumped down. "Lady, no!"

"Those soldiers have no chance. Their weapons are useless," she argued. "We have to try."

"That's crazy," Duessa gasped. "Spells aren't helping." She couldn't bring herself to watch as Elldri swallowed Ar-Kyanon's struggling form. Yet another man who had betrayed her.

"We aren't using their spells," Tisha was calm, her gentle determination at odds with any rational grasp of the situation. "Come with me if you want to, Cylass. Bettain, you come, too."

"Me?" Bettain muttered, confused.

Sethamis got the wagon to a lurching stop, and the three of them jumped down. Lorrah reached down from Torch, steadying Alemin as he got down from the diver's bench. Duessa hesitated, torn between joining them and keeping herself safer. Tisha advanced with a dancing stride, raising her hands as if about to perform in the minstrel show.

"What do you plan?" Zathi turned her sorrel about. "Easy, Ember."

"Catch her first," Tisha answered after a small hop and kick. "Bettain, I know you care for Elldri. Call to her. See if she'll come to you."

"All right," Bettain agreed doubtfully.

"We'll enclose her in a sphere," Tisha instructed Lorrah and Alemin, hips swaying. "Not tight, don't scare her more than she already is. We'll try and soothe her while Bettain talks her down."

Behind her, Duessa heard Sethamis' anxious words. "It'll be hard to get the boys moving again. I hope they know what they're doing."

"If we don't trust our mages —" Zathi shook her head, for once uncertain.

"I think I get what Tisha plans," Duessa said, though she kept a sharp watch in case any of the enemy soldiers tried to come at them. "Elldri blew up when the guards hurt her, and when Kyanon rejected her. So if we do the opposite..."

She trailed off, unsure. Violence was easy. Anyone could see how to lash out, what to target. What was the reverse? Singing Elldri a lullaby wasn't going to help.

Duessa knew what Elldri was doing to Ar-Kyanon, the sheer horror of it. Ar-Lizelle swung her fire whip, demanding that she let him go. Lorrah gave a kind of yelp as Elldri turned on Ar-Lizelle.

"Elldri!" Strain was clear in Bettain's voice as she strode forward. "Elldri, over here. Look at me, love!"

Duessa hardly dared to believe it when the creature that had been their friend did pause. An echo of Ar-Lizelle's panic rang in their minds, but once Bettain had her attention, she kept talking.

"That's it. Elldri, love, we're here." The older woman spoke as if to a very young child. "It's going to be all right. We're all here and we're so worried for you."

"Help her," Alemin murmured. "We're all in the bond. Think it together with Bettain."

It was awkward, but Duessa focused her newly

cultivated meditation on Bettain. Not so much the words, a meaningless babble of reassurances, but the feeling of caring. Alemin, too, tried to reinforce Bettain's comforting words.

"There now, stop crying," Bettain called more softly. "I can't understand when you cry. Can you come over? Tell us what you need."

Elldri did not stop crying, but the tone of it changed from ravenous fury to a wail of grief and terror. Slowly she released Ar-Lizelle, who clung to her horse's saddle as it skittered away. The young devourer glided over the air toward Bettain, moving slowly as a child with a scrape on its knee. Devastation flooded through the link, the shattering knowledge of what she had become.

"That's it. Good girl. Stay calm, we won't hurt you," Bettain said.

Tisha, Alemin and Lorrah raised their barriers, forming a sphere to gently enclose Elldri. Or, they tried to be gentle, but Elldri reacted to their power as she always did, with a cry of panic. She lurched forward, tentacles slashing, to crash against the barrier, but then recoiled from touching it.

"Keep at it," Alemin encouraged.

Duessa jumped down from the wagon and ran to join Bettain's desperate chant: "Elldri, love. Elldri, it's all right. Don't fight us. We know you're in there! Come back to us."

Elldri screamed with fury and betrayal. Through her fierce concentration, Duessa saw Zathi urge her horse around to face the opposing forces. A guard she knew from the prison, Groff, was off his horse and bending over Ar-Kyanon. Endole had caught Ar-Lizelle's horse and was begging her to answer him. The other soldiers still had their swords out, but they were in complete disarray. Many were wounded, and riderless horses were running about.

Zathi surveyed the mess and barked out, "Men!"

They halted, instinctively turning toward her. Even though she wasn't their sergeant, they needed the reassurance of command. More quietly, Zathi said, "Get them out of here."

"What are you going to do?" a soldier asked. It was a challenge, yet also a fearful plea.

Zathi gave a curt laugh. "I'm not doing anything. This is for the mages to handle. Take your wounded to safety."

~ ~ ~

Ar-Lizelle was drowning in a swamp of everyone else's feelings. The world around her was gray and dim, Endole's anxious voice muffled.

"Warden, can you hear me?"

Somehow she dragged herself free enough to realize that Elldri was moving away. Ar-Lizelle's mage robe was slashed all over, the crimson renewed by bleeding from dozens of stinging wounds. Her ears rang with a hollow buzz. Yet her soul, it seemed, was still in her body.

A woman's voice came, as if over a vast distance, telling them to take their wounded and go. Ar-Lizelle wobbled upright, though her many cuts deepened their nagging sting. Color was starting to come back into the world. With it came her own, honest anger.

"No," she panted and dragged her horse around to confront the opposing sergeant. "You don't give the orders here. I'm in command!"

"You're still alive?" The sergeant shook her head a little. "Lorrah will be glad, I suppose."

"Don't say that name to me," Ar-Lizelle snarled. She was upright, but too shaky for battle. Her men couldn't be allowed to know that. "Endole. Groff. Report."

"Ar-Javan's dead, shot. Four of the Ebruc squad are down," Endole replied.

Groff continued the grim tally. "Ar-Kyanon's breathing, but I don't think much longer." A rattling sigh from the ground reinforced his prediction.

Ar-Lizelle tried to think. Behind the woman sergeant, the mages were in a tight cluster. They had imprisoned Elldri in a sphere made of several barriers. That was good, keep her contained. Keep those mages busy, too. This was the perfect time to strike, if only she had the power left after Elldri's attack.

The female sergeant drawled, "I hope you don't plan to interfere." At her sharp gesture, the renegade guardswomen began to fan out between the two sides.

Within her prison, Elldri keened and crashed against the sides, only to shrink away in agony. With a start, Arl-Lizelle realized she no longer felt the girl's emotions. Nearby, Duessa and Bettain clasped hands and reached toward the imprisoned revenant, calling Elldri's name. Come back to us, or some such nonsense.

Then, of all things, Alemin turned toward Ar-Lizelle. "You have to help, too."

"What? She'd never," Bettain scoffed, and Ar-Lizelle shrieked with scornful laughter.

"Help you? A bunch of traitors?" She was laughing too hard, even hysterically, but there was no end to this renegade's ridiculous notions. "The only thing I'll help you with is going back to prison."

"Don't be such a bitch," Lorrah yelled, though her teeth were gritted in concentration to hold Elldri.

"We're all bound through the Larder. I know you feel it," Alemin pleaded.

But she didn't. Ar-Lizelle was alone in her own mind. It was a tremendous relief. Yes, the connection had been useful, but she had had enough of it.

"You saved us once before," Duessa called. "Why would you do that, except that we're connected. As shitty as it is, we need you."

And Bettain, the most surly of them all, added, "Come on, Lizard, be useful!"

"I am not wallowing in your ridiculous sentiment," Ar-Lizelle snapped. She sat rigid in the saddle to conceal a shudder. Ar-Kyanon's soul had been torn away, and she had come terribly close to suffering the same fate. The Ebruc soldiers were regrouping, frightened but waiting for her command.

She knew exactly what that command should be, but if she gave it they would all see how much of her power had been leeched away. There was no way out of this!

~ ~ ~

"We can't wait for her," Tisha declared. She still swayed gently, hips and arms curving against the dusty air. "Elldri can't stay like this. It's too dangerous."

"I'm talking to her, but she's not calming down," Bettain said.

"I know," Tisha replied. "Lorrah and Alemin, can you hold her?"

"For a while," Lorrah promised. Duessa sensed a bit of wobbling as Tisha shifted her focus, but the sphere remained intact.

"We have it," Alemin said.

"What do you want us to do?" Duessa was ready to try anything. Time was running out. Lorrah and Alemin were already sweating with the effort of keeping Elldri contained. If those soldiers attacked while they were all busy, Elldri was going to get loose. She'd lay waste to all of them.

"I'm going to try and heal her," Tisha answered. "Lorrah and Alemin have to concentrate on the sphere. You and Bettain try to call her back to what she was."

Elldri's tentacles were flat against the barrier, pushing wildly and digging with saw-like teeth, only to gasp and jerk back. She hovered for a moment, no longer keening, with all her tentacles coiled around her and flicking to try and shed the pain.

"Focus on Elldri. Think of your friendship," Tisha coached. The familiar golden light was rising around her, sweeping in curlicues that met and merged into the sphere. With it flowed the soothing power of *vitalis*, softening and soothing everyone's raw nerves.

"Everything we went through," Duessa murmured, feeling Bettain's chapped fingers linked to her own. She didn't actually remember deciding to do that.

"All those days we sweated and starved and watched out for each other," Bettain said.

An image appeared, Alemin's memory of Elldri trading him for an orange wedge at breakfast. "You're a good person," he whispered to her. "This isn't you."

Tisha's healing power flowed through everyone in the linkage. It was cool and warm at once, a gentle breeze matched with a slowly flowing stream. Everyone in the Larder's circuit poured in their love, care and concern. The broken creature writhed, weeping, as if their compassion was burning her.

"My kids are gone. You're my kid now," Bettain told Elldri, all her jaded skepticism cast aside. "Don't leave me."

"We care about you," Duessa pressed into the mix. "Don't turn into this thing."

"Come back to us," Alemin said.

Duessa's own fears dissolved among that flow of power. Elldri's pain was jagged and terrible, but they didn't let her go. With Tisha guiding them, Alemin, Bettain and

Duessa sent her love, peace and healing.

The black energy, *voromnil*, bubbled and boiled away in the golden light infusing the sphere. Tentacles slowly gathered back to their original human form. Elldri slumped on the bottom of the sphere. Her face streamed with black tears.

~ ~ ~

Compassion. Reassurance. A will for healing. Those soft emotions circulated among the mages, a swelling tide that wanted to drag Ar-Lizelle under. She couldn't believe someone would care enough to try and save a wretched creature like Elldri.

Yet, it worked! Elldri struggled and thrashed as the blackness of her corruption burned away. Under it was clean brown skin, a shave-headed girl in ragged commoner clothes. Alemin and Lorrah looked exhausted as they carefully lowered their sphere. The sobbing broken thing was just Elldri, crooking her fingers into the dust and wailing with grief over what she had become.

"They... saved her," Groff muttered. Endole hit his shoulder with a clang. "Snap out of it."

"I don't believe it," Ar-Lizelle growled. "This is some trick."

The renegade mages converged on Elldri. Bettain pulled her unresisting form and wept as she rocked her. Duessa and Alemin jumped in. The fool donkey came trotting back and darted around, trying to get back to whose ever it was. The beautiful woman who had been dancing now leaned against it, visibly tired. Her bodyguard hurried to place himself between her and the soldiers.

Ar-Lizelle couldn't deny there was a seductive allure to the thought of being part of something so incredible. That was probably just what these renegades wanted. They would erode Ar-Lizelle's personality, neuter her fierce drive to victory, and replace it with their degrading softness.

"Ugh!" she cried, shaking the temptation away. There was no place in Skaythe for such disgusting sentiment. They were all asking to be killed. Well, Ar-Lizelle wasn't going to be part of it. The minstrels thought they were doing something nice, but it only showed how evil they really were.

While that sloppy drama went on, the guards from Ebruc had come into lines to face the renegade guardswomen. Despite a number of looks over their shoulders, the guardswomen kept their minds on more important things. Their sergeant caught Ar-Lizelle's eye.

"Well," came her cold brisk voice. "Do we fight on?"

Oh, how Ar-Lizelle wanted to! "I suppose you think we're cowards," she spat.

"Not at all," the female sergeant replied. "I just wonder if now is the time."

The answer was obvious. Ar-Lizelle had lost almost half her force, including the other two mages. The survivors were shaken by the disaster of what had seemed an easy victory. The renegades were tired and distracted, but they still had almost their entire crew. They must be riding high, inspired by that dancer's success. Even now, Lorrah jumped back up on Roxalen and rode up to join the sergeant's line.

"Maybe not," Ar-Lizelle admitted. The words were bitter ashes in her mouth. Behind her, she felt the mixture of consternation and relief among her guards and those from Ebruc. Nobody wanted to admit they had failed. Maybe she was just nervous, or still raw from the emotions pouring over her, but she felt them all questioning her decision.

She was about to turn, blazing at them all not to judge her, but Lorrah walked her horse up slowly past the others. "Lizzie," she said.

"Don't call me that!" Ar-Lizelle screeched. They hadn't used such childish nicknames in a decade. "We're not little kids, *Lorrie.*"

Lorrah ignored the taunt. "I know you hate me, but I don't hate you."

"That's a stupid thing to say," Ar-Lizelle ranted. "Of course I hate you! You cost me everything — twice!"

"I made a choice," Lorrah answered. Around her, the guardswomen's sharp eyes watched to make sure nobody had moved. "You can choose, too. Let the past be past."

"You're not only stupid, you're naive." Of all the things, Ar-Lizelle could never accept the offered truce. Not when her highest priority was finding someone else to bear the curse of the Larder. "In Dar-Gothull's name, I will bring you down."

"Will you just stop?" Lorrah burst out. "You could have died." There was bitterness in her voice, but in her dark eyes there was sadness.

"Do you expect me to think that you care?" Ar-Lizelle snarled. "It's six years too late for that. You and your emotional tricks are nothing but sick illusions. But fine. I'll let you go. Try to fight the invincible wizard-king. Go and die!"

She reined around hard, had to control her squealing horse, and told the surviving soldiers, "Salvage what you want."

As they scrambled to obey, Ar-Lizelle stiffened her back and trotted slowly away. Let the fools catch up if they wanted to. It sounded like the renegade sergeant was moving her people out, as well. Space grew between their two groups. Just for a moment, Ar-Lizelle actually missed that lost connection with her prisoners. How ridiculous. They didn't care about her. Elldri, Elldri, Elldri was all any of them thought about. Elldri, the horrible baby revenant.

Ar-Lizelle trotted past the handcart those minstrels had left behind. She pulled up beside it and glanced over. The Ebruc soldiers were stripping the fallen of their armor and personal items, but they obviously needed more time.

Infuriating! Ar-Lizelle shoved with her foot, trying to tip the cart over. The wheels remained stubbornly planted. Spitefully, she backed her horse away and set the cart on fire.

~ ~ ~

Now that the fighting was over, Sethamis risked jumping down to check on the oxen. The guardswomen stayed mounted, but they stroked their horses necks and tried to rub off some of the sweat. Murmured praises formed a backdrop to Alemin, Duessa and Bettain getting Elldri up in the wagon. Tisha took a moment to fuss over Riprap, too, before she looked at the slash Giniver had taken on her shoulder.

Through all that, Jaxynne and Zathi stayed on guard in case the other side changed their minds. Except for Ar-Lizelle burning Tisha's cart as she rode away, there was no further hostility.

"The boys will be all right as long as we go easy," Sethamis told Zathi. "If we can find water, the animals need a good drink and a proper rub-down."

"I bet we do, too," Razeet said, wincing in sympathy as Tisha finished tending Giniver's shoulder.

"Let's not sit here in the open any longer than we have to," Zathi said. "We should try to camp under the trees tonight."

"Yes sergeant," the driver climbed back up to her bench. "Up, boys. Easy does it. Good boy, Star. Steady on, Moon."

It was a quiet group as the wagon got moving. Alemin, on the front bench, leaned back with his eyes closed. Lorrah stayed on her horse, though she yawned often. Duessa and Bettain cuddled Elldri between them in silence. The girl slumped listlessly, eyes open but not focused on anything the rest of them could see.

Tisha, last on the wagon, sighed as she looked back at her handcart blazing viciously in the middle of the road. "We weren't going to pose as rag pickers any more, I guess," she murmured to Cylass, who walked behind with the donkey's lead.

"Probably not," was his stoic agreement.

"Or a circus," Keerin said. "Your tent was in the handcart, wasn't it?"

"No, Riprap has it. At least we have shelter," Tisha said.

"She didn't have to be such a bitch, though." Lorrah looked back with disappointment and disgust.

"That isn't your fault," Zathi told her.

"Not everyone can just change," Duessa said. She was thinking of herself, how hard it had been to take up *vitalis* even when she was interested. Bettain seemed to take it as a poke at herself.

"Not everyone wants to change," she snorted. "Besides, I'm not sure what anybody could do with a sister like that."

"We couldn't have kept up the pretense much longer," Zathi said.

"Word was getting out," Jaxynne agreed.

Except for Elldri, everyone on the wagon nodded glumly. After a moment, Alemin woke up enough to say, "It wasn't always pretend."

"I know." Zathi leaned forward to stroke her horse's neck. "Good work, Ember." The sorrel bobbed its head and whiffed to her.

"We couldn't have avoided that fight," Duessa said. "If we gave up, you know what that would mean. The Badgers and Cylass would be executed, and we mages would be marched back to the Larder." Her heart thudded and her stomach felt sour, just thinking about it.

"We'd be agreeing that Dar-Gothull is right," Tisha said. "That people are just insects to be crushed, and mages are rightfully his food."

"And that the Larder is where we belong. That we deserve to be there." Bettain vibrated with fury at the thought. "I couldn't do that, could you? Go back with open eyes."

"Into my sister's prison?" Lorrah grimaced at the notion. Alemin's profile was rigid. Duessa shook her head with grim denial, and between them, Elldri's dark eyes gleamed with haunted memory. She still didn't say anything.

"I know you feel bad," Duessa told her softly, "and I have no idea how all that... could have happened, but you saved us, Elldri. Don't ever forget that."

~ ~ ~

Shonn knew they were well into Pulgoll when the coast bent farther to the east. The high mountains they tracked around gave way to flatter land, where the mangroves once again extended their braided channels. Glad as he was to get under the humid shade of the mangroves again, he knew Piyaro and his men were not so fond of it.

As they set camp beside the last of the landings Shonn had been told of, Cothyr complained, "When will we walk on solid ground?"

"Probably tomorrow," Shonn told him, "and then we're all going to miss the shade."

"As long as my feet stay dry," Rowlan put in.

"You whine like a bunch of women," Piyaro scolded. "Be grateful we've had a good enough guide through all that." He nodded to Shonn, a gesture he appreciated.

"Excuse me," Nyette coughed wryly. "It isn't the

woman who's whining here."

Several of the men chuckled at her wisecrack. They had all gotten used to each other over the past days, and Cothyr was no longer the only one to flirt occasionally. Sergeant Piyaro just gave her a look.

"We are coming close, though," she added, and gazed speculatively to the north and east.

As Shonn had predicted, the character of the land changed while they moved farther along the coast. Swamps gave way to a thin band of dunes with tufts of coarse grasses in the dips between them. The dunes were broken by patches of brush alternating with slopes of tumbled stones. On the third day they saw the far shore of a shallow bay where a river met the sea. Beyond that, patches of fog flowed down another rubble slope.

"Here's where we turn inland," declared Piyaro, who had spent the early morning with Nyette, in intense study of his charts. Shonn remembered wondering why he was so stressed about it. "We'll come to a waterfall, Weeping Falls. Opshar is just a short march on from there."

"How do we get up all that?" Nyette regarded the unsteady scree with skepticism.

"There's a sort of trail." Shonn pointed it out to Piyaro, who quickly put his chart away.

"Right. I see it." The sergeant led them up a barely perceptible trail across more layers of rubble, rising toward rugged hills where scrubby trees trailed down from the highest ground. The squad toiled after him. Shonn found a place near the middle of the file, after Nyette. It was odd to give up his role as their leader. He didn't quite know what to do with himself.

The going was slow. Shonn's woven sandals, so well suited to the damp marsh, were inadequate to the rough terrain. Every step must be tested, and still he stumbled when the stones shifted under his feet. Curses echoed up the slope along with the clink and thump of falling rubble.

Going along with the Hawks had been easy, when he had only the urgent goal of catching up to Meven. Now the reality was closer. Worries pinched him, like land crabs reaching out from under a bush if he stepped too close. What if he'd come all this way and Meven wouldn't talk to him? Or if she wasn't even here?

His chest and legs ached with the difficulty of the climb, and a reflex of his old anger rose along with the rocky land. He wanted to see Meven. To touch her, to have her. He would take her back to Fang Marsh where she belonged. She owed him, after he'd come all this way.

Shonn tried to shove those ideas away. That kind of thinking was what made him break her trust. It was why he had to leave home and find her.

At last, the squad reached stable ground. A scant but visible trail led them across a relatively level hillside. Brush gave way to broad-leaved trees of a kind Shonn didn't know. Murmurs of relief scattered up and down their line.

"I told them they'd miss the shade," Shonn panted to Nyette. She glanced over her shoulder, narrow-eyed. "What's wrong?"

"We have work to do, Shonn." Saying no more, Nyette focused only on where she was stepping.

Reaction rippled through the ranks of toiling guardsmen. Like Shonn, they were surprised by the change in her bearing. Looking back, he remembered how she marveled at the ordinary world when he first took her through Fang Marsh. This journey was an opportunity for her to relax, have friends, and take in the world with curiosity. Now that time was over. This was the Nyette he first met in the temple school, fiercely concentrating on something he couldn't see.

Their trail was about to crest a rise when Nyette called softly, "Sergeant."

"Something?" Piyaro paused, no doubt as glad for a moment's rest as any of them.

"Let's keep low as we come over this." No longer a passive traveler, she was a mage who sought to direct them.

"You sense anything?" Piyaro's brows twitched as he took in the difference.

"The sun is full up and that fog hasn't moved," Nyette answered, but then allowed a moment of humor. "That, or I'm over-eager."

Everyone glanced back and down, where the calm surf folded itself in gleaming arches toward the shore. They were high enough up the hillside that distance muted the noise of waves, but there wasn't enough spray to explain the strands of white drifting lazily from beyond the river mouth.

"All right." Piyaro dropped to a crouch and motioned Rowlan forward. Everyone else was glad enough to crouch farther back from the edge. Some puffed and pressed their hands to their sides. Others sipped from water skins or pulled out rags to blot the sweat from their faces. Shonn was hot enough in his swamp linen sarong, with its loose overshirt. He didn't know how the men could stand it in their heavy plate armor.

Rowlan moved slowly to avoid kicking up any dust. Nyette tucked her skirt in and bent low to follow. The two raised just their heads to peer over the edge. Then the mage girl turned back to stare at Shonn. She tilted her head expectantly.

It took him a moment to understand what she meant. Fog? There had been fog around Meven's tower in Fang Marsh! He crouch-crawled up beside the others, and stopped abruptly. His heart pounded in his ears, and he couldn't seem to get a full breath. Then he forced out a low laugh.

White, shining, covered in mist...

"What is that?" Rowlan asked warily.

"Ice," Shonn breathed. There was an ice wall on the other side of the valley. Distance made it look skinny as a fence rail, but he knew it must be many feet tall. Meven was here, and no mistake! He still had a chance.

"Like on top of the mountains?" the guardsman frowned, confused.

"Exactly like that," Nyette said firmly.

"But what's it doing here?"

"That is an excellent question," Nyette replied.

With a disgusted grumble, Piyaro came up beside them. After his first rush of emotion, Shonn tried to think. Meven had put that wall up for a reason. He pulled his eyes away from the glittering slabs of ice and tried to see how they fit into the landscape.

The scene was at once strange and familiar. The ice wall was the familiar part. He had never looked upon this wide green valley before, all caught between two mountain ranges. Farm fields were visible off to his right. Before them, a wandering river divided the land into lopsided halves. It ended in a circular lake which drained out as curtains of water and spray, then went splashing down another rubble slope.

"There's Weeping Falls," Piyaro said.

"I've never seen a lake like that," Nyette murmured. Shonn just nodded.

Closer to the lake, a single farm house stood on a ridge surrounded by fruit trees. Terraced fields ranged below it, only a few of them with crops in the ground. Beyond the river mouth and the fertile bottomland, there was a gap between sea coast and mountain range. The ice wall blocked that space with its dramatic planes and towers. It shone, dazzling white against the earthy tones of grass and mountainside. The drifts of fog Nyette had noticed flowed out some distance from it before evaporating in the day's heat.

"Just like in Fang Marsh," Shonn said. "There's never any more or less fog."

"Why would she put it there?" Nyette wondered. "And look, there are more." She pointed more to the right, where several other stretches peeked around the edge of the hillside.

Now Cothyr moved up beside them. "What's on the other side of it?"

"It's the next county, Dunsaph." Piyaro thought about that. "It seems like your ice witch wanted to block anyone coming through."

"You think Dunsaph is getting into the middle of this?" Cothyr asked warily.

"I don't know who else would be coming that way," Piyaro answered.

"Traders?" Rowlan suggested.

"If it's Dunsaph, couldn't they sail around the wall?" Nyette asked.

"No, look behind us," Shonn said. The bay shimmered, streaked with lines of foam. "That's all reefs and shoals. You might get through with a small boat or a raft, if you knew the waters, but a ship big enough to carry troops would be wrecked for sure."

That was hardly the most important thing, anyway. Now Shonn knew he had been right. Meven was here. His heart soared, even as he dreaded facing her.

Piyaro and Nyette looked ready to study the vista for a long time. Impatiently, Shonn urged, "Let's go find her. Instead of guessing, we can ask."

Then a new voice cut in. "I have a better question. Who are you, and why are you sneaking around up here?"

XII — RECKONING

I t was maddening to slink back empty-handed to the same rustic tavern Ar-Lizelle had left so eagerly a few hours before. She hated that sense of loss and shame. If the remaining guards had known of another inn or outpost anywhere nearby, she would have commanded them to lead her there. Instead, she kept a stern face as the same nervous tavern maid greeted them.

"How wonderful to see you again." The wench smiled widely around the fear in her eyes.

"We will be staying the night." Ar-Lizelle gave no other explanation.

The maid's dark eyes took in their gloomy faces and bloodied gear. She must have realized not everyone who left had returned. Awkwardly, she offered, "Mistress, will you need a healer to stitch you up?"

Ar-Lizelle huffed irritably. Yes, she had many small cuts, but nothing that needed such tending. However, her escorts were another story. Three of the six were either pressing bandages to wounds or leaning on their fellows. She grimaced at the thought of her flattened wallet.

"Yes, send for him." The tavern maid scurried off to make the arrangements. Ar-Lizelle told the guards, "We'll rest here overnight. You've earned it. But keep what happened to yourself. Count Ar-Kilohn won't want rumors spreading about that revenant."

"Yes, Lady Ar-Lizelle," they answered, variously relieved or sullen. They began to trail inside. Endole and Groff waited until Ar-Lizelle entered before coming inside after her.

In the common room, a few locals looked at them with dismay and quickly shuffled out. Ar-Lizelle seated herself apart, while Endole and Groff joining the Ebruc soldiers. Both tables were quiet as they considered their losses. Ar-Lizelle especially missed having Ar-Kyanon at her left hand. She had come to depend on him making these minor arrangements, and for giving rational advice.

The tavern maid brought ale for the soldiers, and wine for Ar-Lizelle. Other tavern workers rushed about, bringing water and rags. Guards who weren't injured helped the others get their armor off and began to tend their wounds.

Ar-Lizelle drummed her sharpened fingernails on the tabletop and wondered if she should have her own injuries cared for. They stung and itched, and the heavy lethargy of Elldri's attack still clung to her bones. Realistically, though, those small wounds weren't going to matter.

Victory had been so close! She had been certain this day would repair her mistake at the Larder. The traitors would be dead or in chains, where they belonged. Instead, she had to explain why she had failed. For the second time, Alemin and the rest of them got away. Dar-Gothull could kill her, and she could hardly argue. As one who valued honesty, she didn't see any good way to excuse herself.

"Mistress, your room is ready." The barmaid curtseyed anxiously.

"Very well." Ar-Lizelle swept up her wine to follow. Chairs scraped behind her, and she knew her two guards were trooping after her. The maid took her upstairs and back, to a pair of chambers that, from the smell, must be above a stable. The maid lingered apologetically until Ar-Lizelle waved her away. "This will have to do."

In truth, it was barely acceptable for a mage of her rank. However, Ar-Lizelle doubted she would have to suffer the indignity for long. Endole and Groff moved to join her, watching over her as if nothing had happened. But everything had changed, and there was no way to make this easier. She stopped her guards at the door.

"Wait outside," she said. "I must report. No matter what you hear, don't come in until I call for you."

"Warden," Groff began, but then trailed off. She paused a moment longer, wondering if there was any other instruction she should give, but it all seemed futile.

"This is mage business. Don't try to interfere." Ar-Lizelle shut the door on their concerned expressions. It was only two steps to the bed. She sat, rubbing her hands nervously over her knees. This was bad, very bad. Dar-Gothull would be waiting for news of the prisoners, and what could she say? Dire predictions swarmed her mind. She was certain she was about to die.

For some reason, Lorrah's outburst came to her mind. Calling her Lizzie, saying "you almost died," as if the little bitch cared. And, "let it go."

There was no letting this go. Ar-Lizelle was no whining renegade, distraught over the problems of others. She was a mage, proud and fierce. She could not, and would not, try to change now.

Yet as she prepared to face her fate, her mind went absurdly blank. How did you call out for Dar-Gothull's attention? Normally she tried to avoid the wizard-king's notice. She settled her mind, picturing her office in the Larder. The familiar desks, chairs and shelves. Serene and orderly, everything in its place. Would she ever return there?

A deadly chill swept over her. Moments later, the office door opened and the revenant glided in. He smiled, all shark teeth.

"How did you fare?" Dar-Gothull taunted, as if he

didn't know exactly how the battle went.

"Regrettably, I was not able to capture the fugitives." Ar-Lizelle tried to report as if this was all about someone else. Still, her words rasped from a dry, tight throat. "Count Ar-Kilohn and his son, Ar-Ishahl, were helpful as your majesty had predicted. It seemed that we had them, but then a creature... Forgive me, another of your kind appeared."

The revenant glided around the office, hands clasped loosely behind his back. She hurried on.

"Elldri tore us apart. The minstrels restrained her, and it seemed that they restored her to something like normal. However, my force had to retreat." Ar-Lizelle went quiet, waiting for Dar-Gothull's retribution.

"I appreciate your honesty. It is one of your best qualities." The tyrant rewarded her with a sharp and kindly smile. She winced a little at the way he touched on her own inner thoughts. "Never fear, Ar-Lizelle. You did exactly as I hoped."

"Majesty, I don't understand. I... failed." She forced the words out and braced herself. The lacerations of Elldri's attack ached and stung in anticipation of another lash from shark-toothed arms.

"All is well," he replied. "You made them fight for their freedom. Now they may become careless. Even better, you forced young Elldri to reveal herself."

"Majesty?" Ar-Lizelle couldn't believe Dar-Gothull wanted the fugitives to slip free. He must be toying with her.

"Elldri is like me, you're correct." The revenant spoke as one explaining to a child. "She is a young devourer. While she was in the Larder, I did everything I could to bring her to my side, but she rejected the truth. This will force the issue."

Although she was reluctant to undermine something Dar-Gothull was pleased about, At-Lizelle said, "The minstrels burned her corruption away, or so it appeared."

"Yes, I'm sure they think they can save her with love and kindness." He shrugged, contemptuous. "There's no changing what she is. They'll turn on her soon enough."

Change? Again, Ar-Lizelle thought about Lorrah, who apparently wanted to change their relationship. She pushed that aside. This was no time to be distracted.

"As for those fugitives," Dar-Gothull continued, "you will play this game for me. Pretend to retreat. Let them think they have escaped. Ar-Kilohn will be expecting you to join his forces in Ebruc. Be prepared to march with him."

"You do not wish to crush them?" Ar-Lizelle dared to ask.

"Of course I will." He flicked a hand before him as if shooing a fly. "These minstrels will believe they are safe. It will be even more shocking when we arrive at their secret refuge in the Hornwood." He spoke the words in a mocking sing-song. "I know where they are going, you see. I want them demoralized. They will realize complete despair before I destroy them."

The revenant sighed with anticipation that turned Ar-Lizelle's stomach to a knot of fire.

"What a feast I shall have," he gloated.

~ ~ ~

The sudden interruption made Hawk Squad jump to alert. Men cursed and grabbed for their swords. Piyaro straightened slowly, controlling his own surprise. Whatever this was, he would not be cowed. By the time he had fully turned, Cothyr had the men into battle lines with Nyette behind them. Shonn had drawn his bush knife.

"Easy there." The speaker stepped out from the tree cover a short distance up the slope. Piyaro eyed him, a deceptively ordinary man in rugged leather jerkin and tall thick boots. Black hair was twisted into a knot held by something like pieces of antler. "This doesn't have to be trouble. I just want to talk."

The fellow kept his voice bland, hands spread away from his paired knives. Piyaro noted his easy stance and unusual confidence in the face of superior numbers. Subtle movements in the brush hinted that he was not as alone as he appeared to be.

Taking a similar tactic, Piyaro asked, "Why would it be trouble?"

"I don't know." A hint of mockery lit the black eyes. "We saw you tracking around the point. You hid from boats at sea, but not eyes above you."

This drew an indignant gasp from Shonn. The Hawks stood tense, not relaxing their guard.

"What do you mean by we?" Piyaro asked.

"Just some people." The fellow shrugged. "The locals, you know. We live in the mountains. In times like these, we make it our business to know who's coming and going."

Locals, he said. Times like these. Piyaro clearly remembered Captain Jorus mentioning a gang of raiders who claimed these mountains, though he'd thought that was quite a distance from Opshar. They must be using the confusion of Sand's uprising to make some sort of power play.

"Are you bandits?" Piyaro challenged.

"Tsk, such a harsh word." The fellow shook his head slightly, but he didn't deny the accusation.

"We're on the count's business. I don't suggest you get in our way," Piyaro told him bluntly.

"Well, that's part of the puzzle, isn't it?" The fellow angled his head, unimpressed by the threat. "You wear Pulgoll's colors, yet you wish to move unseen. There aren't enough of you to put down the rebellion. We're curious, is all."

"About things that don't concern you," Piyaro said. Around him, Hawk Squad watched his reactions. Nyette had drawn up straight, a cold look in her eyes. Her hand was tucked against her side, with a pale glow about it.

"We're a fine set, aren't we? Nobody wants to say our business." The stranger gave a little snort. "Well, it seems like you're heading for Opshar. We've been watching the village for some days. We just might have information you'd like to know."

Now that was tempting, but it could obviously be bait for a trap. He glanced to Cothyr, a silent exchange. Was it worth the risk?

"What do you get out of it?" Piyaro asked.

"Someone... has an interest in events down below. If you'd care to accompany me, I'm sure they will want to tell you more. Maybe even come to an agreement."

"I'm not here to negotiate with raiders," Piyaro answered coldly.

"Tsk, so rude," sighed the bandit. Despite his mild manner, Piyaro didn't miss the threat.

"Actually," Nyette interposed. Piyaro made a note to himself to find out why her manner had changed so much.

"Fine words," flashed the bandit, but then he controlled his tone. "You don't know what's going on down there. Your boys seem sturdy and all, but it'll take more than a handful of men to settle this."

"Excuse me!" Nyette broke in sharply. When everyone jerked around, she flatly stated, "Depending on what you have in mind, it's not impossible that *I* may be able to negotiate."

The bandit eyed her, puzzled. Nyette wore no mage robe, but she clearly spoke in that tone. Piyaro frowned for a different reason, which had to do with those suspiciously moving bushes behind the bandit.

"Give us a moment," he said.

"Take your time, talk it over." The fellow turned his back with a sardonic air. He strolled a few paces up the hill, where some taller brush offered shade. A faint quiver suggested he was having a muted conversation with someone hidden there.

Piyaro stepped back, not taking his eyes from that spot. Nyette had been helpful so far, but he knew very well she was hiding something. What had she said to Shonn — 'We have work to do?' Regardless, the fellow's words concerned him. What exactly were the ice walls were for, and what other events were going on 'down below?'

In a low voice, Piyaro asked her, "Is this something in your instructions, or are we chasing some whim of your own? Because I won't abandon Ar-Azlor's service."

"I don't have whims," Nyette answered flatly. "I can't afford them. It's true, my instructions don't include this exact situation. However this unexpected turn may be an opportunity."

Shonn fretted, "This is taking us away from Meven."

Of course that was what the lad worried about.

"That's not our only goal," Nyette told him.

This, Piyaro agreed with. He glanced to Cothyr, who murmured, "We don't need these guys."

Nyette pushed back. "We don't agree to anything just by going to talk. If Countess Ar-Torix was here, I think she would want to hear what they're offering."

Recalling his one encounter with that lady, Piyaro suspected she would turn on her charisma and have the lot of them at her feet. Lacking such an option, Piyaro weighed both ideas. Reluctant as he was to cooperate with bandits, he knew full well that, after water and food, information was a soldier's most precious resource. So he growled, "I'm trusting you, Nyette."

Before she could respond, he turned back to the bandit who watched them idly. "All right, but I'm not dividing my force. We all come or no one comes."

The fellow flashed a wry grin. "Well then, this'll be extra fun."

"How far is it to your friend?" Piyaro asked curtly.

"Just a step up the hill, Sergeant. Come along now!" With mocking cheerfulness, the bandit waved for the Hawks to follow him.

~ ~ ~

"So this is the Hornwood," Alemin observed.

"This is it," Jaxynne said.

Duessa peered around warily as Sethamis guided the wagon over rocky patches and between thorny thickets. There were all kinds of rumors about the Hornwood, but it had been very far away from her home in Busaren. This was the first time she'd been near it.

The fabled hornpines rose, gaunt and majestic, with few branches widely space on their tall trunks. The Badgers had seen isolated trees, but there were a lot more of them now. Shadows somehow gathered beneath the pallid trunks. The air felt cooler than it should, scented with dry earth and unfamiliar vegetation. Sethamis had to go carefully through the many obstacles. The only one who seemed enthusiastic about being there was Riprap. The donkey eagerly snatched at rascalweed along the way and seemed fearless of the sharp bloodthorns he was trying to browse.

"Do you think we'll be safe here?" Duessa asked Jaxynne, who rode near that side of the wagon. There was so much cover, Duessa could readily imagine the savage beasts who were rumored to lurk in the Hornwood, and caravans being waylaid by bandits.

"Relatively," the guardswoman replied. "There's no sign of any more guards following us, at least."

At these words, Elldri stirred a little. Duessa quickly looked around. The girl had been resting between her and Bettain, either sleeping or pretending to. Using a lot of power always left mages spent. At the moment, Elldri seemed dazed, half awake. Her dark eyes wandered listlessly.

"It's okay," Bettain reassured her. "I'm here, you're safe."

Elldri's glance flicked to her, and then anxiously to Tisha, before she settled back again. Her shadowed eyes rolled closed. Duessa met Bettain's worried gaze, but then the older woman looked away, too.

"We can't assume safety," Cylass answered quietly. Then he pulled at the donkey's lead. "Come on, Riprap. I thought you were so afraid of being left behind."

Tisha rested, too, after bearing the greatest burden in purging Elldri's *voromnil*. With her back against the guardswomen's cage, she stretched her legs out, first the left and then the right. "Cylass is correct. When we passed through on the way to Seofan, there were parasitic wasps." She grimaced at the memory.

"Last time, we fought a giant badger," Keerin said with mock cheerfulness.

"I remember Razeet saying that," Lorrah said. "What happened?"

Perhaps she hoped for a story, to distract everyone from the battle earlier, but Zathi put up a cautioning hand. "Let's stay alert. We're still on the run."

"Later." Razeet shrugged.

"Keilos sensed it coming that time," Giniver added.

"So you mages keep your ears open for that, all right?"

Duessa shook her head. "This is not encouraging me."

Nor was the silence that gripped all the mages. Yes, they were recovering from the battle, but there were things that needed to be talked about. And soon.

~ ~ ~

Shonn sent Nyette a surly glance as they followed the bandit up a trail even less visible that what they had been using. None of this was helping him get to see Meven. He'd thought Nyette understood how important it was to him. That she was a friend he could trust. He should have known better. This was just what you'd expect of a mage.

Only, after a few steps, Shonn sheathed his bush knife. Meven was a mage, too, and he reminded himself to stop thinking like that. It wasn't Nyette's fault that the whole squad had been tracked by bandits. She just didn't have to be so abrupt about it.

Their bandit guide led them along a narrow trail that crossed the side of the ridge in a way that wouldn't be visible from below. Weaving through trees and brush, Shonn heard rustling and muffled footfalls behind the squad. They were being followed. Piyaro seemed to know it, and he didn't like it. However, he didn't call for a halt. The trail crested the ridge, turned again, and they emerged into a gap among the trees. Rutted remains of an old road led to a wider space where rock walls rose unnaturally straight toward the sky.

"Some kind of old stone quarry?" Cothyr guessed to Piyaro.

Ahead of them, scattered rock slides partly blocked the way. "Those look random, but I don't think they are," Piyaro answered.

Their guide threaded a path confidently through the obstacles. As they passed, Shonn silently agreed that the slides had been set up as a line of defense.

"Why so nervous?" The bandit gave them a sarcastic look for all the whispering. Nobody answered.

The old road curved around a last outcrop and they walked into an area where great stair-steps carved the hillside. Trees and brush filled in some of the layers. In other places, a system of lean-tos enclosed the angles. Ladders were propped between them for easier access, all the way to the top, where a spy perch was nestled among the trees. Their guide hadn't been lying about keeping an eye on the valley.

A sizable number of people inhabited the lean-tos. Shonn glimpsed men cooking or relaxing near small fires that burned with little smoke. When they saw Hawk Squad come in, some of them jumped up and came to the entrances with wary stares. No two of them had the same armor or weapons, although for the most part these appeared better cared for than he would have expected from a bunch of raiders.

The men of Hawk Squad watched around them, tense and alert at the number of potential enemies here. Nyette observed them with a sharp eye. Shonn didn't understand how she could be so calm. She really had changed from being so interested in the world she was denied while in the Temple School, to this aloof determination.

"Chief." Their guide stopped near the center of the quarry. A crude wooden stair led up to a larger lean-to one level above.

Before long, their leader came out. "Chief Huld," their guide said to Piyaro.

Legs wide and arms crossed, Huld surveyed the visitors below him. He was an older man, dressed like the others in mismatched but well maintained gear. A pair of knives hung at his sides. Shonn would have expected a bandit chief to be big and burly, perhaps with menacing scars. This man was small, almost scrawny, his hair done in a simple topknot. Yet he had the same air of leadership Oberim did when he was aboard *Otter*. The others looked to him, just as Hawk Squad did with Piyaro.

"Well, Skeelon." Huld nodded to their guide. "You made contact, I see."

"They're very cooperative folks." Skeelon stepped aside a few paces. "This is..?" He paused with a questioning expression.

"Hawk Squad. I'm Sergeant Piyaro." The squad leader settled back into a cautious tone and stance. "We serve Count Ar-Azlor."

"And a few friends." Skeelon extended a hand to Nyette.

The student mage stepped up beside Piyaro, brows furrowed in concentration. Shonn saw her hands grip each other tightly behind her back.

"Nyette. I'm a senior student in the temple school at Eshur. Currently, I'm acting as a liaison for Countess Ar-Torix."

A series of whispers hissed around the quarry at those words. However, Huld didn't answer right away. Like Piyaro, his posture was neutral. Brown eyes probed their group with quick intelligence. He paused a moment on Shonn, the odd one, in his swamp linen. Shonn's back tightened at the knowledge that an unknown number of bandits now surrounded him.

"You wanted to talk to us." Piyaro's voice was tight. "Something about the valley situation?"

"More like, we want you to talk to us," Huld answered. "Why have you come here and such."

"I've said we serve Count Ar-Azlor," Piyaro's face revealed nothing as he repeated the information. "Who are you to ask his business?"

Huld chuckled, though without much humor. "I've been more in charge than your count for these past several weeks." Around the quarry, men took note of the verbal fencing. Skeelon ambled a bit farther aside, and a number of the bandits slunk over to join him. Shonn didn't like that.

"How about we skip this nonsense," Huld went on. "Hawk Squad was here a couple of weeks ago. You started this whole rebellion."

"We came with a writ." Piyaro sounded unaccountably tense to Shonn's ear.

"And left the village in an uproar. We heard." Huld shifted to fold his arms the other way. "The rebellion you started has spread down the valley..."

"We didn't start it," Piyaro argued. "That renegade, Sand, has them all on his side."

"I can believe that," Huld said. "The headman, Aulgrip, he's been working to calm the people down, but they won't have it. Seems they're tired of being bullied and taxed."

"This isn't about taxes." Piyaro sounded irritated. "Your man said you know things. Tell me where this renegade came from, then."

"Why would I know that?" Huld's question sounded genuine. Nyette, too, listened with interest.

"You had a woman named Yamaya working with a mage, but they both dropped out of the fight a while back." Piyaro was pressing some sort of advantage, Shonn thought. He'd scored a mark, too.

"Yamaya was teamed with Gabrith," Huld acknowledged. "They both left Cutrock Canyon over a year ago. I hear Gabrith's dead, anyway. This Sand has nothing to do with me, nor the others."

"That's not what Captain Jorus thinks," Piyaro said.

"Ar-Azlor's head bully?" Huld waved a dismissing hand. "He's not shown his face in these mountains for a decade. Like I said, the count's taken a hands off approach. So much that some of Aulgrip's kin decided to press the matter." He glanced toward Skeelon. "Get Kinson out here."

"Okay, Chief." Skeelon and a couple of his men ducked into a different lean-to.

"Wait." Piyaro frowned. "Kinson, Aulgrip's nephew?" Huld raised a brow, inviting more information. "He's the one who sent to Ar-Azlor wanting Sand to be arrested. That's what started the rebellion."

"He's a ballsy brat, you have to give him that." Huld chuckled again, in an even less friendly way. "That family of Aulgrip's, they think they own the valley instead of Count Ar-Azlor. But when you try to do business, they cheat."

Skeelon returned, two of his men holding a prisoner between them. Kinson stumbled with his arms tied behind him. His trousers and shirt must have been fine once, but now they were stained and coated with dirt. Frizzy black hair hung loose over reddened eyes. Those eyes darted anxiously at everyone around him. His upper lip was swollen, and he winced when his tongue touched it.

"Kinson here was traveling through the mountains on his way to Deeve," Huld cocked an eyebrow at Piyaro. Speaking to Kinson, he said, "This here is Ar-Azlor's man. Care to explain to him what you were planning to do?"

Kinson straightened to give a petulant complaint. "Count Ar-Azlor wasn't doing anything about the rebels. He didn't send anyone to help us. We can hardly leave our homes. Everyone hates us!"

"Go on," Piyaro had a dangerous glint in his eye.

"Then a couple more renegades turned up," Kinson said. "The count didn't care. I was going to get help from someone who would take it seriously."

"The help was in Deeve," Huld added, in case Piyaro hadn't figured it out. "Good thing he didn't make it past my boys."

Kinson glared defiantly. Even Shonn, who wasn't part of the land folk's politics, understood how hollow his bravado was. Personally, Shonn was much more interested in the couple of other mages who turned up.

"You thought you could invite the count of Deeve to invade us?" Piyaro's voice rose a little. "Just like you thought you could send to Ar-Azlor because Sand was coming between you and Yamaya?"

"That bitch and her mage boyfriend were squatting at Weeping Falls," Kinson retorted. "My uncle didn't know they were renegades when he rented it to them. They need to get out of there so decent people can work that land."

"Watch what you say about my daughter," Huld's voice was no longer even a little pleasant.

Skeelon spat on the ground. "My sister's a bitch, but she's worth ten of you."

Piyaro regarded Kinson as if he was a hog to be slaughtered. Finally, the man had the sense to shut his mouth.

"Forgive me, I'm a little confused." Nyette broke in with a strident tone. "Huld, you said that Gabrith and Yamaya left your band a year ago, but Gabrith has died since."

Huld nodded. He eyed her curiously, this self-declared liaison, who claimed to be a mage but wore commoner's garb. Nyette turned to Kinson with firm intensity.

"Sand arrived later, but you said now there are others. How many mages are in Opshar at the moment?"

"A woman and a boy came through," Kinson answered, sullen. "She asked at the tavern, but the barkeep there said she was already looking toward Weeping Falls. They didn't even pay for a meal," he complained once more.

"A woman and a boy?" Shonn's heart sped.

"That means something?" Piyaro asked impatiently.

"That's Meven. It has to be." Shonn caught a questioning glance from Huld and explained, "Meven is the ice witch. She has a boy named Ozlin. Claims he's her son, but he's a mageling she picked up somewhere."

"In Eshur," Nyette supplied. "That fits. Before you ask, Sergeant, finding Meven is one of my tasks."

Shonn had guessed as much. Now he wasn't sure how he felt about it. However, he wasn't going to be left out of this discussion.

"I need to find her, too. You think she went on to Weeping Falls?" he demanded of Kinson.

"I assume," the prisoner said, piously indignant. "That's why we... the village council, I mean, were so worried about having another mage up there."

Nyette regarded Kinson in silence for a moment. Shonn thought she didn't see him — or any of them — as people. They were only problems to be solved.

The girl mage turned back to Huld, "When did the ice walls first appear?"

The bandit leader waved a hand to indicate her peasant clothes. "You say you're a student mage, but I guess you're in charge of all this?"

Piyaro frowned at that. Nyette returned boldly, "Let's call it s a coalition. Sergeant Piyaro and his men have their skills, as Shonn does, and as I have mine."

"Very nice," Huld said, but he pressed back, "You're

from Eshur, then? Pulgoll and Eshur, allied against Deeve. Well, well."

"The ice walls?" Nyette repeated, without confirming or denying anything.

"What do you think," Huld glanced at Skeelon. "Six days?"

"Five," that man replied. "I remember because we caught Kinson the next day. He told us one of his cousins headed north, into Dunsaph." Kinson looked down, scowling. "Then Minyin in the north reach sent word there were troops moving southward, with a couple of mages in charge. Either Sand or this ice witch must have guessed what was coming. The ice walls started going up the day before."

"Yes, it's possible one of them sensed another mage approaching," Nyette mused. "How far do the walls extend?"

"My men can show you from the viewpoint," Huld offered. Shonn didn't trust that he was being so helpful.

"Sand told me he plans to stay in Opshar, that it's his home." Piyaro wasn't happy about that. "It sounds like this Meven will, too, and they decided to defend the valley on both sides."

"I still need to talk to Meven, but both of them together would be even better. How far is it to Weeping Falls?" Nyette asked Huld.

Huld answered her with a long, considering look. Nyette's back tightened, and Piyaro shifted his feet restlessly.

"Maybe I'll just take you there myself," Huld finally answered.

Shonn bit back a cry of alarm. He couldn't go up to Meven with a bunch of bandits! Piyaro also frowned, but Nyette kept her cool. "Why would you do that?"

"My daughter is there," Huld answered with dark simplicity. "She's in the middle of some rebellion, and now your 'coalition' is going to muck things up even more."

"Nah, tell the truth," Skeelon suddenly grinned. "Yamaya just had her baby, and you want to cuddle him." The younger bandit mimed rocking a baby, and the rest of the gang burst out laughing.

"Quiet, you," Huld growled with mock anger. To Piyaro he explained, "Yamaya was the one who left, I don't argue that, but the situation has changed. Gabrith isn't there to protect her any more."

"Protect Yamaya," a bandit snickered in the back.

"Understandable," Nyette nodded, and looked to Piyaro. "Sergeant?"

The Hawks' leader turned a hard look on Kinson. "What about him?"

"You want him? Take him," Huld shrugged with every appearance of generosity. "We've learned what we could from him, and my band doesn't keep hostages. Too much trouble."

"Thank you for your kind offer," Piyaro said, though it clearly grated. He beckoned to Cothyr, who stood ready when Skeelon pushed Kinson toward him.

"Just take me back to my uncle," the young man whined. "We have money..."

"Quiet, traitor," Cothyr cuffed him. Hawk Squad made space for their prisoner, with no one showing any sympathy as he stumbled again.

Huld waved his men up the stairs for a discussion of who would stay on guard and who would accompany him. Shonn fidgeted restlessly. All this talking and delay were driving him mad!

"Can't we just get going?" he asked Piyaro, then realized he sounded like Kinson whining and shut up.

"Your girlfriend will still be there," the sergeant answered drily.

Hawk Squad chuckled at his embarrassment, except for Nyette, who let a glint of understanding show past her fierce resolve. Despite her bold facade, Shonn suspected she was as nervous as any of them. He could almost forgive her for this side trip and all the complications.

~ ~ ~

Out of necessity, the women of Badger Squad ranged a little farther from the wagon than usual. Each one sought a path for it, which Jaxynne would look over before telling Sethamis it was safe or not. Sometimes they cut brush to clear the way, but they managed not to backtrack and steadily wove their way north. Or possibly west. The tree cover made it hard for Duessa to keep track of the sun.

Eventually, Jaxynne spotted a dim glow under the dusk of the trees. A silvery road! Everyone in the wagon murmured relief as Sethamis carefully coached the oxen down a bank and onto smooth pavement. The guardswomen happily guided their horses back into the regular formation. Soft conversation began to flow.

"Does the forest feel different to you?" Keerin asked Razeet.

"Like it's lighter," her sister agreed. "Not so forbidding."

Duessa glanced around at the forest gloom. "This is lighter?" she murmured to Bettain. Her friend gave a one-shouldered shrug.

"I wonder what's changed," Giniver said.

"It's still the Hornwood," Zathi cautioned them. "Don't take anything for granted."

And Tisha said, "Remember, we must be careful with our spells."

"Who's casting anything?" Lorrah sounded grouchy.

"I'm still tired," Alemin yawned.

For all the complaints, the passengers on the cart were starting to stir, reviving from their efforts in the battle. Only Elldri didn't react to the noise and movement. The girl hadn't roused since that brief moment in the afternoon. Duessa turned to check on her, and experienced a moment of panic when she thought Elldri wasn't breathing. Then a faint sigh reassured her.

Carefully, Duessa opened herself to the energies around them. Bettain had used the least *lethentros,* and was already fully recovered, while Tisha, Alemin and Lorrah gleamed faintly with their depleted *vitalis*. But Elldri didn't even jump at Duessa's probing. Sensitive as she was, she should have.

This couldn't be right. She focused her senses. The girl felt hollow, like an empty water jar. There was no hot, jagged *lethentros*, nor the sticky sludge of *voromnil.* No wonder the girl was in a daze. She seemed to be drained of all magic.

After seeing what Elldri could become, the last thing Duessa wanted was to provoke her. She looked to the other mages. Bettain seemed unaware of the problem. Alemin had reached up to join hands with Lorrah, the two of them sharing thoughts Duessa had no wish to intrude on.

It was Tisha who met her gaze. Even weary as she was, she seemed to understand the problem. Duessa rolled her eyes toward Elldri. Tisha shook her head somberly.

"I don't know. This is all new to me."

That wasn't encouraging, but Duessa didn't get to pursue it. Sethamis exclaimed, "Hey, is that water?"

The highway passed between two low mounds covered with thorny bushes, and as they emerged, a low rush tickled their ears. The pavement ahead glittered differently.

The scent of water woke Duessa more than anything since the battle.

"It sure is." Jaxynne looked to Zathi. Until that moment, everyone had been putting thirst aside in the urgency of escape. Now even the tough sergeant seemed ready to rest. The horses were pricking their ears and giving anxious little snorts and whickers.

"We'll halt here," Zathi said. "Giniver, cross to the other side and keep watch. I'll hold on this side."

There was a small creek running down from the opposite side of the road. It flowed across and formed a small pond. There was an eager shuffle as Sethamis slowed the wagon and let the oxen dip their broad muzzles into the shallow water streaming over the pavement. Guardswomen spread out around the pond, each horse having its own bit of bank. Riprap fairly dragged Cylass past.

"Wait, you blasted beast!" the bodyguard swore.

"It's all right," Tisha chuckled. "We know where he's going."

After a moment's struggle, Cylass released the donkey's lead so he could help Tisha down. As soon as the wagon stopped, Alemin jumped from the driver's bench. Bettain dropped off the back and turned to wait for the others. Only then did she realize Elldri wasn't stirring.

"Hey Elldri," Bettain called. "Come on, there's water."

"Wake up for a bit," Duessa rubbed Elldri's shoulder. Her throat felt coated with sawdust, but she didn't want to leave her friend there.

The wagon bounced a little as Bettain pulled her bulky self back up. Elldri's eyes fluttered open, blinking with confusion. Crouching beside her, Bettain said, "I know you're tired out, but you can't just lie here. You'll feel better if you walk around a bit."

"Come and get a drink. I bet your throat hurts," Duessa coaxed. That was as close a reference as she wanted to make to Elldri's mad screaming during the battle.

"Sethamis might need help with the oxen." Bettain got her arm behind Elldri's back. Slowly and stiffly, she sat up. "Lean on us. Easy does it."

Between them, Duessa and Bettain got Elldri down from the wagon and walked her toward the stream. Duessa's throat was on fire with thirst, but she held herself to Elldri's pace. All the time, she wondered what it meant if Elldri was so spent that she couldn't even walk.

XIII — HOMEWARD

H uld's men led off, first a pair of scouts and then the bandit chief. The rest of his men followed in a close file. Their number was exactly equal to Sergeant Piyaro's, a sort of courtesy. It was still embarrassing to trail after a bunch of low-lifes. There really was no choice, though. The gang from Cutrock Canyon knew the ground, and Hawk Squad didn't.

The path wove its way out of the hidden quarry, between more artfully placed rock slides and fallen tree trunks. Still hidden by broad-leafed trees, the trail trended downward at a steep angle. Piyaro felt the jolt of each step in his knees, while part of his mind puzzled over what Ar-Azlor would want him to do with this situation.

When gaps in the cover allowed, he scanned the valley below them. The deep green of reed beds was parted by the silvery gleam of a running river. Upstream, almost behind them, were the tamer patches of tilled fields. Opshar was a huddle of stone houses within a curve of the river. Paired wagon tracks led out to the fields, where wisps of rising dust suggested a harvest was being dug.

He recognized that area, having marched up the road not long ago. What he'd never seen were the icy walls, spaced out in irregular slashes between the far hills and the river. Piyaro frowned a little. Like the fallen trees of the quarry, they seemed random. Yet, even if mages were crazy, why waste energy on odd structures? Several steps behind,

Shonn questioned the same thing.

"I don't get it." The young water-folk waved a hand, indicating the scattered ice walls.

Nyette studied the vista, and eventually said, "I think it's a maze. Sergeant Piyaro said there's a gap into Dunsaph. These walls push any invaders away from the village."

"There's a road," Shonn countered.

"It's blocked now." Kinson couldn't resist a complaint. "That ice witch says it's to protect us. Local people who know the land can make their way through on the river."

"Shut up," Piyaro told him. Still, it made sense. Once you started a rebellion, you'd need defenses. "The ice won't melt?"

Nyette shook her head, and Shonn said, "The ones in Fang Marsh had been there for days, when we left."

"So they either come on the river, or they get directed back into the mountains," Cothyr said.

"I told you she's clever," Nyette murmured.

"I already knew that," Shonn grumbled.

Eventually, the bandits' path leveled off and broke into the open. They crossed a low hill and approached that one farm, alone on the ridgetop. A slight breeze carried the scent of damp stone from the shimmering waterfall beyond it.

The house itself was concealed among a copse of fruit trees, but several distant figures toiled among sweet potato and melon vines that grew in terraced fields below the orchard. A young boy with a skinny frame marched across the field, hefting a melon larger than his own head, and proudly deposited it into a wheelbarrow.

Moments later, one of the adults straightened, and

Piyaro felt a tightening in his gut. A man, conical hat — it had to be the rebel, Sand. Or Berisan, if Countess Ar-Torix was right. Two other, skirted figures rose also. The boy ran up to stand beside Sand with his hands clenched defiantly. All four of them hurried up from the fields. The shortest figure took the lead, despite the baby carrier on her back.

Chuckles drifted back from the bandits. Yamaya having a baby seemed to amuse them all greatly. Piyaro wasn't sure why.

Huld now strode ahead, approaching boldly across the slope. He halted several paces from the trees and waited with arms folded, as he had in the quarry. With more space to maneuver, Piyaro beckoned his squad to move forward. A slight tightening of Huld's brow warned him to halt a few steps behind the chief's position.

Yamaya came out of the trees, without the baby on her back. Sand followed her. The other two lingered farther back under the trees. If Shonn was right, that would be Meven and her mageling boy. There was also the shadowed outline of a fenced chicken coop. Yamaya stopped, hands on hips. She wore the same paired knives Piyaro remembered, over her plain peasant dress. Sharp black eyes followed their doubled line. She was still beautiful, and apparently still angry.

From the back of the Cutrock line, Skeelon waved sardonically. "Hi, sis!"

Yamaya rolled her eyes. "What are you doing here?" The occupants of the chicken coop made their own indignant comment. Sand, meanwhile, stood relaxed and took in their numbers with bland interest.

Huld gave his lieutenant a quelling look, then said, "Well, girl, I heard you started a rebellion."

"*We* didn't," she corrected acidly. "We just want to be left alone." She glared at Piyaro, who held himself back from responding to the blatant lie.

"That's not always an option," Huld answered in the tone of a patient father. "And, I've missed you."

"Don't start that with me," Yamaya warned.

"Well, that's the thing," Huld said. "When you came down here, Gabrith was with you. A good team, I'm not arguing that." He held up a calming hand. "But things are different. You don't have Gabrith. You do have a rebellion here. I just want to make sure this is where you want to be. That you feel safe, away from the canyon."

As they spoke, Piyaro watched the shadowy figures in the grove of trees. The ice witch, Meven, stood very still. Another conical hat shaded her face. Beside her, the young boy was poised with clenched fists.

"It's him." Piyaro faintly heard the boy snarl, glaring at someone in the Hawks' formation. The silent woman merely rested her fingertips on the boy's shoulder.

In almost the same moment, Nyette murmured with excitement, "Is that her?"

"Yeah. That's Meven." Shonn seemed to force the words out. Piyaro wished he could see the man's expression, but his attention had to stay on Yamaya, who was furious at Huld's question.

"I am not going back to Cutrock Canyon," she burst out. "You gave me to Gabrith like... like a sack of sweet potatoes! You think you can do that to me again? I'm a farmer now. This is my land, and I am not leaving it."

Yamaya's words explained some of her anger, but Huld brushed the accusations aside.

"I have to offer," he said. "I wouldn't leave you on your own."

"Yes you can," Yamaya corrected him forcefully. "And you'd better —"

Skeelon interrupted again, with a wider grin. "Oh,

come on. We came all this way. Let us see the baby."

Huld scowled at him, but Yamaya's hostility had shifted slightly toward puzzled irritation. Noting her reaction, Huld admitted with some chagrin, "I did want to. Your second mother, you know. She'll have my balls if I don't tell her the little lad is well and healthy."

"So you say." Yamaya's eyes remained sharp as obsidian blades. "That explains you, Huld. Then why are all of them here?" She flung out a hand toward Piyaro's side of the hill.

"We came to talk to... Sand, I think?" Piyaro addressed the renegade, who watched Yamaya's conversation quietly.

After a brief moment of concern, he answered calmly, "It's Berisan, actually." Yamaya didn't react, so she must already have known he used a false name. And Countess Ar-Torix had good information. That was encouraging.

"Last we met, you said you'd talk if Ar-Azlor came. Well, he sent us." Piyaro would have felt better with his own instructions, not depending on Nyette's translation. "This is Nyette, and Ar-Torix sent her to talk also."

In her brassy tone, Nyette declared, "My Lady Ar-Torix has questions." Her gaze went back under the trees, seeking Meven. "Depending on the answers, there may be a basis for further discussion."

Berisan shifted a little, glancing back into the orchard. The young boy tensed, but Meven herself showed no reaction.

"And him?" Yamaya's black eyes were fixed on Kinson, held among Hawk Squad's ranks, with even more scorn, if that was possible.

"A traitor, and our prisoner," Piyaro replied.

"Are you here to talk, too?" Yamaya mocked.

"We're escorting Nyette," Piyaro said. "However, Hawk Squad are sworn to Pulgoll's service. If the border is threatened, I will defend it, even if it means unusual allies." He glanced to Huld, who replied with something between a nod and a shrug.

From farther back, a faint whimper crept between the trees. Yamaya half-turned, sharing a glance with Berisan. "He's hungry."

"Well," Berisan suggested casually, "maybe we can offer our guests shade and cool water while you see to his needs."

"Fine by me," Huld agreed, and Piyaro also nodded. With this many competing factions, resting under the trees was probably as good an outcome as anyone could expect.

~ ~ ~

Shonn tried to pay attention to what Nyette and Piyaro were saying, but it was hard with Meven just a few feet away. She might be half-hidden, but he would know her anywhere. The stillness of her, turning away always. She wore a sarong of pale green swamp linen, with the hat of woven reeds. Seeing her brought back a sharp joy and familiar challenge.

Addith, as he'd known her then, hadn't been friendly the first time, either. Shonn had had to work his way around her, until she finally rewarded him with a cautious smile. Cold as she appeared, asking for nothing, Meven also had a keen and ruthless sense of humor. Shonn wanted fiercely to make her smile again.

A moment later he saw the boy, Ozlin, focused on him with a mage's mad glare, and the impossibility slapped his face. Much as he wanted to see Meven, Shonn was ashamed for her to see him. Oz had it right. After what he'd done, how was he even worthy to speak to her?

The men around him started moving, and Shonn walked with them absently. Under the row of fruit trees, Huld and Piyaro got into a discussion about whether the threat was most urgent from Dunsaph or Deeve. Then Yamaya swept back over, a crying baby in her arms. The bandits swirled toward her as she opened her blouse to give suck.

This effectively left Piyaro and the hunter guards separated from the bandits. Hawk Squad spread out a little, drinking from water skins or chewing on bits of salted fish. The mages, Berisan, Meven and Oz, retreated toward the farmer's hut. Shonn followed them with his eyes. His knees felt tight. Should he go after Meven — with all of them there?

"Come on," Nyette declared. Shonn glanced back to Piyaro, who motioned Cothyr to go with them. The student mage lengthened her stride to catch up with the other mages. "Where can we speak privately?"

"We should have a few minutes while everyone ogles the baby," Berisan answered mildly.

He motioned them to join him inside the farmer's house. Shonn studied the structure, with its stone foundation and walls of woven twigs. The thick, tight thatch of the roof was angled to shed rain into a stone cistern.

Such trivia he focused on. Anything but look at Meven, now that he was so close.

Berisan and Meven seated themselves on folded mats on the far side of a small cooking pit. Nyette sat facing them, straight and stiff in her nervous dignity. Shonn and Cothyr lingered outside the door, while Ozlin scurried closer to Meven. The boy wore the same short sarong from the swamp. A few small shells adorned the headband holding a bush of frizzy curls back from his face. An arc of silvery scars across his narrow chest and left shoulder showed where the mudmaw had grabbed him, those months ago.

Ozlin still clutched the monkey puppet, Eelee, that Meven had given him. Scowling at Shonn, Ozlin made it stick its tongue out. The gesture of defiance brought an unexpected, fond amusement. Shonn would have been angry, before, but now he understood some of the boy's resentment. Becoming closer with Meven was all well and good, but it couldn't have meant banishing Ozlin. Shonn had been an ass to even think it.

Meven seemed to hear the click of Eelee's tongue popping in and out. "Oz," she chided in a soft, dead voice. Shonn winced at her defeated tone. Still hugging his toy, the boy settled against the wall, kicking one foot restlessly.

Of them all, only Berisan sat relaxed, a slight slouch to his shoulders. He softly asked of Nyette, "You have a message?"

"I have a question," Nyette answered with brittle formality. She spoiled it by fumbling slightly, "Well, two questions. Ahem. You will have heard about the three rituals all mages must endure, which bind us to the will of Dar-Gothull."

"You haven't done them," Meven stated, as if this was obvious.

"No, I'm still a student," Nyette said, but then she pushed back. "I assume neither of you have, either. Your renegade life would not be possible if you had. Countess Ar-Torix wishes to know: can you break this bond?"

A startled glance passed between Meven and Berisan. Even Cothyr seemed to catch his breath. Shonn didn't know what they were talking about, but the reactions made him uneasy.

"Ar-Torix and Ar-Azlor. They wish to be free?" Berisan asked carefully.

"Can any of us say we don't wish to be free?" Nyette spoke with a trace of honest indignation. "The people are abused by mages and those who serve them. The students are prisoners in the schools. Bandits and renegades do more to protect people than the counts. Hunter-guards hound anyone who dissents, while the Temple priests tell us there is no other way."

"We all hear tales, that Dar-Gothull can devour souls across any distance," Meven said.

"Nobody wants to find out first hand, I'm sure," Berisan said wryly.

"Indeed," Nyette agreed. "The counts boast of their power, but with Dar-Gothull reaching into their minds, they are in some ways even less free. Whatever their own opinions, they can do nothing as long as they are bound by the rituals. Can you sever the link?"

There was a brief silence before Berisan admitted, "I don't know. None of us ever considered it."

He glanced to Meven, who answered steadily, "As a tactic, I suppose it could be effective. Dar-Gothull would lose control over some or all of his forces. However, whether we succeeded or not, the attempt would certainly expose us."

Watching, Shonn wondered how Meven could be so calm. Only her hands, folded in her lap, tightened a little. Was she afraid? Shonn couldn't tell. Ozlin, however, was kicking his foot a bit faster.

Nyette coughed gently. "We are having this discussion because you've already been exposed." Berisan frowned slightly, concerned. "Countess Ar-Torix informed me and Sergeant Piyaro that the warden of the Larder, Ar-Lizelle, was gathering reports on your minstrel group. I'm told she even captured one of them."

"Do you know who?" Berisan blurted. Even Meven couldn't hide her alarm at this news.

"I don't, and it may not matter," Nyette went on. "The countess also heard that someone broke the prisoners free. That's hard to believe, but I'm certain it would make Dar-

Gothull take notice of your minstrel group."

There was another brief silence and Shonn watched Meven's detachment turn even bleaker. She asked, "If it is possible to release a mage from Dar-Gothull's bondage, what would Ar-Torix or Ar-Azlor intend to do?"

Berisan added, "Are they the only ones allied together?"

"I suspect not, but can't say for certain," Nyette replied.

"What do you *suspect* they intend?" Meven pursued.

"I can infer," Nyette spoke each word cautiously, "that they also intend to rebel. This is based on Countess Ar-Torix sending me, a student who is not yet bound to Dar-Gothull's will, and Ar-Azlor sending Hawk Squad, who are not widely known as his soldiers. That would also explain why Ar-Azlor has held back from marching out to crush this uprising. He may hope the villagers remain alive, to fight under his banner."

Shonn's mind was momentarily a horrible, whirling blank. He remembered Nyette saying she felt trapped in the temple school, but this — open rebellion? He glanced at Cothyr, who stood stunned on the other side of the door. This was why the water-folk stayed out of land-folk business! Somehow, he had to warn his people. And how could Meven sit like a statue, listening to such madness?

"This brings me to the second question," Nyette continued. "Count Ar-Azlor wishes to know what you intend, here."

"I didn't intend anything," Berisan sighed, aggrieved. "Opshar is my home, Yamaya is my boss." Meven gave him a look, and he sighed again. "I told you, we're not lovers. Nobody can run a farm alone. When I got here, she had no one. I've dealt fairly with the villagers, hoping they would let me stay."

That word, *lover*, shocked Shonn in a different way. If Yamaya wasn't Berisan's lover, then maybe Meven was. His old jealousy surged, that she might have found someone else so quickly.

"I understand," Meven told Berisan. "I thought I found a safe place, too." It was her first slight reference to Shonn's presence, and it made him pause. Being jealous had caused a lot of trouble. He had to stop doing that. Anyway, the two of them didn't look at each other in quite that way.

Nyette, however, was not to be put off. "As Sergeant Piyaro tells it, he came with a writ and they immediately rose up."

"I didn't plan that!" Berisan protested, half guilty.

"Yet Meven left Eshur quite suddenly, possibly on the very same day," Nyette said.

"I did not come here to start a revolt," Meven said flatly. "That is not our purpose."

Shonn couldn't stay silent any longer. "We saw a strange creature in Fang Marsh," he interrupted. Ozlin scowled, and Eelee stuck its tongue out. Shonn realized he sounded more accusing than he meant to. He tried to soften his tone. "It was beautiful. It glowed... But then you were gone."

He didn't mean to let the hurt show, the bewilderment of being left behind. Meven did look at him then, a brief moment. She purposely turned back to Nyette.

"It was a warning I received, that we should not linger so near to Dakadoz."

"Who was the warning from?" Nyette asked. Both Meven and Berisan looked uncomfortable. "It must be from someone you trust. Another of the minstrels?"

"None of your business!" Ozlin burst out. Meven quieted him with a glance.

Berisan said to Nyette, "It's too soon to trust you with that, I think."

"Regardless," Nyette grumbled a little, "the rebellion has begun. I don't claim to know Ar-Azlor's mind, but it seems Countess Ar-Torix regards this as a useful turn of events."

"Is Ar-Torix who we want to be useful to?" Berisan asked Meven.

"Ar-Torix thinks everything is about her," Meven answered with a tinge of sarcasm.

"She's a highly ranked mage, and she can do that," Nyette responded. To Berisan, she asked, "When you say you dealt with them fairly, what did you mean?"

"Well, I drove some bandits off." He sounded awkward about it. "I heal their injuries. Before the fighting started, some of them came to ask my advice."

"Protection, healing, advice. These are powerful things, even without magic," the young mage said. "People remember who is kind to them."

"Then how would a revolt be useful?" Meven asked coldly.

"You said you've received a warning not to be near Dakadoz," Nyette pursued. "What is the most dangerous thing in Dakadoz, if not the wizard-king himself? To me, your warning implies that he will take some action. If so, then surely he will call on the counts for troops and supplies. If Ar-Azlor is fighting a rebellion, then he can credibly hold back. As can the neighboring counts and countesses. They can all claim to be vulnerable if the uprising spreads."

"It won't." Berisan sounded exasperated.

"Or if it was simply unresolved," Nyette countered. "One might learn a lot by observing who goes to Dar-Gothull's side when he calls to them. However, it all depends on the answer to the first question. Can you break their link?"

Again, Berisan and Meven shared a long look. "I don't know," Berisan confessed. "That isn't helpful, I'm sorry..."

"Why should they, anyway?" Ozlin broke in, his young voice shrill. "That lady came over threatening us. We don't have to help her."

"Oz," Meven murmured patiently.

"Because then we might not have to be enemies," Nyette said.

Berisan added, "It is always better to have friends, Oz."

"I do have a thought," Meven said slowly, but then she darted a wary glance toward Nyette. Berisan seemed to immediately understand something.

"Why don't you let us think it over?" he suggested. "Evening is coming on. Yamaya will want to know who's staying here and decide where to put you all."

"I agree." Meven spoke with a trace of relief. "Oz and I need to walk the walls and make sure there's been no change."

Nyette looked very interested in that, but Berisan diverted her.

"We'll give you an answer tomorrow," he said.

"Very well," Nyette rose swiftly. "Thank you for hearing me out."

She strode between Shonn and Cothyr, down the steps. Shonn sent one uncertain look into the farmer's hut before he followed them. The angle of the sun had changed, sending the trees' shadows down the hill in long streaks. He couldn't believe they had been talking for that long.

Beside him, Cothyr muttered, "I have to tell you, most of that made no sense to me. But there are a couple of things I'm sure Sergeant will want to know."

"Uh-huh," Shonn mumbled a reply, but his thoughts were flying around again. What if it was a trick of Meven's, this walking the walls. Was he really going to let her get away again?

～ ～ ～

After Dar-Gothull withdrew, Ar-Lizelle sat in a daze. She had failed completely, and yet Lord Dar-Gothull had seen fit to spare her life. How could she believe it? Clumsy hands groped to find the bottle of wine, which she had brought with her to this hovel of a room. She put it to her lips and drank deeply.

Too many thoughts fought for space in Ar-Lizelle's mind. Yes, it was good that she wasn't dead. It was even not too much of a trial that she would have to wash out her cuts after all. Torn as her mage robe was, she would have to get one of the tavern maids to mend it. Such details were menial and boring, a waste of her intellect.

Ar-Lizelle drank again.

Elldri had shifted everything crosswise. The girl had always seemed so meek and obedient, afraid to even speak. How could such a nothing suddenly manifest as a revenant? Ar-Lizelle supposed it was fortunate the minstrels had had a counter for it. Otherwise, she would be as lost as Ar-Kyanon.

She couldn't make herself feel gratitude, though. That disgusting flood of emotions still hung on her, sickeningly sweet. As the crowning touch, that outburst of Lorrah's. Calling her Lizzie, saying "you almost died," as if the little bitch cared. That was just a move in her game. It had to be.

"Almost died," Ar-Lizelle mocked the silence, and drank again.

And now, what was she supposed to do? Dar-Gothull

expected her to report to Count Ar-Ishahl in Ebruc's seat. He would not appreciate the loss of four men, common guards though they were. Guards could be replaced, but there was no one to replace Ar-Kyanon. Unless she stumbled over Illen or Noluss somewhere, and they would be willing to make a deal. All she had left from the Larder was Groff and Endole. It was hopeless.

Ar-Lizelle's bottle was soon empty, and muffled voices were intruding into her room. Groff's voice, anxious, and Endole's prim rebuttal. Honestly, those two were like a couple of squabbling brats. She rose stiffly and yanked the door open. Her two guards jumped, relief etched on their faces.

"You're all right!" Groff cried.

"I know you said to wait, but we hadn't heard anything for —" Endole began.

"Bring me more wine." Ar-Lizelle shoved the empty bottle at him.

"My lady," he fumbled to catch it. "You should get your wounds looked at."

"That's what the wine is for," she snapped, and slammed the door on them.

Footsteps shuffled away and down the stairs. Ar-Lizelle returned to the inadequate bed. Her head was heavy, and she wanted to lie down, but there was no way to get comfortable. The cuts had mostly stopped bleeding, but her robe kept sticking to them. They pulled and stung with every movement.

"Warden?" Endole knocked and opened the door for Groff, who balanced a pitcher, cup, and bowl that smelled of river grain and broth. Ar-Lizelle rolled to her feet and snatched the pitcher, only to find it contained plain water.

"I said wine," she scowled.

"You don't need any more wine," Groff said as he set the rest of it on the small table.

"That is not your decision," Ar-Lizelle said angrily, but then realized she couldn't even speak the words precisely. She must sound like a fool. It was unbearable to be so weak in front of her underlings.

Endole hovered in the door, where he waited to get by Groff. He held another small bowl and a handful of rags. "You can trust us, Warden."

The two of them had been loyal, she grudgingly acknowledged. Ar-Lizelle seated herself at the table, scowling at the plain fare Groff set before her.

"What is this?" she demanded. Groff didn't quite look at her.

"Before Captain Morthem took me on, I did some pretty rough fighting," he told her. "So I know you need those cuts taken care of, and you need to eat. It just can't be anything too heavy or spicy." He poured her a glass of water, and the rest went into Endole's bowl.

"You might not care how much you drink now, but tomorrow you will," Endole reasoned. "You don't want to lose your dignity in front of those other guys."

"Very well," she sighed harshly. Losing the battle was bad enough. Ar-Lizelle could not endure Ebruc's soldiers seeing her in a drunken haze.

While she ate the simple meal, the two guards carefully loosened her mage robe enough to slip one shoulder off at a time. Fortunately, most of the damage was on her back and outer arms. Endole quickly washed the cuts and patted them dry.

Groff, standing guard at the door, asked, "Did you hear how they were talking about Ar-Javan?"

"They really hated him," Endole agreed, then warned,

"I have to press a little harder here, Warden, and make sure the bleeding has stopped."

Ar-Lizelle kept a stern face through the pain, though she was glad enough to be distracted by their conversation. "I hated him, too. He tried to get into my head. I don't tolerate that."

"He was lazy, is what they said," Endole answered. "Tried to get people to do his fighting for him."

Ar-Lizelle could imagine. It wasn't that different from Lorrah and her friends, flooding kindness into everyone nearby. Disgusting.

"What do they say about Ar-Ishahl, or the count?" she asked.

"Count Ar-Kilohn is strict, but the men respect that," Groff replied. "Ar-Ishahl, it's pretty much what you figured. He's putting himself forward, wants to be sure he takes over from his old man. If he could throw us out and catch Alemin's bunch himself, he'd definitely do it."

"Alemin is mine to take," Ar-Lizelle growled over a drink from her glass.

"That's right, Warden," Endole said behind her. "The Larder will handle our own."

"They say Ar-Talvoy's been spreading a lot of gold around," Groff went on. "Buying friends and such. No one is sure where he's getting the gold from."

"He doesn't want to be passed over." Ar-Lizelle remembered her impressions from the mages' dinner. "If Ar-Ishahl is that much of a glory-hound, it's pretty much self defense."

Endole made a neutral grunt and pulled Ar-Lizelle's sleeve back up over her shoulder. "That's that, Warden. You don't need any stitches, so it's not too bad."

"Good." Ar-Lizelle meant that as a dismissal, so she

could finish her meal in peace, but Groff had more to say.

"Speaking of defense," he glanced at Endole, "we should take turns watching tonight. Those are Ar-Ishahl's men downstairs. They hate him, too, but that doesn't mean they won't try to carry out his wishes."

"They were watching you on the way back," Endole agreed as he folded his rags and took up the bowl of bloodied water. "If they can put us out of his way, they will."

Ar-Lizelle couldn't hold back a sarcastic laugh. "Did they not see what we fought against?" Still, they had spoken her own worry, that the Ebruc soldiers would think her an easy target.

"Elldri's not here now," Groff said. "They know she took you down some, and if they decide to test you, they still have numbers on us."

"It's too bad we lost Ar-Kyanon," Endole said, "but the Larder stands together. We'll fight for you if it comes to that."

Of course they would, Ar-Lizelle thought. But all this talk about hating mages made her wonder if they hated her, too. Endole's hands had been gentle enough with her cuts. It would be better not to alienate her last remaining allies.

"Very well, I accept your recommendation. And get some food for yourselves, as well," she said.

"Thank you, Warden. We'll take it in turns." Endole left. Groff followed, but paused before closing the door.

"For now, Warden, you should try to rest," he said. "We need you strong."

Strong? What a joke. If she went down, they'd go down with her, that was all they cared about. Ar-Lizelle finished her food and eased herself back on the bed, hoping she'd had enough wine to sleep without any more nightmares.

~ ~ ~

By the time the mages were done talking, Chief Huld was already leading his troops back up the hill. They would return to their camp in the old quarry, while Hawk Squad pitched their tents on the level ground of a farm terrace where Yamaya hadn't planted any crops yet. Shonn helped out, but he kept an anxious eye on the farmer's hut. As soon as Meven and Ozlin came out, he called, "Be right back!" and hurried to intercept them.

A faintly trodden path led behind the hut, and between stacks of rock that seemed to be meant for the foundation of a second hut. The path led down the slope, toward the shimmering curtain of Whispering Falls. No one was in sight among the brush on the hill.

"Meven? Wait," Shonn called. How could they have vanished so quickly?

It was Ozlin who burst around a fold of the hill, clutching his puppet and blocking the path. "Leave us alone!"

"Whoa. Oz!" Shonn scrambled to a stop, irritated that the boy was in the way again. And yet, he wasn't surprised. "I have to talk to her."

"You don't get to talk. She said to stay away." Even at his young age, Ozlin was all man, determined to protect his loved ones. It was stupid, but kind of cute. However, the wild spark of mage fire in his hands was not at all cute.

"Oz, it's okay," Shonn tried to calm him. "Turn your fire down. You'll burn Eelee."

That diverted the boy long enough to step back and check his toy for damage.

"I'm not going to hurt you, Oz," Shonn spoke softly. "I know what Meven said. I was a fool, but there has to be some way to fix it."

"You stabbed us in the back," Ozlin yelled. "We were hiding, and you turned us in. You can't fix that."

"I know," Shonn admitted. "I made a mistake, it was bad, but I have to try."

Ozlin scowled at him. The words Shonn had been rehearsing tumbled out. "I thought I was doing the right thing. The countess would be angry if I kept it secret. She'd come after my family."

It was what he'd told his parents, afterward. That he was doing it for them. But those words weren't true. He'd never thought of that, only that he wanted to punish Meven for not sleeping with him. The problem was, this boy could sniff out a lie like ants on over-ripe fruit. Under Ozlin's hostile eyes, he had to admit the truth.

"It's what I said, but really... I was jealous. Meven is so incredible. I really like her." Shonn gazed across the valley, where the ice walls gleamed in the lowering sun. "I like her so much, and I thought..." He sighed. "You were in the way."

"I was attacked by a giant mudmaw!" Ozlin cried. Even with Eelee in the crook of his arm, he swept a hand out to point out his scars.

"I was there, I remember." Shonn tried not to sound so defensive. He stepped aside to slump down on some of the foundation stones. "That was the most stupid thing I did. Of course if a kid is hurt, that's more important. Even if you weren't hurt, I shouldn't have expected her to ignore you for me." Again he gazed over the valley. "My mother was so mad. And my sisters, they wouldn't talk to me, you know? My father wasn't happy about it, either."

"So?" Ozlin, who had no family, failed to see the importance of their approval.

"So I came to apologize for that," Shonn said. "I guess I can start with you."

Ozlin glared at Shonn. His narrow chest rose and fell behind the toy monkey clutched in his tightly folded arms.

"Meven told me you were on your own for a while. Then you finally found someone you could trust" Shonn said. "What I did could have taken that from you. So I'm sorry, Oz. You didn't deserve that."

A swish of fabric against grass warned them both a moment before Meven swept around the corner. Ozlin jumped, startled, but Meven did not seem surprised to see Shonn. As if she had known he was there, or simply expected him to show up. It's what he did the first time, tracking her through Fang Marsh until he found her.

Neither did she react, especially. "Oz? I've been waiting."

"Meven!" Shonn jumped up from his seat on the rocks. The words he'd brought forth for Ozlin seemed to dry in his throat. He pleaded, "I'm sorry. I know what you said, that you don't want to see me, but I had to —"

"Ignore my words and come anyway?" At last, there was an edge in her voice, the sarcasm he knew so well. It stung, but it was better than her impassive chill.

"Apologize! I came to apologize." Shonn steadied himself. "I was wrong, I was stupid. I shouldn't have done that."

"Yes, yes and yes," she agreed with blunt scorn. "Jealous of a child? That is wrong and stupid."

"Oh. Uh..." Shonn winced. Had she heard all that? "Well, I am really sorry..."

"I could have died," Meven answered flatly. "Oz, too. If it was anyone other than Ar-Torix, we both would have been killed."

"I know." He couldn't meet her gaze. "What can I do? How can I make it right?"

She opened her mouth to speak, a sharp little frown in her eyes, then stopped. Oz gazed up at Meven, no doubt disgusted that she wasn't shooting Shonn with ice spikes. Finally she said, "I need to think about this."

"Then..." Shonn grasped at hope.

"Come on, Oz. The sun won't stay up forever." Meven strode on down the path, offering no further encouragement.

"Wait!" he called. "You're going by yourself?" She glanced over her shoulder, an inscrutable reproach. "Take someone with you. One of the guards, Rowlan or..."

"I don't know them," she pointed out, clearly annoyed, before turning away again. Ozlin scampered after her, pausing just once to make Eelee stick its tongue out again.

Shonn watched them go, still concerned that she was going into the rebel valley with only a malnourished brat at her side. Even if she was a mage, it was a risk. Oz would say it was none of his business. Shonn just didn't want her to leave so soon.

Just for a moment, there had been something in Meven's eyes. She always had kept her feelings close. It was almost a compulsion with her. So much that Shonn couldn't be sure, back then, if she was flirting with him. But now, today, he struggled to understand what she was feeling. Was it anger, that he had come against her wishes? Or, did she share the ache over what could have been?

All his emotions were at war. The joy of seeing Meven again, his concern for her safety, against the pain of knowing how badly he'd messed things up. Meven's shoulders were supple beneath the rim of her reed hat. The folds of her sarong swept gracefully behind her. He wanted her so badly, and now she walked away.

Faintly, her voice drifted back up the slope. "Show me your witchlight, Oz. If it gets dark, I might need you to light the way."

The boy clutched his toy monkey with his right hand, while his left lifted palm up. A ball of reddish light sputtered in and out. Soon they disappeared in the spray from the waterfall.

Slowly Shonn sat on his rock again. He could have gotten Meven killed. Bad as it was to be reminded of that, she hadn't gone at him with ice spikes. She must have heard some of what he said to Ozlin. Depending on what part it was, maybe there was hope. To show her that he understood how badly he'd messed up. To regain her trust. He clung to that, like the slimmest of vines dangling above a tidal surge.

XIV — ELLDRI SPEAKS

T he creek water was fresh and cold, a relief to Duessa's rasping throat. She scooped it eagerly, and further revived herself by taking off the cloth she had wound around her head, soaking it, and washing some of the dust and sweat from her face. *Vitalis* tingled in the roughness of her scars. At least they weren't hurting any more.

"Good idea." Bettain said, and she did the same. Elldri sat between them, sipping once or twice but otherwise not moving. "This will feel better."

Bettain wiped the girl's forehead and the back of her neck with gentle efficiency. Elldri twitched anxiously, but didn't resist. Duessa ran wet fingers through her own growing curls before re-wrapping her head cover.

Jaxynne scouted a short way ahead on Cinder. Returning, she told Zathi, "The ground is rough ahead, and dry. There's no water that I saw. This could be our best place to camp."

"I was hoping to keep moving." Zathi's keen black eyes swept over them. The guardswomen were just getting their horses away from the creek, and the oxen were still drinking. Everyone was off the wagon and wandering around. Tisha took Giniver aside for a moment, to continue healing her injured shoulder.

"We're all tired, especially the animals," Lorrah said. "How much farther do you think we'd get before dark?"

Cylass observed, "There's not much room for tents here."

"That's not hard to manage." Duessa scanned the surrounding trees with a moon runner's eye. "If there's space behind those rocks, it will block our light from the road, and we can lay branches over the tents to hide their color."

"I'll have a look." Jaxynne glanced at Zathi for permission, and guided her horse in that direction.

"Moon and Star need a good rub-down," Sethamis said.

"So do we," Keerin snickered.

"Elldri, come on. We can help Sethamis," Bettain urged. Still downcast, Elldri passively went with her.

In the end, Zathi relented. The rock formation Duessa had spotted extended farther than she realized, forming an uneven curve that allowed the camp to be mostly hidden. Sethamis had the guardswomen stake their horses down closer to the tents than usual, keeping them within the protection of the stones.

While the daylight lasted, they returned to the brook in groups to wash themselves and their clothes, as needed. Lorrah and Alemin stayed by themselves longer than the rest, which earned them a good deal of kidding.

Once darkness gathered, watches were set and the lantern glowed cheerfully. It was Keerin's turn to cook. Razeet and Jaxynne had shot a couple of hares early in the day, before everything went off kilter. Now they simmered in a pot with dried beans and a few vegetables. It wasn't very spicy, but there was enough for the group to share. Normally the travelers spread out, eating with their particular friends, but as the night lowered, they clustered closer to the stove's warmth.

Everyone ate with intense concentration, especially the Larder mages who were still making up for many short meals. Only Elldri gazed at her food as if she didn't quite know what it was for.

Bettain nudged her shoulder. "Eat something."

"I'm not hungry," Elldri whispered.

"Pretend we're in the Larder and you've been scrubbing the stairs all day." Duessa reminded her of a least favorite chore.

Alemin chuckled wryly. "I'll never take a good meal for granted again, I assure you. Or even a bad one." He raised his bowl briefly toward Keerin, before wolfing it down again.

"What are you saying?" The guardswoman put her hands on her hips, jokingly angry.

"I think you know what he's saying," Razeet teased.

But Alemin's eyes weren't the only ones on Elldri. The mages were openly worried, and the guardswomen kept looking to Zathi for what to do if Elldri erupted again.

"You should eat," Tisha urged gently. "It will help."

Elldri set her bowl down with a kind of desperate stubbornness. Her dark eyes stared at the ground, and a miserable thread of sound emerged. "Nothing helps. You should kill me."

'No!" Bettain choked. "Don't even think it."

Duessa's chest tightened suddenly. What could anyone say to that?

"I didn't rescue all of you, so we could kill you later," Lorrah cried, indignant.

Alemin reasoned, "It was a bad day, but not worth dying over."

"We are not going to kill her." Zathi spoke, quiet but stern. "I have too many questions."

"That's right." Duessa said.

"Nobody wants to hurt you." Tisha still sounded tired. "We need to understand, so we can help you."

"No, you have to!" Elldri's shrill tone was all too like the screaming they had heard in the Larder for so many years.

"Stop saying that!" Bettain set her half-eaten bowl down, and reached to embrace Elldri. The girl ducked away, scooting back from the group.

"You saw." Tears welled in her eyes. "You all saw it — what I am. I'm not safe."

"Oh..." Too late, Duessa understood something. "Is that what you meant? When you told us the Larder was safe? Not that *you* were safe, but that *we* were safe from you."

Elldri drew her knees back up to her chest. "I know what he said to the rest of you, back there. That he would eat you."

Alemin shuddered, and Lorrah quickly threaded her arm through his.

"He never said that to me," Elldri went on, barely audible. "What he told me was that I am just like him. He would show me the best way to take your souls. How good it would feel."

Duessa winced and caught a hissing breath. Elldri turned a guilty glance toward her and Bettain, but quickly veered away. Around the lamplight, the guardswomen ate slowly, barely chewing before they swallowed, caught in the fascination and horror of such words.

"I always said no, it wasn't what I wanted." Elldri drew a quivering breath. "But I already knew how. There were times when I couldn't stop myself. Look what I did. You saw — "

"What you did was defend yourself," Zathi

interrupted, in the same stern but calm tone she used to correct one of the guardswomen for some goof in training.

"That's right," Giniver said. "Those guys were hurting you."

"Well, it was pretty extreme." Razeet sounded almost admiring.

"Maybe so," Zathi agreed, but then gave a shrug. "The end result is no different from sword or crossbow."

Duessa listened, startled, and saw the same surprise on Alemin's face. The minstrels spent so much time trying to comfort people and not hurt them, it was easy to forget not everyone felt that way.

Jaxynne nodded. "We're warriors, Elldri. Our work isn't gentle, no matter what tools we use."

"Yeah. We don't exactly want to kill people," Keerin said. "It's what we must do, to survive."

"See?" Bettain bumped Elldri's knee with her fist. "That's what I'm telling you."

"But Elldri isn't using a sword," Lorrah said. "We're mage born, and we feel the pain of others in a way that warriors can't."

"Ar-Thea taught us that," Tisha said. "The whole purpose of the temple schools is to crush our empathy and turn us into monsters. We minstrels fight against that."

"As if you know anything about it," Bettain snorted. "Everyone's your enemy there."

"You don't look at people the same way after that," Duessa said.

"That's my point," Tisha said. "We aren't at a temple school. Elldri has choices."

"You don't have to live that way." Alemin smiled encouragingly. Elldri stared at all of them as if they were speaking a strange language.

"You stopped yourself, right?" Lorrah said. "Bettain called you, and you came back."

"That time," Elldri lisped. She shuddered. "But it never goes away. I'll lose control again, and you won't be able to stop me. You've all been so good to me. I don't want that."

"We aren't going to kill you!" Alemin cried.

"That's right," Bettain insisted.

"And we're not abandoning you." Duessa still felt the anguish of Ar-Lannon's betrayal. "There's got to be a better way."

"Of course there is," Tisha said. "We can stop you without killing you, Elldri."

"How can you know?" Elldri whispered, paralyzed by the fear of what might happen.

"We already did, because we shared a connection," Tisha explained softly. "Bettain and Duessa, Alemin, Lorrah, and me. That can help you. Not just one of us, but all." She paused a moment, looking around the circle. "The *voromnil* is gone now. You have no power at all. Am I right?"

Elldri gazed at her, speechless. Duessa said, "Yes, I think that's true."

"The space inside you where the *voromnil* was is empty," Tisha repeated. "Before it returns, we can fill that space with something else."

One of the listening guardswomen muttered, "Huh. You think it's that easy?"

But Bettain cried with disgust, "You're not going to make her into one of you!"

"Is that the worse thing?" Lorrah retorted. Bettain stuck her tongue out and gagged.

"No, it won't be easy," Tisha answered the guardswoman. "Healing is hard, and Elldri's *voromnil* comes from a place of deep suffering. However, I believe we can, all together, fill up the space so there will be no need for *voromnil*."

Duessa wasn't as confident. "Based on my experience, it will take her months to learn."

"Do we have that much time?" Jaxynne asked.

Duessa shrugged, but she said to Bettain, "She can't stay the way she is."

"We could begin, if Elldri is willing, with the burden of pain you carry." Tisha regarded the younger mage seriously. "Naming the burden will give you power over it. But a thing you will not name has power over you, instead."

"What do you mean?" Bettain demanded.

"Right after we escaped the Larder, Alemin said she has to tell someone what happened to her," Lorrah said.

Alemin nodded. "You have to face whatever brought you to a situation where you choice was to die, or to... become that."

"We can help you carry this burden," Tisha said softly. "Will you try?"

Elldri nodded silently. Tears streaked her face, but this time they were not black. That was something, Duessa supposed. Elldri breathed heavily, unable to speak. Her eyes were wide and dark as one of the ox's.

"I know I said I'd kill whoever it was that hurt you," Bettain spoke in an unusually gentle tone. "Maybe this revenge would be better. Name their names, like Tisha said. Make them guilty instead of you."

"Take away their power to control you," Sethamis said.

After a long silence, Elldri swallowed and rasped out, "I said... Remember? That I wasn't sent to the temple school. My parents kept me at home."

Duessa remembered that. "And it wasn't as fun as it sounded."

"I was seven when I first got my power. They both hated me for it." Elldri spoke slowly, as if each word cost her dearly. "Father said I was evil. Mother said, something so foul couldn't have come from her body."

"If that's what they thought, why didn't they send you to the temple school?" Tisha asked quietly.

Elldri was pale beneath her brown skin tone. "They kept me home so they could sell me."

Bettain tensed. "To men?"

Dark glances passed among the watching guardswomen. No one was eating any more.

"Not only men, but mostly," Elldri said. "They didn't all want me for sex. Our count, Ar-Makian, was really bad. He taxed us so hard, and his soldiers were always killing people. They'd burn your house and hunt you down. You never knew why. So everyone hated mages, and when they knew there was a mage they could hurt back..."

"They took it out on you," Alemin shook his head, expression grim. Duessa felt slightly ill. What parent could whore their daughter out?

"They weren't supposed to do anything that would hurt me permanently." Elldri went on, a dull recitation. "No blades or whips, that might have stopped them from selling me. Mostly they just punched me, or pulled my hair, or called me a whore, even while they used me that way. I remember one of our neighbors, Velima. Her only son had been killed by the guards, and she came just to scream at me... Like it was my fault."

"Your own parents allowed it," Lorrah murmured.

Elldri couldn't stop, now that she'd started. The mages winced as grief and terror flowed to them through their link.

"One of them, Uvid, he used to choke me until I blacked out," Elldri sobbed. "Then he would slap me awake, and beat me again."

"Bastard," Sethamis hissed.

"Finally, when he started to choke me again, I... did that. I tore the soul out of him," Elldri choked. "It was the only time my mother ever said anything that wasn't mean. Father was mad, but she said the whole village was better off without Uvid."

"You can say that again," Razeet cried growled.

Keerin punched her shoulder. "Shut up!"

"Ow," Razeet complained.

"But that wasn't the end of it?" Tisha asked somberly.

"Once I started, I couldn't help myself. I killed anyone who hurt me. Father said he would beat it out of me, and I killed him. Mother was afraid. She didn't sell me after that." Elldri gave a strangled laugh. "She was trying to find someone who would marry me so she wouldn't have to look at me any more."

Duessa saw rage and disgust reflected among the guardswomen. First prostituting a child, then trying to marry her off?

"Count Ar-Makian heard about it," Elldri went on. "When he came, everyone was so scared. They thought he would kill then for what they did to me. Only first, he said I was mad, and too dangerous to live, and he was going to put me down. When he tried to burn me —"

"You killed him?" Bettain asked hopefully.

"Sounds like it was overdue," Giniver said, but the others shushed her.

"No," Elldri said miserably. "Ar-Makiar brought hunter-guards with him. He ordered for me to get taken to the Larder."

"So you were seven then?" Alemin asked, appalled.

"I lost track," Elldri said. "Maybe I was nine or ten."

"That's..." Duessa trailed off. Elldri had been her friend for years. Whatever she thought she knew, this was so many times worse. Everyone in the squad wore expressions of shock or disgust.

"You are very brave to tell us." Tisha reached out, carefully, to press her hand against Elldri's white grip on her knees. Cylass tensed, ready to jump to her aid, but Elldri didn't react. "Nobody here will judge you."

"They'd better not," Bettain looked around, daring anyone to speak a word.

"It must have been awful," Tisha said, "and scary, and so gross. It's no wonder you lost yourself."

"She did what she had to do," Jaxynne said grimly.

"That's right," Giniver said.

Elldri shrugged, her face still downcast. She didn't seem to hear them.

"Listen, Elldri. You don't have to worry about anything else right now." Bettain leaned closer, speaking softly as she had that afternoon. "I'm going to take care of you, the way your parents should have. Let me carry the burden. All right?"

"We'll all help carry it," Duessa vowed.

"You just rest," Alemin said, and Lorrah said, "You're not alone."

Zathi said, "You're a very strong girl to live through so much. Don't let anyone say you deserved it. No one could."

Elldri rubbed her face slowly, as if waking up. Smears of snot and tears glinted on her sleeve, but finally, she let her knees back down and picked up her bowl of stew.

"That's right," Bettain encouraged as Elldri took a tiny bite from her meal. Duessa was surprised how relieved she was to see Elldri do something as ordinary as eating.

"Now the rest of us," Zathi went on crisply. "Elldri's story might bring back some bad memories for us, too, but they can't distract us. Finish eating and get to your watches. Rest if you can. We travel on tomorrow."

The squad began to stir, some finishing the meal quickly and others preparing for nighttime chores. Nobody talked much. The forest around them was almost completely dark. Pale tree trunks loomed beyond the rocks that sheltered them, and skyberries shed an eerie glow among the high branches.

Once reminded of her body's requirements, Elldri ate hungrily. Bettain stayed beside her. Soon Alemin withdrew into a huddle with Tisha, Lorrah and Cylass. Duessa caught only a murmur of someone wishing that Keilos was there. It was her turn to wash up, but she couldn't do it until Elldri had finished. Once she started the water heating, she returned to join her oldest friends.

"You know," Duessa said to Bettain, "maybe sometime, you could tell us what happened to your kids."

Elldri paused, extending her tongue to lick a drip of broth from her chin. Bettain's expression hardened. "It was a long time ago. I can handle it."

"I know," Duessa said, "but you don't have to handle it alone."

~ ~ ~

Piyaro rose early and stirred up the fire. It was somewhat before dawn, and the line of Hawk Squad's tents faded gently into drifts of ocean fog. Rowlan, on sentry duty, was barely visible at the far end of the line. Somewhere in the distance, a pale gleam reflected from Meven's ice walls.

Piyaro twisted on a folding stool, trying to reach the last couple of buckles on his breastplate. Before this, it had been enough of a challenge just to get to Opshar. Now that he was here, the problems he struggled with had only doubled.

What Cothyr and Shonn had told him of Nyette's proposal had kept him awake long into the night. There was no way Count Ar-Azlor would be part of that scheme. To break his bond with Dar-Gothull and join a rebellion? It was madness, purely madness!

It was little comfort to recall he had suspected something like this when Nyette told him that she and Hawk Squad had all been selected because their associations weren't known. How could Ar-Azlor not see the danger?

Every hand would be against him. His own junior mages and half of his guard would turn. Ar-Azlor would be ringed with enemies, just like Berisan and the other golden mages. That he was a fair count, worthy to be followed, meant nothing. It only made the situation more tragic.

The worse of it was, Piyaro had no way to know if Nyette was even telling the truth. He'd suspected that the girl had her own agenda. This must be her way — or maybe Ar-Torix's way — of luring Ar-Azlor into their deadly scheme.

Piyaro tossed another chunk of wood on the fire and watched the sparks spiral skyward. Compared to such a looming disaster, his other problems were almost comforting in their lower scale.

As a soldier, his obvious priority was to defend Pulgoll's border. His clash with the locals, those weeks ago, was a complication. They might not want his help. If the alternative was an invasion, he could only trust they would change their minds.

Another difficulty was the prisoner, Kinson. The fool ought to be hanged. It wasn't pleasant, but Piyaro had dealt with deserters before. Hanging would have been the easiest solution, yet it tied back to the roots of Opshar's revolt. After spending a few hours in his company, Piyaro couldn't see anyone really liking Kinson. Still, he was their neighbor and Hawk Squad were outsiders. Swift justice might just as quickly sour any chance of the locals cooperating.

Continuing to hold Kinson was hardly ideal. Any time the fool wasn't gagged, he pestered them to take him home and talk to his uncle. Presumably, Headman Aulgrip would ransom his thick-headed nephew. It grated to think a traitor might walk free.

Certainly it would be possible to march the man back to Pulgoll and let Ar-Azlor deal out justice. It would also give Piyaro a chance to speak with the count about Nyette's "question." The border would be undefended, but if he had to choose between guarding the border and protecting Ar-Azlor, there was only one choice. Even then, he could picture Captain Jorus asking why he didn't do what obviously should have been done in the first place?

Piyaro grunted to himself and dragged irritated fingers through his short, tight curls. Somehow, amid this massive tangle, he had to keep his squad together, paid and trained and fed. Oh to be a lowly foot soldier again!

With Shonn, at least, Piyaro knew what would happen. The lad wasn't one of his soldiers. He'd spent most of the night before casting hopeful glances toward the farmer's hut. Shonn would want to stay where Meven was. Since he had succeeded in getting them through the mangroves, maybe he had earned that.

Dar-Gothull knew, somebody had to earn something honestly on this trip!

Sunrise now tinged the fog with gold. Piyaro concluded he had been brooding long enough. He stood and stretched his arms above his head. But as he looked upward, what he saw made him frown. In the west, the moon set through a veil of mist, but the sky he gazed into was still dark. Where did this light come from?

Footsteps suddenly scuffled in one of the tents behind him. Fabric rustled as the tent flap opened abruptly. Nyette burst out, barefoot and wearing only a chemise. Her startled gaze veered around to focus on that false sunrise. In silence they stared up the hill, beyond the orchard and Yamaya's hut.

"I hope that's what I think it is," Nyette breathed, not really speaking to him. The thin fabric of her chemise swirled as she darted back in.

"What do you think it is?" Piyaro demanded, knowing the tent's stout cloth would do nothing to muffle his voice. He already had a horrible suspicion.

Nyette dashed back out, stamping into her shoes. Her hair flowed loose in inky waves, and she was still fastening her brown robe. Ignoring his words, she dashed up toward Yamaya's hut. Piyaro jogged after, determined to keep the witch in sight. He cursed under his breath for mages who wouldn't answer a plain question.

Brighter rays pierced the mist as they reached the orchard. Twigs on the trees appeared suddenly to claw at him. He ducked between them and veered around the chicken coop, where the gray hens clucked drowsily. The crest of the hill was plainly visible as a dark divider against the shimmering light beyond.

Ahead of him, Nyette stopped. She released a little startled laugh as he came up to the top. Piyaro paused, blinking against the flood of light. Though the morning air was cold, what he saw put that right out of his mind.

The fog thinned out below, revealing the pond in its perfect circle. Two figures stood on the bank, silhouetted against the brightness cast by the impossible creature facing them. It was huge beside the humans, long and lean and scaled as a fish, but it had the head of some animal he didn't recognize. Piercing eyes shone beneath a great bush of mane where two forked antlers jutted back.

Piyaro couldn't help enjoying Nyette's stunned expression. "I guess that isn't what you were expecting?"

"I thought a ritual or..." Nyette seemed to realize she was speaking too freely. She broke off.

"This must be what Shonn saw." Piyaro recalled the wild tale of a glowing creature in Fang Marsh. He considered calling over his shoulder to get the lad up here.

Already Nyette had recovered her poise. "Something new to learn," she murmured.

The mage girl started down a narrow trail toward the pond. Piyaro followed, watching his footing among the rocks and brush. He studied the outsized creature as they approached. Vivid stripes pulsed slowly along its corded body. The posture was calm, offering no suggestion of a threat. Only its size remained daunting.

Berisan and Meven stood in fearless silhouette on the bank. A smaller figure crouched nearby was probably the mageling, Oz. The two mages clasped hands, and each of them raised a hand as the glowing beast lowered its head toward them. Nyette caught her breath when they pressed their free hands to its muzzle. She would have gone closer, but the mageling boy jumped up to block her path.

"Get out of here," he challenged.

"I'm not going to hurt them," Nyette answered patronizingly.

Himself, Piyaro had no trouble heeding the boy's warning. This was far too big a creature to rush up to, and the aura coming off it was horribly familiar. It was just like when the golden witch danced in her circle, spreading that sense of lulling peace.

Nyette paused, listening intently as Meven spoke aloud. "It would mean changing them, Keilos."

"A change they asked for," Berisan reasoned.

"Without understanding it," Meven said. Ozlin glanced over his shoulder, as confused and suspicious as Piyaro felt. Keilos might be the kind of creature, or a name for this individual. Piyaro was certain Count Ar-Azlor would want to know about it.

There was a longer pause. The two mages relaxed, as if the golden beast gave some reply. If it did, it wasn't anything Piyaro could hear.

"What do you mean, change them?" Nyette made no effort to hide her avid curiosity. Piyaro was so used to her being a sneak, he could forget how young she was, focused on what she wanted. No wonder she and Shonn got along.

Meven and Berisan lowered their hands and stepped aside. Nyette's back stiffened as the mighty creature bent its head toward her. Piyaro took an involuntary step back, while Oz darted to Meven's side.

"What did you mean?" the mageling whispered loudly.

"It is wrong to alter people's thinking and force them to do what we wish," Meven spoke a little sharply. "Only an evil mage would do that."

"Oh." Ozlin hugged his toy monkey. He didn't sound convinced.

The eldritch creature flowed closer to Nyette, a cloud of golden light surrounding her. Piyaro knew he should grab her and pull her away from that looming presence, but his sense of self-preservation kept him rooted. The young mage stood gazing into the blazing eyes. Her face was slack, eyes wide and unfocused. Then he saw a shimmer of tears welling up in her eyes. Nyette's lips moved, but she couldn't seem to speak.

"You're certain, Nyette," Meven said. "This is what Ar-Azlor wants?"

"It... I didn't think it could be real," she murmured. Not answering the question, as usual

"Wait, now." Angry words broke from Piyaro. "I don't know what you're talking about, but if you're going to do something to Ar-Azlor, I have to..."

He trailed off as the great beast turned its attention to him. As his mind bleated panic, a sense of gentle amusement penetrated his thoughts. There was nothing to be afraid of, and anyway, what was he going to do against all these mages and a drakanox?

"If he's asking for this, we wouldn't be compelling him," Berisan said to Meven. "It sounds as if he's already made the decision."

"And if it's a trap?" Meven said doggedly. "They lure Keilos to them, and —" She hesitated, rubbing her forehead before murmuring heavily, "The biggest thing in Dakadoz is Dar-Gothull."

Piyaro was enormously relieved when the drakanox withdrew its presence. He also appreciated Meven asking a sensible question. Yet other worries gnawed at him. How exactly did he know that this was the drakanox? That legendary creature was supposed to have vanished a century ago. Yet somehow it was here, and apparently its name was Keilos.

"If it's meant to be a trap, I don't know about it." Nyette blotted her eyes with the sleeve of her brown mage robe. Unexpectedly, she begged, "Please, you must teach me this!"

"All right," Berisan agreed immediately. "But we have a few other things to do first."

All of Piyaro's concerns surged anew. Berisan had no idea who Nyette really was, yet he was willing to agree without so much as a thought. How could he be so trusting?

Maybe this was how it had gone in Opshar. Someone asked a question and Berisan just agreed to it. No wonder the locals fell at his feet. Piyaro could almost understand why Kinson got his back up. Not that it was Piyaro's business, if his count decided to set a trap. A creature as big as the drakanox could worry about itself.

"I understand." Nyette sniffled, trying to regain her composure. "Then if Keilos would take me to Pulgoll with him, we can see if Count Ar-Azlor can be helped. Sergeant Piyaro can stay here, with you, to defend the town if Dunsaph or Deeve invade."

The drakanox angled its glowing head in what might have been disagreement.

"No!" Piyaro burst out. "We aren't prancing up to the count with a giant glowing beast. Do you know what that would look like?"

Treachery, Hawk Squad leading this monster to attack his count. Piyaro had spent years guiding and training these men. He couldn't do that to them.

"Keilos does stands out," Meven said wryly.

"This was the point of my coming," Nyette flared. "If Count Ar-Azlor learns you've interfered..."

"How do I know that?" Piyaro batted the implied threat aside. "There's only your word for half a thing you won't say out loud."

"Cothyr was there when I talked to Berisan. I knew he would tell you," she retorted.

Meven and Berisan exchanged wary glances. Yes, Nyette said it was something Ar-Azlor wanted, but she had nothing to back up her claim.

"You can't go there anyway," Piyaro told them. "You don't have travel documents."

"I have a letter..." Nyette began, but then broke off. "No, you're right. I gave it to that soldier. What's his name... to Amren."

"Keilos can't help Ar-Azlor over a distance," Berisan looked up at the monstrous phantom. Piyaro had the impression of growing impatience.

"Then how can we get Ar-Azlor into the same place with Keilos?" Meven asked wearily.

To that, Piyaro might finally have an answer. Not that he liked it. "Easy. We have a rebellion going on here." Berisan started to say something, but Nyette interrupted.

"Yes! I know, Berisan, you didn't intend to start an uprising," she hastily soothed him. "If Count Ar-Azlor wants to maintain the fiction of a revolt, as we discussed, then he could come in person and seem to fight it."

Piyaro couldn't help hoping Count Ar-Azlor would not just seem to put down the revolt, but would actually do it. There were entirely too many schemes afoot in Opshar.

"Then he would be close enough," Berisan looked to Keilos and seemed to receive some reply.

"If Sergeant Piyaro is willing to escort me back to Pulgoll," Nyette said with excessive courtesy, "I can explain to Count Ar-Azlor what may be possible."

"That would allow me to get more clear orders," Piyaro said. Which would be welcome, and if Nyette was playing some game of her own, Ar-Azlor and his own hunter-guards would be able to deal with it. In fact, if they took the traitor, Kinson, back with them, Ar-Azlor could decide whether to hang him and it would be one less problem for Hawk Squad.

Somehow, Piyaro didn't think it would all turn out so

sweetly.

"How long will it take to get to Pulgoll?" Meven asked, all practicality.

"By the ordinary road, five days?" Piyaro guessed. "I'll bet Huld's people can get us through the mountains faster."

"I knew it was a good idea to negotiate with them," Nyette said smugly.

"Then the count would have to muster his forces, and they'd have the trek through the mountains again." Meven nodded to herself, and turned to gaze up at Keilos. After an extended silence, the great creature bent its head down to her. Meven and Berisan again rested their hands on its glowing muzzle. This time it had the air of a farewell.

The drakanox lifted away, coiling in the air like an eel in water. It dove into the circular pond without a ripple, lighting the water to a shimmering haze that abruptly faded. Nyette stared after it with baffled longing.

"All right then." Piyaro turned to trudge up the hill. True sunlight was beginning to lift the morning fog from the Opshar valley. It was time to get his squad up and ready for travel.

~ ~ ~

The morning found Ar-Lizelle with a sour-tasting mouth and dull headache. Bleary eyes turned across the room, before she remembered that Ar-Kyanon was gone. There was a hole inside her that would never be filled. Absurdly, she considered that perhaps she should have slept with him when she had the chance. Ar-Lizelle curled around herself for a long moment, hating herself for such weakness and self-pity. The tight squeeze made all the cuts across her back itch and sting at once.

Properly goaded, At-Lizelle sat up tall. She was no child, to snivel over a loss. Not when there were six guardsmen of uncertain loyalty waiting for her in the common room. Rising, she tipped her glass back for the last mouthful of tepid water and swished it around before swallowing. Then she frowned down at herself.

She had never gotten around to having the tavern maids mend her mage robe. The crimson folds were pierced by many small cuts, and darkened by blood. Her father, Ar-Evaus, would have been disgusted. He never appeared publicly in less than immaculate style. Well, it was too late for mending now. Besides, Ar-Lizelle had an idea that this flaw might be useful.

Although she couldn't dress according to her late father's expectations, at least she would heed his words. *"Never admit you're at a disadvantage. Seize control of every situation."*

Ar-Lizelle opened the door and found her two guards waiting. With a crisp nod, she informed them, "I have a plan." Then she swept past them, headed for the common room.

No locals were present at this early hour, only the tavern maid and six bruised and surly guardsmen from Ebruc. Some of them looked even more hung over than Ar-Lizelle felt. It didn't appear that they had eaten.

"Will you be leaving right away, or..?" The tavern maid asked nervously.

"Food, then leaving." Ar-Lizelle made no mention of payment. Behind the girl, the barkeeper scowled, no doubt thinking of his own flat wallet. "Unless you prefer the count hear of your poor hospitality?"

The man no longer tried to meet her gaze. However, Ar-Lizelle felt the Ebruc soldiers' eyes boring into her back. Watching her, as Groff had warned. Ar-Lizelle drew a deep breath, allowing her headache to transform into fury. Slowly and deliberately, she turned to face them. One by one she met their gazes — wary, sneering, speculative — until each one looked away.

"Yesterday," she began, and paused, allowing them to remember those events, "was a test. Ar-Ishahl thought he could throw us away. That we would face *that* —" another pause "— and conveniently die."

Had Ar-Ishahl known of Elldri's nature? It was unlikely, but Ar-Lizelle didn't have to prove it. She only needed the guardsmen to doubt.

"We did not die," she went on, "but we did lose friends. Ar-Kyanon, your Sergeant Thessal. Now I have new orders. We will return to Ebruc and join Ar-Kilohn's forces for the next action."

Ar-Lizelle stood before them, her torn, stained robe demonstrating how she had fought beside them against the horror. She met each pair of eyes again. "You have shown your worth in an extraordinary trial. Because of that, I invite you to consider serving the Larder instead. If that is your wish, you may speak privately with Sergeant Endole during our journey."

Surprise rippled through them. Without their own sergeant, they would be shoved into random units, or sidelined into something less desirable. Here was an opportunity for better, although with risk. And for Ar-Lizelle, as well. Two guards were clearly not enough for the situation she was about to confront.

She turned to sit down, putting her back to the Ebruc guards and daring them to attack. As she did, she caught Groff's congratulatory thump on Endole's shoulder. Groff took up a guard position, while the newly made sergeant seated himself across from her.

"Thank you very much, Warden," he murmured.

"Your advice was well spoken," she gave the compliment grudgingly.

However, Endole's gaze was already focused past

her, assessing those six guards with a careful eye. The tavern maid approached with trays of steaming food. Ar-Lizelle thought she might be able to eat heartily after all.

~ ~ ~

"Get moving, you bunch of slugs!" Sergeant Piyaro shouted from the edge of the trail.

Dust rose over the farmer's fields as the guardsmen broke their camp down and packed up to leave. Shonn watched, confused and anxious. Tent poles clattered and dirt flew as they filled in their fire pit. The men grumbled a bit at having to move on so soon. Shonn certainly agreed with them. The squad had barely reached Weeping Falls. He'd hardly spoken a word to Meven, and now they were leaving?

Nyette emerged from her tent, dragging her bulging waypack. Her dark eyes sparkled with excitement. "You'd better grab your things," she warned.

Rebelliously, Shonn demanded, "Where are we going?"

Passing the other way with an armload of bedroll, Cothyr told him, "Go talk to Sergeant."

Irritated, Shonn stalked over to the edge of the dirt path leading from their section of terrace up to the farmer's hut. Piyaro watched impassively as his men worked.

"Get your stuff," he said as soon as Shonn was close enough.

"Why?" Shonn's frustrated cry took in all his disappointment over being dragged away from Meven. "We haven't even been here a day."

"Don't argue with me." Piyaro scowled back at him. "You aren't coming with us, so put your back down."

"Why..." Shonn faltered, annoyed and then relieved. "I'm not?"

"You did your part. You got us here. It's obvious you only had one goal." Incredibly, the sergeant actually smirked a little. Then he barked, "Rowlan! Shake the dirt off before you roll the tent." After glaring at his guards a moment, he added, "Are you saying you want to travel on?"

"No! No, that's all right," Shonn grinned back at him.

"Then go get your things before we march off with them."

Shonn hurried to do that, though he had little enough to fit in his shoulder bag. Just the hammock he could string between trees, a bit of dried fish, and his bush knife. With that secured, he pitched in to help Hawk Squad. The squad was escorting Nyette the rest of the way to Pulgoll, he learned as they worked. Remembering what Nyette had been talking about with Berisan and Meven, Shonn was very certain that he didn't want to know any more about that.

Soon enough the Hawks had everything packed up and were shouldering their packs. They fell into lines, with Kinson somewhere in the middle, well guarded. Shonn walked with them when they headed up to the farm house. Berisan and Meven were waiting.

"We'll be back as soon as we can," Sergeant Piyaro told them.

"Don't rush on my account," Yamaya strode down from her hut. She swayed gently and patted her baby's back, all the while watching the guards sharply.

"Be careful," Berisan warned unnecessarily.

The squad moved on, but Shonn deliberately stepped aside from their line. As he walked toward the farmers, Cothyr called out, "Good luck with your girl!"

Shonn choked a little. He could imagine Meven's expression at the cat-call, and the way the rest of the soldiers grinned as they passed.

"It's not luck," he managed to call back, a lame reply.

Then suddenly the squad was walking away. Shonn felt oddly adrift, as he had when he watched the Otter pole off from Oyster Rocks. He'd traveled with these men for days, shared jokes and swimming lessons, and now he was on his own again.

But his goal was still the same. Resolutely he turned toward Berisan, who wore an expression of mild concern. "Look, about you and Meven," the man began.

Shonn tensed. Here was this stranger, one of Meven's oldest friends, and his darker side wanted to demand exactly how close their friendship had been. He swallowed those words. "I'm trying to fix it, all right?"

Yamaya broke in with a knife-sharp demand. "Did you ask if you could stay here?" Too late, Shonn recalled that it was supposed to be her farm, not Berisan's.

"May I stay on?" Shonn asked humbly. He carefully didn't look at Meven. Nor did he try to answer the many questions on Berisan's face. A moment later, Ozlin burst down the steps from the hut.

"No, make him leave!" the boy cried.

"We talked about this," Meven answered quietly. Shonn would have loved to know what she said, but Ozlin was furious.

"I don't care!"

Yamaya laughed harshly. "The kid's got fire."

"Literally," Shonn joked without thinking. Berisan might even have smiled at that, but Yamaya's baby began to whimper and her mood soured.

"I'll bet you don't know a thing about farming," she accused.

"No," Shonn admitted. He gathered his wits, afraid

that his chances were slipping away. "But I notice you have some stones laid out to add another hut, and I saw where some grass trees are growing in the mangroves. They're good for building, so if you'd like I can bring them up here. Or I'll forage something else in the swamp. I can get fish, oysters, land crabs. There's fruit, too."

Shonn didn't dare look at Meven. That was how he'd courted her before, bringing gifts of catfish according to water-folk custom. There just hadn't been such a crowd around, then. But this time was going to be different.

Yamaya stared hard at him, swaying and patting her baby's back. Reluctantly, she asked, "What's a grass tree?"

"Oh. They're tall and straight, with narrow leaves like grass," Shonn explained. He was surprised Yamaya hadn't heard of grass trees. They were an important building material among the water-folk.

"It's real," Meven added, while Ozlin went on scorching Shonn with his eyes. "And we need it." It obviously galled her to admit he was right, and Berisan's expression made Shonn wonder what Meven had told him about their past entanglement.

He kept talking. "When it's green, the wood is flexible, but it dries tough and durable. So your house, I notice it's built with driftwood. The pieces are crooked, and you had to fit them together. With grass trees, the trunks are the same shape, so you can line them up easily."

Yamaya grudgingly nodded. "It sounds useful. Bring some up and then we'll see."

"All right." When no more questions came, Shonn gazed back down the slope, measuring the walking time to the mangroves. "I'll be back by late afternoon."

He hitched up his shoulder bag and headed down the path toward the beach. Behind him, Ozlin yelled, "Don't come back!"

"Oz," Meven began sternly.

Shonn paused, remembering how Ozlin had always been so hungry. He turned back to ask, "Do you want to come with me? There's lots of food in the swamp. Meven was teaching you, before. I'll show you some more, if you want."

Ozlin recoiled with a curl to his lip, as if Shonn had offered him a bag of fish guts. Meven kept her face carefully blank.

"No!" The boy jerked around to put his narrow back to Shonn.

"All right," Shonn answered. He caught an expression of wary approval from Berisan before beginning the long hike down to the beach, and the dark mass of mangroves on the near horizon. The trail was better than what Hawk Squad had the day before, but Shonn was fairly sure he would need to gather reeds and braid a new pair of sandals by the time he finished.

Meven would be worth it, no matter how many pairs of sandals he had to make.

XV — THE HORNWOOD

D amp air closed around Shonn, cooling him under the shade. It was a relief to move among the mangroves without a bunch of guards crashing after him. Every breath brought rich, green scents. Swamp and tide surrounded him with their familiar sounds and soothing touch. Up the hill, Yamaya's farm was too dry and dusty. Whispering Falls hardly counted as water. He didn't know how Meven could stand it there.

He made his way first to Frog Marsh, the last small landing where Hawk Squad would have camped if Yamaya didn't let them stay. It was more of a fisherman's rest than a family camp. The low dock was half-sinking into the lagoon, and the single hut was hardly in better condition. Still, it would do as a base to gather whatever he could forage. Besides, if he could find some reason to get Meven down here alone... The place had potential.

Invigorated by the thought, Shonn set off to find the grass trees. Two or three shoulders of land stood up among the swamp, too high for mud-loving mangroves to sprout. Sure enough, the tall, spindly stalks waved in an ocean breeze. While finding a way over to them, he gathered the vines he would need to manage them, and plucked a few fruit to eat later.

Once among the rustling grass trees, he studied them as Oberim would have, to find the thickest, straightest stalks that his bush knife could manage. You didn't want flimsy wood for a hut, especially one Meven might be living in. Remembering the custom, he would take no more than four stalks from each cluster. Otherwise, they might die.

After thoroughly sharpening his knife, he set to work. The wood was tough, but hollow inside. It wasn't hard to get them down. They weren't very heavy, either, just awkward with their length. Whenever his arms ached or his shoulders throbbed, he thought of Meven and worked with fresh vigor.

As he felled the stalks, Shonn dragged them over and laid them down parallel, until he had a dozen that would make a basic frame. Using the vines, he tied each one individually, and then wrapped the cord around to secure the lot. A last twist and loop of vines gave him something to hold.

He rested then, ate his fruit, and studied the mangroves to find the best way through. By early afternoon, he was swimming through channels to the landing with the bundle of grass trees floating behind him. Glancing at the sun, Shonn calculated that he still had enough time to fish a bit. He gutted his catch, a pair of medium catfish, wrapped them in lotus leaves, and tucked them into his shoulder bag for the walk up hill.

The trek was as much of a pain as he remembered. The long bundle dragged behind him, leaves hissing over the ground as if annoyed. Occasionally the stalks caught on something and he had to yank them loose. He frequently switched hands, and even pulled the tow loop over his shoulders for a while.

The hike had blurred into an endless round of pushing legs and panting breath by the time he felt the first wisp of moisture from Weeping Falls. Not long after, he rounded a terrace and saw the low mounds of sweet potatoes stretched along the hillside. Berisan stood among them, leaning his chin on the handle of a rake. His mournful expression alarmed Shonn. Had something happened to Meven?

Shonn was glad enough to drop the tow loop for a moment. "Everything all right?"

"Hmm?" Berisan blinked. "Yeah, just... Seeing Keilos like that..." The mage shook his head. "What've you got there?"

"Grass trees."

Berisan came over with interest. He ran his fingers through the long, narrow leaves and flexed one of the stems experimentally. Together they dragged the bundle up the last stretch to the farm.

"Boss. Shonn's back," Berisan called as they stopped in the yard. Shonn looked around, hoping to catch sight of Meven, but it was Yamaya who came out of the hut, wiping her hands from some chore.

"This is the grass tree?" She eyed it doubtfully.

"Long and straight, just like he said," Berisan agreed.

"Huh." Like Berisan, the farmer knelt to run her hands down the green stems. She grabbed one to flex it, and watched it snap back. "Might as well try it, I guess."

"Let's get it over there," Berisan said cheerfully. Grabbing the loop, he began to drag the grass trees around the side of the hut, where the new foundation was taking shape.

"I brought you something else." Shonn passed over his parcel of catfish wrapped in lotus leaves. "As thanks for your hospitality." Yamaya flipped back the topmost leaves before she nodded briskly. Shonn walked after Berisan, wondering if every woman in Opshar was this suspicious, or if it was only his luck.

Like Shonn, Berisan had been busy during the day. The foundation stones were built up higher, with steps taking shape on one side. Thick mud stuck it all together. An empty bucket and a faint trail in the grass showed how Berisan had been carrying the mud up from the riverbank below. The newest portion, where the mud was still damp, had added several deep sockets for the posts to rest in.

While Berisan checked those, Shonn knelt and untied the vines. Berisan kept eyeing him while he coiled the vines for later use. It was no surprise when the man began, "So. You and Meven."

"Me and Meven," Shonn affirmed, holding back a reflex of annoyance. With honesty, he had to add, "If I'm lucky. She must have told you what happened."

"Some of it." Berisan's face held a question.

"I'll bet Oz told you more."

That won him a grin. "You changed your mind?" Berisan persisted.

Everyone wanted to hear this, it seemed, so Shonn got on with it. "I was an ass. Is that what you need to hear? I told the Countess' guards where she was. And yes, that was the law, but that wasn't why I did it." Berisan's expression was serious, but he didn't interrupt. Shonn went on, "I was trying to punish her for... I don't even know. But then I couldn't tell her I was sorry because she was gone."

Shonn trailed off bleakly. He gazed across the valley. Meven must be out there somewhere, avoiding him like he deserved.

"So you came to find her." Berisan seemed to get that much. "Then why are you giving presents to Yamaya?"

Shonn retorted, "You said Yamaya isn't your lover, so what does it matter?"

"I'm trying to decide if I like you, for Meven's sake." Berisan was getting a little heated. "And Yamaya's my friend, too. Believe me, her knives are too sharp for you to be messing with her."

"Ugh. I'm not messing with her!" Shonn walked back

and forth a moment, rubbing the back of his head where his ponytail always itched. "It's our custom, in the water-folk. When a man wants to court a woman, he gives her presents. He fishes or gathers clams or fights a mudmaw, to show he has the skills to provide a good life."

"Okay," Berisan said in a slightly confused tone.

Shonn went on, "If the woman is interested, then she might give him a gift in return."

Berisan eyed him. "Did Meven ever give you something?"

It was a fair question, but hard to hear. Meven had always been reticent. Except for on that one day, when she'd given him several kisses.

"Sort of," he smirked, but then went sober. "If the man is really serious, or... if he messed up really bad... then he brings presents to everyone." Shonn swept a hand toward the house. "Like fish for Yamaya's cooking pot. And he gives bigger gifts, like building a hut."

Berisan's expression had cleared. Shonn pulled one of the largest grass trees out of the stack.

"This'll make a good main support, I think." He started hacking the spindly branches and leaves off the top. They worked in silence, lifting the cleaned stalk upright and taking it to try in one of the sockets.

"A little loose," Berisan observed. "We can pack the gap with mud."

"Better than too tight," Shonn replied.

As they lifted the post and set it aside, Berisan asked, "So Meven knows all this?"

"She's water-folk," Shonn said, though instantly there was a doubt. He didn't actually know if Meven had told the truth about herself. Berisan claimed to know her. This was a chance to get some answers. "Lake Bilseng, right?"

"I think so." Berisan was already pulling out another of the stems for Shonn to clear of leaves. "She ran away from the temple school at Ortach, before Ar-Thea found her. Ortach is right near Lake Bilseng."

"So she was part of your group?" Shonn slashed at the top of the grass tree, eager to hear anything more about Meven's past.

Berisan hesitated for a moment, but seemed resigned. "I guess it's not much of a secret any more. We're renegades, Shonn. Our mentor, Ar-Thea, taught us that Dar-Gothull's regime is a perversion that withers all the life and joy from Skaythe."

"That sounds dangerous." Shonn paused with his work knife poised. He couldn't argue that it wasn't true.

"There were six of us," Berisan said. "We traveled about as minstrels, trying to help people who were hurt by the regime. One day, we hoped enough people would be inspired that Skaythe could change."

"Meven did?" She had always been so closed in. Every day in Fang Marsh, all she wanted to do was hide from the world. In a way, it was what the water-folk did, too. Staying on their houseboats, not getting involved in problems on the land.

"Sure," Berisan said. "She did a puppet show with folk stories."

Shonn continued gaping. He couldn't believe Meven did something so romantic as trying to change the world.

Berisan shrugged, embarrassed yet defiant. "It was worth it. People are worth it."

Even if it meant starting a rebellion where those same people were sure to die? Shonn couldn't agree with that. Yet, if it meant he gained approval from one of Meven's oldest friends, he vowed to keep his mouth shut about it.

There was a hut to be built.

~ ~ ~

The oxen couldn't be moving any faster than before, yet Duessa felt as if they were flying with impossible speed on the silvery road. She kept a careful eye on their surroundings. It was easy to see why so many scary tales were told about this place. Hornpines crowded ever closer to the road. The few gaps between them were blanketed with bloodthorn and other brush. Deep shade and thick vegetation muffled the sounds of wagon wheels and horse hooves.

Yet, Duessa didn't have a sense of danger. It was as if the Hornwood deliberately drew a heavy curtain to shield them from the dangers of the world beyond its reaches.

Zathi maintained their training routines as the group moved westward. After their recent battle, the practice was oriented toward mounted combat and the mages casting shields over the wagon. Horse training continued, as well.

The evening's meditation now consisted of Duessa, Tisha, Alemin and Lorrah in a circle, with Elldri between them. All of them drew in *vitalis* and focused its warmth on her. Duessa couldn't have said it was filling the void at the girl's core, but Elldri did seem to sleep better. She took more interest in things around her, especially after Tisha suggested that she might eventually be able to work healing magic on the oxen and horses.

Midway through the fourth day after the skirmish, the highway widened into a fork. The new branch headed directly south and curved out of sight, while the main road continued to the west. Sethamis halted the wagon while Zathi reined Ember in beside Jaxynne's Cinder.

"We went south when we were leaving the tower," Zathi said. "It would take us back to Lithole, eventually."

"Yes, I see it here." Jaxynne drew a folded chart out of her saddle bag. Duessa stood up to see it, but could only make out vague outlines.

"How far do you think it is to the center?" Razeet called from her position slightly ahead of the wagon.

"When we left, we weren't stopping to get exact measurements," Jaxynne retorted.

"We're closer than not, though?" Keerin asked hopefully.

Giniver looked to Zathi. "It can't be that much farther."

The sergeant made no promises, just handed the chart back to Jaxynne, who refolded it and tucked it away again. "Let's keep moving."

Dense forest couldn't darken the guardswomen's mood as the wagon jerked into motion. Duessa saw them peering ahead eagerly. Even she had a sense of something drawing them onward. The only thing that made the guardswomen pause was when rays of sunlight slanted into the gap where several hornpines had fallen into a tangle. A light skein of mist shimmered against the gloom.

"Nobody feels any acid burning you, right?" Keerin joked, half-anxiously.

"No," Zathi answered curtly. "There's no drakanox here."

Bettain and Duessa shared an interested glance. Everyone had heard the legend of the drakanox, Dar-Gothull's most dreaded minion. It had destroyed all life in Seofan Valley. Zathi claimed it had been involved in Keilos' death, too.

"Did you really meet it?" Duessa asked Sethamis.

The driver nodded as she urged the oxen into motion. "Nasty beast. The mist had gathered on the branches, and it dripped down on us like snot. It burned when you tried to wipe it away."

"Keilos took care of it," Giniver said, partly reassuring herself.

"What if there's more than one?" Bettain persisted.

"Then we'll deal with it," Zathi answered tersely, without saying exactly how.

Of course, Razeet had a wisecrack. "Everybody yell Keilos' name, really loudly."

Zathi frowned at her, but everyone else laughed. The tension broke and they spread out, taking their usual positions before and beside the wagon.

After a short time, Lorrah asked, "Can you remind us what we expect to find when we get to the center of the forest?"

"There were a couple of strange buildings," Giniver recalled. "They were long and low and empty. No furnishings, even, except for what was in a tangled pile all in one room."

"It was something between a storehouse and a barracks," Sethamis said. "They all connected to a very tall tower that had no doors. Like spokes to the hub of a wheel, I guess."

"We tried to get into the tower, but we couldn't find a door." Keerin took up the tale. "There was a blank wall, and a couple of side rooms with some mummies."

"Mummies!" Bettain demanded. "You're taking us to a graveyard?"

"I don't know if it was meant to be a graveyard," Giniver said. "Keilos thought they were left from the Shining Ones, ages ago, but there was no burial. Or, no one left to bury them. They're just sitting there, hand in hand." The guardswoman slanted an eye at Lorrah. "Kind of like how you all sit together, working with Elldri."

"Really?" Alemin actually sounded intrigued.

Duessa shoved his shoulder. "Quit being so weird."

"Anyway," Keerin went on, "the wall looked blank, but when Keilos brought his magic light close to it, all kinds of marks appeared. Some kind of writing, we thought, all done in curves and circles."

"Razeet made a joke that people wrote their names on the wall," Sethamis said. "Keilos wrote his name with his light, and that was how he connected to the power inside."

"What do you mean, connected?" Tisha asked.

"Well, I'm not a mage," the driver answered, "but he said they had to commit themselves to being part of the tower."

"I think I get it." Alemin quickly turned on the bench, looking for Tisha. "In the Larder, I was so tired all the time, I leaned on the walls and tried to meditate. That was how I connected to the spirits in the Larder there. Through touch."

"Are we sure there's no revenant defending this one?" Bettain muttered darkly.

"If there is one, it will be Keilos. He died there." Zathi spoke with muted emotion. Duessa studied her expression, trying to decide if the sergeant was angry, or something else.

"Let's hope he's still there," Tisha murmured.

"I really want to see what he got himself turned into," Lorrah added pertly.

~ ~ ~

In contrast to Ar-Lizelle's fast and exhilarating pursuit across the plains of Ebruc, this retreat was endlessly slow and depressing. Groff and Endole kept pace with her as always. The six Ebruc soldiers trailed after them with a semblance of obedience, yet also kept a visible distance.

Ar-Lizelle was surprised. She had thought it was a

good speech. She'd praised their valor, hadn't she? Yet the soldiers showed no interest in her offer. As the days went by, she heard only a vague rumble of their voices behind her. It didn't sound like they were coming around.

Echoing her thought, Endole murmured, "Warden, I don't like this."

"No one's spoken to you?" Speaking crisply, Ar-Lizelle confirmed the obvious.

"No, and they aren't happy when I try talking to them, either," Endole said. "That's not the problem. It's the way they're riding so close, watching us."

"You think they have a plan?" Groff asked from the other side.

"We're getting closer to Ebruc Holl. They know the area." Endole shrugged, a suggestion of more.

Indeed, the square towers of Ebruc's keep were visible on a rise on the far side of a broad, well-cultivated valley. The roads here were wide, but still crowded with pack trains and carts. Her group had even encountered a small herd of cattle moving between pastures. Of course the commoners let a mage ride through, but unless Ar-Lizelle's group galloped, they were unlikely to reach the keep until sometime the next day.

Ar-Lizelle mulled Endole's advice, that the Ebruc guards were watching her for weakness. She was tempted to gallop, if it got this bunch of malcontents back to their barracks where someone else could deal with them. On the other hand, it was possible they would blab about her fault for the loss of Ar-Javan, Ar-Kyanon, and their sergeant. That was unacceptable.

Raising her voice just a bit, Ar-Lizelle asked, "Didn't you mention, a few days ago, how easy it is for tragic accidents to happen when traveling?"

Endole made a slight move, as if to look behind

them, but caught himself. "Er, yes, Warden. We must be on our guard."

The voices behind them went quiet. Groff chuckled softly.

A short time later, a steep slope dropped away before them, partly screened by a patch of trees. The road turned, skirting the trees, then angled as if to begin a switchback. Ar-Lizelle glimpsed movement and heard noises under the cover of the trees.

"What do you think that is?" She scanned the grove as wary tension gripped her shoulders.

"Wood cutters?" Endole pointed out a narrow track, where a half-loaded wagon was pulled under the branches. The noises, now that she understood them, were clearly made by axes striking tree trunks. It was nearly a fatal distraction.

She barely recognized the thunder of oncoming hooves and rattle of harness as the Ebruc soldiers charged.

Groff called, "Look out!"

He and Endole spun their horses, protecting Ar-Lizelle. She felt a moment's alarm — how had the slinking fools come so close, so quickly? — but to her own surprise, it wasn't true fear she felt. Instead, piercing joy soared through her.

"Oh, good," Ar-Lizelle hissed. She had been wanting to destroy something ever since Elldri revealed her monstrous nature. Steel flashed as the yelling Ebruc guards tried to force her two away from her. Without haste, she summoned her flaming whip.

Ar-Lizelle could see at a glance what the traitors' plan must be. On one side, the trees would hamper their movements. On the other, the slope was dangerously steep. Just as Endole predicted, they knew the area well. Riders crowded together, their horses squealing and kicking. Metal clashed as her loyal guards defended her, but it was six to two. One of the attackers had already slipped past Endole.

Ar-Lizelle smiled as she saw his slashing blade. She reined her horse just enough to avoid the strike. Her flaming whip spun about his blade and up the arm. The man was armored, so she couldn't burn him directly, but the reflex of man and beast was to escape from fire. He yelled and tried to drop his sword, while his horse whinnied in terror.

"Oh, what's the matter?" Ar-Lizelle taunted. "Is it too hot for you?" She held tight, with will and hands, as the man's horse jumped out from under him. He screamed and fell in the dust. She banished the flaming whip long enough to ride over him a few times. That upset her own mount, and she had to rein aside and get control of it.

By the time she did that, Endole and Groff had taken down one of the Ebruc soldiers and were each facing another. The remaining two were moving to flank them. Ar-Lizelle studied the scene for a moment, and summoned her flaming whip. She kicked her horse toward Groff.

"On your right!" She slashed downward between Groff and his second opponent. Sparks began to shimmer in the short grass. As Groff obeyed her, the Ebruc soldier snarled defiance.

"Do you think we'd turn on Lord Ar-Ishahl? You bitch!"

Why did people insist on calling her that, as if there was something wrong with it?

"That's right," Ar-Lizelle screeched. "I am a bitch." She flicked her lash toward him. He blocked it with his shield. After a couple of casual strikes scattered more sparks around, she feinted toward his sword-hand side, forcing him to turn so that he kept the shield between them.

"Why should I care what you think," she sneered. "I needed more guards, but you're too much of a coward, aren't you?"

That goaded him into an attack, which Ar-Lizelle met with lash ready to coil up his arm, just as she had done before. This man actually was a bit sturdier than the other, or perhaps he realized the padded gambeson beneath his mail was protecting him from the heat. He kept pressing, despite the protests of his horse. Ar-Lizelle backed her mount away, forcing the soldier to follow her along the brow of the hill. All the while, she focused her rage and hate to pour more heat through her whip.

As the pain began to penetrate, the fellow cursed and tried to pull away. "Let go, damn you!"

With a mocking laugh, Ar-Lizelle granted his request. She loosed his arm, but aimed the lash at his horse's flank. The beast was already wild-eyed and dripping foam from its mouth. It plunged forward and disappeared over the edge. The rider's curses abruptly stopped. No doubt he had met the very fate he meant for her.

Endole and Groff had both finished off their opponents and were facing the last two. Ar-Lizelle trotted her horse up behind them. A ball of fire seethed above her hand. Suddenly both Ebruc guards reined around. They galloped off in different directions.

"Hmph," Ar-Lizelle snorted. "I wonder if they'll report what happened, or just desert?"

"Well fought, Warden," Endole came to Ar-Lizelle's side, while Groff rode to the edge of the hill and peered through the screen of rising dust.

As if she needed his praise. Ar-Lizelle's heart was pounding, her breath coming hard, but she felt alive and powerful. Finally she had a victory to salve her pride.

Groff followed the retreating foes with his eyes. "Should we go after them?"

"Tempting," she said, but with only three of them, it was too risky to divide their forces. "Let their count deal with them. Come."

She turned her own sweated and wild-eyed horse to walk it slowly along the trail, giving it a chance to cool down. Her two guards followed obediently.

"Truly, it's been a tragic day," she intoned with sarcastic gloom. The Ebruc guards' horses were scattering, but their bodies still lay about. "Do we want to take anything from them?"

"I doubt it," Endole said. "What happened to the one who went down the hill?"

"Horse ran off," Groff reported. "The man's down, wasn't moving, but I don't know if he's dead."

"Are there switchbacks below?" Ar-Lizelle asked.

"Yes, Warden."

"Then we'll find out soon enough."

Farther back, she glimpsed a group of wood cutters running out around their wagon. They clutched their axes as if they didn't know what to do with them.

"Want some horses?" she called mockingly. Remembering that she was still all but penniless, she told her men, "Grab anything we can sell."

"We could sell the horses," Groff immediately suggested, but Endole shook his head.

"They'd be known as the count's stock. We'd have to take them out of Ebruc, and we don't have time for that." Endole glanced at Ar-Lizelle for confirmation.

"Just hurry up and search their bags," she told them. "I need coin, and then I want a word with Ar-Ishahl."

~ ~ ~

"Who's this?" Captain Jorus eyed Kinson with wary disinterest.

"A traitor," Sergeant Piyaro answered flatly. "He's

from Opshar, but he was caught sneaking a message into Deeve."

"Is that so," Jorus growled.

As Piyaro had hoped, Huld's bandits had brought Hawk Squad through the mountains in only three days, leaving them nearly at the outskirts of Pulgoll Holl before they vanished back into the landscape. Kinson was still bracketed among the Hawks, swaying slightly in his torn and grubby finery. The man had finally given up on persuading anyone. He now peered up at Pulgoll's guard captain from hollowed eyes.

Before Jorus could ask for more details, Nyette strode up beside Piyaro. She'd straightened her brown mage robe and combed her hair into a sleek knot. Her butterfly hair clips glittered like a crown.

"Kinson is not important," she declared loudly. "The rebels in Opshar are incorrigible. We must see Count Ar-Azlor immediately."

At least one passing soldier paused to stare at her. Piyaro gritted his teeth at her nerve. This wasn't even her city, to be making demands like that. Captain Jorus was equally unimpressed.

"You're the liaison, I suppose."

"Correct," Nyette answered, all brass. Piyaro expected the captain to brush her aside, but he only nodded.

"What took you so long? We've been waiting." Without allowing a response, he turned to one of his nearby guardsmen and jabbed a thumb at Kinson. "Put him in irons until the Count can deal with him. You two are with me," he added.

"Yes Captain." Piyaro waited only long enough to see Kinson led away before he passed leadership to Cothyr. "Get some rest. I'll be back as soon as I can."

Jorus was striding away, with Nyette right on his heels. Piyaro hurried after them. There was no way he'd let Nyette get away that easily. He had too many questions.

For one thing, it didn't make sense that Captain Jorus would come down himself when he heard Hawk Squad had returned. He could have sent a runner with a message. Maybe Jorus was telling the exact truth when he said they had been waiting. Given what Piyaro knew of the secret letters being carried around, that might be a good thing. But it probably wasn't.

The captain led them through the outer defenses. Piyaro caught brief glimpses of the sergeants he had met. Amren turned with an inscrutable expression to watch them pass. In the busy fortress, other men stood on guard or went about with purpose. Piyaro remembered his first impression, that everyone here was haughty and unfriendly. Now that he knew more, he wondered if Jorus and the other sergeants were in on Ar-Azlor's scheme. Naturally, they didn't trust a bunch of roving hunter-guards like Hawk Squad.

That was assuming Nyette's carefully worded speculations had any truth to them.

If they did, what then? The count must had been planning this for some time. He would have pruned away those who disagreed. Still, it seemed impossible that everyone in the castle and county would be willing to turn against Dar-Gothull's regime. Surely there would be those with a motive to strike on behalf of the wizard-king.

Captain Jorus led them across a courtyard, walled on all sides and overlooked by snipers. Piyaro tried not to be obvious as he looked around for some hint of what was coming. He saw only the same superior confidence as before. Was that pity in their eyes, or scorn? Silently he grappled with his options.

Piyaro had gone through the maelstrom of a mage war once already, in Sloram. He shuddered to recall the chaos. How could he ask Cothyr and the others to go through that again?

All too soon, Piyaro followed Jorus and Nyette up an exposed stair and under the yawning gate of the keep itself. There was another courtyard hemmed in with spy perches, and an armored portal into a large hall. Like Ar-Torix's chamber at Eshur, the walls and ceiling were hung with banners, and there were guards posted at several side doors.

However, the throne on the dais was empty. A murmuring crowd milled about, as if the session had recently ended. At one side of the chamber, a group of secretaries appeared to be making notes of who still wanted their petitions heard.

"Wait here," Jorus told them, and strode over to one of the guards.

Piyaro found it hard to concentrate on their surroundings. If Nyette was wrong about Count Ar-Azlor's intentions, that would be even worse. The count would be the one who turned. He'd make short work of a student like Nyette. Piyaro and his men would be down in irons along with Kinson before they knew what was happening.

Except... With a slight start, he realized that Captain Jorus had not demanded that he give up his weapons this time. Piyaro had the means to prove his loyalty in a different way.

He glanced aside, where Nyette stood stiffly in her false dignity. The obvious solution was to strike the girl down himself, ridding his count of a traitorous viper.

Yes, Piyaro knew her. They had traveled together for weeks, sharing scant rations and damp nights in the marsh. She seemed to be an ordinary girl, following orders and trying to stay alive, like everyone. He reminded himself that it wasn't true. Nyette was a mage with ambitions. Even if he did kill her, would it be enough to save Hawk Squad?

Captain Jorus was back. "This way," he clipped out, and led them through one of the side entrances. A staircase wound higher, then passed an armored door, currently open. Beyond was a foyer with richer furnishings. Through an open door Piyaro glimpsed several ladies in fine gowns laughing over a game table. These must be the count's family quarters.

Piyaro found himself sweating, and not just from climbing the stairs. Jorus knocked on another door. Though framed by elaborate carvings, the door was metal, strong. Pressure tightened around his throat, as it had when they approached Sloram Keep with Count Ar-Dayne on his stretcher. There had to be a way out of this, for him and Hawk Squad.

A servant opened the door, well dressed as befitted a count's household. "Captain Jorus, my lord," he murmured, and held the door open wider.

Beyond was a sitting room, where a row of narrow windows cast bright light over the wall hangings, thick carpets, and carved furniture. Three junior mages stood or sat around the room. Three was the customary number, Piyaro recalled from his years in Sloram. Enough mages to keep a harsh eye on each other, but too few for any to sneak away on their own business.

These three stared past Jorus to study Nyette with veiled hostility. That, too, was intimately familiar. At the desk, Count Ar-Azlor wrote quickly into a ledger before him. The servant took it and bowed out, shutting the door quietly.

Piyaro was last in the room, overlooked by all this scrutiny. Nyette was directly in front of him, her back turned. Conflicting knowledge buzzed in his mind.

As Ar-Azlor's man, he should trust the count. Let him make the decisions. He also should not allow Nyette to voice her treason. He should silence her before she destroyed them all.

Having her here was Ar-Azlor's responsibility. It was

Piyaro's, too. He was the one who'd brought her.

Without his wishing, his hand inched toward his sword's hilt.

~ ~ ~

"I feel like I've been in this wagon forever," Bettain grumbled as she tried to stretch out her legs without kicking anyone.

"I know," Duessa murmured. "I've lost count of how long it's been since we got out of the Larder." Days and weeks blurred together into one extended ride, interrupted only by the minstrels' performance at the way station. Even their battle with Ar-Lizelle seemed like a long time ago.

"When will we get there?" Lorrah teased in a whining sing-song. Everyone chuckled.

It was strange, though. Duessa knew they should be hurrying. It was only a matter of time before someone else caught up with them. Yet there was an odd serenity to the silvery road, rolling on between the sheltering trees. As if it were truly endless and they somehow traveled outside of time itself.

Duessa frowned a little. Zathi kept saying to keep their eyes open, that the Hornwood was dangerous. Could this sense of ease be part of another trap? She turned back, where Tisha had begun walking beside Cylass and the donkey. Then, abruptly, she scooted over to dangle her legs off the back.

"I'm going to walk for a while," Duessa said.

"Don't let me stop you," Bettain snorted. Elldri was dozing and said nothing.

The oxen went so slowly, it was hardly a jolt to jump down. Duessa landed on her feet and spent a moment scuffing the road surface. Her sandals made no impression, of course, yet there was a sort of resonance beneath her feet.

Staring behind, she wondered if she imagined a pale glow beneath the shadowed trees.

"Something wrong?" Ever alert, Cylass stopped beside her.

Shaking her head slightly, Duessa knelt to press her palm to the smooth paving. It should have been cool with the shade of so many trees falling on it. Yet she felt a familiar, steady warmth.

Straightening slowly, she asked Tisha, "Is it just me, or is there some sort of spell?"

"What are you sensing?" Tisha stopped and Riprap stood twitching its ears impatiently.

"Everyone is so calm." Duessa began to walk slowly. Sometimes, with Ar-Lannon, she'd done her best planning while they were on the move. "We shouldn't be. Ar-Lizelle is still after us."

"That's for certain," Cylass predicted dourly.

"There is a feeling in the air," Tisha admitted, "but this is the Hornwood. Who knows what's in here, just out of sight."

That was not a pleasant thought. Yet the fear of hidden dangers was almost the opposite of what Duessa sensed. She thought again of the gentle heat beneath her hands when she touched the road surface.

She blurted, "Could there be *vitalis* in the highway?"

Tisha gazed at her, startled. "They say it was made by the Shining Ones." She paused, just as Duessa had, to press her hands to the pavement. "Hmm. I think you're right. There is an energy below us. It seems to be flowing, but slowly. Like a spring that only trickles from the ground."

The guardswomen were starting to look around, probably wondering what they were up to. Duessa said, "Let's not stop everyone."

Tisha nodded, and the three of them moved on. Within moments, though, Alemin had also jumped down and was walking back to them. Zathi caught Lorrah riding past, and Duessa saw the girl's sweet face also watching them.

"What's going on?"Alemin asked, and Tisha quickly explained.

"It's probably not important," Duessa said.

Alemin frowned thoughtfully. "In the Larder," he said slowly, and just the name of it raised a few hairs on Duessa's arms, "I learned that the highways were conduits for *vitalis* to be shared all over Skaythe. Did I tell you that?"

"I don't remember," Tisha said.

"We talked about a lot of stuff at once," Duessa reminded him wryly.

Cylass asked, "Do we know where this part of the highway goes?"

"I haven't got a good look at Jaxynne's charts," Alemin said, "but from what Zathi was saying, there's a large well of *vitalis* and nothing has been drawing from it. If the roads are all connected, the flow could reach as far east as Seofan Holl."

"You think so?" Tisha asked, startled. "It's just a slight flow, but I only awakened a few of the oleya trees."

"They wouldn't pull much. Dar-Gothull was able to cast his mind into the Larder, too." Alemin was getting excited.

"That's Dar-Gothull," Duessa said. "He's ancient. He has to know all about it."

"The whole network must still be there, just waiting for someone to tap it," Tisha marveled.

"But can we trust it?" Duessa seemed to recall Tisha herself saying they shouldn't cast too much around the highways.

"It's from a long time ago," Alemin answered.

Duessa stopped listening for a moment, trying to imagine what Alemin was saying. A network of channels, spreading *vitalis* all over Skaythe? She pictured the landscape of her home. These ancient highways penetrated even Busaren's high mountains. Duessa recalled an old tower where Ar-Lannon's crew had camped between jobs. She was sure it had the same elegant, rounded shape as the Larder. She remembered, too, the broken, crumbled highway they had bumped across when they were fleeing the mages' prison. If Alemin and Tisha were right, the Shining ones had build them all. That was if you believed the Shining Ones had been real, which Duessa greatly doubted.

"How far does all this extend?" she asked.

"Supposedly, all of Skaythe," Tisha said.

They all fell silent again, thinking about what it could mean. Then, because it felt good to move, Duessa just walked along with Alemin and the others and tried not to feel the subtle drift of *vitalis* beneath her feet.

The high fringe of hornpines was just tickling the sun's disc when Jaxynne and Keerin, who had been scouting forward, returned at an eager trot. "I think we're close," Jaxynne called to Zathi. Everyone came to alert, even Elldri, searching the trees for a sign of the fabled tower.

"It feels about time," Zathi agreed.

"Where?" Bettain asked after a moment. "All I see are trees."

"The ground is rising," Razeet jumped in. "Look over there."

Duessa frowned in that direction. It was hard not to agree with Bettain. There seemed to be nothing there. However, it was possible that the land was rising before them and they just couldn't see past the wall of trees and brush crowding endlessly on either side of their narrow slot road.

"There will be a sharp curve ahead that doesn't straighten out," Jaxynne predicted. "Then we'll know we're almost there."

"Don't look with your eyes," Lorrah suggested to the other mages. "We should be able to sense the *vitalis* before we see anything."

Bettain grumbled at that, but Lorrah may not have been wrong. One of the horses snorted anxiously.

"Oh calm down," Jaxynne stroked the neck of her red roan, Spark. "There's nothing to get fussed about."

Spark was always the most excitable horse, Duessa had noticed. He might not be wrong, though. Razeet's bay, Tinder, started to toss its head, too. Badger Squad might not be near the tower, but the horses were definitely aware of something they didn't like. Duessa immediately thought of more soldiers. Out of caution, she strode forward to get back up on the wagon.

"Get in position," Sergeant Zathi called. Tisha and Alemin followed Duessa's lead. Cylass pulled Riprap forward to tie its lead to the back of the wagon, and pulled himself up to watch behind.

"Too bad there isn't another way around," Keerin said, as her dun began to caper. "Smoke, calm down."

"Hurry, let's see if we can get past it," Zathi said.

"Yes Sergeant." Sethamis snapped the reins and called to the oxen. "Get up, boys. Get now."

All the horses showed signs of nervousness, but there really was no other path to take. True to Jaxynne's prediction, the highway began to curl south. Duessa held the wagon's rail with an ever-tightening grip. The land was definitely rising sharply ahead of them. With the dense forest, it was hard to see more than that.

It was also hard to see the danger until the trees thrashed up ahead of them, and a giant beast bounded out of the forest.

"Shit," Sethamis yelled, hauling on the reins.

The guardswomen burst into curses as all of them fought to control their frantic horses. Lorrah, whose mount was the best trained, stood in the stirrups to gaze down the road. In an awed voice, she cried, "Is that the giant badger?"

XVI — REVELATIONS

L ike a bandit in the mountains, Piyaro focused on his target and waited for an opening. Oblivious to the danger, Count Ar-Azlor nodded courteously to Nyette.

"Welcome in friendship," he said. Piyaro studied his bland expression, trying to understand the count's intentions.

"Thank you, Count." Nyette stroll forward, bold as ever. "Unfortunately, the news from Opshar is dire. Another mage has joined the uprising. You must ride yourself, to defeat the rebels."

How she twisted the truth to suit herself! Piyaro ground his teeth.

"Must I?" Ar-Azlor inquired with the arrogance of a dog being given direction by a rat.

He didn't seem to be contemplating rebellion against Dar-Gothull. So Nyette was lying after all. Piyaro slid forward. The well oiled leather made no sound as he drew his blade.

"You wrote to Countess Ar-Torix with a question. I have a partial answer." Nyette glanced around at the junior mages. With a hint of belligerent challenge, she said, "I assume everyone here is aware of the issue?"

A heavy hand fell on Piyaro's shoulder. He jumped. Jorus growled in his ear. "Put it away."

Piyaro hissed back, "She is a viper. I must..."

"Don't be a fool," Jorus snapped.

Their muffled conversation alerted the junior mages, who jumped to readiness. Ar-Azlor saw past them, startled. Then Nyette reacted to everyone else and turned. Piyaro saw the quick flash of hurt in her eyes.

"You have something to say, Sergeant?" Ar-Azlor was calm, commanding attention.

Fury warred with Piyaro's shame and fear. "She claims that she speaks for you, but what she advocates, it is treachery. How can I know this is your will?"

"Because he says it is," Nyette interrupted.

"He never said that," Piyaro bit back. "You hinted at promises, twisted words to snare everyone. But I..."

"Out of caution," she cried, exasperated.

"Put it away," Jorus ordered.

The other mages glared at Piyaro. His steel was pointed at Nyette, who wasn't a friend but was still a fellow mage. In some way, already, she was one of them. Worse was Ar-Azlor's bland consideration, stroking his beard and weighing something that Piyaro could only guess at. A sour ball gathered in his stomach, but he held it down.

In an ashen whisper, he appealed to his count. *"How can I know?"*

"All you had to do was follow orders." Jorus spoke with the old contempt. Black eyes went to Ar-Azlor with a message of finality.

Nyette saw it, too. "Stop. I want more of an explanation."

The nerve of her! Yet Piyaro discovered he wasn't quite ready to die.

"What more?" he choked out. "All this hinting and secrecy leads to one thing. To war. I've done that once. In Sloram." His hand was shaking, and he hadn't yet let go of his blade. "After that, with the golden witch, we carried Count Ar-Dayne back half alive and they all... exploded." His throat closed up, so he could barely get the words out. "There was fire and lightning, blasts everywhere. We grabbed the servants and family and stuffed everyone into the lower keep, while the whole place shook over our heads. We could hear the smashing and the screaming, there was smoke coming in. It was nothing a common swordsman could fight."

Nyette's expression softened, but it was Jorus he appealed to. Surely a commander of men understood the responsibility Piyaro had faced. The man's broad face showed no sympathy.

"We gave you a chance," he rumbled, disgusted, "and this is your loyalty."

"No," Ar-Azlor spoke at last, in the slow way he had when he'd told Piyaro his squad wouldn't be going anywhere. "This *is* loyalty, Jorus. To question a decision that might lead me into danger. But, Sergeant, I do know what's at stake. Even better than you."

He and the junior mages nodded among themselves. Piyaro remembered how Nyette spoke of breaking the rituals that bound them to Dar-Gothull. He finally flexed his fingers enough to allow his sword to slide back into its sheath.

"You take this risk for all of us," Piyaro spoke up for his guardsmen, even for Ragis, who he hadn't yet seen and now wondered about.

"It is a necessary risk." Ar-Azlor spoke with finality, yet also turned a hidden question to Nyette. "You say I, personally, must go to Opshar?"

"The ringleaders are there. You can settle it once and for all," Nyette resumed her noisy confidence. It was her pretext to get Ar-Azlor close enough to that sorcerous beast, the drakanox. Yet, Piyaro could see now, it was partly a performance. A show, to ward off discovery. That didn't make it any better.

"Then we'd best make plans. Nyette and Jorus, stay." Ar-Azlor beckoned to his junior mages as well. "Sergeant, Hawk Squad has seen these... ringleaders?"

"Yes, my lord." Piyaro nodded, feeling slightly ill.

"Then you'll have to come with us," the count decided. Which was probably wise, to get him out of Captain Jorus' sight for a while. "I imagine you've been marching for days. Go get some rest."

Piyaro seethed, futile and hopeless. "Yes, my lord. Only... Nyette will tell you, if you are truly determined, that there is a faster way through the mountains. If you are willing to talk to Chief Huld."

"Huld?" Jorus burst out angrily.

"Yes sir." It was on Piyaro's tongue to repeat Huld's brag that he had done more to secure the valley around Opshar than Pulgoll's official government had. He immediately decided he was already in too much trouble to stir up more. He saluted and left.

Jorus scowled, but he couldn't chase Piyaro down. He'd been told to stay in the meeting. As Piyaro shut the door, Nyette was smirking again. Piyaro remembered the hurt in her eyes and wished he could regret causing it. But this was still her fault, even more than his.

He'd been wanting a definite answer about Count Ar-Azlor's intentions. Now he had one. He just wished it wasn't a completely insane answer.

~ ~ ~

"I didn't think it was real," Lorrah gasped.

"Oh, it's real," Keerin groaned.

"Okay," Razeet made a tense wisecrack, even as she nocked a bolt in her crossbow. "Now is when we all yell for Keilos."

"Quit goofing around!" Zathi barked. "Get in formation."

Duessa clung to the side of the wagon and stared, while the guardswomen got their anxious horses under control. She didn't see how this beast could be real, either.

The giant badger stared down the road at them. It had a long body, wider than it was tall, with shoulders brushing the lowest branches on the hornpines. Shaggy gray-brown fur covered it except where streaks of black and white ran up its long muzzle. The small black eyes framed there held a glint of eerie intelligence.

Despite the protests of their horses, Zathi, Giniver and Keerin surged forward. The three warriors formed a barrier in front of the ox wagon. Jaxynne and Razeet came up behind them, raising their crossbows. The mages on the wagon watched anxiously as the giant badger raised its muzzle. Black nostrils flared as it scented the air.

"What do you want us to do?" Tisha called to Zathi.

"Everything!" Razeet laughed a bit hysterically.

"Quiet," the sergeant snapped, but then added. "Whatever you think will work on such a beast. Just don't blast any of us."

"What fun is that?" Bettain stood, summoning the power of flame to her hands.

In an anxious voice, Sethamis said, "Keilos made it pause before when he lit a light in front of its eyes. He pulled its feet out from under it, too. Can any of you do that?"

"Witchlight? I think so." Alemin looked to Lorrah for confirmation.

"Light? Boring," Bettain scoffed.

"I'm still tired from saving Elldri," Tisha glanced an apology to the girl.

At this, Cylass let Riprap's lead go and vaulted up to the bed of the wagon. Stepping up behind Alemin, he ordered, "Trade places with me." Once again, Cylass placed himself between Tisha and any threat.

While they did that, Duessa watched the road anxiously. Everyone seemed to expect the badger to come at them. The muzzle wrinkled in a snarl, but it didn't move.

"Don't worry, we can manage this," Lorrah said, perhaps reassuring herself. "I'll shield the oxen and the wagon. Alemin can summon the witchlight. Bettain and Duessa can throw power at it."

Elldri had been staring down the highway in awed fascination. For the first time all day, she spoke. "It's like me," she lisped.

She broke off as the giant badger fell back a pace, shaking its head. It turned and trotted down the highway. Duessa watched incredulously as fading sunlight gleamed off its fur.

"Looks like it remembers us!" Keerin whooped.

"Maybe, but it's going the same way we are," Jaxynne said.

Zathi stared suspiciously after the beast. "This is too easy." Just as it was passing out of sight, it stopped and stared back at them.

"If I didn't know better, I'd say it wants us to follow," Sethamis said.

"I don't care what it wants." Zathi hissed out a sigh. "We have to go that way. There's no other path."

"We can't cut through the trees?" Duessa asked.

"That worked because we were on the fringe of the

Hornwood," Zathi answered. "We can't risk it here. Move ahead slowly, Setha."

"Get up then," Sethamis snapped the reins and the two oxen leaned into the yoke. The riders moved forward at a cautious walk, keeping a good distance between them and their strange guide.

As the wagon began to roll, Tisha said to Elldri, "What were you going to say? It's like you..." she prompted.

"It was empty," Elldri stared after the lumbering beast. "Now, it has light, but it doesn't feel right. It doesn't know what to do."

"Huh." Bettain sat down, disappointed. Alemin traded placed with Cylass and reached out for Lorrah's hand. Cylass settled beside Tisha, his arm around her.

"I'll stay here a bit," he said, but his eyes never turned from the giant badger's tail swishing down the highway in front of them.

~ ~ ~

Ar-Lizelle claimed that she wanted to confront Ar-Ishahl, but as the hours passed, common sense reasserted itself. If, as she suspected, the count's son had sent along men he knew would try to murder her, then she would be wiser to stay out of his sight. Let him think his ploy a success, and hope the two who escaped wouldn't spoil her trick.

The one she wanted to see was Count Ar-Kilohn. If he hoped to hold power, he couldn't let another mage outshine him. Not even his own son. Ar-Lizelle needed to convince him that Elldri posed a greater threat. Then he'd be more likely to stop his son making another try at her.

Ar-Lizelle frowned as she studied the ever-increasing traffic around them. There were no open fields to cut across now. Every path was closed in by fences, and every crossroads was backed up as Ebruc's guards searched wagons, hand carts and waypacks. She wondered cautiously what they were searching for. The fugitives, probably.

The Larder team managed to move steadily, though not swiftly, because Ar-Lizelle didn't hesitate to pull rank as a mage. She also had their travel documents to back it up. Otherwise, they would have been as mired in security as the peasants were.

Ebruc's main city, and the keep on a bluff above, became less of a distant mirage and more of a solid reality as the afternoon passed. The closer they got to it, the more she recognized a similarity with that border post to Unthur. Ebruc was swarming with guards.

"This is unpleasantly familiar," Groff muttered behind her.

"I know." Endole replied.

Ar-Lizelle glanced back and nodded. There was a lot of soldiery around. Large squads of 20 or more marched through in orderly ranks. There were also many single mages, like Ar-Lizelle, with a handful of armed men trailing behind. All of them seemed to be heading for the keep.

"The inns are going to be jammed, Warden," Endole said. "Should we try to find a room and start asking around?"

"The inn, yes." Ar-Lizelle had been thinking the same thing. As soon as Endole said it, she understood what they were seeing. "Don't bother with the questions. They'll only make us look suspicious. It's obvious what's happening."

After a moment, Endole asked cautiously, "Warden?"

"Dar-Gothull has summoned the mages to battle, and Count Ar-Kilohn is mustering his forces." At least, she sourly reflected, there wasn't much worry about avoiding Ar-Ishahl. He'd hardly notice her among so many. All they had to do was move along with the rest.

Ar-Lizelle smiled without mirth. "I suspect we'll be seeing our friends again, very soon."

~ ~ ~

"Get out of the way, you stupid beast," Keerin grumbled.

The giant badger seemed determined to block their way. It plodded ahead of them, stopping to look back when the ox cart got too far behind. The guardswomen worked constantly to stay in control of their sweated and balky horses. The calming flow of *vitalis* beneath their feet and hooves was just enough to keep everyone sane.

The situation wasn't much better, though. The sun had dropped below the trees, and they should have been searching for a place to camp. Nobody had mentioned that yet. How could they?

"I don't understand why it's staying on the road," Lorrah said thoughtfully.

"You're right." Duessa had been wondering the same thing. The creature's great size didn't seem to hamper its movements. "If it came out of the woods, it should be able to go back in."

"Maybe it likes us," Razeet teased.

"Don't ask me," Sethamis snapped.

"Take it easy," Alemin said softly. "Didn't you say the first time you saw it, it came right at you? If it's holding back now, maybe Elldri is right and Keilos has some kind of influence on it."

"We'd better hope so," Bettain muttered.

Just as Jaxynne had predicted, the silvery road curved ahead of them in a slow inward coil. The shortened sight line made the badger stay closer than anyone would have liked. But to their left, which would be the center of the coil, that rising land was obvious now. So was the steady pulse of *vitalis* As they passed, there was a low hill that extended toward it. Not a natural form, either. The sides were too straight. A spoke of the wheel, as Sethamis had described it.

"We must be getting close," Giniver said. Zathi grunted in agreement.

"I think it's leaving!" Jaxynne called in a cautious tone.

Everyone stared ahead as the giant badger's shaggy back and sloping tail shimmied out of sight. Brighter light ahead of them suggested the trees were thinning out. When they got to that place, the highway straightened out and entered a broad wedge of clearing framed by two long hills.

"This is it," Zathi declared unnecessarily.

The space was level, and unnaturally clear of vegetation, just like the highway that flowed into it. The long hill Duessa had seen stretched on to their left. To the right, the giant badger stood by a dark gap in one of the hills. It gazed at them a moment longer before shaking itself and disappearing into the gap.

"Finally," Keerin groaned.

The wagon vibrated as people began to drop off and look around. Alemin, Tisha and Lorrah clustered in close conversation, while Sethamis jumped down and dug out a stick of sugar cane. She cut chunks for the guardswomen to feed their horses, while they stroked their necks and praised them for being so brave. Even Zathi had nothing ominous to say for once.

Duessa stayed where she was, studying the edifice before them. Brush and trees covered the flanking hills, but the tower rose straight up, smooth sides coming to a rounded top. There were no windows that she could see. Its elegant simplicity matched that of the Larder, though this one was bigger around, and stood higher than the hornpines. The last daylight bathed it in rich gold. Layers of drifting mist wreathed the smooth sides, like nets drying around a fishing boat on a lazy afternoon.

More than a beautiful vista, though, it held her eyes and tugged at her heart. *Vitalis* was everywhere here, not just beneath them but warming their skin and filling their lungs with every breath. Duessa could see why the badger grew large, living in a place that pulsed with life. Even knowing the dangers that followed them, and with the giant badger nearby, this place felt peaceful. As if nothing bad could ever happen here.

Cylass led Riprap over to Tisha. "Lady, shouldn't we make camp?"

Tisha seemed to shake herself. "You're right. It's good to be here, but night will close in soon."

Jaxynne glanced at Zathi, but she was still distracted, seeking something in the depths of the forest. "Sergeant?"

"What? Oh. Yes." Duessa expected another dour warning about the dangers of the Hornwood, but Zathi only nodded. "Spread out and look around. There may be an entrance into another of the hills."

"What," Razeet quipped. "You don't want to bunk up with our namesake?"

Laughing, the guardswomen spread out to search. Zathi remained beside the wagon, wrapped in her own thoughts, until Lorrah drew up beside her.

"Are you all right?"

"Just memories." Zathi replied tersely.

Tisha approached to ask, somberly, "Which of these hills is... is Keilos in?"

His body, she meant. Duessa had forgotten about that. Alemin and the rest had lost a good friend here.

"One more over, I think." Zathi pointed curtly past the giant badger's den.

"You know he's been dead for months," said Sethamis, who had stayed with the wagon.

"We still want to see him." Alemin seemed undeterred by the thought of a months-old corpse.

"And that wall of names," Lorrad added.

Zathi looked unhappy at the prospect. "Daylight would be better."

Unexpectedly, Bettain walked over. "If you want a proper funeral, we could stack some of this brush up and I'll light it for you."

Alemin nodded his appreciation. "Thanks, Bettain."

Impatiently, Zathi asked, "Can we get a lantern going, at least?"

Something tugged at Duessa's mind, distracting her. A subtle movement drew her eyes back to the main tower. Although the sun fell ever lower, the soft glow hadn't changed. Slowly she understood.

"That's not sunlight. It's coming from the tower." Duessa hadn't realized she was speaking out loud until everyone turned to look at her.

"You're right," Lorrah turned in the saddle. "Is it all *vitalis*?"

"It must be. There's no other power here," Tisha replied.

"What's it doing?" Bettain demanded warily.

Pale golden mist was swirling lower, condensing into thick coils. The shape reminded Duessa of the tentacles from Elldri's nightmare form. Others exclaimed with recognition. Zathi raised a hand to her mouth and whistled the sharp pattern to recall her squad.

"This isn't what I felt in Seofan," Tisha answered despite Cylass trying to push her back behind the wagon.

"Please stop. There's no evil here."

"It's pure *vitalis*," Alemin confirmed.

"It's Keilos," Zathi said in a strange, breathy voice. "He's still here."

"How can that be?" Duessa asked. Zathi had clearly told them the renegade mage was dead, and she acted like she was grieving.

The roaming guardswomen cantered and trotted the short distance to form around the wagon. Demands for information and what to do fell silent as Giniver cried, "It's the drakanox!"

"Look!" "Yes, it's him!" Excited exclamations greeted this news. Strangely, the horses showed none of the alarm they had when the grant badger was nearby.

The coils of mist lifted from the tower and glided gently toward them. The drakanox, if that was what it was, gathered form as it came. It was oversized, like the badger, with a billowing mane and branching antlers followed by a long, fish-scaled body. A mighty tail swept behind it.

Most striking were the eyes, glowing pale yellow like the sunrise on a clear day. The drakanox surveyed them all with joyful recognition, yet mingled with sorrow and regret. Its emotions pervaded the air, just as the *vitalis* did. A choked noise came from Elldri's direction, but Duessa couldn't untangle herself from what she — what everyone, together — was feeling.

Tisha was right. There was no sense of danger here. However, it was still intimidating when the huge creature hovered a few feet from them.

"Keilos, my friend." Alemin stepped toward it, and the great muzzle dipped slowly toward him. In moments, Lorrah was down from her horse and running to join them. Tisha would have gone, too, but Cylass dragged on her arm.

"My lady," he cautioned, alarmed by the idea of her running up to such a thing.

"You are here. All of you?" The drakanox's voice pressed into Duessa's mind delicately, as if it feared to hurt them. The mages answered in a similar way, with affirmations and concerns of the mind, not the ears.

"We didn't find Berisan or Meven —" Lorrah began, but Zathi cut her off.

"Yes, damn you!" Zathi, who was no mage, spoke aloud. "I went out and found them. I brought them back for you."

"Oh my friend," came the soft reply. Duessa expected words of gratitude, but instead the impression was of sorrow and regret. *"This is not your fault."*

There was more that Duessa didn't catch, something private between Zathi and Keilos. The hard-bitten Sergeant scrubbed angrily at moisture on her cheeks.

"Keilos, I'm sorry, too," Tisha cut in, ragged. "We shouldn't have split up."

"We weren't there when you needed us," Alemin's fists were taut at his sides.

"Don't," the drakanox replied. *"This is what we decided. All of us, together. Remember?"*

"We agreed to follow your premonition," Lorrah cried. "But we didn't decide you should die alone!"

"My visions were clear. If we hadn't made that choice, the whole troupe could have been taken."

"Wait a minute!" Razeet's horse skittered forward. Incredulously, she demanded, "You knew this would happen?"

"Not exactly this." The drakanox ruffled its scales with wry humor. *"I foresaw I would be arrested. There's*

usually only one end to that."

"Oh, come on," Bettain half-accused. "Nobody volunteers for the Larder!"

And Keerin followed, aghast. "How could you do it?"

"Don't be stupid." Jaxynne snorted lightly, the way she had when Elldri spoke of her murders as something to be ashamed of. "Any one of us would take a hit for the others."

"Most soldiers wouldn't," Cylass said with dark certainty. Tisha turned a moment to rest her hand on his arm, where the vivid red scars swarmed.

"So that my friends would survive," Keilos answered Keerin and Bettain. *"If we hadn't separated, Ar-Thea's dream would have been destroyed for another generation. Everything you've learned and done since then would never have been achieved."*

The guardswomen stared up at him, much the way Duessa thought she must be staring. It was impossible to think that anyone knowingly gave their life for someone else. Nobody in all Skaythe was that noble.

Yet she acknowledged the irony, that she herself had been a sacrifice for her band of moon-runners. The difference was that it hadn't been her decision. Ar-Lannon and the others had chosen for her, when they abandoned her.

"Seofan Valley would still be cursed," Keilos went on. *"The Larder would be feeding your power to Dar-Gothull. Meven and Berisan have made alliances that are fragile, but they wouldn't exist at all, otherwise. And you —"* he projected great tenderness and humor *"— you lethal and insanely brave women, would still be prisoners, too."*

Now it was the guardswomen who chuckled at some joke that the mages weren't part of.

"Yeah," Giniver grinned. "You're going to have to tell us how you tamed that giant badger."

"It was magic," Keilos explained, as if he was telling some great secret. They all laughed again. Zathi was first to recover her stern bearing.

"I assume you have a plan?" she asked.

"That... is complicated," Keilos replied. *"You need to set camp, I think. We'll have time to figure it out."*

Surprised by the reminder, the gathered warriors and mages looked around them. The glow Keilos shed had concealed that the dusk was deepening steadily around them. Without him, they would hardly be able to see. To Duessa's mind, that wasn't the most important thing.

"How can it be complicated?" she burst out, exasperated. This was just like when they got out of the Larder. "Either you have a plan, or you don't."

"The plan won't be for me," he answered, again with that rueful tone. *"Come on, I'll show you where you can camp."*

The drakanox trailed its glow toward the hill opposite the giant badger's den, and the squad had little choice but to follow.

～ ～ ～

They were almost too late in finding an inn. Coming in from the north as they were, Ar-Lizelle chose to halt at a wretched farming hamlet still some distance from Ebruc Holl. There was only one inn, and with Ebruc so full of soldiers it should have been noisy with their revels. Instead, it was strangely quiet as they approached.

Ar-Lizelle knew better than to think her luck was so good. When she saw the banner curling lazily in the breeze of dusk, she knew the reason why. It was red, of course, with a silver panther prowling across it. A hiss of displeasure slid between her teeth.

"Warden, is that..." Endole began.

"Ar-Gammord." She cut him off, and cursed softly. Why couldn't it be Ar-Khoreen of Yergha, or Ar-Nikolus of Kamuril. She could have worked with them. Perhaps not gladly, but well enough. The paranoid count Ar-Gammord would never have been her choice of allies.

"That explains why it's so quiet," Groff muttered.

Beneath the wide porch, guardsmen stood watch at the door. Vague shadows of figures flickered past lamplight inside. Ar-Lizelle wondered ironically if everyone in the inn had to take their shoes off, or if Ar-Gammord tolerated some deviance due to conditions on the road.

"Do we seek elsewhere?" Endole clearly hoped so.

The guards were staring at them, no doubt agreeing that they not attempt to enter. This sparked the memory of Ar-Lizelle's annoyance during their brief visit to Unthur Holl, and it reminded her of something else. Ar-Gammord controlled his household so strictly, she doubted he had many other mages with him, or many guards. His paranoia wouldn't allow it.

That created a possible opportunity. Even one more mage, with only two guards, could be a valuable addition to his retinue, if she could persuade him to agree. It also served her interest in not traveling through Ebruc so lightly defended.

"I won't leave without trying," she announced. "It's getting dark."

Yet, the blatant failure of her most recent effort to gather allies could not be brushed aside. In a calculated gesture, Ar-Lizelle swung down from her horse. She led it slowly toward the inn, where one of the guards hurried to intercept her.

"Forgive me, my lady." He cleared his throat nervously. "Count Ar-Gammord of Unthur is in residence. He will not allow anyone other than his own household."

"I am known to the Count." Ar-Lizelle gritted teeth a little, recalling how touchy that man was. "I assume Ar-Vennic is here?"

"Yes, my lady. But..." The guard faltered.

"Let me speak to him. I believe we can come to an arrangement." Her dark eyes bored unto him, until he gave way.

A short time later, the anxious Ar-Vennic led her to an upstairs chamber. Endole and Groff waited below, while Ar-Lizelle quelled her natural commanding presence and minced along in stocking feet. Ar-Gammord sat in a humble chair near a brazier. Its radiant glow was the only element of cheer in the gloomy chamber.

He must have been even more alert than Ar-Lizelle supposed, for he demanded, "Who is that?" before Ar-Vennic even had the door open.

"Warden Ar-Lizelle wishes to speak to you, my lord," Ar-Vennic murmured, bowing low. Ar-Lizelle mimicked the gesture, moving slowly and gracefully.

"It's a pleasure to see you so well." She made an effort to soften her high, harsh voice.

"Huh. You look like a vagabond," he sniffed, reminding Ar-Lizelle yet again that she needed to have her torn robe mended. "What is it now? We've been called to war, if you didn't notice. I've no time for your stupid prisoners."

"Allow me to explain, my lord. This is all about my escaped prisoners."

Ar-Vennic winced at her contradiction, but Ar-Lizelle quickly detailed her pursuit of the fugitives. She emphasized the treachery of Ar-Ishahl, sending along his men to assassinate her. That immediately brought up the mad light she hoped to see in his eyes. But the real effect was when she described Elldri's horrific transformation, and how quickly both Ar-Javan and Ar-Kyanon had been killed. Ar-Gammord didn't care about their fate, but Ar-Vennic certainly was paying attention.

"It was that same battle that left me so ragged," Ar-Lizelle concluded, trying to sound apologetic. Of course, she omitted the fact that it was Alemin and his friends who called Elldri off, not anything she did.

"Lord Dar-Gothull had this revenant imprisoned in the Larder?" Ar-Gammord demanded, his voice rising with alarm, quickly turning to fury. "That is what he sends us after?"

"We all must do as the master commands," Ar-Lizelle demurred.

"He'll throw us in front of that thing as bait," Ar-Gammord seethed.

"It seems to be good fortune that Warden Ar-Lizelle found us again," Ar-Vennic inserted carefully. "We would have no warning, otherwise."

That brought the count back to himself, at least as much as he ever was. Narrow-eyed, he glared at Ar-Lizelle.

"How do I know this isn't a trap?" He turned the accusation on Ar-Vennic. "She could be a spy!"

"She has given us more information than Lord Dar-Gothull did," Ar-Vennic replied.

"It is not *my* trap," Ar-Lizelle emphasized. "Yes, obviously, I come to you hoping for an alliance. As you so wisely observed, this is war, and I am greatly disadvantaged. My aide Ar-Kyanon is dead. I have no one else to trust."

This fact was disgustingly true, and both mages seemed to realize it.

"Another ally might make all the difference," Ar-Vennic suggested. For him, too, Ar-Lizelle realized. When they met before, he hadn't spoken up nearly so much.

"Huh," Ar-Gammord glared at her a moment longer, then snapped to Ar-Vennic, "Get her a proper robe at least. I won't be followed around by some shabby beggar."

Ar-Lizelle bowed again, hoping to hide her fury at the insult. "My lord, you are most wise."

"Smooth words from a so-called ally." He pinned her with his stare. "I'll be watching you, Ar-Lizelle."

Somehow she managed not to laugh in his face. "Of course. I expect you to."

Ar-Gammord was a difficult personality. That was widely known, and because of it, everyone would be watching him. Consequently, they would overlook her.

As she followed Ar-Vennic in his solemn exit, Ar-Lizelle considered this interview as a partial success. She had secured safe lodgings going forward, and a new robe, but that was the least of it. The most... could be much more. It would depend upon whether Ar-Gammord's mental state was as volatile as she suspected. And whether Ar-Vennic was tired of creeping around in his shadow.

~ ~ ~

The usual bustle of setting camp was very subdued. Keilos did keep his promise by showing them an opening in the hillside opposite the giant badger's den, but then he left them. *"I'm waiting for word from Berisan, and I must listen."*

"What about?" Alemin immediately brightened. It took Duessa a moment to remember that Berisan was his younger brother.

"Whether some of the counts are ready to reject Dar-Gothull's law." With that tantalizing suggestion, Keilos lifted away. The travelers watched him leave with various expressions of disappointment or indignation.

"The counts are always trying to figure out how they can overthrow him," Bettain said sourly.

"I don't think that's what he means," Zathi murmured. The sergeant lingered longest, while Keilos returned to hovering about the highest part of the tower. "We have to trust him."

It sounded like she was reassuring herself. Duessa was starting to wonder if there had been something between Keilos and Zathi before he turned into the drakanox. She shook her head a little. Just thinking that sentence was hard to understand.

With Keilos' departure, it was darker than ever. Lorrah, Tisha and Alemin made their witchlights blaze brightly, so that the warriors could work at cutting brush back from the entrance. Fortunately, the gap this revealed was wide enough for Sethamis to coax the oxen through. Bettain found a pair of sturdy branches and lit them for torches. With these spitting and flaring, Duessa, Elldri and Bettain followed the guardswomen into the hillside.

Beyond was a cavernous vault, stretching in both directions beyond the reach of the lights. The air was cold and still, lightly scented by pine needles and other forest debris that had blown in over decades. The three mages brought their witchlights in. Even then, the feeble glow hardly made more than a golden bubble amid the smothering darkness.

Duessa tried to ease the mood by teasing Alemin, "I guess your Shining Ones weren't too worried about leaving their doors wide open."

He shrugged. "They aren't my shining ones."

"Anyone could have opened it since then," Lorrah added.

"I'm not sure about that," Keerin said. "Did you see the size of those stone wheels that close it up?"

"That was a fun time, moving those," Giniver chuckled.

Jaxynne interrupted their banter. "Let's get the horses in and settled."

"Find our lantern first," Zathi directed. "I'd forgotten how dark it gets in here."

In truth, the horses weren't very happy about coming into an unfamiliar, dark place. Even with *vitalis* giving a soothing background thrum, Sethamis and the guardswomen had to work it slowly, persuading them that this place was safe. The skittish red roan, Spark, resisted everything Giniver tried, until he realized the rest of the horses had gone in and he was going to be alone outside.

The horses' drama gave the mages time to explore a little. That long aisle followed the spine of the hill. It was edged on both sides by shoulder-height walls creating individual alcoves. The ones nearest the door were drifted with pine needles that seemed well suited for horse bedding. There was no indication what they had really been meant for.

"What do you think," Duessa asked Bettain as they followed Tisha and her light along one silent aisle. Cylass, as always, lurked in her wake. "Cubbyholes for the individual mages?"

"It's not much room. Even the temple school gave us more," Bettain answered.

"They were a different culture," Tisha's soft voice came eerily from the darkness. "Legend says they shared everything. Maybe they didn't want much space of their own."

"I don't see where they cooked anything, or washed up after," Cylass remarked warily.

Duessa couldn't help agreeing. This place was so at odds with the glorious tales of the Shining Ones and their paradise. Yes, it had been a long time since they were gone, but there should have been something left. This emptiness was eerie.

"Let's get back," Elldri lisped, and nobody argued with her.

The evening routines felt just as unsettled. There was only one lantern — Tisha's had been lost when Ar-Lizelle wrecked her hand cart — and the stove set up by the door shed little additional light. Eating, clean up and maintaining their gear were difficult in the echoing darkness. They'd run long and fought hard to be here, but what happened next? And why didn't Keilos want to talk about it?

XVII — REALITIES

N obody was happy the following morning. Duessa couldn't sleep. In the vast darkness under the hill, the single lantern only emphasized the gloom. The Badgers had spread out, two or three sharing each alcove, but the loud crackle of pine needles beneath their bedrolls spoiled the stillness whenever anyone stirred. By first light, it was almost a relief to sit up and stop pretending to sleep.

Outside that gap in the hill, daylight crept slowly over the bare paving. Duessa gathered with the others around the meager warmth of the portable stove, sipping listlessly at the boiled grain Giniver put together. Maybe it was natural to feel let down. They had all been counting on Keilos to be wiser and more powerful. They expected that he would know what to do. But he said he didn't, so now what did that mean?

Hence, the general sleeplessness.

Once it was well light enough to see, Zathi had them all out in the plaza. She didn't send them on the usual run, but they did begin their morning stretches and horse training. Ironically, the giant badger emerged at almost the same time. It shook itself, flicking a wary ear toward the squad.

Elldri stood up from where she was crouched in the doorway. She began walking across the plaza, slowly but with determination. The badger's shaggy head snapped toward her.

"What are you doing?" Bettain grabbed at Elldri's arm.

"I just want to see," Elldri murmured.

Duessa had been seated with the others, meditating in hopes of reviving her faded energy with the *vitalis* flowing all around them. She was pretty certain Elldri didn't mean seeing with only her eyes.

"Are you crazy?" Bettain gripped harder. "You can see it from here!"

"Wait," Alemin said. "I think we should trust her."

"With that thing?"

Duessa studied Elldri, whose eyes were still haggard. Even after Tisha's efforts, and with *vitalis* permeating the area, she was emptied, shattered, unable to fill.

"Nobody else knows how to help," Duessa said. "If this is something Elldri needs, we should let her try."

Elldri said, "I need to understand."

Someone among the guardswomen gave a sniff of disbelief, but Bettain reluctantly let go. The girl walked on toward the badger. Despite its great size, the animal eased back before her. Its muzzle twitched in a brief snarl. Elldri stepped closer, her shoulders visibly stiff and tight. The badger turned in a restless circle.

Duessa understood Bettain's distress. Elldri was so young and slight, and the shaggy mass of that huge animal loomed over her, a living wall of death. Around them, the guardswomen watched anxiously with hands on their swords and crossbows tightening slowly. Bettain's fist was wreathed with glittering sparks.

Zathi held up a hand, motioning them back. "This is her trial."

Elldri reached up, her brown fingers like tiny splinters against the black furred muzzle. Fearsome jaws dipped toward her, nostrils flaring. Then it skittered back from her, surprisingly light on its feet for such a massive beast. Rounded ears flicked forward and then back. Suddenly it spun away. The sweep of its tail sent Elldri stumbling. It bounded into the trees, ducking to pass beneath the lowest branches, and vanished over the hill. The thrashing of brush faded quickly.

"Are you all right?" Bettain's heavy form raced across the clearing.

"It didn't hurt me." Elldri was already on her feet, brushing at the back of her skirt.

Zathi lowered her hand, and the guardswomen murmured among themselves. "Was she really going to tame that thing?" And someone else said, "Better than having it run wild."

"It'll be back," Sethamis said encouragingly as Elldri and Bettain returned.

"Does it have to?" That was Razeet, sassy as ever.

"That's its den," Sethamis pointed out sharply.

Before the guardswoman could respond, a soft voice came from all around them. *"The badger must return. It is bound here."*

A frisson of excitement went through the group as Keilos swirled down to them. The stately tower glowed gently in the sunrise.

"We were nowhere near here when it attacked us before," Zathi objected.

"The badger's name is Ruen," Keilos said. *"It resists captivity. That is its nature. Though it roams, it cannot truly escape."*

"What else do you know about it?" Jaxynne asked,

practical.

"We speculated, once, over whether Dar-Gothull made the drakanox or only enslaved what was already present." Keilos gazed at the tower, its light beaming above them. *"I have learned that so much* vitalis, *the pure life force of the world, creates its own life. Ruen and the drakanox both are such spirits. There once were many others, living among the Shining Ones as allies."*

"That was a spirit?" Lorrah frowned.

"And the giant wasps we saw?" Tisha asked doubtfully.

"Spirits of the Hornwood," Keilos told them. *"They were meant to be guides, not guards."*

"Until Dar-Gothull captured them," Duessa said.

"When the Devourer came, so long ago, he drained this tower completely. The Shining Ones and most of the spirits were consumed. He spared only a few, the ones he thought most deadly. In their weakened state, they couldn't resist his domination. Instead of welcoming those who came to the tower for healing, or to serve their communities, Dar-Gothull made them guard the tower and attack anyone who came here."

"Is that why the drakanox kept attacking us, back when... before..." Giniver stumbled over the fact of Keilos' death.

"Yes. Even for me, it isn't easy to resist the compulsion. That is why any plan cannot be for my sake. It must be for you."

"You can't ever leave here?" Alemin asked.

"I can, but only for a short time. Like Ruen, I am bound," Keilos said. *"Still, I will do all I can to help you."*

Something nagged at Duessa. "When you said that last night, it didn't sound like just leaving was all you meant."

"You are right." Keilos settled in a glowing coil, though some part of his mane or tail was always moving. The humans gathered around, listening intently. To Tisha and Alemin, he said, *"You may have been counting on me to foresee events, but I am sorry."*

"You have no more visions?" Tisha gasped, dismayed.

"No, for I am no longer human." Regret again colored his tone. *"The drakanox simply* is, *endlessly. It... I... am a spirit. I will not grow and later die. The needs of my body, to eat, to rest... They are fading. Past and future no longer mean what they once did."*

"For you, there is nothing to foretell," Alemin finished with reluctant understanding.

"What about the rest of us?" Sethamis asked.

Everyone around Duessa looked a little sick and scared. Herself, she wasn't surprised. No matter how much they expected Keilos to lead, it had seemed obvious he wouldn't. For those who had sought him much longer, even the radiant *vitalis* couldn't soften the blow.

"You still have your mind, don't you?" Zathi made a cutting gesture with one mailed hand.

"I would never abandon you, dear friends," Keilos spoke urgently through his supernatural calm. *"I will help in every way that I can, but I cannot tell you how to go forward."*

"That's not much help." For all her cynicism, Bettain sounded truly disappointed. "What did we come all this way for then?"

"We came to fight," Zathi snapped, angry now. "Do not question that we will."

"It's not like we could avoid it," Giniver said wryly.

"We've tangled with everyone on the way."

Jaxynne grimaced. "Don't remind me."

"We broke them all out of the Larder," Keerin groaned.

"I fought with my sister," Lorrah lamented.

"They're all still after us." Duessa's heart hammered in her chest, the way it had all the way to the Larder.

Looking around, she could see how despair weighed on them all. The seven warriors and six mages had bulled their way through so much to get here. And maybe spent all their strength to do it. Fears and disappointment tore at their unity.

Then Zathi drew herself up. "Well, so what? We always meant to fight." She prowled fiercely across the pavement. "After we lost Keilos, we went to find his friends. Why? Because it's unbearable, the way things are. We found Lorrah, and then Alemin and the others. Every step has led us to this." She turned to rake the group with her fierce gaze. "Yes, they are coming. Dar-Gothull and Ar-Lizelle and the counts and their hunter-guards. What of it?"

"Are we going to back off now?" Lorrah took up the call.

"No." The murmured reply swept through the group. "No!"

Duessa watched anxiously as Keilos drifted a bit above them, easing back, turning over command to Zathi. Maybe it had always been his plan.

"We came to fight for a better future," Giniver said.

"Just didn't think it would be so short," Razeet joked.

"It was our choice to come, too," Tisha spoke for the Minstrel side of the squad. "All of us believed in a better way, because our teacher Ar-Thea believed it." She swept a hand to the tower above, and the gentle tide of *vitalis* everywhere. "Look where we are. It's an accomplishment for all of us just to be here. This cannot be a dead end. I won't believe it. We will find a way."

"Yes. We also came to fight, but not with swords." Alemin, reached to take Lorrah's hand. "We mages fight with our hearts and souls."

"Not with killing rage, which they understand all too well, but with compassion and love, which are beyond them." Tisha drew a deep breath and gazed up to Keilos. "They said you wrote your name on the wall of the tower. If we do that, can we draw from the tower's reservoir?"

"Yes, but there is more there than even you understand, Tisha," Keilos told them. *"You could still scatter again, try to evade Dar-Gothull's forces, and go back into hiding. Once you commit yourselves, the power comes, but a change will also come."*

"We'd be like you?" Lorrah frowned doubtfully as she looked up at him.

Cylass was immediately concerned. "Lady, the risk."

Tisha didn't even look at him. "We won't abandon you," she vowed to Keilos.

Abandon. That word pierced Duessa like a sword.

"Would we become like those trapped souls in the Larder?" Alemin was understandably concerned.

"Maybe you'd turn into spirits, like the giant badger." Bettain almost seemed interested.

"I do not know what the change will look like for you."

"What's the choice, really? Like Zathi said, we have death closing in from five directions," Duessa said. This was inevitable, she thought. It terrified her, but having once been deserted, she couldn't turn her back on her friends. "Where's this wall we write on?"

Jaxynne said, "While they find the wall, we can spread out. Get the lie of the land and come up with a plan for defense."

"Good," Zathi nodded. "You mages must make your own choices, but all those counts will come with squads of guards. That's for us warriors to worry about."

~ ~ ~

The next few days took on a pattern of their own. Each morning, Berisan and Meven sat quietly, meditating in the first dawn light. Ozlin tried to join them, although he couldn't seem to sit still for more than a few minutes at a time. Yamaya would be cooking inside, while Shonn sharpened their tools for the day ahead.

After eating, Meven and Oz would head out to the ice walls. Shonn and Berisan worked in the fields or on the new hut. Yamaya let them scramble around her hut and study how the roof was put together. They tied many knots in cords to measure the length of the pieces. Their partnership wasn't exactly close, but it did get easier. The building took shape with satisfying speed.

Between them, they set the upright posts and wove enough vines between to hold them steady. Thatching couldn't be worked in until they had a floor to stand on, so Shonn took several more trips down the hill to cut enough grass trees for it.

He continued fishing and foraging for other supplies, which he handed over to Berisan or Yamaya. He also tried to give fruit and other treats to Ozlin and soon learned that the boy wouldn't take anything from his hand. However, if they were set out prominently in Oz's vicinity, they would quickly vanish.

Shonn tried, too, to hold baby Gabrith and play with him as often as Yamaya would allow. When the baby started fussing, Shonn searched out a firm fruit called kani, that the infant could gum on without a risk of choking.

Although willing enough for the respite, Yamaya did ask, "Why are you so interested?"

"Everyone takes care of babies, among the water-folk," Shonn explained. "It isn't just the women's job. Children should grow up knowing everyone in their clan. Knowing who they can trust," he added, thinking of the frequent hostility from land-folk.

"I guess I can see that," Yamaya said. She might have more of a farm crew than a family, but the principle seemed to apply.

As he spoke, Shonn raised the baby above his head and twirled gently. Only when he slowed down, he saw Meven watching from her usual distance. There was a moment's awkwardness as he wondered if she thought he wanted children right away. Fortunately, the infant gurgled his approval and Shonn went back to playing with him.

It was rare to have any time with Meven. She and Ozlin always seemed to be waist-deep in sweet potato vines or prowling about the valley on business of their own. In the evenings, she really only talked to Berisan or Oz. Despite this, Shonn was always thinking of her. Everything he did was for Meven. Just seeing her always made him happy.

Still, it was just as well that work kept him too busy, and too tired, to dwell on his longings. They still might too easily flare into jealousy.

On the fourth morning, Berisan carefully arranged the grass trees for the floor, turning them to fit with the smallest gaps between them. Shonn sat on the steps beneath the skeletal walls, sharpening his bush knife with a whetstone he borrowed from Yamaya. Something flickered in the corner of his eye. Straightening, he gazed across the valley with its lacework of ice walls.

"What do you think that is?"

"What's what?" Berisan followed his gaze, just as a second fiery streak rose on the far side of the valley. Berisan tensed. "That's Oz. It has to be. Meven wouldn't use fire."

"What is it, though?" Shonn asked.

"A signal flare." Berisan kept watching that spot across the valley, under the jaws of the shark-tooth mountains.

"You have signals?" Shonn didn't know whether to be surprised or approve of the practicality.

"Since it seems that I started an uprising," Berisan answered with some irony, "we developed signals. Meven's been keeping watch on that gap into Dunsaph."

So that was what she and Ozlin went off to do. Shonn wished he could be surprised. Beside him, Berisan went still for a moment, breathing in deeply. Light gathered to his hand and he flung it upward, a rising comet that pulsed brightly against the day.

"What does the signal mean?" Shonn was almost afraid to ask. They'd fallen into a peaceful routine, here at Weeping Falls Farm. The rebellion at Opshar was suddenly much nearer and more dangerous.

"They've seen movement approaching," Berisan answered. "When they get a better look, there will be more flares to tell us numbers. Come on. I'd better warn Yamaya."

Shonn gazed across the valley, wishing he could see what was happening. He jittered just thinking about Meven out there with Ozlin, and who knew what was coming down on them. Shonn hurried after Berisan. The floor of the hut would have to wait.

~ ~ ~

Tisha led Alemin and Lorrah in a grave, silent procession down the long aisle at the center of the hill. Cylass stalked close behind Tisha, as always. Overhead, a string of witchlights glided with them, revealing the succession of mysterious alcoves on either side of them. A trail of boot prints caked with dried blood stood out against the silvery paving. This was what the mages followed into the darkness. Far ahead of them, a vivid golden blur came slowly into focus. KEILOS was written there, with a showman's flair.

Awkwardly, Duessa followed the three minstrels. Cylass kept close to Tisha, while Bettain trudged farther behind. Duessa sensed her uneasiness at the errand. It wasn't their friend who had died here, after all. However, Alemin was a friend, and he had been close to Keilos. For Alemin's sake, they came to help gather the body. It was sad that Elldri had refused to come along, but there was no persuading her to come any closer to the *vitalis* tower.

The strangeness of the second-hand obligation made Duessa's shoulders itch. Keilos was not truly dead. They'd talked to him for a long time, just this morning. How could you have a funeral for someone like that?

Duessa kept expecting a charnel stink, the rotting of flesh left lying in the open. From the way Cylass kept looking around, he was waiting for it, too. Though slightly stale, the air remained ordinary. Even a large rat's nest in one of the alcoves they passed hardly reeked of manure. One more for the list of oddities about this place.

Keilos' name seemed to float in the air, ghostly bright. As the witchlights drew near, she saw a smooth wall stretching up into the darkness. The boot prints went straight to it. There were two sets, both leading away from the wall. Duessa puzzled over that, until the lights got closer.

A large dark blotch appeared against the base of the wall. Something huddled in the midst of it, slightly off center. The man's body was propped up, hands on the knees in a meditative posture. His chin had fallen forward on his chest. Curls draped forward, obscuring his features. He seemed to be wearing mostly black, and seated on a black carpet. As they came closer, Duessa realized his simple tunic was heavily stained with blood. The "carpet" was a pool of it that had completely dried and crackled like mud from an evaporated puddle.

Slowly Tisha stepped over the blood and knelt beside the body. Head bent, she rested her hand on one of the dead palms. Alemin and Lorrah moved to follow, all of them joining hands. Thoughts flickered among them. Loss, sorrow, a sense of disbelief, knowing their friend was dead and still shocked to see it. All the while Cylass, Duessa and Bettain loitered awkwardly, with nothing to offer but their presence.

Bettain conspicuously turned away, shunning the sight. Duessa, too, wanted to turn her eyes anywhere else, but she fought it. Death was coming for all of them, soon, and probably painfully. She had to accept this, so she could resist its despair.

She made herself study the body. Keilos' corpse showed no bloating or discoloration. Rather it was becoming a dry husk. Duessa allowed her eyes to turn long enough to see a pair of archways on either side. Jaxynne had warned them there was a circle of mummies in one of the chambers.

Before Duessa could really wonder about the mechanics of it, something else drew her eye. Some kind of reflection of the light on the wall? No, it was like art or a mural, drawing itself out where the witchlights hovered. The display grew as she watched, a succession of graceful shapes like vines or coiling serpents. Circles and arcs overlapped each other, yet combined into a balanced whole. They were all made of letters, scribed in a language she didn't understand yet felt she should know.

The other mages straightened as the light grew, spreading wider and higher up the face of the wall. Alemin stepped back a little, taking in the scope of it. Duessa moved closer, tantalized by the *vitalis* radiating from the wall. Such a large building should have been chilly, but she sensed only the warmth and comfort of a loving welcome.

"Are you sure about this?" Bettain's harsher voice distracted her for a moment.

"Of course not," Duessa answered, exasperated. Her old friend's scornful face was sketched by the rising glow. Was she sure? Keilos said it would be a change, and he didn't know what it would look like. Anyone with sense would be unsure. "This is what we came here for. I can't turn around now."

"That's not what I mean." Bettain rubbed her arms restlessly. "Alemin says we're already connected to the Larder. That means the Lizard, too. Will she be able to... I don't know... interfere?"

The three minstrels had been gazing at the wall, seemingly drinking in the possibilities. Alemin now turned toward the other Larder mages.

"That's true," he said. "We are already bound together, but it..." He gazed back at the wall. "It's hard to know, but from the spirits of the Larder, it seems their circle was only a small part of something greater. This must be it, the heart of the Hornwood."

"It's like a great tree," Tisha mused. "The Larder was a sapling that grew from its root. Rather than pull us away, Ar-Lizelle may be drawn in with us."

"Could she?" Lorrah asked hopefully.

"I haven't felt her since the battle," Alemin said. "She may have broken the bond when she rejected Elldri's pain."

"But she's done the rituals. She's bound to Dar-Gothull." Duessa was immediately concerned. "Would he have access to all this?"

Softly but firmly, Tisha said, "Dar-Gothull could not use this power. He can only consume it."

"That would keep anyone else from having it,"

Cylass said. "Maybe that's enough for him."

"If my sister does feel it, maybe it will be easier for her to let go of her anger," Lorrah murmured.

At this Bettain gave a little snort. "She will not let go of her anger."

"If she won't, then we will." Alemin clasped Lorrah's hand and softly asked, "Together?"

She gazed at him with shining eyes. "Yes, always."

With no more hesitation, they each stepped close to the shimmering wall. Witchlights swooped down to them, and they moved them over the surface. Alemin spelled his name in a glittering golden trail beside Keilos' while Lorrah, who was shorter, wrote beneath his. They rested a moment, palms to the wall. Duessa could have sworn there were ripples in the golden tapestry, as if they had touched clear water.

Cylass had been watching it all silently. He darted up to Tisha as she raised her hand to write. "Lady, wait!"

Tears she had shed for Keilos still glittered as she faced him. Cylass caught her in a sudden, fierce embrace. Duessa and Bettain both strolled aside a little, trying to respect their privacy, but there was no way to avoid hearing his ragged question.

"Lady, would you leave me?"

"I am glad for what we've had. I hope it will not change," Tisha answered. "But this is what I have trained for and lived my whole life to be. I am a healer born. Not only for you or some other — I can heal all of Skaythe." She gave a sad laugh, muffled by his shoulder. "What confidence. That's what Ar-Thea would say."

Duessa flicked a glance in time to see Tisha withdraw from Cylass' embrace. Her heart went out to him, the worry and grief as he watched his lover go to the wall.

All of Duessa's doubts closed in at once. Tisha had a natural gift, and a lifetime of preparation. What was Duessa compared to that? Just a worthless smuggler and fugitive. She didn't deserve the minstrels' respect.

For a moment, she could feel all it had meant to be in the Larder. The smell of hot stone and sweat. Hunger and exhaustion, every moment stifled by walls that bled nightmares.

Bettain was at her side, gruffly anxious. "You don't have to do this. Just because they're fools..."

With sudden clarity, Duessa understood two things. First, that the Larder wasn't something you left behind. It lived in her still. Traumatic memories chained her to it. Worse, Bettain was speaking with the Larder's voice. Even their long friendship was another loop in the chain.

"I can still feel it. Can't you? The smothering of the Larder..." Duessa shuddered. "That oven of a courtyard, guards always treading on our heels. It was how Ar-Lizelle controlled us."

"Every moment of every day." Bettain's eyes glimmered with emotion. "We're out, but we're not free." She was afraid, Duessa thought. Like Cylass, she feared being left behind in that prison of the mind.

"Don't worry, I'll still be your friend," Duessa said. "And we will find a way to help Elldri."

Before she could lose her nerve, Duessa turned and went to the wall. She didn't need a lifetime of training or a brilliant talent to break free. A moon-runner's scrappy will was enough. That, and knowing when to take bold chances.

Tisha, Alemin and Lorrah stood wrapped in a close embrace, just as they had when the Badgers finally caught up at the border spring. Cylass walked aside with shoulders slumped. Defiantly, Duessa stepped up beside the others. Her witchlight was a feeble spark compared to theirs, but she couldn't let that stop her.

DUESSA, she wrote, placing her name in an arc on the opposite side of Keilos' name.

She felt the connection instantly, but it wasn't the invasion Duessa had feared. *Vitalis* didn't overwhelm her senses. A breath eased in. The power came as a slowly rising river. It was like the time Gauer shared a flask of stolen wine behind the moon-runners' cart, and Duessa felt that she was floating away.

Deep inside her, the Larder tried to burrow in with its memories of a dark prison cell. Old nightmares screamed in the walls as *vitalis* flowed in to light every corner. Black shadows clung to her with tearing claws, only to be lifted away. Duessa didn't hear the Larder any more. Instead of screaming, she was welcomed with joy after a long isolation.

Her eyes prickled with hot tears that she would never shed for anyone, least of all herself. This was everything she had hoped for. No more paying for her power with a price of pain and fear. No more running from the law and living on empty dreams. Warmth and comfort filled her core.

Duessa stood for a moment, just breathing. She didn't know how long it had been since she felt so relaxed. Then she reached out to touch the wall, stroking it lightly as a wounded duckling. Streaks of golden light flowed down to her, bringing the circulation of glad relief from Alemin, Lorrah, Tisha and even Keilos. When she lowered her hand the connection sparkled away, but she knew it would always be present.

They had a bond now, with her and within her. Each one was distinct, like colored strands woven into a belt. It felt peaceful and natural. But when she turned to Bettain, her friend took a half-step back.

"What happened?" Bettain blurted.

Duessa chuckled. Surely that was obvious. "It doesn't hurt," she said, a lame reassurance.

"Not that," Bettain spat, disgusted. "You're all lit up!"

"Because it doesn't hurt," Duessa repeated with emphasis. "The teachers at the school said if you want power you have to suffer. They were wrong. It isn't power that we need. It's magic. They're different."

Doubts and fears flickered in Bettain's eyes. Duessa felt a stinging disappointment, which the flow of *vitalis* rushed to sooth away. Recently Bettain had spoken of trying the Minstrels' way, but she obviously hadn't meant it. Or maybe she just couldn't. It was too much, too soon.

Bettain shook her head, unwilling or unable to understand. "What about the Larder?"

"It's gone," Alemin said. "Can you feel us?"

"No," Bettain shrugged, "but I was never one for sensing stuff."

Duessa was distracted from Bettain's answer, because she was staring at the other mages with fascination. There was light in their eyes — not poetic or symbolic, but an actual light with the pale gold of *vitalis*. It glowed in the waves of Lorrah's and Tisha's hair, and even in the shorter curls where Alemin's shaved head was growing out. Cylass stood nearby, gazing at Tisha with a stunned expression.

With an oddly shy smile, she reached out her hand. "It's all right. I'm still here."

He quickly moved to embrace her again, but the crinkles of his forehead betrayed some of the same doubts Bettain was feeling. Duessa looked down at herself. Radiance picked out every fold and stitch of her peasant dress in the cavernous darkness. She raised a cautious hand to touch her face. Even her scars felt smoother, less stiff.

"Huh," she murmured. "When I heard the story of the Shining Ones, I didn't think they were *literally* shining!"

~ ~ ~

Yamaya listened to Berisan's description with a

closed expression. "All right," she said. "You go watch for more signals. I'll call for our people."

Rising swiftly, she adjusted the cradleboard on her back where baby Gabrith was curled up asleep. Taking a burning stick from the fire, she strode out of her hut. Shonn hesitated, but he couldn't send up any magical flares, so he trailed after Yamaya.

There was a fire pit lined with stones on the eastern slope, just past her orchard. Chunks of branches and other farm debris were piled high inside. Shonn hadn't really noticed the pit before. He'd assumed it was for burning trash. Yamaya moved around the edge, holding her stick close enough to ignite the smaller twigs. As little flames twinkled with sparks, she worked her stick into the center. The crackling of fire quickly grew louder, and a thick plume of smoke began to rise from the fire.

"Get your gear on." Yamaya spoke curtly, as if he should have already been doing this..

Shonn watched, puzzled, as she swept past him. "Gear?"

Yamaya cocked an eyebrow at him over her shoulder. "You plan to fight, don't you? Impress that girl you're after."

"Yes!" Shonn scowled as he realized she was taunting him over Meven. But he had to rest a hand on his work knife and admit, "This is it."

She stopped completely, her stare growing impatient.

"We don't fight against land folk," Shonn sputtered, defensive. "It would be suicide. We keep away from them."

"Really? You run from everyone?" Yamaya regarded him with incredulous pity.

"We stay in the swamps," he said. "There's plenty of food and materials, but metal isn't one of them. They can't find their way through the mangroves, and —"

Yamaya waved such reasoning aside. "All right, come on. I have a jerkin you can use."

Shonn followed her, balancing his resentment with the knowledge that Yamaya seemed to know what she was doing. He wondered if all farmers on land were experts in arms and armor.

In her hut, Yamaya had Shonn help move two large crocks full of water and river grain, then lifted a trap door to reveal a compartment in the foundation. Out of this she handed him a heavy bundle wrapped with a folded cloth.

"I salvaged this from the last fool who thought he was going to take over my farm," she explained casually. "See if it fits."

Shonn unwrapped the thick leather vest. It had no sleeves, but a brief cap over the shoulders, and a higher collar with something stiff sewn in. There was an overlap at the front, also reinforced, and a row of buckles across that. The bottom came to his upper thighs, so that it fit easily over his shirt and sarong. As Shonn did the buckles, Yamaya got the baby off her back and nursed him while she strode around the bonfire and studied the land below.

"Move around, swing your arms," she coached.

The jerkin felt heavy over his light swamp linen, but it wasn't as stiff as he thought it would be. The leather was supple and well cared for. There was just an unfamiliar whiff of someone else's sweat.

"Mogrok was bigger than you," Yamaya said with a shrug. "Could be worse."

Afterward, she let Shonn hold Gabrith long enough to buckle on a jerkin of her own. Her two knives were prominently displayed, as ever. Shonn took his turn to watch the bonfire, and something else caught his eye. Yamaya's blaze was now sending up a thick plume of smoke. Far down the valley, another column of smoke drifted in answer. The fires were another sort of signal, Shonn guessed.

When he pointed this out to Berisan, the mage replied, "Good. They'll be here soon."

Belatedly, Shonn asked, "You didn't want to use this, did you?" He plucked at the base of the jerkin.

"Him, fight?" Yamaya gave a bark of laughter.

Berisan shrugged laconically. "It's fine. You need it more."

The wait stretched on. Yamaya was uncharacteristically quiet, focused on playing with little Gabrith and cuddling him more than usual. Shonn hadn't thought she was so sentimental, but perhaps it was ritual of her own, to spend as much time with her baby as she could before the battle.

Himself, he prowled restlessly, uncomfortable with the reality. Yamaya's reaction to the typical water-folk strategy reminded him how tenuous their survival could be. And he could admit, privately, that he felt very conflicted. Part of him thought this was foolish and dangerous. Tracking down mudmaws in a swamp was hardly the preparation to go up against armored warriors.

Yet part of him was jumping, ready to fight for his woman. In fact, if the people Yamaya mentioned didn't get here soon, he was going to take off and try to find Meven on his own. He'd follow every inch of those ice walls if he had to.

"Shouldn't we go?" Shonn growled anxiously to Berisan.

"As soon as Lilia gets here," the man answered calmly. "They're almost here, look."

In fact, there was movement on the slope facing toward the valley. A pair of men and a young woman toiled up to them. Lilia, it seemed, was the helper who cared for baby Gabrith while Yamaya was busy. Her brothers were only slightly older, and there to protect her. According to the brothers, a group of men from Opshar were already heading toward where Ozlin's signal had come from.

There was a last bit of turmoil as Yamaya transferred the baby into Lilia's care. While they hastily talked over his needs, Shonn took the older of her two brothers aside.

"See that trail?" He pointed to the path he had been using to go up and down to the swamp. "If you have to run, that way takes you into the mangroves. There's a shelter where you can hide out for a few days."

Berisan, who was listening, nodded approvingly. Then they were off down the slope, racing toward Meven's position. The jerkin rubbed against Shonn's neck, its unfamiliar thickness like an extra weight of the spirit. But this was the way it had to be. Whatever was coming, he had no intention of leaving Meven to face it with only a permanently angry mageling boy at her side.

～ ～ ～

The trip back to Opshar was strangely easy. Piyaro had been dreading another trek through the mountains, this time without bandits to guide him, but things were different in a noble's retinue. Count Ar-Azlor could simply order up enough horses and be off. Riding was a strange luxury to Piyaro; Ar-Dayne had always made the common guards run to keep up with him. Piyaro's legs and back ached at the unfamiliar posture, but the speed was worth it.

Hawk Squad was in front, since they had recently used the back trails. There was also the possibility that Huld's people would recognize them and defuse any confrontation. Ar-Azlor then followed with two of the junior mages, Ar-Norius and Ar-Sessall. Nyette was seated proudly among them. Another forty of Pullgoll's guard followed in as close a formation as they could manage.

Narrow mountain trails made for slower travel, but there was no contact with the bandits. Another strange and fortunate turn. Or perhaps even Huld wasn't bold enough to go up against such numbers. They camped one night in a fogged-over hanging valley, and crested the spine of the mountains early the following day.

When they emerged from the mist, Piyaro signaled a halt. He turned in the saddle for Count Ar-Azlor's confirmation. From this rocky height, the valley spread out green and gold with the village of Opshar in the near distance, nestled in its curve of river. It was a peaceful scene except for the column of smoke billowing up from the middle of the town.

Already there were whispers among the mages. Someone asked, "Are we attacked?"

"Not likely," Piyaro answered. "It's a single fire, not the whole town."

"If the attackers came across the valley, outlying farms would be burning, too," Ar-Azlor agreed. "It must be a signal."

"But who is signaling, and to whom?" Ar-Sessall asked.

Ar-Norius pointed down the valley. "What is that?"

"Meven's ice walls," Piyaro reported. At the western end of the valley, you could just see the white arcs shining in the morning light. Even when he knew what they were, the brightness was startling. Another column of smoke rose on the south side of the valley. "That will be Weeping Falls, there."

"The rebel headquarters," Nyette hastened to insert herself. "But there are others starting, too." Across the valley and to the east, plumes of smoke were just beginning to show.

"It's a call to arms," Ar-Azlor declared, with

suspiciously dramatic flair. Still keeping up the pretense that the uprising was what he had come here for. "The rebels gather their forces."

"Against us, or someone else?" Piyaro wondered aloud.

"Wait," Nyette stood in the stirrups, squinting. "Is that a fire bolt?"

They all stared toward the western valley, where a series of faint streaks blazed against the whiteness of the ice.

"Someone trying to get through the ice walls?" Cothyr suggested.

"It's too high, that just wastes *lethentros*," Ar-Norius argued.

"Yamaya and Berisan were concerned about encroachment from Dunsaph," Piyaro offered.

"Yes, I recall you said that." Count Ar-Azlor smiled without humor. "I guess we'd better go see who it is."

XVIII — THE ORDEAL

Y amaya led the way, with Berisan running at her heels. Shonn came last, watching ahead and behind for any ambush. Yamaya had kilted her skirts, revealing sturdy boots that kicked up bits of dirt behind her. They skirted the circular pond, where the footing was soft, and then followed a narrow track through the tangling reeds. Shonn panted to keep up, and tried to ignore the unfamiliar chafe of stiff leather against his neck.

For a woman who had birthed a child less than three months ago, Yamaya set a remarkably fast pace. Even from behind, with her tightly braided hair bobbing in front of them, Shonn could see a difference in her bearing. The so-called farmer was always forceful, whether she was pulling weeds or cooking for her crew, but she was also restless and easily went to alert. Now, at this run, she was ironically more relaxed than Shonn had ever seen her. Yamaya moved with purpose and skill, not racing headlong but pacing herself. This was her true self. He wondered how someone like her had ever decided to settle down on a farm.

The trail they followed dipped to cross a narrow stream, and turned toward the shore. The land fell in stair-steps here, layers of rock obscured by thick brush. It was still some distance to the glistening blank of the ice walls, but Shonn felt the cool draft as they passed through the first drift of fog that trickled off them.

With a glance over her shoulder, Yamaya called to

Berisan, "What do you feel?"

"Movement between the walls," he called back to her. "A mage must be leading them." As if summoned, a fire bolt rose from midway down the slope, among the rocks and brush. A second one followed it. "Two mages," Berisan corrected.

A distant hail caught their attention. "There they are."

Yamaya ran again, following the edge until she found a trampled path to slither down. Shortly they joined a group of men dressed in bulky coats and carrying farm implements. Shonn assumed these were the villagers from Opshar.

"Berisan," they all greeted the mage with relief. Yamaya was met with a slightly wary, "Farmer," and Shonn received many suspicious glances. With no hint of his former reluctance, Berisan moved among them, touching a shoulder here and shaking a hand there.

Yamaya interrupted, "Where's Meven and Oz?"

"The ice witch told us to wait," one of them grumbled, but they did point toward the lower wall. Yamaya strode off in that direction. Shonn hesitated, torn between wanting to hear what else they said and needing to see Meven. He quickly chose Meven, and hurried after Yamaya.

The fog was thicker and the chill harsher as they approached the ice wall. Muffled sounds began to echo from behind it. There was a muted rumble of hooves or running feet, and faint angry voices.

Yamaya half vanished into the mist, and Shonn heard her impatient call. "Hey — witch!"

"Meven?" He added his own call, though the cold air rasped in his throat.

A reddish flickering glow appeared, somewhat to their right. Yamaya headed toward it. Moments later, they found Ozlin striding toward them. The boy's fevered gaze reflected the globe of fire hovering over his fist.

"What do you want?" he scowled.

"I'm here to help," Shonn assured him.

"Let it be," Yamaya said to Ozlin. "We need everyone we can get, and we need to set battle lines. Where's Meven?"

"Here." A shadowy form emerged from the drifting fog. "I've just been strengthening the wall."

Shonn was struck by how straight and stiffly she moved. Her eyes were only partly focused as she strode to them, unhurried. Calm, emotionless, seemingly unaware of the cold around her. And yet, she was beautiful in an unexpected way. Like Yamaya, she was living as her true self.

For the chill didn't come from the ice. No, it came from Meven. Wisps of cloud followed her. The stark chill grew ever more painful as Shonn stood there. It radiated, too, a sense of dread mixed with the chill. It was right to love her, but right also to know fear.

Ozlin's angry heat was almost welcome. Shonn joked, "It's really cold. Can I stand by you?"

"No!"

"Hey, Oz." Pebbles rattled down as Berisan appeared on the edge above them. "You signaled two mages. What else can you tell us?"

"The two, plus about twenty riders," Meven said. That wasn't good. Shonn hadn't counted up how many villagers were here, but he knew it wasn't twenty. Worse, the mounted warriors would have a big advantage against simple farmers and peasants.

"Twenty isn't enough for a real raid," said Yamaya with a thoughtful frown.

"There has to be more to their plan," Berisan agreed, but Yamaya waved that aside.

"We can't get distracted by something they might be doing somewhere else," she said firmly. "There's enough to deal with here." As if to demonstrate her point, there was a distinct crackling thud. Smoke coiled up above the wall, and shards of frost glittered as they fell.

"At first, they were just riding around between the walls, trying to find a way through," Meven said. "I set the walls close enough together that it's hard to get turned around or change position. Once they realized it's a dead end, they've been working together and trying to break through."

"You've been keeping it up?" Berisan asked the obvious.

"So far." Meven did not seem especially concerned.

"If they're all in the maze, can you close it up behind them? Just let them freeze," Yamaya said. Shonn, who was still feeling the intense cold, shivered in unwilling sympathy.

"I thought about it," Meven said, "but we'd rather not kill them. There's a hex of fear in the ice. The longer they stay, the greater the fear."

"I felt that!" Shonn exclaimed.

"Why not kill them?" Yamaya looked at her as if she was crazy. Some of the villagers had come up to the edge above them and were listening anxiously. A few of them appeared to agree with Yamaya.

"It's our way," Berisan said. "If we can get them to leave without violence, that's what we want them to do."

Meven was unapologetic. "The gap into the maze is still open. They can get out the way they came in."

"Besides," Berisan said mildly, "we don't have twenty fighting men. I know you're brilliant, Yamaya, but you can't win this on your own. I can't keep a shield over everyone, either."

The two mages stared at Yamaya patiently. The bare sense of it gave Shonn a chill inside that had nothing to do with the temperature around the ice wall. The villagers looked worried.

Yamaya gave a kind of growl. "Fine. Then if they start breaking through, try to let them out a few at a time. And make it about there." She jabbed a finger toward the second step down from the valley, a narrower layer that was almost more of a ledge than a terrace. "I'll set our people up above, where we can shoot and throw rocks down on them. Then Oz, with his fire, can try to shy their horses."

The boy straightened eagerly at that. Meven and Berisan didn't look happy about it. Another large explosion shivered through the ice walls. Faint yells of alarm suggested that the blasts were coming too close for comfort with the invading troops.

"Don't be fools," Yamaya scolded. "Maybe they're scared, but they aren't going to just walk away. If we're lucky, we can push them off that bank and they'll fall toward the beach. The footing will be worse on sand."

Meven had turned back to focus on the wall, and a fresh blast of freezing air made Shonn step away from her. Berisan nodded reluctantly to Yamaya.

"I trust you," he said.

Yamaya rolled her eyes and called, "Listen up, everyone."

She made to climb back up to where the villagers had gathered, but there was a stirring among them. Someone suddenly yelled, "Riders approaching!"

~ ~ ~

Something was different. Ar-Lizelle shifted uneasily in the saddle, where she rode among Unthur's entourage. She tried to look around without making it obvious.

It hadn't been her idea to ride so close to Count Ar-Gammord, but when she tried to hang back, it provoked his suspicions. "If you sense that creature nearby, I want you to tell me!" he demanded sharply.

"Of course, my lord," Ar-Lizelle had replied through gritted teeth. Now she rode at the center of the file, just behind the unstable count. A senior guard led the way, holding Unthur's banner aloft. Ar-Vennic was beside her. More guards flanked them and brought up the rear. Her own two from the Larder had barely managed to squeeze in behind her.

Allegedly she was in a more protected position. To Ar-Lizelle, the warning was clear. Whenever the count turned to glare at her, she made sure to nod in recognition. It was tiresome, but better than waging a pointless battle. The rest of the time, she searched the near horizon for some indication of what she sensed.

The swarm of soldiers and guards over the plains of Ebruc were even more obvious than they had been before. Half a dozen other columns were visible in just this area. Though they avoided coming too close to each other, all of them converged into a rough ring around the edge of the Hornwood.

"Something wrong?" Ar-Vennic's cautious tone was nearly lost among the thudding of hooves as they rode.

Reluctant as she was to reveal any weakness, Ar-Lizelle had to answer. "I don't know. It's subtle. With so many other mages nearby..." She trailed off, hoping the suggestion would distract him.

"Somebody from Ar-Ishahl's household could still be working against you." Ar-Vennic joined her in looking around. He wasn't nearly as discrete as she would have liked.

"It could be any of them," Ar-Lizelle replied. He nodded with grim understanding.

Dar-Gothull's will drove them all — Ar-Lizelle felt the compulsion as much as any. The wizard-king's intention moved them relentlessly toward the Hornwood. Even so, the mages would be sizing up their rivals, looking for flaws to exploit. What she didn't want Ar-Vennic to know was that her intuition led her in a different direction. Not of an imminent attack, but of something invisibly shifting. An unknown change. But how?

Worse yet, Ar-Lizelle couldn't sense her escaped prisoners any longer. The fugitives she hated so much, but whose connection had drawn her on and given her purpose — it had slipped away. Backtracking to Ebruc Holl had cost her that.

She would see them again. Ar-Lizelle promised herself. Between Dar-Gothull's will and her own, it was certain. All she had to do was wait.

Ar-Lizelle despised waiting.

~ ~ ~

Ar-Azlor's troop stopped only briefly in Opshar. There they found the beacon fire in the market square, amid market stalls that were being set up as healing stations. Only women and children were in the area, and they scattered with shrill cries on sighting the mounted warriors. After a few minutes of confusion, Headman Aulgrip emerged from his tavern, loudly claiming that he had nothing to do with the rebels.

His story, if it could be believed, was that Yamaya first signaled for aid. The village men had put together a crude militia and were on their way to the ice walls. Count Ar-Azlor assigned ten of his men to secure the village with a stern warning: "Keep your hands to yourself." Another ten were to ride eastward and find out if those beacons heralded a separate incursion out of Prizom.

Now Hawk Squad galloped toward the ice walls in the fore of Pulgoll's force. The footing was uncertain, with thick reeds hiding many small channels beside the river. Piyaro rode stiffly, waiting for the moment that a horse would go down, but they emerged safely onto drier ground. The ice walls loomed over them, a featureless white bulwark that radiated frigid menace. It was easy enough to see the crowd gathered near them.

Shouts broke out as the rumble of hooves alerted the rabble. They started scrambling into a defensive knot, but Ar-Azlor ordered, "All slow," and the men approached at a steady trot. By the time they halted, Berisan and Yamaya had joined their fighters. A moment of tension stretched, until Piyaro barked,

"All hail Count Ar-Azlor!"

"Hail!" Ar-Azlor's own men lustily repeated the cry, but the villagers shifted uncomfortably. Yamaya's mocking laughter pierced their quiet.

Berisan gave her a chiding glance before calling, "Welcome, Azlor."

Piyaro's stomach clenched, remembering another mage who dared flout tradition and call a count by his bare name. Anger rumbled among the mounted warriors, but Ar-Azlor ignored the insult.

"People of Opshar," he called in a steady tone, "I am glad to see you here. It is good that you have the courage to defend your homes." The count paused a moment before acknowledging, "There have been difficulties. Let us put those aside for a time. Opshar is also my home, as all of Pulgoll is my home. These invaders must be defeated before any other problems can be resolved."

While he spoke, Piyaro caught Berisan's probing gaze into Ar-Azlor's guard. When he saw Nyette, he tilted his head a little. The girl mage replied with a secretive nod.

"You speak with wisdom," Berisan replied, but the villagers shuffled anxiously. There was no trust in their faces. A muffled boom sounded on the other side of the ice walls. Piyaro glimpsed Meven and her mageling boy hurrying toward it. Count Ar-Azlor also turned his eyes in that direction. In the lengthening silence, a horse stomped restlessly.

"What do we know," the count asked after a moment. "Who comes, their numbers?"

"Two mages and perhaps twenty more riders." Yamaya answered that. "Meven has them trapped in her maze, with a way out if they choose to take it. So far —" Yamaya broke off as another bang echoed from behind the walls. She shrugged, as if that explained everything.

"Two mages?" Ar-Azlor turned to Ar-Sessall, who nodded.

"That feels right."

Piyaro's knees were clenched so tight around his saddle that they started the tingle with lack of circulation. He couldn't believe they were all talking so casually to a bunch of traitors, and a mage who was leading them all to catastrophe.

Besides, they were asking the wrong questions. "Why did you leave them a way out?" Piyaro demanded.

"Yes, could you explain about that?" Ar-Azlor asked. "I'm told that you don't seek out conflict, but it isn't always possible to avoid."

"Violence is easy," Berisan replied steadily. "It's the obvious choice. Everyone in the world thinks you should do it. What's harder is to wait, and hold your hand, and let them think better of their actions."

"They're already attacking," Ar-Norius protested. "How can you not fight back?"

Around them, the villagers and soldiers stirred with restless agreement. They wanted to trust Berisan, but there were all these guards looking more and more nervous.

"I am doing something." Meven's voice drifted up from below, sharp with impatience. "I'm doing it right now. Or what do you think all this is?"

Piyaro looked around, startled. He hadn't even seen the woman at first. When he did spot her, standing near the ice walls, it didn't look like she was doing anything at all. Except, the graceful folds of her sarong gleamed with particles of frost, and there was a quickening skiff of breeze that carried a bitter edge. Streams of mist poured off the ice walls to coil about her feet. Shonn, who was lingering close to her, scuffed his sandals in the dust, as if it pained him more to leave her side than it did to stay near her.

"You've blocked the way into Pulgoll." Nyette frowned, as if this was a particularly difficult puzzle and they were hiding the clues on purpose. "You're making them cold and afraid..."

"But they haven't left," Ar-Norius argued. And Ar-Sessall agreed, "They're still there."

"The way out is open to them," Berisan explained patiently. "When the pain is enough, they may make the choice to leave on their own."

Among the mages and guardsmen, there were whispers of doubt and confusion. Even Hawk Squad, who had been exposed to this nonsense before, were hesitating.

"How long will that take?" Piyaro demanded.

"If you want me to do more, you will all need to step back." Meven's voice was smooth as ice, and almost as friendly.

"No," Berisan turned to protest. "You can't hurt them."

Yamaya laughed, harsh and shrill. "Do you think they care about hurting us? I say, let them through! We should fight it out."

Count Ar-Azlor leaned on his saddle horn, poised as a serpent at rest. "No, let them do it their way. I want to see this."

Frustration surged in Piyaro's gut, yet he also heard a note of challenge in the count's voice. It seemed not everyone was so persuaded by Berisan's absurd methods.

~ ~ ~

"Shonn, Oz." Meven spoke in a gentle monotone. "You need to move away."

"What?" Shonn protested. Yes, he was jittering, trying to keep some feeling in his hands and feet. His thin garb did nothing to stop the chill boring ever deeper into his bones. Even with the leather jerkin it was becoming really painful.

"No! There are too many guards." Ozlin argued, though his narrow brown shoulders were hunched against the cold. The ball of flames that hovered above his fist flickered in tempo with his shivering.

"Oz is right," Shonn said. "You need us."

Meven regarded them both under the edge of her reed hat. The dark gray of her eyes was lit with silvery fire. "What I need," she pronounced distinctly, "is to know that I won't harm you."

Before Shonn could process her words, bright movement caught his eye. He just had time to glimpse the searing arc of a fire blast coming down on them.

"Look out!" He dove toward Oz and scooped the mageling up with one arm about his waist. Skinny legs flailed as Shonn rushed them both out of the way.

"Aagh! Let go!" Ozlin's cry was lost in the bang of a fire burst erupting in the place where they had been standing. Cries of alarm came from the slope above them. The villagers ran closer to Berisan, while the guardsmen spurred into protective formation around Count Ar-Azlor.

"Meven?" Shonn let the boy go and staggered a few steps back toward her. The ice witch had hardly moved. A shallow crater smoked among the short grass and pebbles, but any sparks were quickly fizzling out.

Ozlin gave a piercing scream of rage. Flames enveloped his head and shoulders. Shonn ducked, thinking the boy was mad because he'd picked him up, but Ozlin's rage was focused on the other side of the ice wall. He gathered the flames and with another screech he hurled his own fireball back over the wall.

"Witch!" Yamaya reappeared at the edge. "Don't stay in one place. They're targeting you."

Ozlin stood panting and seething, and Shonn wondered if he even recognized the people around him. Then Berisan called out, "Ozlin, that's it!"

Shonn kept an anxious eye on the mageling boy while Berisan's voice came from above them.

"Meven's walls keep them out, they haven't gone away," Berisan explained to those nearby. "They're too proud, or too afraid of quitting. We need to show them we have strength to oppose them. Throw our blasts over the wall, together."

"They'll see there are four of us here." Shonn couldn't see Nyette, but he immediately recognized her proud voice.

"Seven," Yamaya snapped back. "Don't leave us out of your tally."

"Those are convincing odds," Piyaro's voice came, grudging.

"All right, we'll try that." A man who could have been the count spoke up. "There's just one more thing they need to know."

The mounted guards jostled each other, and a mage

emerged in rich red robes, ornamented with gold and pearls.
Shonn's stomach flipped nervously. That was definitely the
count.

"I am Ar-Azlor, Count of Pulgoll!" he shouted, and
there was power projected in it. He would easily be heard
regardless of any noise on the far side of the wall. "If your
Count Ar-Hespaas though he could send you to steal my
land, he was wrong. Go back and tell him to stay off my
border and leave my people alone!"

As Ar-Azlor spoke, a fiery globe grew above his
raised hand. He flung it upward to soar over the wall. Three
others followed closely. Ozlin hastily added his own blast,
and Berisan sent up a smaller golden flare. Yamaya stood
with hands on hips.

"That's it?" she scolded Berisan. "You're just going to
yell at them?"

Angry shouting also echoed from behind the ice
walls. A moment later, two more fireballs arced into view.
This time Berisan stepped forward and raised his hands. A
pale gold barrier flared up in front of the attack. Shonn heard
a slight grunt as the blasts struck the barrier, but then Berisan
pushed back. Burning particles deflected down on the far
side of the wall. More cries of alarm echoed past it.

Shonn watched anxiously. If there was ever a time
for betrayal, this was it. Berisan had his back turned,
attention focused on the defense. The villagers were in
disarray, unable to protect him. Shonn flexed his fingers,
trying to keep them from growing numb, and looked for a
path to get up there if Berisan needed help.

But the yelling beyond the ice wall was already less
distinct. There were more hoofbeats than shouting. Everyone
above was turned toward the wall, poised to respond to
another volley.

"They are withdrawing," Meven confirmed as the
noises grew obviously fainter.

Berisan turned and made a little bow to Yamaya while gracefully gesturing toward the wall. "Occasionally, a few well chosen words can be good enough."

A nervous cheer rustled through the villagers. The tight knot of guards around the count loosened up, and Count Ar-Azlor urged his horse forward at a careful walk.

"An interesting approach. Thank you for the demonstration." Ar-Azlor nodded to Berisan, then called down to Meven. "Are you certain they've given up?"

"It appears so," she answered.

"Then, the people should return to your homes. My guards can support the ice witch here." Ar-Azlor scanned the wary villagers. "I know you have grievances. We can discuss them back in the village."

"No way you're splitting us up," Yamaya retorted. "You'd surround us and take us all separately."

Shonn glimpsed Sergeant Piyaro's hopeful expression, but Ar-Azlor patiently answered, "If that was my intention, we would already have done it. You have my word that my forces will not draw steel against you today, and that we will meet to confer in the village. However, there was a private matter I had hoped to discuss before that."

The villagers appeared cautiously satisfied, but when Yamaya saw Ar-Azlor looking at Berisan, she immediately grabbed his arm.

"What's this about?" Yamaya demanded.

"It's a private matter," the count repeated with slightly less patience.

"Yamaya, it's all right. And please let go," Berisan murmured. "That hurts."

She reluctantly released him, grumbling, "What a baby."

The crowds started to loosen up, villagers watching Berisan as he edged between the mounted guards.

"If you are certain, it's this way." Berisan reached up to guide the count's horse. In his grubby trousers and tunic he appeared as much a humble farm hand as a powerful mage.

However, Meven called up after them. "Azlor, be aware. If you choose only to save yourself, then this will not be as easy as you believe."

"We have to let them try," Berisan said.

The count replied, "If you are not bound as we are bound, then you don't know what we think is easy and what is hard."

~ ~ ~

Slowly, with solemn purpose, the newly made Shining Ones formed their barriers and lifted Keilos' rigid form from the dried oasis of blood. Duessa followed as they carried him into the next room. There was the circle of mummies, as Jaxynne had described them. They carefully set Keilos beside the ring. It wasn't a perfect match. Keilos wasn't nearly as mummified as the rest of them. Yet, it was a true fit. Keilos belonged with those ancient ancestors.

It was the living who didn't belong. They still had a terrible challenge before them. Even Keilos' best friends seemed eager to leave the darkness of the tower behind. Only their hovering names marked their presence.

When they emerged into daylight, Keilos was waiting. *"Welcome, my friends."* Duessa sensed his thoughts with no effort, and she felt the urgency that made his ghostly body shimmer and swirl.

"What is it?" Tisha immediately asked.

"Berisan calls me."

"Why? What's happened?" Alemin demanded.

"Some of Dar-Gothull's mages have asked to be freed of his bonds."

"Is that possible?" Lorrah asked, and Duessa didn't have to guess that she was thinking of Ar-Lizelle again.

"I'm going to see if it can be done," Keilos said. *"The wizard-king is fearfully strong. Wish me well."*

Already the shimmering coils lifted away, wafting to curl about the tall tower. Instead of merely hovering in a silent halo, Duessa felt Keilos merging with all of the power there. She received the strangest sensation from him, as if the tower itself stretched in multiple directions, farther than Duessa could understand.

It was almost a relief when Bettain's voice broke into her thoughts. "Well, I guess they've been busy."

Shaking her head and blinking, Duessa looked around. Cheerful voices echoed through the forest around them. Sethamis had the oxen hitched to a makeshift travois, instead of the wagon. Keerin and Razeet were hard at work hacking down the tough bloodthorns and piling them on the travois. Others of the squad wedged the thorny brush tightly between the hornpines.

"They're making a wall?" Lorrah realized.

"It's a good idea," Cylass said approvingly. "We need defenses, and the green brush will tangle anyone who tries to rush through it. Not to mention the thorns."

Tisha squeezed his hand. "Go on and help them."

"We should all help." Alemin voiced the new instinct that connected them. The Shining Ones always worked together, because this was a task to benefit everyone.

As their circle moved toward Zathi, Duessa hesitated. Someone was missing. It took a moment to realize who she didn't see working along with the squad.

"Where's Elldri?" she called.

~ ~ ~

Piyaro would rather have been anywhere else. Berisan led Ar-Azlor and the other mages across the valley at a fast walk, which the horses easily matched. Others of the Pulgoll guard remained to watch over Meven and her mageling at the wall, but Hawk Squad was ordered to stay with their count. Last of all, Shonn trudged after them. He hadn't wanted to leave, but Meven insisted. She wanted him to come back right away with word of what happened.

From ahead of them, vague snatches of talk drifted back. It seemed the mages were asking questions. It would have been encouraging, if they hadn't already made up their minds to take this mad risk. Piyaro could only follow orders and hope to stay alive.

An unwelcome thought nagged at him. Dunsaph was very close. If worst came to worst, there might be some way to shed their livery and slip across the border. Piyaro tried to shake the idea away. How could he speak to Hawk Squad of loyalty, if he did such a thing?

All too soon, they reached the circular pond below Weeping Falls Farm. The signal fire sent its black plume of smoke upward from the ridge. Piyaro saw the silhouette of someone keeping watch beside it. Farther up the valley, the river water was clear. Here, the water was dark and completely smooth. There wasn't even a hint of current leading to the waterfall.

Berisan directed the mages to dismount and space themselves out along the rim of the pond. None of them were in arm's reach of the others. Piyaro had his men lead the horses aside but keep them near. Yamaya prowled around to the far side of the pond. After a moment's hesitation, Shonn went to join her.

Berisan was at the center of the arc, Ar-Azlor on his left. The two junior mages flanked them, with Nyette as the odd one at the end. Just for a moment, her determined eyes met Piyaro's. She straightened her shoulders and focused on the still waters.

Piyaro told himself not to be taken in by her childish hurt. If their friendship mattered, she would never have encouraged Count Ar-Azlor to this point. Instead, Piyaro watched the mages' faces and body language. Berisan was calm, but then, Piyaro had never seen him get upset. Count Ar-Azlor's face was the grim mask of someone who was about to begin mortal combat. Ar-Sessall and Ar-Norius fidgeted and constantly looked to the count for reassurance. Only Nyette stood with confidence, eager for what lay ahead.

The sun above was bright and high. It wasn't easy to see at first, but the water began to glow. Hawk Squad murmured as the light increased.

"Sergeant?" Cothyr's low question reminded Piyaro that most of his men hadn't seen the mysterious creature before. What they did see was that pale golden color, from the witch in the grove.

"Hold steady," Piyaro snapped. He meant to say something — a reassurance, perhaps — but the drakanox arrived.

The massive beast emerged in a corona of light, but the pond itself barely rippled. Piyaro blinked against the glare. He'd forgotten how big the drakanox was, how strangely put together with its long, scaled body mismatched to the mane and horns.

Around him, men uttered shocked curses. Gloved hands opened and closed to grab weapons that would obviously be useless. Shonn, too, gaped at the creature that had drawn him so far from his home in Fang Marsh. Oddly enough, the horses were unconcerned by the looming phantom. After a quick look, they went back to grazing the lush grass growing among the reeds of the valley.

Moving slowly, the drakanox bent toward the mages. It seemed there was a conversation, and then Ar-Azlor spoke distinctly. "Yes, this is my choice."

Piyaro should have cursed, too, but the drakanox radiated serenity. The creature's every hair and scale blazed with shimmering gold. But it blurred, losing definition as it spread out across the pond. Sheer golden vapors enveloped them all, mages and guards and horses, too.

Piyaro tried to hold his breath, not inhale that... stuff. Something settled against his skin, a wisp as light as a spider's web when you crossed it. He twitched at the contact.

Around the circle pond, the mages made no effort to resist. Piyaro watched their faces as the drakanox swirled among them. Ar-Azlor stared ahead with a guarded expression, while his two assistants stood with eyes closed and fists knotted at their sides. Nyette's shoulders rose as she drew in a greedy breath.

But as Piyaro watched, their expressions softened. Stiff backs relaxed a little, tight fists eased. The drakanox circled among them, drawing a pattern Piyaro couldn't see as the breath he held clawed at his chest. A delighted half-smile bloomed on Nyette's young face. Count Ar-Azlor nodded at some thought he did not speak.

Piyaro's held breath escaped in a puff. He couldn't keep himself from gasping in a mouthful of air softened by golden mist. At once, the tension inside him began to let go.

The drakanox returned to the center of the pond. All the mages focused on it, transfixed by an unfamiliar sensation they somehow craved. Piyaro's whirling thoughts slowed. The other men of Hawk Squad had stopped cursing. Yamaya stared at her hands as if she had never seen them before.

Yes, this was everything Piyaro had feared. The memory of Sloram Holl was painfully vivid. The danger and terror had been real. Yet that was in the past. Somehow he could look back on them with acceptance instead of fear.

This was not so easy for the mages. Their eyes were

still focused on the drakanox, but growing fear and remorse twisted their faces. Ar-Sessall, nearest to Piyaro, breathed heavily, his closed eyes shadowed by tortured brows. Count Ar-Azlor's lips moved as if he was speaking frantic words, though Piyaro heard none of them. Beyond him, Ar-Norius bent forward with a whimper, hands pressed to his temples. Berisan and Nyette maintained their steady focus on the drakanox. Tears ran from the girl's eyes.

A keening moan began to rise. Ar-Azlor and his aides staggered, even though they had been so firm in their purpose. Groans gave way to shrill wails. They bent forward, or fell to their knees, then thrashed backward with arms crooked skyward. In an awful chorus, the possessed mages roared, "THESE ARE MINE!"

Piyaro was no mage, but he felt a terrible will intruding from outside himself. It mocked his sense of peace and acceptance. Dark images poured through his mind. The men he had recruited by force. Harsh discipline to make them heel like dogs. Training that was little more than beatings. How could he think he deserved forgiveness, after how he treated them?

Everyone around the pond was moaning and crying. Rowlan bellowed, "Papa, I'm sorry!" Shonn was whimpering, "I didn't mean to do it!" "It's only for a little while, dear," Cothyr moaned. Piyaro found himself weeping, too, because he had never even wondered if his men had left family behind when they were exiled from Sloram. The men had let the reins drop, and the horses scattered away from the sinister presence at the pond.

If the guardsmen were upset, the mages were in paroxysms. They spoke together in a strange, gargling drone. "I give my body to Dar-Gothull." Count Ar-Azlor's eyes had gone black as ink. Ar-Sessall flung his head back with a gurgling cry. Dark fluid spewed from his mouth.

Berisan whirled to help him. Golden light blazed his eyes. "Let them alone!"

The three mages wailed as one, "I give my mind to Dar-Gothull." It was the same kind of noises that Piyaro had heard from Ar-Dayne's workroom when he carried out initiations.

On the other side of Ar-Azlor, Ar-Norius was on his knees. He gave an even more terrible cry as his whole body appeared to be splintering into bloody tentacles that whipped around him. Barely recognizable words echoed among them: "I give my soul to Dar-Gothull."

"No, don't listen," Nyette begged as she ducked a flailing tentacle. "You can be free!"

The drakanox moved swiftly among them. As it brushed by, Piyaro felt a resurgence of tranquility to balance his guilt. If there were words, he did not hear them, but he received the belief that there always was time to seek forgiveness.

Ar-Azlor stood rigid as a post driven into the ground. Piyaro felt the same compassion the drakanox had shown to him. And he remembered that this man was their only hope. If they lost him, Hawk Squad would be done for.

He stumbled past the spasming Ar-Sessall, to Count Ar-Azlor's side. Sightless black eyes stared into nothing. Through a grimace of self-loathing, a few words came clearer. "I should die."

Under any other circumstance, Piyaro wouldn't have dared to touch him. Now he grabbed the count's arm. "No, don't say that!"

"After the things I've done. The people I hurt. All of it. I should die," Ar-Azlor could only get out a few words at a time in that death-like rasp.

Chaos reigned all around them. Both junior mages were on their knees, vomiting blood or worse, shrieking incoherently. Nyette had a vivid slash across her face, and Berisan's tunic was soaked with the black fluid Ar-Sessall was spewing.

Piyaro shook Ar-Azlor's shoulder. "We still need you. My men, and the people of Pulgoll. Don't you leave us here."

The count turned toward him in a series of stiff, jerky motions. He blinked rapidly. "I can't..."

On the other side of him, Nyette was half tangled in Ar-Norius' writhing tentacles."Stay with us," she cried frantically. "It isn't too late!" The girl mage seemed to be pouring some sort of golden light from her hands. The tentacles sizzled furiously and a stench of burning flesh billowed around them.

Berisan was on his knees beside Ar-Sessall. He, too, blazed with light. "You don't need his power. Your spirit is enough."

The younger mages twitched and howled together, "MINE!"

The mighty and perilous drakanox descended suddenly, a curtain of light made solid. Piyaro felt hot wind buffeting him, yet still there was no sense of danger. This was protection, a denial of the wizard-king's evil will. Shimmering magic went through them, as it had during the eruption of light in Seofan Valley.

In a strange chorus of their own, Berisan and Nyette rejected Dar-Gothull's claim. "LET THEM GO."

"Let us go!" Ar-Azlor coughed, but his roughened voice grew stronger. "I reject you, Dar-Gothull. I put you out of me."

Berisan and Nyette jumped to their feet, racing to grab his hands. Golden light now flared from the three of them. "My body is my own," they cried together. From beside Piyaro's feet, Ar-Sessal added a feeble whisper. "My mind is my own. My soul is my own!"

"You fools," shrieked the monstrosity that had been Ar-Norius. "There is no such thing as freedom. You are mine, and I will have you again!"

The drakanox's light flared brighter still, and with a final shriek of rage and agony, Dar-Gothull's puppet was consumed. Even the black fumes evaporated as that corrupted and ruined man seared to bubbling tar.

It was quiet, suddenly. The remaining mages glowed with peaceful light. They gazed at each other, stunned. Ar-Azlor frowned in confusion as he looked at Nyette holding his hand. Berisan let go to kneel beside Ar-Sessall. The junior mage lay on his side, barely breathing, but the blackness had cleared from his eyes.

A slightly unsteady Nyette came over to stand near Hawk Squad. "I am so glad I never went through those rituals. Who wants to have that monster inside their mind?" She bunched up a long sleeve to blot her eyes.

This was absurd, Piyaro thought. Impossible, all of it. No one could defeat Dar-Gothull. That was a given of life in Skaythe. No matter what else you struggled against, the tyrant's power was supreme.

Yet here they were, alive, on a reedy bank above a mirror pond, standing in a cloud of golden light. Piyaro was no mage, but he knew there was something different in himself. Hawk Squad had been changed forever. Laughter bubbled up from his gut, rough and despairing laughter that spoke only how glad he was to still be alive.

XIX — COMBUSTION

None of the guardswomen remembered seeing Elldri go anywhere. They had been well occupied with constructing their defenses and hadn't been worried about her. "I thought she must be staying with the oxen," Sethamis said.

"We'd better go look for her," Bettain huffed angrily. Duessa was concerned, too. Just because some of them were connected to the great tower didn't mean it was safe to go wandering off.

Alemin immediately asked, "Do you want us to help?" He and Lorrah both looked ready to abandon the defense project, attuned as they were to Duessa's feelings.

"Bettain and I are her closest friends. Let us try to find her first," Duessa said. "Besides, we don't all need to rush off."

"All right," Lorrah said, "but if you need us, we're here."

Duessa nodded, cautiously pleased. With this bond, she would never be ignored or betrayed again. But Bettain was hurrying away, and she quickened her pace to keep up.

"I wonder if she planned this all along," Duessa said as they climbed back up the long hillside. It was an easy walk with so much of the brush cleared. "Maybe she waited until we were all busy."

"Why would she do that?" Bettain grumbled.

"I don't know," Duessa said. "It's been hard to understand her." Which was absolute truth, but not much of a comfort.

The horses were tied out where they could graze among the hornpines. Giniver kept watch there while the other guardswomen constructed their makeshift defense.

"Have you seen Elldri?" Duessa asked her.

"Nope. When did you last —"

"Hold on." Bettain snapped her fingers. "I know where she'd go."

"Where?" Duessa waved to Giniver and followed Bettain back down to the main plaza.

"Remember this morning?" Bettain started across, heading for the dark hole that was the giant badger's den.

"Oh, you're right." It was obvious where Elldri would go, once everyone else was busy.

The space beyond the entrance was similar to their own refuge inside the hill. Bettain held up a flaming orb to reveal the long aisle going both ways, and the row of alcoves on the sides. There was no animal stink, as Duessa expected, just a suitably large nest of broken tree branches with softer vegetation packed between them.

Luckily, the giant badger had not returned. Unluckily, there was no sign of Elldri, either. They emerged from the hillside, blinking against the daylight.

"Let's keep looking," Duessa encouraged, though she was feeling more alarmed. Where had Elldri gone, and why now?

She walked slowly along the base of the hill, searching the forest with her eyes. Brush was still thick between the hornpines, for even Badger Squad wasn't brave enough to start clearing it right above their namesake's den. It was easy to spot the gouged earth and broken bushes where the badger had gone vaulting off.

"That's where it went," Duessa said.

A moment later Bettain cried, "Look there. It has to be her." A smaller trail of disturbed soil angled up the slope, plainly following the badger. "Let's go after her!"

"All right, but hold on," Duessa said. "We'd better tell Zathi where we're going."

"If she says no, I'm going anyway," Bettain warned.

That, Duessa could readily believe. She didn't see Zathi right away, but Jaxynne had joined Giniver on the crest of the hill. Jaxynne was the second, and she was a skilled tracker. Duessa's legs ached as she climbed the same hill again. She quickly explained where they were going, and added, "I don't suppose you could come with us?"

Jaxynne shook her head. "Sorry. Dar-Gothull's forces are going to get here sometime soon, and we're nowhere near ready."

It was disappointing, but Duessa couldn't argue her reasoning. As she turned away, Giniver said, "Be careful."

"We're both mages, and I won't get lost," Duessa assured her. "The tower is like a beacon for me. I'll always be able to find my way back."

As she headed off to join Bettain, Duessa tried to focus her mind a little, sharing knowledge with the other mages of where they were going. Then they started up the opposite slope, following the series of large divots the giant badger had left. Elldri's smaller trail clearly followed it into the thick undergrowth.

As they pushed between thorn bushes and jumped over fallen wood, Duessa marveled at how different the Hornwood seemed. The forbidding gloom was alive with little sparks of life, *vitalis* gleaming below ground and from almost every leaf. Birds glittered in the treetops, and an ants' trail made a tiny river of fire. It was beautiful in a way she would never have seen before, but it brought them no closer to Elldri.

The woods must have remained dark and forbidding to Bettain. She tripped often, and cursed Elldri for a fool. "I can't believe she did this."

"She's looking for something," Duessa said soothingly.

"From the giant badger?" Bettain scoffed.

"She said that they're alike. That must be what she's counting on."

Bettain made gagging noises. Duessa smiled at her dramatics, and tried to reach out with her senses. All the brightness she had never sensed before was confusing. How could she find one soulless girl among so much life?

"For what it's worth, I don't think she's dead." Yet Duessa was haunted by something more than Bettain's worries.

Elldri had clearly made a decision to leave the camp and search for the badger. As a friend, Duessa wanted to respect her wishes. Yet, she was troubled by the idea that Elldri, essentially, was abandoning her human friends for something that was potentially fatal.

Even if it was Elldri's choice, was it one they could accept?

"I won't give up on her," Bettain insisted. "We have to keep going."

~ ~ ~

Ar-Lizelle rode watchfully among Count Ar-Gammord's entourage. The Hornwood loomed before them in a ragged green wall. It was a haven for traitors and home of monsters. Ar-Lizelle knew well enough that not all the monsters were vague legends. Yet they were not what she watched for.

The true peril was from the other mages, of course. Each small force worked its way separately across the plains of Ebruc. The lines bunched together and then expanded, like strange caterpillars, all determined to reach the tasty treat before them. Ar-Lizelle had a sense that others were coming from the west and east of Skaythe. Taken together, there were hundreds, a voracious invasion. She could almost pity those fugitives who thought they had any hope of escaping.

From time to time — not so often that it would catch her patron's eye — she continued trying to recapture some sense of where her former prisoners were. What had previously come easily, even against her will, now proved elusive.

It made no sense. The Hornwood was where they had to be. Realistically, there was nowhere else for them to hide. Ar-Lizelle refused to believe they were dead. Alemin with his insane optimism, Duessa and Bettain clinging to their alliance — they simply had to be there!

Ar-Lizelle reined in suddenly. There was a warning shudder, a sense of some distant battle raging.

Ar-Vennic clapped a hand to his temple. "What's happening?"

There was no time to answer before fury erupted within her.

"BURN IT. BURN IT ALL!"

She was vaguely aware of Ar-Vennic and Ar-Gammord calling out. Endole and the other guards anxiously asked what was wrong. Ar-Lizelle's voice rose in a shrill cry as she grappled with the overwhelming anger and hatred.

This was not her own cheated rage. It was like the

renegades' flood of emotion that tamed Elldri. Everything in her rejected this compulsion, but she couldn't get free of it. Only one person could do this. Not just to her, but to every mage at once. It was Dar-Gothull's wrath igniting inside them.

Without her will, Ar-Lizelle's eyes and mind focused on the Hornwood's forbidding bastion. There was the hiding place of his enemies. It must fall to flames and ash, as all who defied the wizard-king would fall.

The lost bond of the Larder no longer mattered. Her desire for vengeance and the restoration of honor burned away. Nothing mattered but the imperative to loose her flames and destroy her enemies.

"Burn it," Ar-Gammord howled, and he ruthlessly spurred his horse into a charge. Ar-Vennic followed, screaming, "Burn, burn!"

The count's guards milled uncertainly, then rallied to gallop after them. Ar-Lizelle found herself cut off as Groff snagged her horse's reins.

"Warden, wait!" he cried. Endole's horse crowded up beside hers. "What's wrong?"

For a moment, her mind cleared enough to rasp out, "You are done."

Endole jerked back, and Groff choked some word of dismay. Ar-Lizelle had no time for their pain at her rejection. Yet, these were her loyal guards, the last remaining fragments of the Larder. There was only one thing she could do for them now.

"This is for mages," she gritted, fighting to keep her own will against the rising tide of madness. "Go back to the village. The one where we joined forces with Ar-Gammord. Wait for me. If I don't come, return to the Larder and inform Captain Morthem."

Before they could respond, Ar-Lizelle yanked the

reins out of Groff's hand and spurred forward. Dar-Gothull's fury surged through her in an irresistible flood.

"Burn everything!" she shrieked.

~ ~ ~

The drakanox's magic was like a sneaker wave, dragging Shonn over the houseboat rail. Or it was a warm wind blowing through the mangroves. Except the mangroves were Shonn's body, and the surging wave somehow muffled the awful screams on the other side of the pond. His mind spun so helplessly that it was a mild surprise to find, when his head cleared, that he was still standing among reeds on the bank of the circular pond.

Nearby, Yamaya had gone to her knees, one arm pressed over her eyes. The sleeve muffled her sobs. Shonn understood that well enough. The ugly guilt of betraying Meven still clung to him like water-weeds washed up on shore.

Half way around the pond, Sergeant Piyaro gave a desolate laugh and scrubbed his face with his hands. The horses Hawk Squad had been holding were scattered, although they hadn't gone far before they fell to grazing. Shonn heard Piyaro send the men to collect them. Oddly, he didn't snap out the order. Instead, he asked them if they would do it.

"Yes sir." Cothyr ambled off, about as steady on his feet as Shonn felt.

Near them, Count Ar-Azlor gazed into the drakanox's eyes in a stunned manner. Berisan and Nyette crouched beside Ar-Sessal. Their hands were clasped, and a pale glow suggested they were casting something. The junior mage's eyes were barely open, his skin ghostly beneath its brown tone.

"Gabrith!" Yamaya lurched to her feet. Shonn had a fragmented memory of her saying she didn't love him enough.

"The baby's fine," Shonn tried to reassure her, though he felt half dazed. "Your friend has him, remember?"

"I have to go," Yamaya cried in uncharacteristic disarray. As she hurried past him, Shonn remembered something important.

"If they're not at the farm, try down the trail to the swamp."

Yamaya paused with a more normal scowl. "Why would they go there?"

"I told them there's a shelter there if it looks like things are going bad here."

Yamaya grimaced, exasperated. "Don't help," she snapped, and headed up the slope at a run. Shonn hurried around to join the Hawks on the other side of the pond. The drakanox was gathering itself in a benevolent coil near the center. By the time Shonn got there, Nyette and Berisan were helping Ar-Sessall sit up. As soon as he was partly upright, he lurched over and heaved more black fluid onto the grass.

Ar-Azlor murmured to Piyaro, "I should send the men. Defend the land. They need me..." He trailed off, as if he wasn't certain.

Berisan looked up from supporting Ar-Sessal. "They do need you, but take it slowly. I had years of training, and you experienced everything in a few minutes. It must be overwhelming."

"You were never bound to him," Ar-Azlor said. "You can't know..." He trailed off again.

Nyette bowed her head, voice thick with grief. "I couldn't save Ar-Norius."

"Not all can be saved. We must prepare ourselves for that reality." Shonn and Piyaro both started at the sensation of the drakanox speaking in their minds. *"Yet I also know there is an advantage. Our friends in the Hornwood have*

succeeded in bonding with the heart of Skaythe. It was a blow to Dar-Gothull's supremacy. The Devourer is distracted."

"They did it?" Berisan's eyes lit with joy. "I wish I could be there."

"Alemin wishes it, too," the drakanox said. *"He asks for you. With this, here, we have struck a second blow. It is proof that Dar-Gothull's control is not absolute. But the Hornwood is where he must strike if he hopes to claw it all back. This gives you time, Azlor."*

"What should we do?" Ar-Azlor gathered a bit more focus.

"Just what you said. Prepare to safeguard your people."

"Dunsaph has been answered, but there may be others who seek to use this moment of confusion," Nyette said.

"In Deeve," Piyaro sounded grim and tired.

"Yes, I see it." Ar-Azlor said. "You are gathering the horses, Sergeant?"

"Yes, my lord."

"I must return to the Hornwood." The drakanox was already submerging in the pond. *"Be safe. Take care of each other. There is no greater power than your faith in each other."*

In silence, they watched him sink into the water. A fading glow streaked off to the east. Hawk Squad were returning, each leading two or three horses. Ar-Sessall was on his feet between Berisan and Nyette, no longer so ill.

"We'll need someone to fetch the rest of my guards." Ar-Azlor sounded more alert.

Shonn seized the opportunity. "I'll tell them. Meven

wanted me to bring news anyway."

"Thank you." The count nodded.

Shonn's head reeled again, at the simple gratitude from a fierce and deadly mage. Before he could decide what to say, his feet were carrying him back toward the ice walls. Dark thoughts and guilt tried to keep pace with his steady jog. What did he think to find, if not the cold truth?

He had no claim on Meven, and never would. Everything he had done to woo her was a lie. It was just another way to control her. Shonn shook his head, trying to banish the unwelcome thoughts.

The drakanox had said to take care of each other. That made it practically an order.

It was easy enough to see the squad of guards Ar-Azlor had left at the ice walls. They loitered on horseback, visibly restless without a clear enemy to fight. When they saw Shonn coming, the sergeant trotted out to meet him.

"Did it work?" the man called anxiously. "We heard all this noise."

"Mostly," Shonn grimaced at the reminder of the mages' horrific struggle. "One of them didn't make it. The count wants you back there. He'll explain and give you new orders."

"Very good." The sergeant was glad enough to take Shonn's word. Once the guards rode off, he saw Ozlin swinging his legs over the lip of the stony stair-steps. The boy scampered down to the level where Meven was.

"He's back." The mageling prowled about with arms folded against the chill, kicking at tufts of sparse grass.

"So I hear." Meven turned to measure Shonn beneath the rim of her hat.

His heart seized for a moment at the strange beauty of those seal-gray eyes, and the vision of her strong brown body wrapped in pale green swamp linen against the bold white of the ice wall. All of his guilt flew away and he remembered why he had wanted her in the first place. Meven kept herself apart from everyone, even with Ozlin. But nobody deserved to be so alone.

Something in Meven's gaze was different. Perhaps she was tired from casting. The diamond hard focus had eased. It could be his imagination, but the frigid draft from the ice wall seemed less intense.

"Are you all right?" Shonn blurted.

Meven studied Shonn in return, tilting her head a bit, as if something puzzled her. "What happened?"

"To me? Nothing." He eased down where Ozlin had been and launched into a brief explanation of the events with the drakanox. Even when it seemed obvious to Shonn that he was brushing over the worst moments of guilt, Meven listened without interrupting. Ozlin smirked a little when Shonn described the mages speaking in chorus. "That wasn't creepy at all."

"They really did it," Meven marveled when he'd finished his account. "I thought never..."

"How about here?" Shonn asked. "Those guys didn't change their minds and come back?"

Meven barely glanced at the ice walls. "It doesn't seem so."

"Then, are you going to come back to the farm?" Shonn tried not to sound forlorn. Ozlin scowled, but Meven again gave Shonn that odd stare.

"We'll wait a few more hours to be sure," she decided. "If Oz doesn't signal, we'll be back by mid afternoon."

"Right. I'll tell Berisan." Shonn gathered himself to go. Up on the ridge, the black plume of smoke was turning gray-white and wispy. "Oh — there's supposed to be a meeting in Opshar. I don't know when. Count Ar-Azlor is going to negotiate with the villagers."

He moved slowly, hoping for one more word. It didn't come. With an inane wave, Shonn jogged off toward the waterfall.

In his head, that nasty voice of doubt jeered. What else did he expect? Meven didn't owe him anything. He had to let go of his expectations.

True as that might be, it still hurt to give up his hopes for her. For them.

~ ~ ~

The Hornwood held more rough ground than Duessa had expected. She and Bettain had been tramping through the tangled thickets and rock outcrops for what felt like hours. Duessa's lungs ached as she paused at the base of yet another slope. Then she caught sight of Bettain's face, determined but deeply flushed and beaded with sweat.

"Wait a bit." Duessa patted her friend's shoulder.

"We need to find Elldri," Bettain panted. "I'm not giving up on her."

"I didn't say you should," Duessa answered, "but we're dashing around without knowing where to go. Let's rest. I'll at least try to find water."

It was stupid of them to leave camp without provisions. Traveling as much as she had, Duessa should have known better. Just beyond the nearest thicket, there was a sunny gap where several hornpines had come down in a long-ago storm. They pushed their way through to settle on the lichen-scabbed length of a fallen trunk. Bettain still breathed heavily and flapped the front of her blouse to generate a breeze. Duessa did her best to ignore the distraction as she tried to orient herself.

The tower was a beacon, spreading steady warmth through the dense woodland. Then her senses caught on the cool slickness of water. She turned her head in that direction. Near it was a gap in the shimmering net of life all around them. Duessa probed into that place of silence. The dark hole was definitely large enough to hold a giant badger.

Not wanting to make any promises, she straightened and said, "Let's try this way."

Bettain trudged after her, around the latest outcrop and through a grove of pale hornpines. The crowding trees created deeper shade, and they met a cooler draft that carried the scent of damp earth. There was a downward angle, a gentle turn, and a welcome glint up ahead. Another clearing held marshy pools spreading from a brook flowing down the opposite side. Insects hummed amid tall grass and reeds.

"At least it's something," Bettain grumbled, and she knelt to drink from the nearest pool. "Hey, look!"

Duessa bent to examine the muddy verge. There were many tracks, of deer, small rodents, birds of varying size. Among them was a human footprint. Elldri's, no doubt; she still wore thin leather sandals from the Larder.

"Good eye." Duessa scooped a bit of water for herself while following the prints with her eyes.

Several more were visible beneath a scant fingertip's depth of water. They meandered around another, much larger, paw print that was quickly filling with water.

"They've got to be close." Bettain straightened, drying her hands on her skirt.

"I think they're right over there."

Beyond that the bright sunshine and the glitter of water, heavy shade lurked beneath the trees. Something dark moved within it, and Bettain let go a gusty sigh of relief.

The giant badger was curled up, like a shaggy

bounder, a little bit up slope from the soggy ground. Elldri was perched on the crest of its back. The great striped muzzle turned back toward her. Small round ears flicked restlessly, but there was no sense of danger in it.

Bettain slapped at a whining mosquito, and set off around the edge of the pools. Duessa followed, feeling something in the silence that she didn't understand.

"I guess you dream big," Bettain puffed as they got closer.

Elldri only darted a glance toward them. Her black hair was loose in fluffy waves, the shadows a sort of cloak she could draw around her. The badger snorted, but stayed still.

"This is Ruen," Elldri answered at last, her shoulders hunched and defensive. It was the same name Keilos had given. "I told you, we're the same."

"I can see that." Duessa studied the pair of them. Though different in size, covered in clothing or fur, each had a yawning chasm inside. "You match, don't you."

"If you put aside a few feet of height," Bettain scoffed.

Elldri tossed her chin, rejecting the joke. Dark eyes, gleaming with indignation, focused on Duessa. "You don't match," the girl retorted. "You did something."

Ruen pointed his long muzzle in Duessa's direction. The black skin of his nose twitched. A low sound reached her. It could have been a growl. Duessa stopped, startled by the accusation.

"Yes," she said softly. What did this have to do with her? She faltered, "I did. I want to try a different way."

"She signed on their wall!" Bettain cackled, but there was a tone in her voice that Duessa couldn't place.

"You're like them now." Elldri's voice held a tremor.

"Tattle-tale." Duessa gave Bettain a sarcastic look. Carefully, she explained to Elldri, "I reached for something better. But Bettain stayed as she is, because that was right for her."

"How is it better?" Elldri challenged, but she immediately looked away, murmuring, "We were a team. Through all of that, in the Larder, we were together. But now you're... You did that."

"I chose for myself, to stop being what the world forced me to be. " Duessa's temper began to rise. "So I can have peace instead of always being afraid. Why is that wrong?"

"Yes, for yourself. Not like you need us any more." Bettain spoke quietly, not in her usual gruff tone, as she passed Duessa. Stopping closer to Ruen, she looked up to Elldri."I'm still here for you."

Duessa stared between them. She didn't understand why her friends questioned her loyalty. Holding back indignation, she said, "I'm sorry Tisha hurt you, Elldri. And Ruen." She belatedly acknowledged the giant badger. "She wanted to help, but it was wrong to try and 'save' you. This is who you are. It's who you always were, before we were thrown in the Larder."

Her two friends traded glances. Bettain shifted uneasily. Inside herself, Duessa felt an echo of her other friends, from Alemin or perhaps Tisha, offering words and comfort.

"I accept who you are, Elldri. I accept Bettain deciding not to change. But that's no reason we have to stop being friends. Who said that?" The old ache stung Duessa's heart, of the moon-runners leaving her behind. She couldn't let it happen again. "Yes, my power is different. I guess I'm glowing, and it feels like my scars are going away. I'm finally able to grow the way I should have. This change... It's a beginning, not an ending. Just like you finding Ruen doesn't end anything else."

The unspoken question dangled: could they, in turn, accept who Duessa was?

Elldri was silent as ever, her dark eyes swimming with thoughts. Bettain couldn't meet Duessa's eyes. Instead she looked up at Elldri again, impatience a cover for her worry.

"Can we please go back?" Bettain said. "Nobody is judging you. Zathi said it, they're warriors. Killing is their job. If they blame you, what would they have to say about themselves?"

"You know, you can't really live out here," Duessa added gently. "My gang of moon-runners did that some. It takes more gear than you think. Besides which, you can't eat raw meat, the way Ruen does."

The badger snorted and twitched its ears. Elldri was still tense, but a faint smile pulled at the corners of her mouth.

"All the counts are coming," Bettain pressed, more anxious. "You shouldn't be out here alone." Ruen gave a definite growl at that. Bettain scoffed at him. "Look, you're big, but you're still only two... monsters... against a mob."

Somberly, Duessa said, "I went down fighting once before. If I have to do it again, I'd want it to be together."

"Okay," Elldri spoke in a low breath. "But not yet. Ruen doesn't want to stay in one place too long. We'll... we'll scout the forest."

The great beast came to its feet. Elldri clambered forward to bury her feet in his pelt and held on by handfuls of fur. Bettain groaned with frustration, but Duessa laid a hand on her shoulder.

"See you soon, then."

~ ~ ~

No longer was the Hornwood a dark bastion of lost

lore. The mages had made it a hellscape. Searing layers of red and yellow fire leapt and danced among the gaunt hornpines. Their tall forms were wreathed in flames. Shifting screens of gray and black smoke churned skyward, flecked with bright cinders.

From every side of the hornwood, mages advanced. Fire's guttural roar sounded everywhere about them as flames loosed from their hands. Brush and trash wood that blocked their way was eaten down to ash. A forward wind pushed the fires ahead of them, leaving bare cinders open to their passing.

Ar-Lizelle grinned feverishly as she gazed upon it. This was good. It was right to destroy everything that stood between them and the subject of Dar-Gothull's vengeance.

She had lost track of time, while Dar-Gothull possessed her. The sky above was gray and dim. Was this the darkness of night, or did the bitter fumes blot out pitiful daylight? Nor did she knew how far they had come, except that they were well into the depths of the Hornwood.

It didn't matter. There was farther yet to go. The renegades had a base in the deepest part of the woodland. They thought it secret, but it was no longer safe from Dar-Gothull's attention. There would be no more hiding, no refuge for the idiot minstrels.

Ar-Lizelle saw the place, as they all did, with their master's eyes. There was a high, rounded tower, much like that of the Larder, but this was grander, not ruined and corrupted as the Larder was. This was where they must gather. Skaythe's true mages would stamp out the piercing light that insulted Dar-Gothull's beautiful darkness. Ar-Lizelle remembered the light all too well. The nauseating sweetness that had tried to win her over. She shook her head, a reflex of disgust.

For a moment, common sense penetrated the feverish haze of Dar-Gothull's fury. She was aware of her horse, trembling beneath her. Ar-Gammord's chestnut breathed in deep gasps. Blood streaked its muzzle. Ar-Vennic's beast was matted with foam. It had been chaos when the burning began. Not all the horses were as well trained as others, but Ar-Gammord had good stock. These three had been able to stay together.

However, no guards were near them. Only mages came in and out of sight amid the blowing smoke. The guards had been left behind. She spared a moment's thought for her two guards. They'd better have followed her orders. The last thing anyone needed was a bunch of commoners getting in the way.

Or, was that true? Ar-Lizelle had a momentary sense of being harrowed, her energy poured out by the force of Dar-Gothull's will moving through her. Suddenly she felt the sting of smoke in her eyes. Ar-Vennic coughed repeatedly. But Ar-Lizelle stiffened her spine.

What did such trivia matter? Ar-Lizelle was a mage, her mind disciplined to focus on what was necessary. She would not let this shake her.

"Come. These beasts are foundered," Count Ar-Gammord snarled as he dismounted.

"Agreed." Ar-Lizelle kicked a leg up and dropped from the saddle. Ar-Vennic also slid down. Still coughing, he leaned on the saddle. She paused only long enough to grab her waterskin and a pouch with extra food. Like their guards, the horses were no longer needed. Better to leave them before they fell and took her down, too.

She came up beside Ar-Gammord, who stared into the burning Hornwood with terrible intensity. Yes, it was a hellscape, but it held no terror for Ar-Lizelle. Fire was hers to command. She would order it away as easily as summon it up. If she faltered now, her life was over. And there was something she had to do, a vengeance of her own. By serving Dar-Gothull with her whole being, she would see them both satisfied.

Ar-Gammord settled himself, then turned to summon Ar-Lizelle and Ar-Vennic with his glare. Without a moment's hesitation, she strode after him into the holocaust. It was time to drive their fire right up to that rebel's tower, and burn its contagion from this world.

~ ~ ~

Duessa sensed the excitement even before she and Bettain got back to the tower. Keilos had returned from his errand to Pulgoll with good news. Alemin rushed to tell them how the mages had been freed from Dar-Gothull's control.

"It wasn't easy," he said, "but they did it!"

"That's hard to believe," Duessa murmured, although she sensed no deception.

"The mage must be willing to risk everything," Keilos said, *"and not all are strong enough."*

"But it's possible," Lorrah repeated, trying to reassure herself. Alemin wrapped a comforting arm over her shoulder.

Duessa and Bettain exchanged skeptical glances. It was sweet that Lorrah cared about her sister, but Ar-Lizelle had made her hostility more than clear. Through their bond, Duessa knew Lorrah's conflicted feelings. The anger she still carried against her hateful older sister, balanced against her wish for a better relationship. It seemed futile, but Duessa saw no reason to be cruel. She kept her doubts private.

The mages might celebrate, but Zathi seemed unable to stand still. Storm clouds were clotting on the horizon as she called them back into their working teams.

"If we are to defend this ground, we must know it well," she declared when they had gathered. "We'll use this time as best we can."

For the next hour they did drills, using the squad's empty wagon as a focal point to pivot one way or another, where their stretch of pavement might come under attack. The archers, with few bolts to spare, only sighted along their crossbows, while mage and warrior teams made practice charges toward the bristling brush walls.

Before, Duessa had struggled with holding up barriers. Now she found it simple. Her friends' knowledge wove into her mind, showing her what to do. Working together, they formed ever broader and stronger barriers. It was almost frightening, how easily the power flowed. With an endless reserve of *vitalis*, Duessa didn't get tired as she had expected to.

During one sortie, Zathi identified a low spot in one of the brush walls, where mounted attackers might to jump their horses. She paused the group so that Giniver and Razeet could heap the thorny branches higher, until Jaxynne said, "Wait. Maybe we can use this."

"You mean, let them think it's a weak point?" Keerin suggested.

While the Badgers discussed it, Ruen reappeared from the deep forest. A surprisingly pale tongue lolled as the giant badger panted. He lowered his head to sniff at the tangled brush, then hopped over it with a scornful tilt to his ears. There was a momentary silence when everyone saw Elldri riding along, legs buried in the beast's thick fur.

"My goodness," Tisha murmured admiringly, while Cylass hurried to her side.

Razeet turned in the saddle to grin at Sethamis. "Hers is bigger."

Sethamis sputtered, "Well, mine are cuter!"

Everyone laughed, but a few steps more brought Ruen to loom over them. Elldri leaned over to tell Zathi, "The woods are on fire!"

That startled everyone into looking around. The dirty gray clouds Duessa had noted before no longer hinted at rain. That was smoke ominously rising, and it promised storms of an entirely different kind. Anxious babble rose as mages and warriors gathered.

"Which way is it coming from?" Zathi demanded, and Jaxynne added, "How long has it been burning?"

"It's everywhere," Elldri said. "We scouted to the east, then south and back around west. There's fire on all sides. I don't know how long since it started, but it might not matter."

The mages' flush of success faded as they understood what she was saying. "They're pinning us here," Bettain said.

"Even if it gets this far, the fire will stop at the edge of the pavement," Giniver said hopefully.

"It will take our walls down first," Cylass countered.

"The bloodthorns are still pretty green," Razeet said. "They won't burn too well."

Lorrah inserted, "It won't take every wall." Duessa sensed her thought, just as Keerin blurted, "We planned everything around those walls!" She and the other warriors looked to Zathi with dismay.

"Don't panic," Alemin said soothingly.

"We don't panic," Zathi returned sharply. Duessa's stomach turned over. She had thought there was such solidarity, but would their two teams fall apart this quickly?

"There's more than one kind of wall," Tisha reassured Zathi. Cylass snapped around for a worried glance at her. "I have a thought on this. May we mages have a moment to discuss it?"

Zathi turned a dour eye on the horizon, where the menacing curtain of smoke swept ever higher. Instinctive fear prickled within Duessa as she considered how much fire there must be, and how quickly it was advancing.

"Yes, please do," the Sergeant bit out.

She beckoned Jaxynne over for a conference of their own, while the mages gathered around Tisha. Even Elldri joined them, sitting high on Ruen's back. The giant badger listened with intelligent eyes.

"What's your idea?" Duessa shifted restlessly, shifting her shoulders against the itchy sensation of approaching danger.

"This is very like when I faced Ar-Dayne in Seofan," Tisha began. "I believe my strategy can work again."

"You only faced one then," Cylass objected.

"I'm not alone now," she reminded him gently. "This is how I defeated Ar-Dayne..."

Reaching a hand, she invited Alemin and Duessa to join hands. Bettain reluctantly took Lorrah's hand to complete the circle, so they all received Tisha's memory. Her power had already been up as she danced, trying to revive the moribund oleya grove. Duessa felt the impact of poisoned bolts against Tisha's barrier, and heard the count's increasingly baleful threats.

"We're going to do more than just deflect, right?" Bettain asked.

"What need for more?" Tisha shared her moment of panic as fire poured down on her. Yet the scalding pain gave way to a softer rush as *vitalis* mingled and changed it. "He meant to burn me, but he made me stronger."

"Yes, I see it!" Lorrah cried. Duessa wasn't quite so certain. In the back of her mind, she felt a presence riding on the smoky breeze. Someone she had thought, just this morning, she would never have to deal with again.

"It seems like an awful risk." She spoke aloud for Elldri's benefit.

"Our barrier will be strong, with all of us together

and ages of *vitalis* behind it," Alemin said. "They will spend their strength against it, as Ar-Dayne did."

"I never struck against him." Tisha spoke with serene confidence. "It was he who could not control his rage. He poured out everything trying to get through."

"You think they'll make the same mistake?" Duessa asked doubtfully.

"Who would warn them?" Lorrah said. "Mages like them can't even be in the same room. Even if they knew, they wouldn't tell the others."

"Okay," Bettain said, "but that's just a stalemate. They can stay outside our barrier as long as they want, and like Cylass said, there's a lot of them."

"It's a gambit." The soft voice came from all around them. Everyone looked up as Keilos settled to their level. The strands of his mane ruffled gently in a sourceless breeze. *"If they fail to break through and destroy us, what do you think will happen?"*

Duessa's stomach dropped with horrible realization. Even the reassurance of her mage's circle couldn't ease it. Alemin spoke for all of them. "Dar-Gothull will come."

Lorrah gave a dramatic shudder, but rallied. "I thought you couldn't foresee any more."

"This doesn't take foresight," Keilos answered wryly, *"just a minstrel's understanding of people."*

"Someone who rules through force cannot be seen to fail," Tisha said.

"Alemin is right," Elldri lisped above them. "The Devourer is always hungry. He will see us as tempting prey." Ruen gave a low rumble of agreement.

"Then, when he gets here —" Alemin looked a question to Keilos.

"That will be my task," the drakanox answered.

"You're definitely the biggest target," Bettain laughed without humor.

"I, most of all, am the representation of everything he despises," Keilos said. *"He thought the drakanox was safely chained to his will, but it... I... escaped. He must destroy me, or be destroyed himself."*

If that was true, Duessa thought, then all Dar-Gothull's mages should be coming after Keilos. There was something about that. She couldn't quite bring it to her mind.

"Lady." Cylass's low warning called them out of their close conference. The mages stirred, looking around them. Zathi strode toward them, while the rest of the guardswomen moved about busily.

"More practice?" Alemin mock-groaned.

"No more practice." The sergeant slowly raised her hands to remove her helmet. She shook her head and ran her fingers through the loose black curls. "My old sergeant used to say, if you keep sharpening your sword, it will lose its edge completely. We've prepared as best we can, and we all know what's coming. Once the fire gets here, the mages will be right behind it."

Around her, Duessa saw the mages nodding somberly. Zathi went on.

"Jaxynne thinks we have a couple of hours before then. We're going to rest up and have a hearty meal, and prepare our minds for..." she shrugged diffidently, "whatever happens."

"You are very wise," Keilos said.

Zathi paused, seeming not to know what to say to that. After a moment she snapped, "Get over here and help us."

"You don't have to tell us twice," Lorrah grinned.

XX — DUALITY

T he mages hurried over to the wagon, which seemed to be the center of preparations. Jaxynne had Razeet unloading almost all the food Badger Squad had in store. They brought the portable stove over and got it lit, while Giniver and Keerin dragged several large chunks of wood out to the center of the pavement for a bonfire. Bettain lit it with flair.

There were other preparations, too. Elldri and Sethamis bedded the oxen down inside the hill, in what they hoped would be a safer location. The horses were staked out under the trees. Sethamis divided the last of her grain among them. Giniver asked Duessa to help fill the large water jugs from a nearby pond. As they were coming back, Duessa glimpsed Tisha and Cylass slipping off, hand in hand. In camp, Alemin and Lorrah stayed as close as bark and its tree.

Duessa was slightly depressed that she had no one like that. But Gauer had made his choice to leave her behind, and there was no magic to undo the years gone by.

Soon everyone was gathered around the bonfire, sitting on folding stools or on the gleaming pavement. Razeet was simmering a massive stew, and all the dried fruit was mixed in a bowl. Jaxynne came out with a couple of bottles to pass around. Even Ruen had gone into the

Hornwood and returned with a young boar for himself to tear into.

Duessa found it eerie to lay out such a feast while all their enemies closed in. It was a silent admission that they likely would not have a next meal. Yet, how could she regret sitting down with her friends? It was relaxing compared to the grim fellowship of the Larder, where guards ringed the walls and stared at them while they ate. Nor did she have to skulk around a hidden camp, as the moon-runners did. Water jugs were heavy to lift, but the work was pleasant because she did it with friends.

When everyone had food and drink, the entertainment began. Beside the snapping bonfire, Lorrah played her fiddle and Tisha danced. Alemin's props had been lost with Cylass' hand cart, so he juggled the last few sweet potatoes. The Badgers laughed long and hard at Razeet's funny story, which turned out to be an embarrassing incident from Keerin's girlhood.

With their helmets off, the guardswomen seemed very different. Duessa studied their faces one by one. They'd been together for weeks, but somehow she hadn't known Giniver had three short braids tucked up inside her helmet. Sethamis bore knife scars down the back of her neck. Keerin and Razeet each wore a single silver earring and no other adornment. Such small details, but now they were striking and important.

Keilos circulated during it all, eating nothing, but trailing a gentle breeze that kept off the worst of the smoke. All too soon, dark streamers began to blow through the camp, scenting the air with poignant warning. Billows of dirty gray curled up on every side. Wild birds and animals pelted frantically across the plaza. Duessa wished them well. Even Ruen, with his powerful legs, would have little chance if he did try to escape.

The circle grew quieter as Zathi stood up, slapping a glowing spark off her pauldron. Her dark eyes roved the circle, nodding and acknowledging each one.

"It is time," she said.

No one bothered clearing the dishes. They stacked them near the stove and went to fetch their horses. Mages and warriors were on their feet, moving with haste but no panic. Bettain reappeared, carrying those patchwork robes she had worked on during the long weeks of travel. Duessa slid hers on over her peasant dress, and marveled for a moment at the sight of the six mages, uniformed in gray cloth, just as the warriors wore their gray steel armor.

The Badgers mounted up. They soothed their anxious horses or sighted down their weapons casually, with long accustomed skill. All the while, the flames in the Hornwood galloped closer. Daylight was dimming, beyond what the sun's progress allowed. The bitter stench of smoke was unavoidable. Ruen moved around their line, with Elldri on his back.

"We'll be roving on the outside," she lisped to Duessa and Bettain.

"What?" Duessa cried. This wasn't a plan that anyone had discussed. There was a slight vibration underfoot as the giant badger moved past them, trotting toward the thorn wall. Turning to Keerin, who was bringing Smoke up beside her, she said, "I don't feel good about this."

"Yeah," Keerin murmured darkly as she got up on her horse. "We told you how vicious that beast was the first time, right?"

Zathi's lips quirked with gallows humor. "I hope somebody else ends up in its mouth this time."

Duessa watched Ruen lope away and hoped he wouldn't drag Elldri into the darkness with him.

"Be careful!" Bettain called after them. An impossible request, given the circumstances, but Duessa understood it. Elldri waved once more before her giant steed vanished in the smoke and shadows.

A tense silence followed. Alemin coughed a little. Then his voice rose in a familiar chorus. At the first line, others caught their breath and began to sing with him.

The light of your fire draws me ever,

A tie that no distance or time can sever.

Sure as the sun rises at dawn,

The hope in our hearts will go on.

One or another of the Badgers often hummed this tune, but Duessa was always surprised that a simple song about home and love could hold such meaning. Yet the mages' faces were soft with nostalgia, and Jaxynne reached up to wipe her eyes.

If this was how they died, Duessa supposed you could do worse for an epitaph.

~ ~ ~

Ar-Lizelle strode through the blackened woodland. Charred branches crunched under her boots, and a few fragile shapes of vine or leaf that were preserved in ash crumbled instantly as her robe swept past. She followed the exhilarating rush of destruction, her mind at one with the inferno's endless hunger. She passed some sort of animal, killed in the inferno. The cloying stench of burned flesh only added to the dizzy rush.

Dar-Gothull's bloodlust might be what drove her and the other mages who walked through the smoking debris, but Ar-Lizelle fully exulted in it. This, the unstoppable flame and wrack, was what it truly meant to be a mage in Skaythe!

Sheets of fire and smoke might obscure the trees, but they couldn't hide the renegades' vaunted refuge. How pathetic it was, a high hump like a swollen wound scabbed over with vegetation. It would be lanced and drained like any infection.

At ground level, some kind of pathetic barricade had been put up among the hornpines. Beyond that was a wide opening where a paltry handful of defenders were ranged around the prison wagon Ar-Lizelle remembered so well. A bonfire flickered — how redundant! And what were those robes the mages wore? They looked like old prison garb patched with dyed rags. The sight of it drew a shrill, harsh laugh.

"As if a bunch of twigs and branches are going to keep us out," she crowed. "And are they... singing? What a sad joke!"

"We'll burn it," Ar-Vannic rasped, his voice roughened by the smoke. No more the half-guilty submissiveness he had used to deflect his count's suspicions. Madness now shone in his eyes.

On her other side, Ar-Gammord hissed agreement. "They will die."

Among the scorched tree trunks, flashes of crimson showed the other mages and counts closing around that ridiculous renegade trash pile. Banners of war popped out from the smoke: Lithole, Yergha and Kamuril to her left, and farther back Ebruc, Nimthar, Ortach. Ar-Lizelle snarled a little on identifying Count Ar-Nithal, who had sent her from Prowth in chains, bound for the Larder. There were many others she didn't recognize. Followers of the counts, perhaps, or upstarts who refused to take service. Dar-Gothull's drive to destruction united them all, for this moment, at least.

"Burn it," spat from Ar-Lizelle's lips, and she heard it echo through the forest. As one, the mages raised hands to send forth renewed gouts of flame. Ar-Lizelle expected the puny barricade to kindle at once, tangled branches withering among the blaze.

Only they didn't catch fire. Racing flames came up against something unseen. They faltered and sputtered out. Cries of fury rippled down the mages' line.

"You dare!" Ar-Gammord struck again. Bright flames seared the air, only to die away.

Ar-Lizelle could see it now, a smooth surface outlined in reflections of flame. She knew what this was.

"Little sister," she snarled.

Lorrah was a coward who hid behind such barriers. She and the pathetic minstrels must think they were safe. Ar-Lizelle uncoiled her flaming whip and dragged it along the surface, seeking a weak point. A barrage of thuds and bangs resounded through the forest as mages made every effort to batter the renegades' defenses down. Somehow, each attack dissipated as it struck the barrier.

In the distance, a shout was broken off. Ar-Lizelle ignored it. Lorrah's barrier hadn't been this strong before. Ar-Lizelle side-stepped Ar-Vennic's blast and slammed the wall with her fist.

"How are you doing this?" she shrieked.

"You know something about it?" Ar-Gammord glared an accusation. With a sweeping gesture, he gathered the fire still burning around them, and flung it at the barrier. She glared back at him through a burst of ash and sparks.

"Don't attack me now," she snarled. "It's those prisoners."

Ar-Lizelle paused, breathing hard. This couldn't be just Lorrah. The other prisoners were with her, too — Alemin, Duessa and Bettain. Not Elldri, though. And was that a dancing girl? Ridiculous! She glared through the translucent golden screen, where the mages clustered on their wagon. Mounted guardswomen trotted around them, watching the barricades.

"Yes, your prisoners," Ar-Gammord advanced, gathering more fire. "Is this all some scheme?"

"It's none of mine," she answered fiercely, and screeched, "Alemin! Come out and face me!"

This was infuriating. After everything Ar-Lizelle had gone through to get here, those cowards just sat and waited. Snug in their shell, refusing to join in honest battle. What an insult! She stalked along the wall, darting wary glances at Ar-Gammord.

Again, she heard a cry of pain cut off. It sounded closer. This was enough to hold her attention. "What are those fools doing?" she demanded, annoyed.

"Don't try to distract me." The count reached upward, gathering fire from the lowest branches.

Ar-Lizelle opened her mouth, but the words she spoke were not her own. "COME TO ME." Dar-Gothull's irresistible command burst forth. Ar-Gammord's eyes glazed as he and Ar-Vennic both chanted. "Come to me. Come."

As one, the counts and mages left the barrier that stymied them. Ar-Lizelle, too, hurried to the call. Her robe snagged on a crook of branch and she tore it loose. Others stumbled over loose stones, or collided with low branches. Vaguely, Ar-Lizelle noted a low place in the brush wall. She had no chance to examine that. None of them knew where they was going, only that they must obey.

Mages spilled out of the blackened forest and gathered on a broad swath of silvery highway. On one side, the thorny barricade kept them from their enemies in the plaza. But the pull Ar-Lizelle felt was from the other side, where pavement curved away into the trees. There was movement on the road. No, *within* the road. A trail of darkness warped and bubbled to the surface. Tarry streaks formed just before a crack split the paving. With a stench like burning flesh, a welling of darkness emerged.

It was the nightmare revenant she knew so well, a

manlike form trailing jagged-toothed tentacles. This quickly solidified into that of a man. Dar-Gothull was garbed in crimson, winking with gems and fantastic embroidery. A web of gold chains adorned his bald head. Even without them, the overpowering aura of power and majesty were unmistakable.

Counts and mages bowed or knelt before him. They were but reddish shadows, all of them, compared to the wizard-king. Ar-Lizelle's heart pounded with reverence and dread.

Dar-Gothull smiled with kindly malice. "Let's have this down, for I hunger."

Ar-Lizelle did not try to resist the compulsion as they all raised their hands to strike. Instant obedience was better than being the one to sate his appetite. Beside her, Ar-Gammord twitched as he moved. His eyes were wild with paranoia, but his body obeyed Dar-Gothull.

Once again, flames, lightning and hail battered the barrier. Then, to her left, Ar-Lizelle caught another flash of movement. There was a wild shout. Something gray and hairy buffeted her. Snarling jaws snatched Ar-Vennic from beside her. Even Dar-Gothull was startled by the attack. His compulsion loosened enough for Ar-Lizelle to whirl away from the massive animal thundering past her. It was a badger, terrifying in its massive size.

"Ruen!" Dar-Gothull cried angrily. "You dare defy me?"

The giant badger paused. Ar-Vennic's arms waved wildly between the jagged teeth. With a growl, the beast shook its head. Blood sprayed everywhere. Mages scattered, avoiding the creature. It spat out the lifeless body with visible contempt and whipped around. Its huge tail bashed several mages aside.

Ar-Lizelle stared as it leapt away into the smoldering woodland. Someone was riding that thing!

"Elldri?" she choked with fury.

"Return to me at once!" Dar-Gothull commanded. Somehow he loomed taller and darker than ever.

"You... You!" Ar-Gammord's eyes were white in a distraught face. He babbled incomprehensibly, among which Ar-Lizelle made out, "You lied! You were using us as bait!"

"Don't be a fool!" She darted back, summoning her fire whip, but this time he wasn't accusing her. With a mad cry, he launched his attack at Dar-Gothull.

~ ~ ~

Duessa breathed evenly, humming a song in her mind to keep her spirits up. Multiple impacts vibrated through her bones as dozens of mages tried to burn, blast or hammer their way through. Weaving their shields together with layers of magic and spirit, the four mages created a far greater protection than any of them could have done alone.

Even knowing their faith in each other, it wasn't easy. Dar-Gothull was the nightmare of every mage. From childhood they knew his name, the monster who ruled over Skaythe and someday would consume them all.

They all felt him arrive. His overbearing will gnawed at them even through the barrier. But Duessa kept breathing. She held her concentration. Shards of fear darted through their bond, but the four of them buoyed each other up. They depended on each other, and the Badgers depended on them. If one of them broke, they all would pay the price.

It helped that Dar-Gothull had his own problems. Outside the barrier, Ruen flashed through the attackers' ranks. The next moment, a melee erupted. Duessa hummed to herself, watching the mages turn on each other. Smoke billowed once again, lit by lightning, flames, and other attacks. She couldn't even tell who was fighting who. Bark and branches went spinning off from the nearby trees.

"That isn't going to work," Jaxynne predicted. "The

story says he can devour all magic."

"I guess they haven't heard the story," Sethamis said.

Reactions flitted among the mages. Horror and pity from Tisha, Alemin's disgust, and from Lorrah a reluctant sense of justice. That those who profited from brutality were also prey for it. And Duessa's simple reality. "We can't make them stop, anyway."

Zathi trotted by on her sorrel, Ember. "Don't get distracted."

Duessa refocused on her breathing. There was nothing she could do about those mages. They were outside the barrier, and she was inside, out of reach. It still didn't feel safe.

"Sergeant." Zathi reined around as a golden blur settled around them. *"There is one more vision I had, back then. I thought it was irrelevant because I had transformed, but now I understand."*

"What is it?" Zathi demanded.

"You have learned something?" Tisha's hips swayed gently in a rhythm to support their working.

"I didn't realize," Keilos told them, *"I think that I cannot fight him. Or, not alone."*

Duessa's breath stopped for a moment. This couldn't be right. Keilos was so powerful. How could he fail them again?

"You aren't alone," Lorrah retorted. "He is."

"Let him speak," Alemin said.

Reluctantly, Keilos corrected Lorrah. *"Dar-Gothull is not alone. He is a duality, both human and spirit. The form Alemin saw in the Larder is that of a tortured spirit from the depths of the sea. Dar-Gothull must have bound it to him ages ago."*

Questions and concerns darted among the mages as both Duessa and Alemin remembered the nightmares of the Larder.

Bettain snorted, "Just when you think it can't get any weirder."

Something like a chuckle ghosted through them. *"We each are great in power, but I am purely a spirit. His commands to his followers also tear at me. I fear Dar-Gothull will be able to dominate me. He already did it to the drakanox once before, and his control held for over a century."*

The Badgers seemed to realize something was happening. They trotted their horses closer. Seated on Cinder, Jaxynne said, "That sounds bad."

"It would be." Keilos spoke with greater haste. *"The human I sense in him is smaller, but as a spirit I cannot defeat it. Or, not quickly enough for our situation. I, too, need a human partner, to anchor against his attacks."*

Blazing eyes turned to Zathi and she blinked, startled.

"In order to defeat Dar-Gothull, both human and spirit have to be overcome. As a duality, I can try to release the spirit. My human partner will have to handle his physical self."

Zathi's lips parted in a grim smile. "If he's just a mage under all that, I can deal with him."

"I know you can." Keilos' mental tone was tinged with irony.

Keerin chuckled. "You had to bring that up, didn't you?"

Behind the barrier, a series of loud booms echoed through the forest. Whatever they were fighting about, the violence was spreading.

"We don't have time for jokes." The sergeant's hands

opened and closed on the reins. "How will this work?"

"As in my vision, I fit my shape to yours." Keilos flowed a bit closer, and Duessa sensed words passing between them the others couldn't hear.

"Jaxynne, you have command while I'm... busy." Zathi swung down from the saddle and led her sorrel over to Sethamis. "Look after him."

"Yes Sergeant." They chorused. Sethamis tied Spark's reins to a ring on the side of the wagon. Jaxynne's expression was worried, but fierce pride shone in her eyes.

Razeet said, "You take that monster down, for all of us."

"Count on it." Zathi straightened, facing Keilos. "I'm ready."

Keilos's long, misty body settled and reshaped itself around her. Before the shimmering glow hid Zathi's face, Duessa was certain that she was blushing. At any other time, it would have been hilarious.

Alemin's streak of humor reached her. *"Of course it's hilarious."* Lorrah giggled. Still swaying, Tisha smiled to herself.

Oddly enough, even that moment of laughter refreshed a bit of their strength. Turning her attention back to the massacre outside their barrier, Duessa thought they were going to need it.

~ ~ ~

Ar-Lizelle laid about with her flaming whip, trying to get out of the worst firefight. Ar-Gammord hurled something like metal splinters at the wizard king. Other mages jumped out of the way. Some of them turned on Ar-Gammord, but others had their own ambitions. Across the roadway, Ar-Lizelle was certain one of the mages from Lithole was striking his count from behind.

By far the greatest number swarmed and blasted toward Dar-Gothull. "Now's my chance," they yelled, and "You won't get me!"

Ar-Lizelle ducked and scrambled through a whirlwind of deadly castings. It was stupid of them to try and take Dar-Gothull down, and yet, it was also the most logical thing to do. Dar-Gothull's own teaching was to seize any advantage and grab power while you could. Who wouldn't want to rule over Skaythe as the next wizard-king?

Her own goal was less grand: to get far away from the lot of them. All the mages had gone through the three rituals that bound them to Dar-Gothull in body, mind and soul. He had already shown that he could use that to control them. There was no fighting against that.

Ar-Lizelle stumbled back through the trees. Broken branches caught at her hem and bloodthorns trailed fire along her arms, even through heavy sleeves. She jerked away and kept moving. That low spot in the barricade was back here somewhere.

When she found it, she approached cautiously. Behind her, on the road, there was more yelling than battle cries. Ar-Lizelle didn't know what was happening, and she didn't care. After a quick look to be sure the fight didn't move in her direction, she pressed her hands against the barrier. Not hitting it, that might draw attention. Just pushing, waiting for any slackening of the pressure.

All she needed was a moment. Something would distract Lorrah and her stupid friends, and their concentration would slip. Ar-Lizelle would be ready when it did.

～ ～ ～

The drakanox's cloudlike brilliance settled around Zathi's straight, disciplined frame. The shape of a dragon's head, complete with antlers and mane, rested over her helmet like an elaborate crest. Behind her, the mane trailed down into something like a furred cloak. Scaly wings with clawed tips flexed above her shoulders. Even her expression was different, no longer alert for danger but mild and resolved. When she moved, a subtle glow lined the details of her armored body. The sword she drew shone as if a sliver of the sun itself had replaced mere steel. One of the guardswomen released an awed sigh.

Up on Cinder's back, Jaxynne stepped into Zathi's role. "Stay alert. This still won't be easy."

Duessa breathed steadily. Beyond the thorny barricade, the sounds of battle were slowing down. Maybe the mages had finished each other off, or Dar-Gothull had forced them to stop fighting each other.

Even as she thought so, a shudder rolled beneath their feet. Sooty ribbons stained the silvery pavement, streaming in from the direction of the battle. The paving bubbled and blackened, then split into jagged fissures. A black form oozed upright and shaped itself into a man, magnificent in crimson robes. Worse than his abrupt appearance was the smothering stench of *voromnil*.

"He's here!" someone cried. Maybe more than one of them.

Warriors scrambled back from the revenant. Horses capered, squealing with terror. Duessa could only stare. Nobody had warned them that he could slide right under the barricade!

Yet there were cuts on his face, and his robes were scorched. A finger swept out, as if to spear the radiant duality of Zathi and Keilos.

"What a feast this will be," Dar-Gothull leered. One of the gold chains dribbled down from his head to clink on the pavement. He didn't seem to notice.

"Come ahead and try," they answered, a strange combination of Zathi's and Keilos' voices. The shining warrior moved forward, neither fearful nor angry.

Dar-Gothull seemed to stomp, and a thundering darkness swept out across the plaza. The paving bucked beneath Duessa's feet, and searing agony burst in her head. She went to one knee with a cry of pain. Her concentration shattered under the onslaught. And not only hers.

"Hold on," Lorrah gasped, but something else hit Duessa. A physical blow, tearing through her robe and into the flesh of her back. She cried out as the shield they were holding slipped and went down.

~ ~ ~

It was several hours yet until the evening, when Ar-Azlor was supposed to meet with the villagers in Opshar. Until then, Piyaro kept his squad busy. They set up their camp where it had been before. Ar-Azlor and Ar-Sessal rested in the partly-built hut. Once Yamaya was reunited with her baby, she and Berisan talked with her friends from the village. The friends headed back there, possibly to gather ideas ahead of the negotiation.

The bandit Skeelon loped in with a couple of his buddies. According to him, the signals from the far end of the valley were for more forces attacking from Dunsaph. However, Count Ar-Oshtur of Prizom shared that section of border. He had sent soldiers to hold them off. Chief Huld thought Ar-Azlor would want to know. After that, the Pulgoll soldiers insisted on riding patrols through the rest of the Opshar Valley. Piyaro set out extra sentries around Yamaya's farm.

Shonn had posted himself at the bonfire, watching to be sure the flames stayed where they were supposed to be. It seemed he wanted to be alone. Hawk Squad ended up joining him anyway. None of the Hawks were saying much. They studied each other's faces sidelong, with a question nobody quite wanted to come out with.

After some time, Berisan suddenly rushed out of Yamaya's hut. He peered down at the circle pond before tapping on the other hut's door frame. "Azlor, Sessal. Are you awake?"

"Uh-oh," Cothyr mumbled. Piyaro and the rest of Hawk Squad jumped up to see what was happening.

"What is it?" Ar-Azlor came out, carefully avoiding an incomplete step. Ar-Sessal leaned on the door frame. His face was creased as if he had aged several years.

"I don't know," Berisan admitted. "It's just a feeling, but I'd like to try and reestablish contact with Keilos. Are you up to it?"

Shonn interrupted. "Should I go get Meven?"

"I'll put up a flare, but if you want to meet her on the way, it would be helpful," Berisan agreed. Shonn immediately took off down the slope, while Berisan lobbed a ball of golden light skyward. "Azlor?"

The count nodded. "I'll come. You keep resting," he told Ar-Sessal.

"Yes, my lord." The junior mage nodded gratefully and shuffled back inside.

This didn't sound like a dangerous situation, but after the count's ordeal earlier in the day, Piyaro was in no mood to take chances.

"Cothyr. Pick two men. You'll stay to watch over Ar-Sessal. The rest come with me."

Count Ar-Azlor caught his eye and nodded appreciatively, then hurried to keep up with Berisan, who had already started down the slope. Hawk Squad hurriedly sorted themselves out and followed.

When they got to the circle pond, the water seemed still as ever. The sky above them was hot and clear. However, Piyaro's wary eye caught a reflection of flickering reddish light that didn't seem to match anything around the pond. The two mages settled at the edge, a hand's reach from each other. Berisan leaned forward, pressing both palms to the silvery stuff that ringed the pond.

Almost at once, he announced, "They are fighting."

A frown stitched Ar-Azlor's brow as he copied Berisan's posture. "He is there?"

"It must be him. This feels like so much..." Berisan trailed off.

Piyaro wished for more information. Did "he" mean Keilos, the drakanox? Their concern didn't make sense for that.

"You haven't met them," Berisan resumed, "but think well of them. Alemin, Tisha, Lorrah and Keilos. They need our support, even if we can't be there."

"Whatever help I can give, they shall have it." Ar-Azlor breathed out slowly, deepening his concentration.

A ripple stirred the pond's bright surface, but no more than that.

~ ~ ~

The barrier shuddered and dissolved beneath Ar-Lizelle's hands. This was her chance!

"Yes!" She blasted out flames and the dry, tangled branches went up in a sheet of flame. Ar-Lizelle summoned all her thwarted fury and pushed harder. Within seconds, the barricade shattered into particles of drifting ash and char. The growing blaze swept off along the packed brush of the barricade. Sweeping the last sparks from her shoulder, she strode through the breach.

At the base of the hill, she paused to orient herself. "Where are you?" she hissed.

Obviously, the counts who attacked Dar-Gothull had failed. The wizard-king was in his hideous revenant form. Saw-edged tentacles flailed through the middle of the renegades. Mages, warriors, and even the horses went down

or ran. But facing him... Ar-Lizelle had to squint to make out
one of the guardswomen cloaked in a blaze of light.

"What are they using?" Ar-Lizelle whispered, but
then angrily shook her head. Dar-Gothull swelled and
stretched as he flowed toward the fiery warrior. No matter
what tricks these renegades tried, he would have them. She
had her own affairs to settle.

Lorrah had stolen her horse, the beautiful chestnut
Roxalen. She could find her by that. The traitor
guardswomen regrouped to protect the mages, who were
staggering to their feet. And there! Lorrah clung to the
saddle, rubbing her forehead.

With that cursed barrier down, mages were burning
through the barricade on the opposite side from the melee.
Several groups charged in, blasting lightning or fire ahead of
them. A pair of mounted archers shot back, and on the
wagon Ar-Lizelle saw Bettain's bulky form. The fugitive was
drawing the flames from their bonfire to fling at the
attackers.

"Get the barrier back up!" someone yelled
hopelessly.

There wasn't going to be an easy way across all that.
Ar-Lizelle strode out, making for that one red horse among
the milling crowd.

Dar-Gothull's tentacles slashed at the shining warrior,
seeking to bind her arms at her sides. His victim side-stepped
with deft economy, and scaly wings flared out to slap the
strike aside. Only on one side, though. Another tentacle
wrapped around her blade. The warrior set her feet, turned
the blade and pulled. Several chunks of that limb fell to the
pavement. Dar-Gothull yelled, more from anger and surprise
than pain.

Ar-Lizelle moved onward, only altering her path to
avoid that duel of darkness and light. Ahead of her, one of
the horses was struck on the flank by a mage's bolt. It went

down, burning and squealing, and took its rider with it. Frustrated, Ar-Lizelle had to shift her path again.

Lorrah had seen her at last, and trotted Roxalen out warily toward her. One fist was raised in suggestion that she had a shield prepared. "What do you want, Lizelle?"

That giant animal — a badger, now she could see it — galloped between them with Elldri still on its back. Ar-Lizelle froze for an instant, hating the idea of being that close to Elldri again. But the beast closed with some of the attacking mages, biting and batting them with massive paws.

When she could see her sister again, Ar-Lizelle taunted, "What's the matter, Lorrie? Are you worried about your friends?"

"No," Lorrah huffed, a fragile lie. "Are you?"

Friends? No true mage had friends. Ar-Lizelle's mocking laughter penetrated even the noise and chaos of the battle. Duessa straightened up painfully. Alemin and Bettain whirled to stare at her.

"You are all going to die," Ar-Lizelle told them with relish, and she uncoiled her flaming whip as she stepped forward. Duessa held her shoulder and grimaced as she cast something. Alemin turned frantically toward Lorrah.

Bettain replied with a nasty fireball. "Shut up, Lizard!"

Ar-Lizelle caught it with her whip and waved the shower of sparks aside. "This is perfect. I can avenge my father and destroy all of you filthy renegades who escaped from my prison."

"Father went down in a battle he started," Lorrah retorted. A sweep of her hand indicated the roadway behind the barrier. "Just like all of them. Don't you want a better way?"

Ar-Lizelle shrieked with laughter. "Nothing is better

than this!"

Her flaming whip snaked across the pavement as she advanced with deliberate malice. The horses snorted and stamped, but their riders controlled them.

Dar-Gothull was still fighting the warrior of light. She had gone on the offensive, pressing with a relentless jabbing attack even through the slashing tentacles. It seemed she was trying to push her foe away from the rest of the renegades. Dar-Gothull swelled again, stretching wide enough to engulf the warrior, but the dragon wings tangled his tentacles. The blazing sword flashed out, and the warrior leaped easily back. Dar-Gothull hunched forward, clutching his midsection. More gems winked as they fell from his robe.

"This... will not be," he snarled.

Ar-Lizelle felt his words inside her, as she had when his fury drove her to burn everything in front of her. Now it was she who staggered. Darkness blurred her vision as a vortex opened inside her, tearing at the very bones of her power. In a moment of panic, she remembered Wharon, the Larder's previous warden, and the desiccated husk that had been carried out of his cell.

She came out of a buzzing haze to find herself on the ground. When did that happen? Vaguely she heard other mages screaming nearby, and realized they too must be caught in the maelstrom. Dar-Gothull was consuming their souls to hold off that renegade warrior.

There was movement nearby, hooves and armored boots striding about. Someone shouted, "Is Jaxynne okay?" and "Where's Tisha?"

Another voice, a younger woman's, called, "Spread out! Put them down while they're helpless."

Lorrah, curse her, cried, "Cylass, no. She's my sister!"

"She made her choice," a man replied. "Let us do our

job."

"You mages need to get that barrier back," the female officer demanded.

The voices were strangely muffled. Ar-Lizelle fought for breath. She wouldn't let the vortex take her. Not yet.

"Lorrie?" Ar-Lizelle quavered dramatically. She could still do this. If her soft-hearted little sister would just come a tiny bit closer.

A shadow darted toward her. Gray robes swirled, and a calloused hand caught hers. It was nothing like the annoying, sticky fingers that used to grab at her dress.

"I'm here. Hold on, Lizelle," Lorrah pleaded. "You have to reject him. Put him out of you. It's not too late."

A spasm of disgust allowed her to snap her fire whip up, coil it around that traitor's neck. "Why would I do that?"

"Stop it!" Lorrah jumped back — or tried to. Ar-Lizelle exulted to see her sister jerk up short. Lorrah screamed as the fine hairs on her neck sizzled and flared. Brown skin reddened and blistered. Ar-Lizelle's hatred scorched the gray robe that Lorrah had stolen.

Somewhere nearby, Alemin yelled, "Lorrah!"

Ar-Lizelle laughed, and heard death's rasp in it. No matter. If Lorrah's pain made Alemin suffer, too, that was worth everything to her. The world narrowed down to Lorrah's agonized tears.

An impact came from somewhere. Ar-Lizelle was hollowed, her life and power ripped away. It was hardly more than a finger's push to send her into the abyss.

XXI — RESOLVED

No music was enough to cushion Duessa's terror. She couldn't see what had hit her, but her shoulder and back throbbed intensely. It felt like something was burrowing into her, tearing its way down to her spine. Tisha's knowledge answered her need, showing her how to heal herself. Duessa tried it, clumsily. The fight wasn't over. She had to get back into it.

All the world was flinging fire or choking on blood. Mounted warriors thundered by, trying to keep the mages away from that side. On the wagon, Sethamis loaded and fired her crossbow with frantic speed. But then the enemy mages staggered. They began falling like petals scattered from a spent flower. When Ar-Lizelle collapsed, too, Duessa breathed again.

Jaxynne's horse, Cinder, was down and thrashing. It was Giniver who stepped up and gave the order to finish off the mages. But Lorrah jumped off Torch and ran toward her sister.

"Are you crazy?" Duessa yelled. She couldn't hear what they said to each other, but her stomach clenched when Ar-Lizelle's fire wrapped around Lorrah's throat.

"Lorrah!" Alemin tried to reach her. Zathi's sorrel was tied to the wagon and slammed him against it.

Duessa lurched into motion. She wasn't even sure what she meant to do. Before she got there, Cylass stepped around and drew his short sword across Ar-Lizelle's throat. The flaming whip fizzled out. Duessa grabbed Lorrah's arm and pulled her away. The younger mage sobbed, clasping a trembling hand to the blackened skin of her neck and chin.

"I couldn't save her," Lorrah wept.

"What's done is done. Can you heal yourself?" Duessa's old scars throbbed in sympathy. There had been no one to help her when the hunter guards tried to make her tell where Ar-Lannon was traveling.

"Lorrah. You're all right now." Alemin was there, folding her into his arms. "Breathe. Just breathe."

Together, Alemin and Duessa pushed *vitalis* in. Lorrah straightened a little, the glaze of pain easing from her eyes. Angry weals faded from her neck, but nothing could erase her grief. Duessa left her with Alemin and turned back to Ar-Lizelle.

The Larder's hateful warden lay inert. Her whole body was shrunken. In a half-crouch, Cylass examined her warily. There was very little blood.

"My lady said he was draining them, using their power to save himself," Cylass said coldly. "Zathi won't win if we let him do that."

"I know." Duessa waved his explanation away. While she had been focused on Lorrah, she had shut out a lot of the noise and confusion. Now it all struck her like a blow. Her back throbbed its own reminder. "Where are we with this?"

Cylass joined her in looking around. It wasn't as bad as it could have been. Zathi and Dar-Gothull were still going at each other, but none of his mages were on their feet. The few bursts of power Duessa sensed were far distant. Giniver had the Badgers move among the fallen, shooting or slitting throats. Keerin limped a bit as she went. Bettain leaned against the side of the wagon, panting, with a shine of sweat on her face.

"Tisha?" he asked.

"Over there." A few yards off, Tisha knelt beside Jaxynne. Healing power rippled around them. Cylass nodded and hurried over. The blue roan, Cinder, was on his feet but with his flank badly burned. He held that hoof high above the ground and wheezed with pain. Taking Tisha's example, Duessa tried again to heal whatever had injured her.

Movement in the Hornwood made everyone snap around, but it was only Ruen and Elldri. The giant badger emerged with a limp red-robed body and dropped it near some of the others. Elldri waved briefly to Bettain and they plunged back into the trees.

It was almost all right, Duessa thought. They would be fine as long as no other enemies burst in.

There was just one problem.

The monstrosity of Dar-Gothull was even bigger than it had been before, gorged with the magic it had ripped away from its followers. The duality of Keilos and Zathi was puny beside its black bulk, though they still blazed with *vitalis* from the reservoir. Dar-Gothull's tentacles were a blur, trying to grab Zathi, and Keilos steadily batted them aside. Zathi leapt at Dar-Gothull with supreme athleticism. The swelling bulk tried to engulf her and was again deflected.

"This is going to take a while," Duessa murmured as Alemin and Lorrah came up beside her.

"We should get our barrier up again." Lorrah was still in pain, even with the hum of *vitalis* supporting her power.

Duessa glanced back to where Tisha worked on Jaxynne. She sensed in the healer's thoughts that Jaxynne's back was injured, and the healing could not be rushed. That left the three of them.

"What do you want to shield?" she asked. "I don't think we can cover the whole plaza any more."

"We could cover the two of them," Alemin suggested. "Maybe it will help Zathi if we keep Dar-Gothull contained."

Duessa didn't know if that would work. "Won't he just slide under it again?" Nevertheless, she joined the others in focusing on their mutual shield.

"I think we took care of all the mages here." Alemin winced at the sheer number of dead. It was something that would haunt them all, if they survived. "There must be others, scattered all over Skaythe. Does anyone know how far that control of his reaches?"

"In theory, anywhere. But I have an idea," Lorrah said. "Do you remember when we held Elldri in that globe?"

Duessa grasped her plan, but immediately saw a problem. "We poured our love for Elldri into it. Nobody loves Dar-Gothull."

"We don't have to love him," Alemin smiled. "Because we do love Keilos and we do love Zathi. They won't reject our aid, and they'll still have it even if Dar-Gothull tries to escape."

"Yes!" Lorrah cried. "We can give them hope and strength against his hate and degradation."

All three of them caught the idea and eagerly took hands. A shimmering dome appeared. Both Zathi and Dar-Gothull paused as the barrier solidified, keeping them separate from the rest of the plaza.

Dar-Gothull scoffed, "Wait your turn."

But Keilos' translucent form brightened, and Zathi spoke in their strangely doubled voice. "What do you fear, Devourer? That you are alone in your darkness, having consumed all you could reach?"

"Alone. What does that mean?" Dar-Gothull returned the taunt. "I will drink up your soul as if it was wine, and snuff your light for good this time."

Zathi smiled oddly. "You will find our souls not to your liking."

Duessa concentrated, slowing her breath until it matched with the others. She didn't know Keilos as well as her friends did, but he had always been honest and kind. Zathi was stern, but she had committed everything to the hope that Skaythe would see better days. Duessa drew on the memories they shared, the practice battles and her stumbling journey toward *vitalis* with these friends always at her side.

Inside the gleaming dome, light and darkness feinted and clashed. The warrior was forced back a step, sword blazing in her hand. Duessa poured in her hopes and strength for Zathi. Yet again Dar-Gothull swept his tentacles out to envelope her.

Life to Zathi, Duessa chanted, as one with Alemin and Lorrah. *Life, strength, hope.*

Keilos' wings snapped out from the billowing darkness. They flared forward, embracing and holding the enemy who wanted to destroy them.

Life to Keilos, they repeated. *Life, strength, hope!*

Opposing dualities struggled together, Zathi and Dar-Gothull each trying to overcome the other. A strangled cry emerged as the surging black billows began to shimmer and turn pale.

"The spirit!" Razeet reined in nearby. "That's how he did it before."

Duessa remembered that. Keilos was trying to separate the enslaved spirit from its human captor.

Life to the spirit, they silently chanted. *Life, hope, freedom for that spirit.*

"You... will... not..." Dar-Gothull tried to break loose, but awkwardly now. His formless mass split into a dozen tentacles, but even that could not wiggle out of Keilos' winged embrace.

"This is the truth of Skaythe." Zathi spoke within the blaze of light. "No matter how you crush it, or tear it, or jail it, our love for each other is stronger."

Streaks of shimmering gold now outlined the tentacles and suffused the black mass of it. Dar-Gothull shrieked, "Filthy renegades! Skaythe is mine, and everything in it! You will not do this to me!"

The mages chanted: *Life to Keilos, strength to Zathi, freedom for the unknown spirit from the deep.*

Tooth-studded tentacles writhed and jerked, but not in a coordinated way. The heaving golden mass abruptly split and fell apart like torn fabric. A human form was revealed among the shreds, naked and howling with rage. Zathi's bright frame leapt into a shoulder bash that rocked him back. Before he could recover she whirled, sword flashing like the first narrow streak of dawn rising above the edge of the world. It dimmed momentarily as she slashed across his belly, then plunged it into his chest.

There should have been more blood. That was Duessa's own thought, untangled from the chant of hope and light. He was so close to the barrier, they should have seen the gory spray, but the withered body slumped and fell. Without the spirit to sustain him, Dar-Gothull was left as Ar-Lizelle was, a shriveled and lifeless husk.

Three minds knotted together, waiting to see if that was all, or if the wizard-king had some way to escape his fate. Glittering mist rose up from the mangled husk of the deep sea spirit. Without Dar-Gothull's malice, it no longer mimicked a merciless shark or squid. Instead, Duessa thought of a jellyfish stranded on the shore, splayed out and helpless. Slowly and weakly, a tentacle groped toward the scraps of its hide.

Keilos lifted away from Zathi, their combined

brilliance shimmering away. No longer a duality wreathed in glory, Zathi watched the fallen spirit's struggle. She knelt to clean her blade on Dar-Gothull's robe, then sheathed it. With armored hands, she gently pressed the spirit's torn edges together.

Keilos drifted up to the barrier. *"It is safe now."*

~ ~ ~

Ar-Azlor, Meven, Berisan and Nyette knelt silently beside the circle pond. Eyes closed, they rested their palms on the silvery verge. The area was eerily quiet. A breeze stirred the reeds, and the waterfall endlessly chattered, but all such noises were muffled in the greater silence. Deep in the pond, elusive rays of light flickered and vanished.

Hawk Squad was spaced out around the pond, keeping guard over the kneeling mages. Expectation coiled around them like a hungry snake. Piyaro prowled between, restless in his vigilance. He passed Shonn, who also lingered nearby. Their eyes met in a moment of shared understanding.

As one, the silent mages tensed. Nyette made a brief whimper. It wasn't loud, but the guardsmen snapped around. Ar-Azlor released a gust of breath. They opened their eyes with varying joy and disbelief.

"They... They did it," Nyette breathed.

"He is dead," Meven spoke as if the words tasted strange.

"I never thought it could be," Ar-Azlor murmured, stunned.

"I did," Berisan answered simply.

Piyaro kicked at a pebble, releasing some of his tension. It would have been nice to know what they were talking about.

Shonn coughed a little and asked, "Who died?"

"Dar-Gothull," Meven said.

Shonn's face went blank with surprise. Silence blanketed the pond. One of the men stammered, "That's impossible."

The dreaded wizard-king who held all Skaythe in thrall... he was dead? The Hawks gathered silently, questions in every eye. It sounded too good to be true. Yet Piyaro saw no evasion in Ar-Azlor expression.

"I don't understand it all, but they split him from a spirit. And then he was just a man." The count drew in another, deeper breath and turned toward Berisan. "This... This is beyond what I hoped for."

The rebel mage nodded. "We all dreamed, but it didn't seem possible."

"I wish Ar-Thea could have seen it." Bitterness and regret colored Meven's words.

"What happens now?" Piyaro cut in. It was all well and good to congratulate themselves, but the implications were frightening. A ruler's death would create vast uncertainty.

Nyette, too, looked to the count. "My lord?"

"The histories say that before Dar-Gothull, Skaythe was made up of many kingdoms." Ar-Azlor trembled a little as he made to rise. Rowlan, who was nearer, stepped up to steady him.

"Yes, I've read them." Nyette hastened to put herself forward. Piyaro wanted to slap her, but Ar-Azlor merely nodded patiently.

"Not everyone has," he reminded her. "Those kingdoms became the counties as we now know them. Without him, I suppose the land will break up again."

"Then it's civil war after all." Piyaro's worst fear loomed before him.

The other mages also climbed to their feet. Meven and Shonn exchanged a glance of some significance.

"Unless there's someone strong enough to unite them," Nyette glanced a question to Ar-Azlor.

The count shook his head. "There was never a succession plan. Dar-Gothull kept us at each other's throats. I assumed it was to make sure we didn't unite against him. Maybe it did that, but his binding rituals also allowed him to consume our souls." Ar-Azlor paused to rub his face with his hands. "It was how he extended his own life."

"He must have thought it would go on forever," Meven said icily. "Thus, no need for a plan."

"Unless..." Ar-Azlor deflected Nyette's question toward Berisan.

Who vigorously waved the idea away. "No! No, I said I'm not in charge of this!"

"They won't follow him," Piyaro cut in. "No offense to the man who started an uprising..."

"Thanks?" Berisan rubbed the back of his head with a wry smile. "I don't think it's all my fault."

Piyaro didn't miss the jab, he stubbornly went on.

"Our loyalty is to you, the count. We don't know these other mages. It's you who holds our trust." Piyaro gestured to take in the soldiers in their protective formation.

"Sergeant Piyaro may be correct," Meven spoke more objectively now. "There will be a power vacuum. The counts will fight each other."

"If they're still alive," Nyette pointed out.

"If not, it's a battle for succession." Piyaro repeated his worse fear.

"The people will gather around someone who has shown they are willing to take care of them." Meven fixed her gaze on Ar-Azlor.

"So your negotiation with the people in Opshar will be even more important," Berisan told him.

"Not to mention Huld's folk in the mountains," Piyaro said, though it galled him. "We may need their blades, bandits or not."

"You all have a ridiculous amount of faith in me." Ar-Azlor's dark eyes roved from face to face. He seemed flattered, but gave a weary sigh. "The next few years are going to be very long."

~ ~ ~

It was a huge relief to untangle herself from the others and let their barrier fade. Duessa's brain felt taut, like a muscle that couldn't unclench. Alemin let her hand go so he could turn and catch Lorrah in a tight embrace.

The three of them turned slowly at the sound of hooves. Giniver and Razeet were still on horses, weapons ready. Past them, Duessa saw Keerin limp over to help Jaxynne sit up. Bettain stood on the wagon's bench, peering through drifts of smoke.

"Elldri!" she called. "Ruen?"

A few yards over, Cylass stood guard near Tisha as she worked to heal the blue roan, Cinder. Sethamis held the horse's reins, soothing him.

It looked like the worst was over. Duessa didn't know if she dared believe it. Dar-Gothull had come with all his forces, and somehow they were still alive.

Zathi knelt by the crumpled heap of the spirit. No matter how much compassion the Shining mages poured out, it didn't seem to make a difference. She had stopped trying to press the pitiful thing back together.

"Sergeant, are you all right?" Duessa stepped closer.

"It had to be done." Zathi spoke crisply as ever, though her expression was slightly dazed. "But this one never deserved to be used that way."

Bettain hurried over. "They're back."

Together they watched Ruen trot easily out of the forest, carrying yet another red-robed corpse to add to the pile.

"You're having a big funeral pretty soon, I can tell," Duessa teased.

"Scatter their bones in the forest, for all I care," Bettain grunted.

What mattered were the scorch marks that criscrossed the giant badger's pelt. One of them forked just short of the young mage who was sliding down from his furry shoulder. Duessa was relieved to see a girl's slender legs and feet, rather than jagged tentacles, under the flaring gray robe.

Seeing their expression, Elldri lisped with a hint of sass, "I'm not turning into the next evil duality, so stop looking at me like that."

"Huh," Bettain rubbed at her eyes. "You never would."

It was Ruen who surprised them. Rounded ears swivelled to focus on the ruined carcass that Zathi guarded. He prowled over, dipping a giant black nose toward it.

"It needs water," Elldri translated.

"Yes, for it is a spirit of the sea," Keilos said.

"We have drinking water." Zathi strode over to the wagon, where at least one large crock still had water in it. "Bring it over here."

Giniver jumped down from Spark to help. Together they carried the crock over to where the spirit lay feebly twitching. They set it down with a grinding thunk and put the lid aside. Giniver edged back, visibly nervous being so close to the sea spirit. Elldri and Duessa helped Zathi fold the cold, sticky mass over on itself.

"Lift that end," the sergeant directed. Together they slipped the pathetic bundle into the mouth of the crock. It didn't seem like the gelatinous mass would fit, but it somehow furled in on itself. The tentacles crept in last — gratefully, Duessa thought — without so much as a drop of water rolling over the edge.

"That is well done," Keilos said as Zathi gently replaced the lid. *"Now, there is one thing more."*

Zathi gazed up at him for a piercing moment. What must it feel like, Duessa wondered, to be part of a duality, fighting completely as one, and now be separate again? The two of them might need a moment.

"Gather, everyone!" Duessa walked apart, dusting off her robe a little.

They responded at once, on foot or on horseback. Keerin and Jaxynne leaned on each other, both limping, as Tisha closely followed. Lorrah had not let go of Alemin's hand.

"What's wrong?" Jaxynne asked.

"Nothing. Keilos says there's something else we need to do," Duessa told her.

"Something else?" Razeet pretended she was going to faint.

Reluctantly, Zathi moved away from the crock. Only Elldri remained with Ruen, who settled his huge bulk to apparently hold a vigil beside the injured spirit.

"The reservoir of vitalis.*"* Keilos was with them, shining out comfort as ever. *"It isn't meant to be hoarded only for those of us here."*

"Vitalis is meant to be shared," Tisha immediately

agreed.

"It goes out through the roads," Alemin said. "I learned that much in the Larder."

"As a spirit, I have traveled through the highways just as Dar-Gothull did. His passage damaged them, but we can heal it," Keilos explained. Everyone glanced over, where a black, corroded hole marred the silvery pavement. *"From here, there is a circulation that reaches all of Skaythe. The pathways weave across each other, but there are end points. Some lead to smaller towers, and some have rings."*

"Towers like the Larder?" Duessa immediately guessed.

"Yes. The towers gather vitalis *and direct it here."* He tilted his antlers at the tower standing serenely over them. *"Vitalis comes from everywhere and mixes together. What the rings draw out is more potent than what came in."*

"In the Larder, the ancients showed me that everyone could draw from it," Alemin said. "This must be how they managed it."

"All right," Zathi said. "Then what will happen if we release it now?"

"All of Skaythe will be full of *vitalis*," Duessa said. "That's obvious."

Perched on Ruen's shoulder, Elldri frowned thoughtfully.

"But what does that mean?" Jaxynne asked impatiently.

"And what good will it do?" Bettain huffed. "It won't change people. They'll still be selfish and greedy. With that guy dead over there, they're going to be fighting over his power. We don't even know how many of his mages are still alive."

"He drained a lot of them," Keerin suggested

hopefully.

"I'm sure there will be unrest," Tisha acknowledged, "but those dark feelings only thrived because Dar-Gothull had killed everyone who might have shown them a different way."

"Or he thought he did," Lorrah smirked.

"Not because people are naturally selfish assholes?" Giniver inserted.

"Only when they're trained that way," Tisha countered. "Remember, it took hundreds of years for him to completely dominate Skaythe. Even if the others try to keep his way, the flow of *vitalis* will change things over time. People will take it in without knowing."

Duessa wasn't sure about that. "We don't know what this will do to them. The story says that everyone was a mage. We can't just make everyone change."

"It is true," Keilos admitted. *"Forcing a change would be as cruel as anything Dar-Gothull did. Yet, we would not be imposing* vitalis *upon the land. It is restoring what should have been there all along."*

"People won't know what it is," Giniver said.

"We didn't know until Ar-Thea taught us," Alemin said. "Just like we didn't know nature spirits could exist until Keilos became one. The spirits would have been around, too, if Dar-Gothull hadn't interfered."

"Maybe we need to send out the minstrels again," Razeet suggested. "Tell the story, so people will understand."

"All right," Zathi cut in. "We'll let the mages decide what to do about this. The rest of us, I see we can all ride or walk. Go over the perimeter for stragglers. I'll take a volunteer to search the bodies for anything useful."

The guardswomen moved off, cheerfully bickering

over their assignments. Who had to wash all the dishes was a particular debate.

"Get to it," Zathi snapped as she untied Ember. "You bunch of babies."

The mages took hands in their usual circle. Even Bettain and Elldri, very hesitantly, came into the ring. Thoughts and ideas flowed among them, melding and adapting almost too quickly for words to follow. What developed was that they didn't want to force anything on people, but there were times when a decision simply had to be made. *Vitalis* was meant to be part of Skaythe. They had to set it free.

Keilos was rising, and their hearts rose with him to seep into the tower. The store of *vitalis* had been pent up for a long time. It needed help to remember where it should go. Elldri dropped out so she could explain to the Badgers. The rest of them filed back into the long hill and sat in a ring, hands clasped, at the base of the wall where their names shone in the darkness.

Each mage drew a strand of *vitalis* into themself, and Keilos showed them how to send their minds into the paving. In the plaza where the Badgers were working, they found that blackened scar and worked together to rebuild it. Before it was even healed, they could feel the branches of the highways tugging them toward places they knew.

Alemin sought the orchards of Kamuril. Lorrah went to that oasis on the border of Ebruc and Prowth, and Tisha to the gentle hills of Lithole. *Vitalis* followed them, drawn into old pathways by their love of home. Bettain was bound much farther, to Dakadoz itself. Perhaps her gift of *vitalis* would smooth the chaos of a capitol that had abruptly lost its ruler.

As for Duessa, her mind turned at once to the peaks of Busaren. Ar-Lannon had a favorite hidey-hole near an abandoned tower whose shape she recognized as she hadn't back then. Would she somehow find him there? If so, she had a few things to say.

After the most beloved home places, there were a dozen more counties, and crossing paths to reach them. No part of Skaythe would be denied this gift of renewal. The work was going to take hours. Duessa just hoped, at the end of it, that some of Razeet's stew would be left for them.

～ ～ ～

Hawk Squad was gathering to escort Count Ar-Azlor up to the town when Berisan's startled cry halted them.

"The pond!"

Piyaro spun to confront whatever the danger was. A familiar glow rose from the pond, vivid rays streaking the glossy water.

"Is Keilos coming back?" Nyette asked as she and Meven hurried to the edge.

No drakanox emerged from the pond, but the water itself swiftly turned to palest gold. That light swelled brighter and with a whispering crackle it spilled over the edge. People jumped away, but couldn't evade the shimmering glow that spread from the pond. Light surged in pulses, rushing faster and faster across the land.

"Is this all *vitalis?*" Ar-Azlor asked.

"Yes!" Berisan exulted, reaching into the water itself.

Meven held up a hand, frowning at its golden lining. "I know they had a reservoir, but..." She gasped. "My tower!"

"That's in Fang Marsh," Shonn said when no explanation followed.

"I can sense it, no matter the distance," she answered absently, and tilted her head slightly, as if listening to something no one else could hear.

All around them the glittering illumination swept past

the waterfall and toward the shore. Waves of it flowed up the slope, toward Weeping Falls Farm and across the reed beds where the ice walls still shed fog against the Dunsaph mountains. Another crest galloped east, toward the farms and village of Opshar.

"It's for us," Berisan murmured. "For everyone."

"What does it mean?" Nyette demanded eagerly.

"It's already fading," Rowlan said, but Piyaro shook his head wearily. The first rush was beginning to dull, but it hadn't gone. The line of radiance was visibly creeping up the jagged peaks.

"There is a current," Meven said, still listening to something far distant. "Drawing in, pushing out."

"Like it's breathing," Berisan said.

It was left for Piyaro to ask the sensible question: "Is this dangerous?"

"No." Nyette seemed startled that he would think so.

"I sense no malice." Ar-Azlor reluctantly turned away from the glow of the pond. "We'll await any wisdom Meven may glean, but this doesn't seem harmful. Come, friends, or we'll delay the talks. That won't make the impression I want."

Hawk Squad mounted up, with Piyaro taking a place just behind Ar-Azlor and Nyette. This new development wasn't ideal, coming on the eve of negotiating with rebels and the possibility of civil war. Yet, this gleaming magic felt similar to what had set Ar-Azlor free of Dar-Gothull's control. It was hard to cling to his fears in the face of all this.

Berisan said, "I'll get Sessal and Yamaya. We'll catch up to you."

"Bring Cothyr and the others, if you would," Piyaro put in.

"Sure."

Meven, slapped her knees to rise. "I need to get closer to the ice wall."

"I'll come with you," Shonn volunteered. After a tiny pause, she nodded.

"It's going to be all right," Berisan assured everyone, and it didn't even sound like he was trying to convince himself.

They trotted out in formation. Remnants from that mysterious wave of power gleamed all around them. Even Piyaro could see a subtle shine lingering on every reed and wildflower in the valley. He wondered if this would help the negotiations go more smoothly.

When he first led Hawk Squad into this village, they had been in bad shape. No liege lord, and few resources. After a lot of hard travel, they had somehow returned to the same village, but everything else had changed.

In Ar-Azlor they had found a leader who could be relied on. The men of Hawk Squad had a secure future with a count who wouldn't blast them down as an inconvenience to his ego. As sergeant, Piyaro didn't have to worry about them, if Captain Jorus was willing to be reasonable. He might even think about retiring from service.

He wasn't sure what he might do then. Take to training, perhaps. Or maybe he could travel back to Sloram and see if his parents still had their farm there. When some bunch of renegades could take down the Wizard-King Dar-Gothull, who was to say what was impossible?

~ ~ ~

Early the next day, Shonn finished the hut he and Berisan had been building. Yamaya and Berisan were already at the village, working out deals with the count, or the headman, or who knew what else. That had nothing to do with Shonn or the water-folk. He did miss getting to hold baby Gabrith, though.

Meven and Ozlin were off at the ice wall. She hadn't mentioned whether she planned to stay in Opshar or not. That in itself was an answer.

For Shonn, the certainty grew that it was time he went back to his own people. After he knotted the last bundle of palm leaves into the thatch of the roof, he went to forage in the mangroves and brought back land crabs, scrown and clusters of wild berries to prepare a traditional water-folk meal. In a moment of defiance, he laid his fire in the new hut. The cooking was well under way when Meven and Ozlin returned in the late afternoon.

"You've finished," Meven immediately noted. Ozlin merely glanced at the hut before moving on toward the orchard.

"Take a look around," Shonn said while he was chopping the spicy herbs from Yamaya's garden.

She did that, but quickly returned, sandals stepping lightly over the dusty ground. "Berisan will like it."

Berisan, but not Meven? Shonn stirred the herbs in with the boiling scrown and casually said, "Now that it's done, I'll be going back."

Meven seated herself on the steps. The valley spread before them, river and reeds shimmering even more vividly since the pond overflowed its magic. Even the mangroves were different. It made Shonn wonder if Fang Marsh had also changed.

"I was thinking," Meven said slowly, "that I should return as well."

He looked up from stirring the pot. "You don't have to..."

"I know," she said, "but my tower is calling more and more. There's a flow of energy around it. I should be there.

Anyway, these dry lands aren't for me." She adjusted the folds of her sarong. "Berisan will stay, though. He's made his place here."

"Oh. Okay." Berisan had explained to Shonn and Yamaya that their friends in the Hornwood were trying to heal all of Skaythe in the aftermath of Dar-Gothull's fall. Shonn heard the words, but they didn't mean much to him. "Is Oz going, too?"

"That's for him to decide. He feels the *vitalis*, but it's hard for him to work with. After so long fighting for every scrap..." Meven shrugged. "The swamp is better for him. Quieter."

"Jorja and Nog were asking when he can come visit," Shonn felt like a jerk, using Ozlin as bait. "Kids should have friends their own age."

Her eyes crinkled in a smile. Shonn felt a spark of fire in his belly. He missed the way she did that.

"I have to admit, I'm curious if Iratorix is all right," Meven said. It took Shonn a moment to figure out she meant Countess Ar-Torix. It was strange to hear a mage named without their proud title. "There may be fighting there. Nyette thinks that Ar-Sudunn in Deeve was just waiting for a chance to invade. She hasn't been able to reach the countess or anyone else she knows in Eshur."

"We'll have to be careful then," Shonn said. "We can stop at Oyster Rocks and see what they know before we try to cross."

Back under the trees, something rustled. It was either the wind, or Ozlin climbing among the apricot and cherry trees. The mageling hardly weighed a thing. Berisan had been sending him up there to prune the higher branches.

Meven, on the other hand, cultivated her ice walls with loving care. She gazed toward them now, white and shining in the afternoon light. They seemed different, Shonn realized. Still starkly bright, but the edges were softer, the spires blunted.

"They're melting?" He was surprised. The maze of ice walls had seemed incorruptible, enduring through all the hot days in Pulgoll.

"They aren't really ice, you know. Or, not only ice." Meven darted him a glance, almost hesitant. "They are made with *isalonis*, and that is born from fear. It's why the ice never melts. There is always something to be afraid of."

"I guess that makes sense." Shonn didn't know magic, but whenever he was near the ice walls, he certainly felt that bad things might happen. "We're water-folk. We have to be afraid of the land-folk making trouble."

"Not only us," she said. "Everyone in Skaythe has lived in fear. We needed it, to warn us and be safe, but now that *vitalis* is returning, that may not always be so. I will know Skaythe is changing when the ice walls have melted."

Shonn had stopped stirring the pot. It now began to sizzle. He quickly added a measure of water and stirred to stop the scrown from sticking to the bottom.

"*Isalonis* has been in me a long time. I am the Ice Witch, after all." Meven's gray eyes were level and calm as ever, but her chin pulled toward her neck in a way that spoke of fragile shyness. "Can you wait a while longer, for the ice to melt?"

Shonn drew a slow breath, hardly daring to believe. It was a second chance, and he didn't deserve it. Carefully, he set the pot aside from the heat. When he turned back, Meven was holding something out to him.

"A gift?" Very carefully, he took it. The bracelet was braided from thin strips of reed from the valley. Small, speckled shells were woven in to it. Shonn could hardly breathe around the joy in his chest. "It's really nice."

He tried not to cringe at the clumsy words. It was all he could do to sit while Meven solemnly wrapped it around his bicep. Her fingers were cold and tentative. A small loop went over the shells at the end, allowing her to adjust the fit.

Shonn wanted so much to kiss her. He could pull her in and light that fire... But she had said to wait. Before he could find the right words, Ozlin appeared in the door with his toy monkey hanging over his elbow. His cry of disgust startled them both.

"Hey!" Shonn tossed one of the kani he'd brought back for baby Gabrith to teethe on. Ozlin caught it, stared at him suspiciously, then bit into it while slouching back into the trees.

That boy was going to be a challenge. And Shonn knew Meven's role as a mage would always come first. But, as long as he knew there was a place for him, he could wait for the ice to melt.

AFTER

The ancient tower still stood, lonely and patient, at the end of a long silvery highway. Its rounded elegance rose oddly among Busaren's craggy heights. A landslide had blocked the highway long ago, and thick forest grew close around it, but Duessa would have found it no matter what. The tower had been calling to her for months.

A sheltered cave was still hidden below it, closer to the rugged shore. In this hidden camp, the moon-runners once rested between escapades. Their furnishings remained in place, rough as they ever had been, and now coated with years of dust and wind-blown leaves. The hideaway was all too empty without Ar-Lannon and the others, but it served her needs all the same.

Every day since her return, Duessa had climbed the path to the tower. Using *vitalis*, she slowly shifted the stones and dirt that clogged the tower's entrance. She gathered gray-white boulders to one side, and moved the earth to another. As she worked, Duessa began to feel the tower's breath. *Vitalis* flowed steadily toward the Hornwood. Even without writing her name on the wall, the tower welcomed her as she had known it would.

Duessa remembered well the fevered elation of the first days after Dar-Gothull's fall. Zathi and Tisha had made many urgent decisions. First, they salvaged wood and put up a defensive stockade. The great tower was no longer their desperate refuge, but a permanent base. There was no way to know who else might turn up, either wanting revenge for Dar-Gothull, or to seize control of the *vitalis* reservoir. Even with Elldri and Ruen as formidable defenders, something had to replace the scorched barricade.

Next, the battered water spirit must be returned to the sea. Zathi had decided to send the crock to Pulgoll in their wagon. Pulgoll was a longer way, but it had plenty of ocean shore, and they knew Azlor was friendly. Sethamis drove, with Giniver as guardswoman. Then Alemin wanted to go along and see his brother, and Lorrah was not to be separated from Alemin. Zathi gave in to that and assigned Lorrah the task of gathering information on who was in control of the areas they passed through.

The remaining Badgers and Minstrels set to work converting the long underground chambers into living quarters. Tisha had insisted on creating space for teaching those who came to investigate the source of the vitalis, while Cylass pointed out it was just as likely that people would come for healing. As Keilos relayed information from Lorrah, Razeet began to agitate for a new team of minstrels who could spread the word about how Dar-Gothull had met his end in the Hornwood,

That needed time for planning, and not everyone was a natural performer. After nearly a year of helping others build, Duessa said goodbye to Bettain and Elldri and the rest. She set off alone, following the persistent draw of the old moon-runner's retreat. And so here she was, patiently shifting rubble. Building and restoring, as a Shining One must.

Despite the tower's isolation, local people began to come by within a few days. The first were a pair of hunters. Then came a wary guard from the nearest village, Liatho — the same Duessa fled to, those years ago, and came into Ar-Lannon's crew. The guard demanded to know her intentions. He didn't seem to believe that Duessa just wanted to care for the old tower, but her gray patchwork robe showed she was a mage. He was afraid to try and drive her off.

Soon enough, there was a steady trickle of visitors. Nobody winced at the sight of her scars anymore. *Vitalis* had healed them nearly to invisibility. That made it easier to trade — for food or housewares, for minor healing, and most eagerly, for news. Duessa swapped them a story for a story.

First she asked about Ar-Lannon and the others. No one had seen them in years. The lack of tidings was discouraging. Duessa would have liked to tell Ar-Lannon how the old myth he struggled to take seriously had been made true — by students of his long-lost friend, Ar-Thea, no less.

But she did learn from the villagers that Busaren's count, Ar-Cadrun, had gone insane without Dar-Gothull. Predictably, the other mages had fought for power. The last one left was Ulivir, who had been an instructor at the temple school. Duessa found it hard to trust anyone from a temple school. However, the villagers said Ulivir hadn't made a claim to be count. He wasn't even using the Ar- prefix to designate rank. *Vitalis* was subtle, but it was having an effect.

Now, at last, the base of Duessa's tower was clear. She could even get up the stairs to the flattened roof. Due to some vigorous bartering, she had managed to acquire basic furnishings. Some men from the village brought it over the ridge in pieces on donkeyback. As thanks, she served them a stew of rabbit from the forest. All during the meal, one of the younger men gazed up at the tower. Clearly he was seeing it in a way the others didn't. Duessa caught him looking sideways at her, too. He took in the glow around her with sensible caution, but also curiosity.

He went back to Liatho with the others, but Duessa was certain he would be back. *Vitalis* had returned to Skaythe, and there would be many who felt its call. Perhaps even the newly freed mage Ulivir would pay her a visit. It was Duessa's duty to welcome whoever came.

She climbed the stairs to the top of the tower and

stood overlooking the raw mess of rocks and dirt she had been moving around. The boulders she had set aside might be useful to make a wall and prevent any more dirt from sliding down. She could also build a terrace and fill it with the loose earth, to grow a few vegetables. A breeze rustled through the trees around the tower. Its soft voice reminded her that there was no need to rush into making firm plans. Duessa wasn't running away from anything. Not anymore.

Perhaps she would keep a few rocks aside, the flatter ones that were good for sitting on. They could form a meditation circle, where new mages took the first steps toward understanding. Duessa might not be as experienced at teaching as Alemin or Tisha, but she had been through the journey herself. She knew how hard it was to push aside Dar-Gothull's harsh laws and change your whole life. She also knew how great the rewards could be.

And if people only came to hear her stories? She had a lot of them, ready for the telling.

She would teach them about the Shining Ones, of course.

About the Minstrels who tried to live up to their legend.

She would tell of Badger Squad, who first served Dar-Gothull but later rallied to the Minstrels.

About a tower armored with ice, and another that swarmed with nightmares.

There was the tale of the Drakanox, whose foretelling had guided them.

And there was a new story, too — one that was only beginning.

PEOPLE AND PLACES
OF SKAYTHE

Places

Skaythe — A tropical island continent.

Fang Marsh — mangrove swamps inhabited by the water-folk

Gavalar Mountains — the highest peaks in Skaythe, where ice and snow persist all through the year

The Hornwood — an area of dry, dense forest in the center of Skaythe, inhabited by the Drakanox and other fell creatures

Temple Schools — training sites where young mages are indoctrinated into Dar-Gothull's laws; Attendance is compulsory

Governance

Dar-Gothull — tyrant and wizard-king, who rules through domination and cruelty

Dakadoz — Dar-Gothull's capital city

The Minstrels — renegade mages who work to undermine Dar-Gothull's tyrannical regime

Ar-Thea, a very wise and kind mage, who trained the Minstrels before she was assassinated

Alemin, juggler and older brother of Berisan

Berisan, juggler and younger brother of Alemin

Keilos, lutenist (deceased)

Lorrah, violinist

Meven, puppeteer

Tisha, dancer and healer

Badger Squad — an independent squad of hunter-guards; women only

Zathi, sergeant and warrior

Jaxynne, second in command, archer and tracker

Giniver, warrior

Keerin, warrior, older sister of Razeet

Razeet, archer, youngersister of Keerin

Sethamis, ox driver and archer

Thersa, warrior (deceased)

Hawk Squad — formerly Count Ar-Dayne of Sloram's personal guard, now independent hunter-guards

Piyaro, sergeant

Cothyr, second in command

Guardsmen: Cylass, company scribe (former), Ennow (deceased), Hyurei, second in command (former), Ragis, Rowlan, Saylor (deceased), Tallon (deceased)

Boar Squad — an independent squad of hunter-guards

Traggan, sergeant

The Larder — a dreaded prison for the most violent wizards

Ar-Lizelle, warden

Ar-Chindu, second in command (deceased)

Ar-Kyanon, second in command (formerly a prisoner)

Guards: Captain Morthem, Endole, Groff, Rhodec

Prisoners: Alemin, Bettain, Calsith, Duessa, Elldri, Ferrant, Haafeth, Illen, Noluss, Wharon (deceased)

The Counties — autonomous, but under Dar-Gothull's control

Busaren

Ar-Cadrun, count

Dakadoz — capital city

Dar-Gothull, wizard-king

Deeve

Ar-Gevant, count

Dunsaph

Ar-Hespaas, count

Ebruc

Ar-Kilohn, count

Ar-Ishahl, son of Count Ar-Kilohn

Ar-Javan, independent mage who sometimes works for

Ebruc

Ar-Talvoy, assistant mage

Eshur

Ar-Torix, countess

Ar-Engil, assistant mage

Nyette, student mage

Ar-Selviss, instructor at Eshur's temple school

Kamuril

Ar-Emuras, count

Lithole

Ar-Sharris, count

Nibbok

Ar-Khavek, count

Nimthar

Ar-Othram, count

Ortach

Ar-Rendon, count

Prizom

Ar-Oshtan, count

Prowth

Ar-Nithal, count

Pulgoll

Ar-Azlor, count

Ar-Norius, assistant mage

Ar-Sessal, assistant mage

Jorus, guard captain

Opshar — a pastoral valley within Pulgoll

Aulgrip, village headman

Kinson, Aulgrip's nephew

Yamaya, a farmer on the outskirts

Seofan — a desolate valley once famed for its nut oil, long ago ruined by Dar-Gothull's vengeance

Sloram

Ar-Jeziak, countess

Ar-Dayne count (deceased)

Unthur

Ar-Gammord, count

Ar-Vennic, assistant mage

Yergha

Ar-Khoreen, countess

ABOUT THE AUTHOR

Deby Fredericks has been a writer all her life, but thought of it as just a fun hobby until the late 1990s. Her first sale, a children's poem, was in 2000. Since then she has published seven novels through two small presses. She self-publishes her short story collections and novellas.

She also writes for children under the byline Lucy D. Ford. Ford's short stories and poetry have appeared in magazines such as *Boys' Life, Babybug, Ladybug*, and *Cricket*. Her middle-grade novel, *Masters of Air & Fire*, came out from Sky Warrior Book Publishing in 2015.

FIND OUT MORE

Follow her blog: wyrmflight.wordpress.com

Official web site: www.debyfredericks.com

Facebook author page:
www.facebook.com/AuthorDebyFredericks

www.ingramcontent.com/pod-product-compliance
Lightning Source LLC
Chambersburg PA
CBHW072012020726
47501CB00006B/1780